Between
Two
Rains

Between Two Rains

Harriet Heyman

Atheneum

New York · 1989

Copyright © 1989 by Harriet Heyman

Atheneum
Macmillan Publishing Company
866 Third Avenue, New York, N.Y. 10022
Collier Macmillan Canada, Inc.

Library of Congress Cataloging-in-Publication Data
Heyman, Harriet.
    Between two rains/Harriet Heyman.
    p.   cm.
    ISBN 0-689-12077-X
    I. Title.
PS3558.E855B48   1989
813'.54—dc19   88-31324   CIP

10 9 8 7 6 5 4 3 2 1

Printed in the United States of America

For CKH, MJM and Jake

1

Mirie Keane was sure she had forgotten something. She opened the Halliburton, where her gear fit snugly into a bed of corrugated foam: two Canon bodies, lenses—28 to 300—flash, battery pack, extra batteries, meter. The plane ticket and the passport were in the new camera bag that was Jonathan's gift; so were the monographs on elephants, the letters of introduction and the sheaf of permissions, her reward for months running a gauntlet of slow-moving clerks and dilatory embassy bureaucrats. The light tripod she would strap onto the Halliburton. The film she'd carry separately in a plastic bag to avoid Third World airport X-ray machines that might fog it.

She dumped out the duffel and rechecked her list. All there, right down to the details—medicine kit; bug spray; extra shirts (Jonathan's hand-me-downs); a small framed picture; a second pair of eyeglasses; sunglasses; tubes of sun block, for fair skin that broiled easily; a compass, to make up for an undependable sense of direction; water bottle; balloons for kids. Cigarettes? Good for tips, old Africa hands advised—buy them duty-free at the airport. She stuffed everything back in.

What had she forgotten? She had a sip of milk and took the glass with her to the bathroom.

She swayed, sending the pulsing shower spray up and down her spine. The fogging mirror reflected suds streaming down a lithe body, a gift of her mother's genes helped by regular attendance at exercise class.

Soap froth slid between her breasts, colors playing on the surface of the bubbles. Once she had photographed soap bubbles to illustrate a chapter in Frank Evans' book on patterns of nature. The pictures showed how six iridescent partitions between bubbles clasped edges at 120-degree angles, all the time and everywhere, whether in shampoo suds or ocean froth. Mirie had only hazily understood Evans' explanation of the rainbow hues. It had something to do with waves of light reflecting off the bubble's skin from above and below, then shifting as the bubble stretched; fugitive colors swirled over the shimmering membrane, exciting the eye for an instant, then vanishing.

Mirie stepped out of the shower. She wiped the steamed mirror with a towel and knocked the milk glass. It teetered but did not tip. She drank the rest of the milk and pictured what had not happened: glass shards and a spiral galaxy of spilled milk in the sink. It was an image from her pictures of cosmic turbulence. She had spent hours before and after work making photographs of milk, ink, glycerin and food coloring sloshed on black slates until Evans agreed that her kitchen images resembled gas clouds and the collapsed star of the Crab Nebula.

She bent over and brushed her wet hair toward the floor. When wet, her dark brown hair looked black like her mother's had been when she was young. Mirie had checked her memory against family photos. Yes, her mother's hair had been black and thick. She had been a beauty, very past tense.

Mirie darkened her lashes and touched shadow to her eyes. One eye was brown, the other blue, as if nature, choosing neither, had opted for both. She put on her glasses, without which the world was blurry around the edges.

She put on the long skirt and the money belt—with Jonathan's loan of a thousand dollars, ten crisp hundred-dollar bills, in case of emergency—sweater and old khaki jacket. She rummaged through the pockets and threw out empty yellow film cartons.

Dissatisfied with her reflection, Mirie put on heels, which

transformed her appearance from Peace Corps volunteer to faded chic. Then a quick straightening of the bedroom, closet door closed, bed comforter smoothed.

She tugged at the duffel flaps and snapped on the canvas strap. The padlock clicked shut. She had packed with care, in the interest of keeping the weight down, but already the three bags seemed a burden. *Yes, sir. Yes, sir. Three bags full.* What was the children's rhyme? Probably, she had overpacked, but it was too much to sort through again. She was as well prepared as she could be. Nothing to do now but call a cab. The nagging sense of something forgotten hung over her like a drop of water not yet heavy enough to fall.

2

From the row behind, a wailing baby shattered Mirie's half sleep. The man across the aisle, having drunk three bourbons, had tipped his Stetson hat low and gone to sleep open-mouthed. Mirie fidgeted in the confines of the seat.

She began a letter to Jonathan. She wrote about her project, a letter about beginnings, but tore it up. It was corny. She settled for a note on a glossy postcard with a 747 on the front.

Dear Jonathan,
   I got off okay, despite the jitters. I am five hours and 40,000 feet from you, and twelve more hours from Simahali.
   I was restless and asked if I could go up to the cockpit. It was quiet. The whole world spread out below me, horizon to horizon, and I could see the lights of fishing trawlers. Remember *Captains Courageous*?
   The on-board movie was a dumb comedy about a murder in suburbia. I watched it without headphones, and that way was better.
   Will write more when my feet are planted on African soil.

Love, M

o o

Jonathan was shooting an industrial video for a brewery. By mutual agreement, he and Mirie had downplayed her trip. They'd shared a split of champagne with dinner before he left for Detroit. He called her as she was in the midst of packing. He told her to look in the storage closet. She opened his going-away presents while he was still on the phone.

She did not expect his life to change dramatically when she was away, except that, knowing Jonathan's aversion to cooking for himself, friends would invite him to dinner more.

Otherwise, he would be back on the phone in his office overlooking the airshaft above a Chinese laundry. Jonathan preferred the space to his pigeonhole office at NYU. He was a terrific teacher, as Mirie knew, for they had met when she took his graduate seminar on the history of film. He liked being onstage in a classroom. His course was always full, and during office hours students dropped in to talk about film esthetics or to seek advice on how to become an overnight success in Hollywood, as if he should know.

Jonathan had misgivings about teaching. After yet another of his film treatments was rejected, he went through a period of savage remorse. His lectures paled, his students caught his ennui. He curtailed his office hours. He blamed teaching for diverting energy from filmmaking. He couldn't bear spongy academics. He lit into Mirie about her job. She helped select photos for *Ecoworld,* a natural history magazine. Jonathan challenged her to get on with the photographic career she professed to want instead of "pissing away years hunched over a light-table for a dismal penny-ante rag." There was a fight followed by two days during which they hardly spoke, passing each other in the apartment like shades in the netherworld. Jonathan's black moods were brief, but they had a lingering contagious effect. After he had regained his buoyancy, Mirie still smarted.

He courted her. He brought home a gift-wrapped box. Inside was a black plastic cat clock.

"What's this for?" She was bemused by the bulging eyes and the rhinestone tail that moved back and forth as it ticked.

"To throw at me. What else?"

They hung it in the kitchen, where it ticked in counterpoint to the old Regulator clock, one of the few things she had kept from her mother's apartment.

Jonathan won back his students the same way. He leavened his lectures with the right amount of empathy and entertainment. When students came to him for advice about work "out there in the real world," he counseled from experience: rejection was not a divine judgment but an arbitrary opinion made by people whose focus was money, not art.

Jonathan had a keen respect for both. He liked the hard-edged reality of New York. He drew his ideas for movies from headlines. His treatment about a murdered real-estate developer was only the most recent, but there were stacks of others that had never been optioned, let alone made into films.

In his office, steamy from the laundry downstairs, Jonathan pored over newspapers, sipping coffee and dragging on cigarettes, as ideas for docudramas, plays, movies and miniseries percolated up from within. When Mirie first came to know Jonathan, she was amazed by the way he could improvise stories on the spot. They sounded wonderful when he told them, but when he put them down on paper, they somehow seemed raggedy. Jonathan said that didn't matter. Once a project was underway, you could always hire someone to flesh it out. He wasn't a detail man; he liked broad creative strokes.

On the wall were his awards: plaques from advertising guilds, honors from obscure film festivals, and—the only one that meant anything—first prize from a long-ago student film contest for his whimsical short on an old painter who fell in love with his neighbor's vixen daughter.

When they first met, Jonathan was not ferreting around the movie business. He was working for public television. He made documentaries on river pollution, on an ex-street-gang-leader-made-good who returned to his old neighborhood to help and was killed, on racial antagonism against Asian immigrants. They were good programs, but Jonathan was dissatisfied. He complained about the well-intentioned ditherers he was working for and the creative and budgetary constraints. It wasn't worth his time. So he switched his focus to commercial movies; he wanted to direct actors. Meanwhile he made money by teaching, and by doing industrials and editing. A certain amount of busywork for good money was the price of creative independence. That's what Jonathan said.

○　○

Dragging the duffel, teetering under the weight of all her gear, Mirie shuffled through customs along with other jet-lagged travelers. She clutched the canvas strap across her breast so it wouldn't chafe.

Her hair smelled of cigarette smoke. Her mouth tasted of stale coffee. She felt dirty. The line moved, sleepwalkers in a queue, oblivious to the baby who was crying even louder now. It moved slowly, punctuated by the customs man stamping passports. Mirie recalled what Old Africa Hands had told her about dealing with these guys: Say little. Be patient. Don't get angry. Dash—a small bribe—if you have to. The line stopped. An Indian man with many boxes was delaying things. He was arguing with the customs man, a slim expressionless African in a tan uniform. Another customs agent appeared and the Indian, very upset, was told to follow.

The customs man examined Mirie's passport, visa and photo permit.

"What do you take pictures of?"

"Animals," she said. She hoped for no hassles and showed him letters from the ministries for conservation and tourism.

"Europeans always like the animals."

"I'm American."

"Yes. Michael Jackson." He actually smiled, then pounded the passport with his rubber stamp and it was over. Mirie drifted along with the other travelers into the arrivals room.

Placards rose above a throng of black, brown and white faces. Group tourists herded up under signs for Aardvark D-Luxe Tours, Rhino Runs, Dik-Dik Safaris and Mountain Sprees. Conventioners gravitated to the signs for "International Diabetes Week" and "Jehovah's Witnesses." An African in a three-piece pinstriped suit led his family to a black Mercedes. His wife, wrapped in a blue paisley-swirled kanga, was trailed by eight small children. The girls wore pinafore dresses over starched white blouses, while the two eldest boys

7

were in somber suits and caps. The youngest boy, about two years old, had on Oshkosh overalls and a red Yankees jacket.

Mirie lugged her gear over to the sign saying WINDSOR HOTEL.

"Welcome," said the driver, an African in a burgundy jacket with the name of the hotel embroidered in gold over the front pocket.

Mirie had read a book on the Windsor, and when she saw the real thing, she was not disappointed. It was a bungalow-style hotel built in the early 1900s when Kwendela, then little more than a swamp, had spawned a hodgepodge of tents and shacks while serving as a way station for British railroad builders.

A terra-cotta roof shaded the long front terrace. A handsome new wing had been added, to replace the one destroyed by a terrorist's bomb on a Christmas Eve some years before. Bright white stucco walls contrasted with dark wood beams. Burgundy cushions covered new white wicker furniture. Everything about the terrace smacked of the good life in the tropics.

The main building led to a courtyard surrounded by airy bungalows. African birds sang from Victorian aviaries. Cannons adorned the lawn, next to rickshaws once drawn by native boys who carried colonials from the railway depot to the hotel.

The book said that the bar on the terrace was named after Lord Northcott, who settled the fertile highlands. His cows died of rinderpest and were stolen by spear-wielding natives who believed that God had made them guardians of all cattle. His crops withered with tropical blight. But he stayed on, and elderly colonials invoked his name as if he were still alive.

Teddy Roosevelt and Winston Churchill had slept at the Windsor, the book boasted. So had T. Boone Pickens and Linda Ronstadt and Floyd Patterson. It was the best hotel in town and the Northcott Bar attracted all sorts: Africans, Europeans, Asians, diplomats and professionals in the aid trades, tourists, British colonial dowagers in ancient finery who sipped gin fizzes, prostitutes, white teenagers and older cowboys who roared up to the hotel on motorcycles, furtive men of all colors, and fiddlers and fixers who dealt in the bizarre commerces of the Third World.

For Mirie, staying at the Windsor was an unaccustomed luxury. One night at the Windsor was the final part of Jonathan's good-luck present. After that she'd be at the tourist camp shooting the brochure.

The porter led her to a room in a newer section of the hotel called, postcolonially, the Singles Block.

"Thank you, Jonathan," she said to herself, flopping down on the bed. The room was twice the size of her and Jonathan's bedroom, and more finished, with curtains and a comfortable reading chair.

Her heart was beating fast—the altitude, she supposed. She was exhausted, but pinpricks of consciousness kept her awake. Max Howden was meeting her. Maybe he'd be late. From what—coming out of the bush? But they had to leave in the morning. Goode, the camp manager, expected them. There had been so many arrangements put in place long-distance. She was planning, rearranging. But the bed was so welcoming.

She was just drifting off to sleep when the phone rang.

"Madame has a visitor," said an African voice in a soft lilting cadence. It was the desk clerk. "His name is Mr. Max and he wishes to meet you in the Northcott Bar. I shall tell Mr. Max this is okay? A few minutes. That is fine, madame. Thank you. Good-bye."

Mirie sat on the edge of the bed, trying to get her bearings.

3

"Africa's very different," Dr. Evans had said. Max Howden had been a student of his twenty years before. The scientist was proud of having encouraged Howden to become a wildlife photographer. Among wildlife photographers, Max Howden was admired and envied. He made a good living doing what he liked to do, he could pick and choose his assignments and his books did reasonably well.

When Mirie had first told Evans her idea, he referred her to *Realm of Giants*. She tracked down the book in the library of the American Museum of Natural History. She came across Howden's picture of the head of a great bull elephant, with twin masts of ivory and ears outstretched like sails against the sky. The photo appeared to have been taken from underfoot. Was Howden in a blind, from which he could shoot unobtrusively, or had he been among elephants for so long that he was accepted as a member of the family? The text talked only about African animals. There wasn't a word on how he took the pictures. Or even a mention of the type of film used, which was a way some photographers wangled free film from a manufacturer. Nor was there a picture of him. The biographical description said only that Howden was born in St. Louis and spent most of his time in Africa. His first book, *Cats at Twilight,* was similarly unrevealing. Nothing about technique. The dust jacket said Howden and his wife and daughter lived in Virginia.

If Mirie had asked Dr. Evans about an animal, he could have described it minutely and summarized its evolutionary history. About his old friend and former student, he said only, "Max is a good man. Maybe he can help you get started. Africa's very different."

ɔ   ɔ

Mirie passed through a courtyard where caged birds keened at the twilight. She didn't know who or what to look for on the crowded verandah. There was a man, a very tall man, leaning against a pillar. He tilted his head to observe her sideways, the way birds do. Mirie glanced around the bar. No one else had the look of waiting for someone, so she approached him. "Are you Max?"

He leaned forward awkwardly, as if in the habit of guarding against bumping his head.

"Good to meet you." He shook her hand briskly.

She followed him to a corner table in the crowded bar. He was well over six feet tall, and his long legs didn't fit under the table or anywhere else he tried to put them. He settled them uncomfortably to the side.

He raised his long arm to summon the waiter. "What will you have?"

She asked for a lemonade. Max ordered in Swahili. Mirie had the impression of a man made of oversize parts fitted together into an ungainly whole. She wondered what his wife looked like.

Max folded his arms across his chest, stretched out his cramped legs, crossed them at the ankles. He observed the people at the bar, as if he had momentarily forgotten her. When the waiter returned, he had to pull in his legs again so as not to trip the man. He paid, leaving the change in the tray. The waiter bowed and left.

"Is this your first time here?" he asked. Mirie nodded. "Dropping out of the sky into Africa. There's a kick in the head." After considering this a moment, he raised his beer glass in the gesture of a toast.

Mirie drank the lemonade thirstily.

"You're smart not to drink your first night here," said Max.

"The combination of jet lag, alcohol and altitude can knock you flat."

"I'm not much of a drinker anyway."

"You may change your mind." He sipped his beer. "It's the national pastime. There isn't much else to do."

Sandy curls fell from a thinning dome, a tonsure in anarchy. His high forehead was marked with a suntan line from wearing a hat. Sun had bleached out his brows and lashes around eyes that fixed on her intently. It wasn't an admiring look, but more in the nature of detached curiosity, as if he were trying to figure out this new creature.

"What sort of name is Mirie?"

"Nothing fancy. My mom wanted to call me Miriam, after her mother. My dad talked her into shortening it to Mirie."

She gestured toward the bar. "I read about this place." The outside tables were taken up mostly by tourists, judging by the new safari garb, while the bar was packed with locals. Above the phalanx of bottles was a portrait photograph of a dour black man with a red rose in his lapel. The picture had been hung over a fading wall mural depicting a hunting party. A settler woman on horseback, with pith helmet and parasol, rode next to her dark mustachioed husband, followed by bearers carrying a dead lion. Their destination was hidden behind the black man's portrait.

"What a shame!" said Mirie. "To ruin the painting by hanging that character's mug over it."

Max's eyes narrowed and he glanced around. "That's the president," he said quietly.

"Really!" She laughed. "He looks like a guy in a wanted poster."

Max stiffened and shook his head. He said distinctly, "The president is very popular," and under his breath added, "today." He sniffed. "You're a long way from home." His eyes questioned whether or not she understood.

The anxiety that stole over Mirie turned into an odd thrill at the idea that she would have to watch what she said in public. She drank down the rest of the lemonade.

"Another?" offered Max. He was still nursing his beer.

"Yes. Thanks."

It took a while to hail the waiter. He was collecting money from a sallow white man at another table. His companion was an African woman with plaited hair. Wearing a tight white blouse, she pressed her breasts against the man while he paid the bill. She whispered in his ear and he shook his head no, then she said something else and he nodded. As they got up to go, the white man glanced around.

They made their way out, past the center table where a fat white man was presiding over a group of Africans in uniform. The fat man raised his glass to the portrait, revealing a pistol strapped under his ham-sized arm. "To the president," said the fat man. "To the president," said his minions, and all clicked glasses.

Max said quietly, "Bwana Matata is celebrating. His contract has been renewed."

"Who is he? A policeman?"

Max considered his words. "His job is to make trouble disappear." Mirie looked at him questioningly. "People make trouble."

Mirie exhaled. "Frank Evans told me Africa was different."

Max smiled at the mention of his friend.

"When he comes here, he knows how to have a good time."

"Dr. Evans?" said Mirie incredulously.

"Last year we traveled together in Kenya. We camped by Lake Turkana for three weeks. There are very few hours when the light's any good for pictures—just after dawn and late afternoon. The rest of the day we'd catch fish and read. He'd swim a lot. The lake is warm and greasy from the soda. The old boy would be out there bathing bare-assed with the crocs."

"Frank is always so decorous!"

"Oh, he likes playing Indian." Max smiled at the recollection.

"When I first told him my idea," said Mirie, "it was as if I'd said I was going to Saturn to photograph unicorns."

Max raised one eyebrow. "There's some similarity."

"But you don't think it's ridiculous—in your letter, you didn't say forget it."

"I wouldn't tell another photographer what can or can't be done. If I'd listened to anyone else . . ." The rest of the sentence trailed off. "Like I wrote you, what you want to do has never been done successfully. It's a matter of luck as well as skill. Elephants breed every four years, and if there's been a long drought, even less often. To come across an elephant in labor, to get an unobstructed view in decent light, to gauge distance and light when they're constantly changing, to assume that you yourself won't disturb the female, and that the second it happens you'll get a good, clear shot—you aren't going to get a second chance. Even in zoos, it happens so fast it's hard to get pictures. The chances are slim."

"But your pictures seem impossible, too . . ."

"There's no trick. I'm always ready, then I wait and I wait and I wait." He finished his beer. He tapped the empty glass on the table. "We'd better say good night. I want to start at sunup, before the heat hits."

When they stood, Max seemed to keep on rising. Though Mirie was wearing heels, he was still more than a foot taller than she. Slightly bent from the waist, he negotiated a path between the tables with a queer uneven gait. Once off the verandah and away from the crowds, he seemed to relax.

"I'll be ready." Mirie gave him her hand. "I've been looking forward to this for a long time. It's great of you to help."

"You're a friend of Frank's, and I have a little time before I go to Zambia. Besides . . ." His brow furrowed while his eyes smiled. "I like people who have crazy ideas. This place . . ." A sweep of his long arm seemed to take in all of Africa. "This place collects them."

4

Africa was a dream that became most vivid to Mirie in the last year of her mother's life. When going up to her mother's apartment on the West Side, she would visit the American Museum of Natural History. She liked best the dioramas of animals that were familiar to her from childhood. She strolled past, not really studying them, but using them instead as fodder for daydreams. The hall of the African elephants dominated Mirie's dreamscape.

She saw herself in the flank of Kilimanjaro, where zebras grazed and lions stalked. The Africa Mirie imagined was very much like the painted dioramas, only bigger. She was aware of the other Africa, the one of coups, droughts, development schemes and calamities that the newspapers wrote about. But those stories had no weight in her life. Her Africa was as constant and unchanging as the dioramas.

o o

When Neil Donner called Mirie at the magazine, to say he had a job for her in Africa, she was immediately suspicious. He had given her name, he said, to a client; he couldn't do the job himself—a scheduling conflict, supposedly.

The real reason, Mirie suspected, was that the job wasn't big enough to suit either Donner's bank account or his ego. For old times' sake, he had tossed Mirie a scrap. No matter; to her it was an opportunity that both thrilled and disturbed her, a means to an end. Here was a chance to work in Africa, to make her dreamscape come to life and fix it on film. The client needed pictures of a big-game ranch in Africa for a tourist brochure. It was April and she was to go in June.

In terms of her job, it was the worst possible timing. *Ecoworld* was being expanded. The small staff had been working ten-hour days and six-day weeks. Everyone had red-rimmed eyes, and her boss, Sam, too tired to drive home to Manhasset, slept on a couch in his office.

Counting travel time, the two weeks of vacation she was due was barely enough to do photos for the brochure, let alone even one good wildlife story. She would have to convince Sam to give her more time off, if necessary a leave of absence. The next question was what stories and for whom? Other than *Ecoworld,* what publication would give her an assignment? She had a respectable news portfolio but a short track record shooting wildlife.

The frog story she had shot in New Jersey had worked out well. Equipped with two strobes mounted on the camera to overpower ambient light, she had shot frogs in a glade. Mosquitoes ravaged her while she dealt with a critical focus. When her subject hopped away, she picked it up, set it back on the leaf, wiped the sweat from her eyes, scratched her bites, refocused, by which time the frog hopped again. This ritual went on for hours, but she did finally come away with good pictures. However, the magazine didn't use her best shots. She asked Jonathan to compare her own selects with the ones Phyllis, the picture editor, chose. But Jonathan didn't want to judge a frog beauty contest. Why, he asked, was she fussing over a little assignment that hardly paid for itself?

Later, on a beach in Costa Rica, Mirie had shot teary-eyed sea turtles laying eggs. Right on schedule, under a full moon, turtles by the thousands had trudged up from the sea, scooped out holes in the sand and dropped their Ping-Pong–ball eggs, unbothered by the gaggle of photographers shooting off flashes at their rear ends.

She was invited on that trip because of the osprey poster, a job she had volunteered to do for the New Jersey Fish and

Wildlife Department. She and a biologist had visited the nesting poles by rowboat. They climbed the poles, teetering above the wetlands. The biologist removed a dead egg from a nest, and in its place Mirie put a warm bony hatchling abandoned from another nest. They then moved to another shaky lookout perch to await the osprey. For the poster Mirie caught an osprey returning to its nest, wings spread six feet, a fish writhing in its talons as a hatchling craned its neck toward its adoptive mother.

The poster was all over New Jersey and on PATH commuter trains, with a credit line that more than compensated Mirie for her work. Though Mirie had won a few awards for her pictures, she had not been able to parlay them into a permanent job on a New York City paper. This was no great disappointment. She'd been a photographer at a small paper in New Jersey, and her heart wasn't in being a newshound anymore.

Instead, she went to work for Neil Donner. Donner was a first-rate commercial photographer, a blowhard and a womanizer. As far as Mirie was concerned, Donner had one strong point. She could learn from him how to shoot in natural light and under difficult conditions.

Unfortunately, he rarely asked her to go on assignment with him. There was a short brawny assistant whom Donner took along to play Sherpa. When Donner hired a helicopter to fly around the Statue of Liberty, the mighty midget accompanied him, not Mirie. The two men went to Utah to shoot hang-gliding enthusiasts for an ad pushing cigarettes. They went to the North Sea to shoot offshore oil rigs for an annual report. In Alaska Donner tickled a caged polar bear pup, which responded to the overture by biting his finger to the bone. With Donner out of commission, the assistant got to take the pictures. Mirie's envy gave her stomach pains.

At an exhibit of wildlife photography, Mirie ran into Sam Gebhardt. He was looking for an assistant photo editor.

"Why would you want yet another job as a glorified file clerk?" Jonathan chided her when she told him about the offer. "You're supposed to be taking your own pictures, not shuffling through other people's."

Over Jonathan's objections, Mirie took the job. It was not the right time for her to try to become a wildlife photographer. With her mother so ill, traveling was out of the question.

When her mother died, three months later, Mirie wanted to feel relieved. Instead, she felt like she was dragging an anchor.

ɔ ɔ

She met Liz at the museum to tell her about the Africa job Donner had thrown her way. In college she and Liz had been gofers at the university press. Now Liz was art director at a textbook publisher.

"Why isn't Donner doing it himself?" Liz asked.

"There's no money in it by his standards." Mirie laughed. "Donner spent a week in Lagos a few years ago. After that he wrote off the whole continent."

"But you want to go."

"Simahali's different. It's set up for tourism. There are a lot of foreigners there. Jonathan says I should do other stories while I'm there, things nobody else has gotten."

"Like what?"

Mirie didn't know. She gazed up at the great elephants that dominated the Hall of African Mammals. Footsteps and voices of schoolchildren echoed through the Hall. "It's worth the trip to see the real thing."

Liz considered the elephants a moment. "What's wrong with the ones at the Bronx Zoo?" Then she said seriously, "Did you know that I tried once to find a picture of an elephant giving birth? There were pictures of elephants with newborn calves, but not the actual moment of birth. I couldn't even find a good picture of a birth in captivity." Liz laughed lightly. After fifteen years in New York she retained the gracious, easygoing manner of her North Carolina upbringing. "Think of that. The largest animal walking on earth. It couldn't hide if it tried. I'd think it would be simple to get a picture of one having a baby. Wouldn't you?"

The conversation drifted to other things, but Mirie felt somewhat distracted.

The next day she checked with stock agencies for photos of an elephant birth in the wild. There were no pictures of the birth itself, and the photos of newborns were mostly amateurish. She came across Max Howden's name on many of the better ones, but even he didn't have birth photos. She combed scientific abstracts for material on "elephant parturition," but there was little to go on.

She was about to broach the subject of an unpaid leave of absence when Sam called her into his office. His shirt sagged from the back of his pants. He removed a pile of papers from a chair and stacked them on his cluttered desk. "Sit. Sit."

She sat. Sam haphazardly straightened the piles of manuscripts on his desk. The phone rang. He ignored it. She assumed they were going to have a picture conference. Phyllis was out sick.

"I like your work, Mirie. Something's come up, and I have a solution that's good for both of us. Phyllis is pregnant. She's quitting work to have her baby and be a mother. Good for her. Lousy for us." Sam shrugged. "But what are we going to do?"

Phyllis and she had worked together for nearly four years. She had confided in Mirie that she and her husband had given up hope of having a baby—she was forty-one—and they were trying to adopt.

And now this. The news set off tremors. She was hurt that Phyllis hadn't told her herself instead of having Sam break the news. She and Phyllis had been friends as well as workmates.

Sam was still talking. "I'm raising your salary twenty percent," he said. "Start looking for a new assistant." He got up part way and extended his hand across the desk. "Congratulations." He made another try at straightening his papers. "Before lunch let me see the critter you're working on."

Mirie went back to the light table where she had left slides of a pangolin, an animal resembling an armored anteater. The droll creature no longer interested her. She was thinking about Phyllis. If Phyllis could become pregnant at the last possible moment, then Mirie, at thirty-three, had perhaps seven or eight more years, and anything could happen in that time.

As her mother's health had deteriorated, Mirie found herself staring at children and at pregnant women younger than herself. Her mother never asked or admonished. She never said a word, but Mirie believed that toward the end her mother had held on waiting for her and Jonathan to marry. Mirie thought of a baby as a new beginning to balance an ending, but she didn't act on her inclination. She did not want a child unless Jonathan did, too. He appealed to her practical side: How could they afford a baby? There was barely room in the apartment for them, let alone a baby. Was she prepared to stay home with a baby all day? Perhaps she wasn't, but before her period, tears came at unexpected moments. Jonathan was sympathetic, but he acted as if her grieving were one of those private women's problems.

Mirie went back to Sam's office with the pangolin selects. After he looked at them, Mirie made no motion to leave.

"So?" said Sam.

"I need some time to think about this."

Sam hunched up his shoulders. "What's to think about? You're promoted."

"I need a vacation."

"We all do." Sam ran his hand through hair that looked like strands of rusty Brillo. "Later, Mirie. After the deluge."

"I can't wait. I have—"

"No vacation. Not until October." Mirie's face fell. "Be happy." Sam smiled, an ugly, benevolent gnome. "You've got a great job at a growing magazine. What more do you want?" Sam rubbed his temples. "May we all survive success."

ↄ ○

She went to Frank Evans, once her professor, now her friend. His quiet deliberation as she told him her idea made her think it wasn't so crazy after all.

"But this thing about trying to shoot an elephant being born," said Evans. He picked up the nautilus on his desk and examined its chambers. "What are you going to do? Follow a pregnant elephant around until she decides to give birth? Why, how would one even know when an elephant is pregnant? Really, Mirie, it's awfully far-fetched." Evans set down the nautilus. "But then, I'm not a photographer." He flipped through his Rolodex, stopped at a card and considered it for a moment. "Get hold of Max Howden," he said. "Tell him I told you to call."

As she copied down the number, Evans asked, "What does Jonathan think?"

"You know he's been urging me all along to stay with photography," said Mirie. "My own photography."

"He doesn't mind your going off to Africa?"

Mirie shrugged. "It's not my first field trip. And two or three months isn't forever."

"Why doesn't he go with you?" asked Evans. "For part of the time at least."

"His idea of roughing it is a day at Jones Beach."

"Why do you want to go?"

"How can you ask? If I don't do it now, when will I? I don't want to wake up one day regretting the career I never had." Mirie bristled at the insinuation in Frank's question. "Jonathan's been wanting me to get back on track ever since we met."

"Going to Africa is 'on track'?"

"Why is it, Frank," said Mirie, "that if a man goes off, it's an adventure, and if a woman goes off, it's an escape?"

o   o

So at Evans' suggestion Mirie telexed Max Howden in Zaire. Three weeks later a letter arrived.

> Dear Mirie,
>
> I've spent years with elephants and though I've come close, I have never seen an actual birth. Once at sunset I saw a female pacing and acting nervous. I left to avoid disturbing her anymore. The next morning I found her with a newborn calf. I've never forgotten that lost picture.
>
> A birth in the wild is not the sort of thing you could go after. It's hard to predict or plan for, which is not to say the picture's impossible. Someday, someone, is bound to get lucky. If you're not discouraged, I'm happy to advise further. Let me know if you plan to come to Simahali—best for working if you time your trip between the rains. Dead dry at the moment. Say hello to Frank for me.
>
> Max Howden

5

The Land-Rover gnashed its teeth on the two-lane tarmac as Max shifted. The morning had started out drab, but now sunlight gilded the lowlands scrub. He stopped for boys herding bony goats across the road who waved sticks in greeting and called, "*Mzungu, Mzungu!*"

"That means a European, or any white person," said Max. "No slur intended. The kids are from squatter villages near here."

"Where are they going?" asked Mirie.

"Nowhere. They're grazing their goats."

"On the roadside?"

"There's nothing left. The rest is owned by ranchers who'd run them off. What little that's left is grazed out. The rains have failed now two seasons in a row. It's going to be a dust bowl pretty soon."

"How do people survive?"

"They're used to getting by on very little—a sack of maize meal and some beans."

"And wildlife?"

"A lot is dying. The vultures are getting fat."

The pungent odor of goats and earth, manure and grass filled Mirie's head. The land seemed limitless, stretching to an endless hemisphere of curving sky that dipped to the horizon as if bent through a fisheye lens. Was she looking at huge trees far away or dwarf bushes nearby? She had no sense of scale. The problem, she realized, was that she had the eyes of a city dweller. Accustomed to the gray, leached colors of Manhattan, she could not fathom great distances. At home colors faded into the monochromatic, fume-clogged canyons of New York City. Here, they leaped out at the eye. Parasols of acacia, silvered spikes of thornbush, piebald goats and African boys seemed to glisten against the red soil.

The Land-Rover bumped along at eighty kilometers an hour. On the far side of the pocked road, a gasoline truck hurtled toward them, veered around a crater and into their lane. Max swerved as the truck roared past.

"God!" Mirie swallowed a frightened chirp. "I thought Costa Ricans were the worst drivers I'd ever seen."

Max's face was impassive, what she could see of it. Curls escaped from under a worn khaki cap. "It is no problem, madame," he said, imitating the locals' musical cadence.

He asked her what she had been doing in Costa Rica, and she told him about the turtle story. They talked shop about equipment, and more about the technical matters she had posed in a second letter.

Max's advice was too general to be of much help: Wait and see about building a blind. No point in setting up a remote shot unless she knew for sure where the elephants were going to be. Exposures were tricky, because elephant hide soaked up a lot of light. Different elephant groups tolerated humans differently: Forest elephants were more likely to feel cornered and charge; plains elephants could see their escape routes and would usually walk off rather than come after you.

She checked her watch. It was only ten-thirty, and the light was already harsh.

He motioned toward her watch. "You won't be needing that. Sunrise and sunset are almost unvarying year-round. All the time in between is elastic."

She thought about this cryptic remark, then asked, "What do you do all day, when you're not working?"

A fleeting smile appeared on Max's face. "I watch all the time. There's an awful lot going on. I don't shut my eyes just because the light isn't right." The eyes, roofed by the cap, stayed fixed on the road.

Was Max shy or arrogant? Here they were, two strangers on a long journey with, if nothing else, their work in common. But conversation didn't come easily. Perhaps he'd been working alone so long he'd forgotten how. Or he didn't feel comfortable around women.

On most other occasions Mirie had found that being a woman, and attractive, gave her an edge as a photographer. She received cooperation from firemen, policemen and politicians who routinely shut the door on men photographers. She didn't flaunt her attractiveness, but recognized it as a helpful tool, there when she needed it. It wouldn't help now, though; elephants didn't care about looks.

ɔ ɔ

Steel dragon teeth barred the road ahead. Soldiers were posted by the barricades. Police inspected trucks while African drivers stood around waiting for a go-ahead. A pudgy Indian man shouted and gesticulated beside his Peugeot. As Max slowed the Land-Rover, he was waved on by the police.

"Is this a safety check?" asked Mirie.

"If they cared about safety, no one would be driving."

"Why didn't he stop us?"

"They let Mzungus go. They stop Africans and Asians. They like to harass Asians."

"Why?"

"It's a game for the moment, but one with nasty overtones. Remember how Idi Amin kicked out all the Indians. They lost everything. There's no love lost between Africans and Asians. More to the point, these guys know Indians are always good for dash. The Asians are a tiny, well-off minority. They're the professionals and the real-estate developers and the hotel owners. The Africans resent their success and insularity. It's always front-page news when an Asian trader is caught spiriting money out of the country, though the African elite are doing the same thing." Max downshifted to climb. "Here comes our friend."

The Peugeot sped around them in the right lane just as an

oncoming truck rounded the top of the hill. A hairsbreadth from collision, the Peugeot zoomed back into the left lane.

"Nice pickup," said Max. "Driving here is sort of a Darwinian sport. You adapt to it, or you won't be around very long." She laughed. "No. Really," he continued. "They drive like it's a game of bumper cars. Are you going to buy a car? You can usually sell it without losing much. And renting's a fortune."

"I'm not sure," Mirie said. "I have to look into it."

"Cars cost a bundle here, either way." He shook his head. "When I first came to Africa—that was in the sixties—I bummed around without one. You can't work that way. I scraped together some money and my parents pitched in so I could buy a used Land-Rover. We were on intimate terms, that car and I. I must have fixed every part in her at least once."

He had traveled around the wildlife circuit shooting stories, he said. *Cats at Twilight* brought in enough money to buy a new Land-Rover and a Leica.

"Your picture of a leopard pouncing a gazelle—I've never seen anything like that," said Mirie. "How did you do it?"

His deceptively simple explanation revealed no trade secrets. "We found a sick gazelle, and followed it. We thought something might happen, but not a leopard—you seldom see them. I was lucky."

Mirie noted he had said "we." "Did your wife always travel with you?"

"Only early on," he said blandly. "I found I worked best alone."

Trying to talk to Max was like walking in a labyrinth. No matter what she said, she ran into walls. So she tried to coax conversation out of him with an admission of her own.

"I've never been in the field alone for any length of time. It's not creature comforts I'd miss"—she didn't want him to think her a wimp—"I'm afraid I'd be lonely."

"You get used to it," he said. "Are you married?"

She was surprised by his directness. "Kind of."

He said nothing.

Ahead of them a small boxy vehicle listed dangerously. Africans were jammed inside, and extra passengers hung out the back and dangled from the sides. Stacked crates skated on top. Suddenly, with no warning and no flash of brake lights, the vehicle stopped. Max slalomed around. Mirie whirled in her seat. Passengers, screaming and laughing, poured out and huddled over something at the side of the road.

"Can we stop?" she asked.

Max checked his rearview mirror. "It's not going to be pretty."

As he pulled over, she took the camera body from the foam-lined case and snapped on a 55-mm lens.

The driver of the vehicle was inspecting wisps of coarse hair fluttering from the caved-in fender.

"This is a *basi,* a bus," Max explained impassively. "The drivers pack in as many people as they can. When these things crack up, thirty, forty, people are smashed."

The Africans hovered over a carcass, chattering excitedly. It was a wildebeest, a shaggy antelope with a sloping back and a head like a horse with a goatee. Altogether, it looked as if it had been stitched together by a deranged taxidermist. A woman ran back to the *basi* for a panga, a kind of machete, which she turned over to a man. He raised the blade over his head and whacked it down on the beast's rump. Blood ran into the dry grass. Mirie edged in closer.

"Why do you want pictures?" asked Max.

"I want to try to sell a photo essay on the drought to the *Beacon,* the paper I used to work for in New Jersey."

"This has nothing to do with the drought. This is normal. Africans don't waste free *nyama.*"

"What?"

"Meat," he said. "That's the general word for animals. The peasants don't share white people's lofty notions about preserving wildlife for its own sake. They're much more concerned with preserving themselves."

It made sense. Mirie shot more pictures, fixed on the image in the frame, the smooth mechanical sound of the camera.

"This isn't even wildebeest country," said Max. "Poor fellow was lost."

She moved in closer. The wildebeest had been reduced to a bloody mess of head, legs and entrails. When she put the camera down, a foul gut odor filled her nostrils. She went white. Perspiration trickled down her.

"I'm not squeamish," she said.

"So I see."

She mumbled something about the heat, made her way back to the car and put her head between her knees.

o   o

The sun was high. Heat waves shimmered off the melting tarmac. Colors withered and hard shadows cut the hills.

The car reeked of bananas. Mirie was torpid but upright. She sipped a warm Coke.

"How about a banana?" asked Max.

Mirie twisted around and dug in the food carton in back. She peeled the skin part way. Max engulfed the banana in two bites.

"Not having one?" He looked at her. "You're still a little green around the gills, aren't you?"

Mirie slid back down in the seat.

"Look! Tommy!" shouted Max. He pointed. "There. Do you see?"

By the time Mirie distinguished the tawny specks from the grass, the Thomson's gazelles were gone. Over the rest of the drive through the dry savannah, Max spotted oryxes, impalas, elands, waterbucks and giraffes. The only animal Mirie was positive she had seen was the filleted wildebeest.

o   o

The askari guarding the gate radioed to headquarters that there were visitors. When the watchman received an okay, he swung open the iron gate that said SWALA RANCH—PRIVATE PROPERTY.

The Land-Rover bounced along the dusty laterite toward the manager's house. There was not an animal in sight, not even a cow, nothing but dry grass and thornbush and an occasional bare baobab, its fat fleshy midriff gouged by elephant tusks.

"This is a ranch?" said Mirie.

"One of the biggest. It has one permanent river, some boreholes, and the rest is *nyika*—wilderness."

"But not even one elephant to greet us!" She feigned disappointment.

Max grinned. "Take it up with the management."

"Tom Goode promised to fly us around so I can check out the herds."

"That's a good thing," said Max. "But you may find that you'll do better down on the ground, and on your own."

6

The servant who was clipping back a torrent of scarlet bougainvillea said Bwana Goode was not at home. He went to fetch "memsahib." Mirie had never seen a memsahib before. She pictured the slim lady-with-parasol from the mural at the hotel.

She did, that is, until a wan woman nestling a bat-eared kitten appeared at the door.

"Hello. I'm Evelyn Goode." Mrs. Goode snuggled the baby caracal. "Tom's hunting lions. Won't you come in?"

She led them to a living room crowded with skins, trophies, plaques and bric-a-brac. A painting of a leopard in stiff repose guarded the fireplace. It seemed to have been done from a paint-by-numbers kit. Colobus monkey and cat skins covered the furniture. Mirie was reminded of the Safari Room at the Prop Shop in Times Square. She and Jonathan had spent hours sifting among the sargasso of theatrical artifacts for *Jumper,* his antic short on a berserk broker who terrorized the Stock Exchange in a kangaroo suit.

Mrs. Goode's musty collection held Mirie's attention only momentarily. Past the open porch was a watering hole from which the bush radiated far to the horizon. Two warthogs knelt drinking, tufted tails sticking up like red pennants.

Evelyn Goode, cat in lap, sat limply in a chair covered with leopard skin. Her forefinger eddied around a bald spot in the fur.

"One of my husband's hunting trophies," she said. She seemed tired and distracted. She called to the servant to bring *chai*. "Or would you like something stronger? I'm having a hot toddy, myself. It's lovely. Very soothing for my cold."

"A beer for me. Thanks," said Max.

Mirie stayed with the hot tea. She was tempted to ask for it iced but suspected that, being British, Mrs. Goode would think her barbaric.

Mrs. Goode asked for news from the city. Mirie first assumed she meant London, but it was about Kwendela that Max spoke.

"Petrol shortages are getting longer. The locals are queued up for hours with jerry cans, waiting for paraffin." For Mirie, Max translated into American: "Kerosene—for lamps." He continued, "The president has declared war on corruption."

"Mmmnn," intoned Mrs. Goode. "He should first dismiss himself."

Max continued: "He got rid of a dozen ministers and replaced them with his cronies. A colonel and a captain traveling together in a government vehicle drove over the edge of a cliff under rather mysterious circumstances. Rumor has it they were becoming too popular . . ."

Mrs. Goode's interest strayed. "Isn't she lovely?" she asked, scratching the wild kitten behind the ears. "I hope she lives. Would you like to hold her, dear?" she asked Mirie. "Oh, excuse me, tell me your name again. Oh, yes, Mirie." Mrs. Goode held out the kitten. It bared needlelike teeth and hissed.

"No, thank you," said Mirie. She was fond of cats, but this one looked decidedly unfriendly.

Max declined as well.

"Surely, you're not afraid of a kitten," Mrs. Goode said coyly to Max. "A big man like yourself."

"Allergies. I'd hate to have a sneezing fit."

"What a pity. She's so endearing—poor little wild creature." Mrs. Goode set down the kitten as the servant arrived with the drinks. The caracal clawed at her ankles. She plucked it up by the collar fur and put it back in her lap. "Are you on holiday?"

Mirie and Max exchanged puzzled looks.

Mirie said, "No, Mrs. Goode—"

"Do call me Evelyn. We're not awfully formal out here."

"Evelyn. Excuse me," said Mirie. "I assumed you knew— I'm here to take photos of the tourist camp. It's for a brochure. Your husband's telex confirmed our meeting today."

Evelyn Goode looked at her blankly. "So you're here to work. That's how I came here, too. Oh, yes, I was pretty like you. It was a lark, my coming here. I took a job as a secretary at the bank. I never intended to stay. Then I met Tom. He was so . . . brave." She scrutinized Mirie. "A woman must be especially careful, Mirie. The servants steal—one has to lock up everything—"

Max interrupted. "That's an impressive backyard you have." He nodded to the view outdoors.

Mrs. Goode stared rheumy-eyed at the empty wilderness. "It is, isn't it?" she said apathetically. "My bachelors should be coming soon." The bachelors, she explained, were a half-dozen bull elephants that were regulars at the watering hole.

Mirie, brightening, excused herself to fetch her camera bag from the car. She did not care at all for Evelyn Goode. Mirie had detected the too-familiar scent of a woman drifting and drinking. She did not relish going back inside, though she could tolerate the woman a while longer if only her husband would show. She wanted to start work immediately, and Tom Goode was supposed to be showing her around. After she had traveled thousands of miles for this job, how could he fail to be there?

"I've had good luck raising leopards and lion cubs," Evelyn Goode was saying when Mirie returned. "After a certain point, though, you can't keep them."

Max rolled the empty beer glass in his large hands. "Do you expect your husband soon?"

"Tom had one of his emergencies," said Mrs. Goode. "Friends ask me how I can live out here, with Tom flying here and there. They say, 'Evelyn, aren't you bored?' What nonsense. Life is never dull here. Henry Tate just lost a prize bull and five cows to lions. He asked Tom to help him get rid of them. My dear husband is still a boy at heart. The only time Tom is happy is when he's in the bush."

She chattered on as she mixed by rote hot water, honey, lemon and a healthy shot of whiskey. The silver spoon tinkled insistently against the china cup.

Max had folded his arms across his chest and gazed outside.

Mirie asked her directly, "Mrs. Goode . . . Evelyn. Is your husband returning today? We had arranged—"

"We have company," said Max.

Evelyn Goode, her face suddenly contorted with rage, leaped from the chair and ran out to the porch.

As silently as ghosts, elephants had invaded her garden. They ripped out tomato vines, dribbling them like spaghetti from their mouths.

She screamed, "Moses! *Ndovu! Kuja hapa!*"

The servant came running, banging a kettle with a wooden spoon. The elephants shook their heads, flapped their ears and retreated quickly from the watering hole.

It was too fast for Mirie. For her first encounter with African elephants, she found herself snapping at six enormous rear ends in retreat. Far away the elephants, red with dust and dwarfed by the expanse of raw land, stopped to wait.

Mirie posted herself on the porch railing.

"I missed them," she admitted to Max.

"There will be plenty of other opportunities. It's much better in your head, anyway," he said. "The colors don't fade." If that was Max's idea of a joke, Mirie could not tell from his deadpan expression. He continued, "They'll come back. They know they're safe here."

Evelyn Goode was marching among the ruins of her brave little bush garden. "They're not going to bully me," she muttered. "Those bloody beasts are not going to run my life."

Max rubbed his cheeks to hide a grin. Mirie turned away until she had checked her impulse to laugh.

When they went back inside, Max dropped out of the conversation, leaving Mirie to respond periodically to Evelyn Goode's ramblings. Mirie kept her eye on the watering hole.

The warthogs scurried off as the elephants returned. Trunks swinging, ears flapping, their motion oddly graceful as if dancing without music, the six elephants arranged themselves around the watering hole. Mirie marveled that they could move so soundlessly.

Now that her bachelor boys were in their proper place and not destroying the garden, Evelyn Goode made herself another hot toddy. She prattled on, taking little notice of her guests' wandering attention, then excused herself to speak with the servant. Max and Mirie went out to the porch. Mirie shot a few frames and edged onto the grass. Elephants sank into the water and emerged glistening dark red against the blue sky. They rumbled deep in their throats. Mirie interpreted that contented sound as an invitation to move closer.

Max said quietly, "Stay here."

"I won't go far." She moved onto the grass, then glanced back self-consciously. Max stood with his arms at his sides, somber as a totem pole. She wished he'd go back inside.

A bull elephant lifted its head, his trunk upraised and ears outstretched. The others did the same. Mirie tried to capture the elephants poised and wary. The group did an abrupt about-face and took off.

They had been magnificent through the lens. She wished she could have had the film developed immediately, instead of having to send it to Europe for processing.

She turned to Max. "That was okay." Her face, however, conveyed the excitement that her words sought to minimize. Downplaying emotion was a defensive trait she had acquired in the male bastion of the newsroom, where anything more was deemed gushy and unprofessional.

Max smiled slightly, shifted his weight and looked up at the bowl of blue sky as if there were a message to ponder.

"I was concerned," he said slowly. "You never know how they're going to react. Every once in a while they'll come after you with no warning."

"I read that at first they only mock-charge."

"I wouldn't count on these elephants having read that book." He frowned and rubbed his neck. "I don't see much point in hanging around."

Mrs. Goode reappeared, along with Moses. The servant carried a rosebush, with roots wrapped in burlap. She gave orders in Swahili heavily laced with a British accent. Moses dug a hole with a long knife and scooped out the loose soil with his hands.

"A friend brought it from the city," Evelyn Goode told her guests. "I've never had any luck with roses out here. The soil is wretched for anything but desert roses. But now I have fertilizer . . ."

"Which is the desert rose?" asked Mirie.

Max knelt before a gnarled shrub. A fuchsia-petaled flower burst from a gray woody stem. "Some say it's related to a baobab."

Mirie touched the silvery stem. It was surprisingly silky, and the plant did look much like a miniature tree, a bonsai of a baobab crowned with a defiantly delicate flower.

"You like those?" Mrs. Goode asked, puzzled. "They're so common I don't bother with them. They don't belong in a proper garden." She attempted to replant a tomato plant the elephants had torn out. When Mirie was finished taking pictures of the rose, Max caught her eye and nodded toward the car.

"Evelyn . . ." said Mirie.

Evelyn Goode peered at them as if she were having some difficulty recollecting who they were and what they were doing there.

"Yes, yes. Forgive me. We'll have some more tea. Tom will be home soon."

Max didn't want another beer, nor Mirie more tea. Already they had waited for several hours. They stayed a while longer on the off chance Goode would return before sundown. Two hot toddies later—Evelyn Goode was serenely drunk—they gave up.

"Why don't you stay tonight?" said Mrs. Goode, her speech slurred. "You can sleep on the balcony. It overlooks the water, that is, if you don't mind the noise of those bully boys . . ."

"Thanks, Evelyn. We have to go," said Mirie firmly. She took Mrs. Goode's hand to say good-bye. It felt damp and boneless.

"Well, another time," she said. "At Tom Goode's house visitors are always welcome."

Max said, "Please have your husband radio us when he returns."

"Oh, yes. Tom's a man of his word," she said vaguely. "And he loves to help . . . charming young women." With both hands she briefly clasped Max's hand. "Lovely to meet you. Do come again."

Max backed away. "Thanks for the beers."

Evelyn Goode gazed into mid-distance. With the kitten clinging to her bodice, she walked them to the door, wound a tendril of drooping vine around the latticework and faded back into her house.

7

They were ten kilometers from the tourist camp as the sun dropped out of sight. Night closed in around the Land-Rover's headlights.

"Isn't it peculiar that Goode wasn't there?" asked Mirie.

"Things come up all the time. A lion killing stock is a lot more important than a travel brochure—no offense."

"Oh, I agree. I just wish we could have gone with him. A lion hunt. It might have made a good feature."

"I doubt they would have let you take pictures. A bunch of white guys hunting? It smacks too much of the old days."

"Is it illegal?"

"No. You can kill an animal that's threatening property or life. But photos would make it look like old colonials having a hunting party."

"Well, even if we only came along for the ride, it would have been better than hanging out with Evelyn Goode."

"She's a sad case," said Max.

"She took a fancy to you." When Mirie's tease met with resounding silence, she repeated his phrase, "No offense," and changed the subject. "Are you really allergic to cats?"

"Among other things."

"Even wild cats?"

"I don't know. I don't make a point of petting them. I'm not crazy about wild animals as house pets."

"She acts like that kitten is her only friend." Mirie sighed. "All that space, all day and all night—it must weigh on her."

"On a lot of people. Miles and miles of bloody Africa—that's what the Brits call it. It gets to people."

"But there's so much beauty here—everywhere you turn."

"Beauty can pierce like an arrow," said Max in his low-key way, and added, lest the lyricism be mistaken for his own, "Some writer said that."

"Who?"

"Can't remember. I read it a long time ago. It was one of those things that stuck—like chewing gum."

His humor, if you could call it that, mystified her. He'd hint at seriousness and fend it off with a joke. Her thoughts turned to the elephants. "I wish I could see my pictures right now. I need to spend the whole day with the elephants, watching everything they do, so I'll know what's ordinary and what's unusual."

"You'll get your chance," said Max. "All you want."

"Is it obvious when an elephant is close to calving?"

"Maybe to another elephant, not to me. If there were a clear sign, it would make things a lot easier. But there isn't."

o o

It was after the dinner hour and they had the rustic dining room to themselves. Max ate avidly. Mirie had soup. Her gear was at her feet. She would not let it out of her sight and had refused to let the porter take it.

The bags seemed to have grown heavier. Max took them for her, as an askari escorted them by flashlight to their tents. They said good night. She stood outside for a moment as Max and the guard continued down the path to his tent, visible as a dim lamp glow.

The porter had lit a kerosene lamp and turned down the bed. The tent was sparely but comfortably furnished: two beds, a table, two chairs, a woven sisal rug on the floor. The bathroom was in a smaller tent in back. A sign posted at the entrance said,"Please use water sparingly." She showered off the road dust by lamplight.

Mirie removed the beaded muslin net from the water

pitcher and poured herself a glass, another and another. She slipped into bed and snuffed out the lamp.

Her body seemed in motion, as if the accumulated momentum of traveling thousands of miles were still within.

She pictured the raiding elephants and whiskered warthogs. They reminded her of Sam Gebhardt—she should write him. To say what? So far so good? She thought about the new *Ecoworld* that would appear on newsstands any day. Through Liz she had found a replacement for herself.

Sam had taken it as a personal affront when she told him she was quitting to go back to photography. He said he had all he could do without having to train two new photo editors while the magazine was being revamped. He accepted Phyllis' departure. But hers, he said, was capricious and selfish. He ranted about the trouble with women, that they wanted everything, marriage without babies, babies without marriage, everything together, careers, lovers, marriage, babies. He railed at her about the folly of trying to grab at not one brass ring but thousands.

Sam shook his head sadly as he delivered the *coup de grâce*. "You young people. You have no ties, no loyalties. I pity you."

When she told Jonathan what Sam had said, he was outraged. "That patronizing turd! How could you let him talk to you like that?"

"I couldn't argue. He says I'm leaving him in the lurch. I suppose I am."

"You gave him plenty of notice, M. Because he's obsessed with that earnest little rag, you should be too? Don't be ridiculous. You should have left a long time ago."

As Mirie put her forehead against Jonathan's chest, he suddenly sprung away. Pulling at his hair the way Sam did, he began dancing madly around the dining table. "*You vill, my leetle koomkwat, peec pictchoors forrr me for eeterrrnity. Hee-hee.*"

Mirie laughed at Jonathan as Sam-the-Svengali. Jonathan did not stop until he had banished all outward signs of distress.

They made love the way she liked, slowly, like a seduction. He fondled her through her blouse. He undressed her, touched her. He kissed her eyelids, mistaking the new round of tears for those of pleasure. But Sam's curse still stung, and she used ardor as a balm. She became a seductress with a vengeance. Jonathan could not know or care at that moment that Mirie's passion was a cover-up. He touched her, made her touch herself. When they finished, Jonathan fell right to sleep. Mirie lay against his chest, listening to his heart beat. She was restless. What did she want? An apology from Sam? To make love again? She had no idea, but she could not let go.

ɔ ɔ

Asleep in the tent, Mirie dreamed of elephants. She was at home in New York, in her mother's old apartment. She had taken out the roll of film, and the pictures were all developed. The elephants came out as wood sculptures tall as baobabs. Her mother came into the bedroom. She was young, not much older than Mirie, in an 1890s dress the color of seashells. Her black hair was pinned up.

Her mother ignored the elephants. "They're only pictures. Be practical, Mirie. Wear a dress." Her mother began to unfasten the dress.

"It doesn't suit me," said Mirie. "I can't shoot in that dress."

"You really should," said her mother airily. "It's the fashion."

"Jonathan likes the way I dress," said Mirie stubbornly.

Her mother primped her hair. "Who cares about Jonathan?"

"But he was with us when you died."

"Oh, how could I forget?" Her mother plumped the pillows and neatened the room, as if Mirie weren't there. She sang lightheartedly:

> *"There's so much to do every day, every day*
> *To make our meetings end."*

Mirie cried out, "Oh, Mom, why don't you remember me?" Her mother continued to sing.

ɔ ɔ

A sound awakened her, a deep heaving sound from the belly of the night. Then it was quiet, so quiet Mirie thought the sound might have been a remnant of her dream. She groped for the matches and lit the lamp. Again it came, the dyspeptic, repeated groan of a lion. It had delivered her from the nightmare, which seemed more real and hurtful to her than any lion on the prowl could be.

Damn Evelyn Goode, she thought, as if the poor lush were to blame. A terrible business, betrayal, she thought, a small family business she had inherited. Be practical, her mother had said. Practicality was an idea her mother had been forced to learn too late in life to do much good. Fully awake, Mirie tried to regain her usual sense. But sense did better in sunlight. It wasn't for a night of lions.

The roaring came again and drifted away. She shone a flashlight out the net window. She wanted to see a lion. For to see a lion was to confirm she was in Africa. She waited for the lion's sound and the shriek of prey. But there was nothing more, until a raspy chorus of frogs broke the silence.

8

Judging by the sun, it was around four o'clock. Mirie put down her binoculars and closed her bird book. She had identified the birds around camp by the illustrations. The iridescent blue ones with white-ringed eyes were junk birds called superb starlings. The comic birds with lobster-claw beaks making a racket in the trees beside the tent were red hornbills. The yellow birds were weavers. They were always busy adding twigs to nests that dangled from the acacias like Christmas ornaments.

Those were easy descriptive names, easier to remember than birds named for their discoverers, who, like Adam, had first choice. She was surrounded by birds she had never seen before. They were extravagantly colorful compared with the drab birds of New York. Identifying them was like detective work; it gave Mirie a sense of mastering her unfamiliar surroundings.

o o

Her father's magnifying glass had an ivory handle. It was kept in a compartment of the roll-top desk. He used it to read the *Daily Racing Form*. Mirie used it to examine yeast grains, dead flies, Arbuckle's shed hairs, anything that might prove interesting under magnification. When she was nine years old, her father gave her a microscope. After Mirie examined paramecia in rotting lettuce leaves and hairy-legged insects in pond scum, she concocted more challenging experiments.

Arbuckle was a lethargic bloodhound who treated her father with slobbering affection and Mirie with indifference, occasionally accompanied by snarls. His main occupation was following sunspots around the apartment all day. His loose skin flopped on the floor. His fleshy muzzle snagged on a tooth as he slept, and gave him a perpetual sneer. Arbuckle whimpered and twitched as he slept. Mirie assumed he was having doggy dreams. There was gray liquid on the tip of his penis.

She had read a children's primer on sex and believed she knew what Arbuckle was up to. She snuck up on the sleeping dog and touched a glass slide to his penis. The dog, suddenly alert, went for her hand, but she snatched it away in time and ran off to her microscope. The results were disappointing. She had expected to see tiny Arbuckle puppies, or even halves of puppies, but there were only wriggling tadpoles. She called her father. He laughed and called her mother. Her mother looked and grew flustered.

"Don't bother Arbuckle. He'll bite you."

"He already tried," said Mirie. "I'm too fast for him."

"Don't discourage her," her father told her mother. "She's going to be a scientist."

o o

She left the shade of the canvas porch to see what car was rumbling into camp. It wasn't Max's, but only a ranch vehicle full of "jolly tourists"—the description on her film log of the rolls she had taken of them earlier.

A week had passed and still no word from the camp manager, Tom Goode. When she and Max had driven by his house, the houseboy confirmed he was still on safari. The assistant manager of the tourist camp, a harried young Briton, sent a radio message to the ranch's head office. The voice on the other end of the static had no information. The assistant, new to the job himself, could offer no advice. But because she was doing work for the ranch, he let her have the field guide on birds for half the inflated price the tourists paid.

Mirie set to work photographing the tourist camp over-

42

looking the muddy river. From the opposite bank she photographed the open wood-and-thatch dining room, as crocodiles, jaws agape, sunned themselves on the banks below. She photographed tourists armed with cameras jostling for space on the sun roof of a Landcruiser. She photographed them at lunch as starlings hopped among the tables stealing crumbs. She photographed them as they rode lethargic horses among an optical confusion of reticulated giraffes and pinstriped zebras. She photographed them relaxing at their tents.

The visitors, a couple of dozen in all, were well-to-do older Americans on vacation. One couple had retired to a life of travel. There were younger couples, too, with money to burn, in search of adventure with a minimum of discomfort. They had come to Simahali "to see the animals before they're gone." They were a congenial bunch, outgoing and eager to talk about themselves, as Americans far from home were wont to do. Mirie mingled with them long enough to get all the pictures she needed.

Max, however, avoided them altogether. She would join him for a game drive at dawn, then he would take off. He might reappear for another drive before sundown, depending on how far away he was and how involved he was in his own work. So far, the only time he had taken out his camera while they were together was when they came upon a group of Grevy's zebras, a rare variety whose thin-striped hide was attractive to poachers. Max and Mirie would photograph from on top of the car. When Mirie was done, she would stay absolutely still in deference to her companion at work.

Mirie picked up her binoculars. Across the ravine an elephant she called Old Joe was scratching his back on a tree. Old Joe was a solitary regular at camp. He was too far away for a good shot.

"Any word from your friend Goode?"

It was Max. She had been so absorbed she had not heard his footsteps.

"Nothing."

"I brought you a present." He handed her a Coke bottle plugged with paper. Inside was a yellow scorpion scrambling in circles, frantic to escape. "I found it in my tennis shoe."

"It's unhappy," said Mirie.

"His brain is too small for unhappiness."

"Is there a brain that small, Max?"

Max considered this a moment. "Set it free if you're bothered, but be careful you don't get bitten. They aren't known to be grateful."

○ ○

The car roof shuddered as Max pivoted on top, scanning the bush through binoculars.

"What's going on?" Mirie got out of the car.

He circled again and came down. "Nothing. Fortunately."

"Why fortunately?"

"No tourists, no poachers, no cows . . ."

"No wildlife," Mirie added. The warm late-day light was fine for pictures, but there wasn't so much as a starling to photograph and she had already taken plenty of landscapes.

"Excuse me." She had to pee and went off in search of a bush.

Max called after her. "Clap."

Mirie turned. "What?"

"Clap your hands. To warn animals."

"Oh, come on."

"As a precaution."

Mirie marched onward, applauding the rustling grass. There was nothing there. Not so much as a dik-dik was disturbed. She felt ridiculous.

"It's safer to go behind the car," said Max when she came back. He started the motor.

"I like being in the grass. It's peaceful."

"Unless there's a snake around."

"Oh, how likely is that?"

"Not very. But it's painful—or fatal—if it happens. I don't mean to scare you. But believe me, you want to avoid trouble when you're out here."

Max's cautionary advice did not scare Mirie at all. She had no particular fear of being in the bush. To her it was a benign place, a huge sunlit canvas on which she had barely begun her work.

Besides, she thought, both she and Max were so well prepared, with extra water, a jerry can of gas, spare parts, medicaments and—Max's indulgence—a renewed supply of overripe bananas. What could possibly happen that they couldn't cope with?

They drove on as the sun, amber and bloated, neared the horizon. The track joined red earth and blue sky, a trick of the brief equatorial twilight. They stopped at a crater where a waterhole had dried up. The soil had shrunk and split into a crazy quilt of trapezoids and hexagons.

Max got on top of the car, scanning through the binoculars. Mirie wandered the field bent over, camera molded to her face. She tripped and barely caught herself from taking a dive into the hard-baked earth.

Nice going, Ms. Magoo, she thought, a real pro maneuver. Max hadn't noticed. Why should she care if he had? If she took pictures standing on her head, what difference did it make as long as they came out?

Mirie ran her hand over the whitened cape buffalo skull she had stumbled over. Spiky larval tubes had colonized the horns.

She called to Max, "What do you suppose happened to it?"

Max looked over. "It died naturally, or it was weak and was preyed on while drinking. It could have got stuck in the mud."

"What an awful way to go." The skull evoked a grisly scenario: the buffalo tried to kick itself free, only to sink deeper, struggled to keep its head out of the mud, then, exhausted, suffocated slowly in the ooze.

She framed the curve of whited handlebar horns against the scarlet field. Seen through the lens, the skull was no longer animal remains but a sculptural form to photograph in the intense light that was the last of the African day.

"Mirie!" Max called to her, his voice low and insistent. She heard him jump down from the car roof.

"One second." She knelt down for a different angle.

"No. Now!"

She looked up, stunned by the sharpness in his voice, and made a dash for the car.

He drove slowly across the crater. She didn't see a thing, just dry grass everywhere. "What is it?"

45

Then she spotted them, a pair of lions poised like bookends. The male got up and paced around the female. His mane was scruffy and his coat thorn-scratched. The female lay still, switching her tail. The male approached from the rear. She snarled and threw back her head when he mounted her.

It was too unexpected, too fast, and the sun was not cooperating. Mirie grabbed the other camera body, loaded it with fast film and fitted a 200-mm lens. By that time the male was settling down a few feet from his mate, surveying the rough patch of universe that was his dominion.

Max cleared his throat. "Sorry about that. I didn't want you to be standing there in case they decided to take a stroll."

What was he apologizing for? she thought. She wouldn't have given his irritability a second thought if he hadn't brought it up. He must have been miffed at himself, for losing his cool, disinterested amiability. A show of feeling, any feeling, taxed him, somehow compromised his privacy. She smoothed it over.

"It's okay. You didn't want me to miss my first lion," she said. "Or be eaten."

"Give the old boy a few minutes. He'll do a repeat performance." Over twenty years he must have observed lions mating many times. Mirie thought he wasn't displeased to be sharing it again with her.

The light waned. The male lion got up, circled the female twice, reconsidered and lay down again. When it finally mounted her, it was too dark to shoot.

9

Dear Jonathan,

The more I see, the more I think of pictures I haven't taken and better ways to shoot the ones I did take. Having to wait to have my film processed is nerve-wracking. I'd run through a hundred rolls a week if the good light lasted longer. Though my days are full, time in Africa goes *polepole,* so slowly it runs backward.

We saw four cheetahs hunting. I didn't notice them—they blended into the grass—until Howden pointed them out. Work would be easier if I had his experience. He positioned the car between the cats and a herd of gazelles. He found the best spot for light and camera angle, while not disturbing their hunting. Shooting logistics are second nature to him. On my own I'm afraid I wouldn't have been able to figure things out fast enough to do the job.

Mirie stopped writing.

ɔ ɔ

The cheetahs had not budged as Max drove in closer. The female was sitting up, while her cubs napped under an acacia.

The mother, a long rangy cat, looked around. She turned one way, and froze sphinxlike except for flicking her black-tipped tail. The car was only five meters away, but she looked right past it and was not bothered by the noise of the camera.

Her golden eyes radiated from round pupils, different from

the vertical slits of other cats. Black lyre-shaped tear stripes framed the muzzle. When she stretched, using a skeletal tree stump as a scratching post, her spine made a strong S-curve over her haunches. As she started for the westering sun, the three cubs roused themselves. They still had a kittenish ruff at the neck. Though they were nearly full grown, they could not yet hunt for themselves.

Max opened his mottled silvery camera box, which he kept in easy reach of the driver's seat. "I think it's dinnertime." He drove in a wide arc, staying slightly ahead of the cats coursing over the plain. "Those cats are skinnier than usual. They can't afford to miss a kill."

Mirie squinted. She had trouble distinguishing the cheetahs from the yellow grass. The car's jolting made the binoculars impossible to use. "They're so thin I can't see them at all."

Max pointed to an acacia. "That's the center of the clock. Follow my hand to four o'clock."

Finally catching a glimpse, then promptly losing them again, she asked, "How do you see them?"

"It's like looking for a flaw in a pattern. I see motion or color that's different from the surroundings. You think I'm good. I've gone out with these old native hunters—I'm blind compared to those guys."

Max stopped the car to have a look around from on top.

"There's a herd of Grant's gazelles," he said, driving on. "And kongoni."

The larger, red brown kongoni reminded Mirie of cartoon animals. They had a dopey, cross-eyed expression on wedge-faced faces, capped by a stubby brace of horns.

The cats took their time, walking and trotting toward the herd. The gazelles detected nothing, even though there was a slight breeze and they were downwind of the cheetahs.

"Cheetahs hunt while there's still light. Even so, I have only one good closeup of a kill."

"The one in *Cats at Twilight?*" She recalled the series of pictures of a cheetah chasing a Thomson's gazelle, where cat and antelope were elongated in flight against a blur of grass, the instant of the kill, and the cat devouring the dead animal.

He nodded. "I'd say I'm due for another . . . I fought with my publisher about that sequence, right down to the mat."

"Why? They were fantastic pictures."

"Thanks . . . We had a big go-around because he didn't want to include the shot of the Tommy being eaten. He said it was anticlimactic and would turn off readers. 'People buying fifty-dollar coffee-table books for Christmas gifts don't want to see antelope intestines.' I argued that if we didn't include the picture, it was pandering to the notion that these cats are savage killers. People think of animals killing in human terms. It's silly. Cheetahs don't hunt because they have a grudge against gazelles." Max gesticulated, his big hands taking up the argument on their own. "I'm not interested in sanitizing nature. I don't want to sensationalize it either. I just wanted to show the point of the hunt. The cats hunt to eat! If they don't kill, they die." Max's gaze shifted. A kongoni had stopped grazing. Max switched off the motor. The dispute over pictures he had published years before was forgotten. His eyes were riveted on the scene before them. The kongoni faced in the direction of the cats and turned to stone.

o   o

Mirie crumpled the paper and took out a new aérogramme.

> Dear Jonathan,
>   I'm busy all day. Nothing happens for a long time, then suddenly you have to act fast. Howden and I followed cheetahs hunting. I felt like I was sprinting alongside. The only trouble was, I focused on the wrong cat . . .

The sides of Mirie's camera were damp where she held it. She used the end of her T-shirt to wipe it dry.

The mother cheetah was out in front. Her slow, careful steps seemed strangely stilted.

Another kongoni spotted the cats. A silent signal swept the herd. The gazelles stopped grazing. They turned toward the cats, their flanks twitching.

"Why don't they beat it?" whispered Mirie.

Max didn't answer.

49

A cub shot off in a dead run, cutting a wide swath through the panicky herd. Gazelles leaped and ran. In the midst of the commotion the mother cheetah exploded in a sprint. As she bored through the herd, the gazelles wheeled and the cub was left all alone in a dusty haze. It stopped, bewildered. It paced nervously, like a petulant runner that had blown the race.

Everything moved too fast. Mirie didn't know where to look, let alone where to shoot.

Most of Max was out the window. Defying gravity, he had braced his feet and contorted his body to shoot from outside the car.

The female, her back coiling and uncoiling up and down like a spring, closed in on her quarry. She tore after a young gazelle, her motion punctuated by Max's motor drive. The other gazelles flew out of the way.

The gazelle dodged the cheetah, once, twice, and made another switchback. Then the cat sank its dewclaw into the gazelle's flank and it went down. The two cubs bounded after the mother. She released her stranglehold on the gazelle and the cubs were on it, tearing at the back end. It managed to get up, dazed and hurt. The mother cheetah clamped her mouth around its throat and killed it.

Her sides heaving, she lay down a few feet away from where the cubs were on the kill. The third cub, recovered from its aborted chase, trotted up to them.

A lark chirruped. Max pulled himself back into the car, grimacing and breathing heavily. "You think you got anything?"

She shook her head. "It was too fast."

"That was a tough one to anticipate." He offered Mirie the water bottle, then took a drink himself. He pointed to a tree. "Black-headed herons," he said. Mirie looked through binoculars. The birds perched close together on an acacia branch, heads pointed in opposite directions like the face of Janus. "In about half an hour, in the final light," said Max, "that would be a nice shot."

How could Max see so much at once, Mirie wondered, while she herself was still dazed from the chase?

Max drove slowly over to where the cheetahs were feeding.

The mother had joined in. While three cats ate, one stood sentinel, its muzzle bloody, on the lookout for lions or other animals that could steal the kill.

"Did you see how the cub almost blew it for them?" asked Max. "The mother cat took advantage of the panic. She ignored all the other gazelles, even ones that were in her path, for the little one. They pick out the prey that they have the best chance of getting. They can't afford to miss, in terms of energy, not after a sprint like that." He wiped his forehead, turned his head from side to side to loosen kinks. "But I guess you've read about all that."

Was he afraid he was boring her, telling her what she already knew? Or was there a hint of poking fun at all the studying and planning she'd done for the trip? In hindsight, it did seem like a useless effort, like trying to experience the succulence of a peach by reading about it.

"It's not the same."

o o

Mirie tore up the aérogramme. "Sorry, Jonathan," she said to herself. "It doesn't work."

She could describe the speed of the cats but not the thrill of tracking them. She could describe the killing, but not how it felt that she and Max were the only human witnesses to it. She could describe the cats devouring the gazelle, so hungry that they had a tug-of-war with the flayed skin, but not her own greedy hunger for a few more moments of twilight and a few more pictures.

The sun sank, the herons flew away, the gazelles moved off to graze.

10

Mirie waited. Her mind filled
the vacuum of time in not always agreeable ways. It populated
the sprawling empty canvas she had reserved for Africa—her
Africa—with things that were old and decidedly out of place.

o o

Jonathan burst through the door, kicked off his shoes and
headed for the kitchen. He inspected a bowl of chicken breasts
basting in sauce, then joined Mirie on the fire escape, where
she was fanning coals on a hibachi.

"Did you have that meeting?" she asked.

He nodded.

"And?"

Jonathan lit a cigarette, watching the smoke curling into
space over the hodgepodge of East Village rooftops.

"Forget the Bogart," said Mirie. "What happened?"

"I think I got a bite."

Mirie's mismatched eyes widened with hope. "Yes?"

Jonathan shifted his weight, pacing in place on the cramped
balcony, trying not to knock over Mirie's flowerpots as he told
her about the meeting with a producer.

"There's no desk in Raskin's office. No one does deals at a
desk. There's a couch and wall-to-wall windows, green plants,
bad oil paintings. Raskin's in his fifties, chinless under the

beard, body of an avocado. He smokes cigars and doesn't move. He and the assistant—his little friend—were on the couch. I walked around. The eyes followed me. That's how I knew he was awake."

"Your lecturing trick," Mirie said.

"Whatever works," said Jonathan, shifting as he spoke, high on his own nervous energy. "I pitched the story."

Mirie squeezed by him to fetch the chicken. She arranged it on the hibachi grate. "What did he say?"

"He said, 'We'll talk.'"

"What does that mean?"

"Who knows? But they were like kids listening to a bedtime story. Raskin's a phone junkie, and when the phone rang—I was telling him about the terrorists at the Statue of Liberty—he didn't take the call. I've got a feeling about this one, M. I can smell a deal. What do you think?"

"I smell barbecue sauce," she murmured, painting the chicken with a basting brush.

"Thanks, M . . ." He tickled her from behind. She yelped and almost tipped over the hibachi. Before Jonathan could duck, Mirie daubed a red stripe down his nose.

He grabbed her wrist. "Truce!" she cried. She pulled Jonathan closer, screwing up her features into a comical grimace. She sighed, "What I won't do for you," and licked off the sauce.

o o

Mirie's mother called her at the magazine to say she wasn't feeling up to the concert. No, Mirie needn't come over. She was going to bed early. Mirie knew what was happening, and knew as well there was nothing more she could do.

Instead of hanging around at the office until eight o'clock, Mirie headed for the midtown editing room where Jonathan was finishing an industrial video.

She picked up Cokes and a pizza on the way. Jonathan had a remarkable metabolism. He could engulf large quantities of junk food. His belly would bulge as if he'd swallowed a goat. The next morning he would be trim again.

When she opened the door to the editing room, she noticed

a scent of irises. Jonathan greeted her. Beside him at the editing console was a woman Mirie did not know. She had pale skin and doe eyes framed by a frizz of strawberry blond hair, and she was enfolded in a challis shawl. A reel was rewinding, turning sound into chipmunk gibberish.

"Thanks." Jonathan took the food from her. "Mirie, this is Diana Lee . . . Diana, Mirie Keane . . . Diana works with Hap Raskin," he said. "I thought you and your mom—?"

"She canceled."

Jonathan looked hard at Mirie and motioned to the hallway. He turned to Diana. "Excuse us a moment . . ."

Diana checked her watch. "Actually, I should go."

Jonathan said suavely, "You won't share our elegant repast?"

"Thanks. I'm meeting Hap uptown for dinner. I'll call you on Tuesday. Nice to meet you, Mirie." She zipped her briefcase and left.

The pizza was cooling fast. Jonathan devoured his first piece and with two hands shoveled up another wilting slice. "That girl, Diana, left me her screenplay." He disengaged a string of mozzarella from his chin. "The trick is to eat it so fast your taste buds don't know what hit them."

"Where are you going to find time to critique a script? You have all those term papers."

"If the little friend of the producer who's about to option my project wants my advice, I'm not turning her down."

"Why doesn't Raskin read her script?"

"Are you kidding? Raskin doesn't read. He has a ten-second attention span. For scripts, that is. Little girls are a different story."

"Is he a necrophiliac? She smells like a funeral parlor."

"What are you so surly about?"

"Nothing. I liked her shawl. Will you come to the concert with me?"

"I'll be lucky if I'm home by midnight." He rolled his chair over to hers. "What are you going to do about your mom?"

"She didn't want me to come over. She's starting again." Mirie didn't feel like dwelling on her mother's troubles with alcohol. "I'm going to see her shrink tomorrow . . . What about your movie idea?"

"She says Raskin is definitely interested."

"That's one small step for mankind."

"It's something."

She put her hand in his. "It's your best yet. I know that. But how do you get these yahoos to notice?"

o   o

A few weeks later Jonathan flew to southern Indiana to shoot stonecutters hewing blocks of granite from a quarry. It paid well for an industrial video, and Jonathan liked the old cutters, who described their work with a Hoosier twang. Rain and gray skies prolonged the trip.

Jonathan called Mirie in the evenings from a motel room where he and the sound man were holed up. Mirie laughed at Jonathan's down-home accent as he told her about the day's snafus. There was little to do for amusement. He had gone swimming in an abandoned quarry in the drizzle. He had drunk beer with the townies. He had read all the local newspapers. In short, he was bored and couldn't wait to get back to Manhattan.

He arrived home at 2 A.M. one night, showered and crawled into bed. They fell asleep, legs entwined, warm and snug.

Jonathan slept through the early-morning clatter of metal garbage cans as the sanitation truck belched and grunted its way down the street. Light filtered in through the tall windows of the tiny bedroom.

Mirie touched a silver hair among the black ringlets at Jonathan's temple. He opened one eye.

"There's another one," she said.

"Pull it out," he said groggily.

"Why? I love you salt-and-pepper."

"I hate it. Pull it out."

She yanked it.

"Shit!" Jonathan sat up in bed.

"You told me to."

"Not that. Do I have a clean shirt?"

"There's one I can iron." She pushed him back down playfully.

Jonathan said, "I have a breakfast meeting with Raskin."

"That's great. When did that happen?"

"Yesterday."

"You talked to him?"

"I set it up with his assistant."

She kissed him. Jonathan looked at the clock. It was still early. He pulled her on top of him.

ɔ ɔ

Mirie laid a clean wrinkled shirt over the ironing board in the bedroom. Jonathan had on pants and a tie draped over his T-shirt. He dumped his suitcase with dirty laundry into the basket in the closet and hastily shut the door before the clothes spilled out. Since he had given up his hole-in-the-wall apartment and they were living together, Jonathan had become almost domesticated. He had had to. Her one-bedroom apartment was too small to accommodate chaos.

Mirie felt Jonathan watching her from behind, watching the way her shoulder blades moved under her nightgown as she laid the shirt over the tapered end of the board. The iron hissed as it glided over wet specks of spray starch.

"Thanks." Jonathan kissed the back of her neck. "I'll put on the coffee."

She supposed there was something in the new can of starch that gave it a cloying sweet smell. But the nozzle was odorless. It wasn't the shirt either. Maybe it was aftershave, or soap Jonathan had taken from the motel. But the smell didn't come from the bathroom. There was a hint of it in his suitcase. Mirie dumped out the laundry basket in the closet. She picked up the white terry-cloth robe, the one she had given him last Christmas.

Irises. She smelled irises.

The stink of burning cloth brought Jonathan running to the bedroom. Mirie was leaning halfway out the window. He dashed over in time to see his robe flutter down six stories to the street below. Jonathan shouted something incomprehensible, and snatched the iron.

56

He was much too late. The shirt was branded with a black scorch mark right over the heart.

o   o

When Mirie appeared at her mother's door, her mother was having her own problems. She had broken her promise. When her mother left her in the living room, Mirie knew she had gone to rinse the sherry out of her mouth.

Mirie would not have minded a glass herself, but the prospect of getting drunk with her mother was too dismal.

She put on the kettle and rinsed two Meissen cups and saucers from the sink of dirty dishes. The kettle shrieked. The jar of freeze-dried coffee was almost empty—Mirie wrote "coffee" on a slip of paper—and scraped out the last two teaspoonfuls.

They sipped their coffee, both skirting the issue of the duffel bag Mirie had dropped in her old bedroom. Her mother lapsed into familiar themes. The plaster was falling, the toilet was running, and the landlord had ignored her calls. A tenant downstairs had fired a gun at a prowler. The police showed up. Tenants accused the landlord of hiring a goon squad to persecute them so they would leave their low-rent apartments.

The three-bedroom apartment was her mother's only asset. It housed the remnants of a more gracious past. The Regulator clock with a brass pendulum ticked in the corner over the roll-top desk. That had been her father's place, where he helped Mirie with her arithmetic when she was a child and read the *Daily Racing Form*. Her father had died Mirie's first year at Columbia.

After his death the desk yielded from its many compartments a trove of IOUs and gambling debts her mother had known nothing about. There was also an insurance policy, the best offered by the firm where her father had been chief actuarial statistician. An old friend from her father's firm said the policy would ensure them a comfortable life. Having never so much as balanced a checkbook, her mother entrusted him with the family's financial matters. He put the money in safe conservative investments: a foundry and a railroad. Two years later the steel business slumped and the railroad filed for bankruptcy, and while it seemed in the latter case that the small shareholders would eventually get their money, the litigation had been going on for years.

Her mother had passed the civil service exam and found a clerical job in the Motor Vehicles Department. For a woman bred to be wife, mother and hostess, her mother showed unexpected resolve. Her husband's fondness for playing the horses and cards she always thought was little more than an amusing pastime, respite from a cramped employment that ill suited his gregarious nature. The disclosure of his debts did nothing to change her line. She confected a past much sweeter than Mirie remembered, a past as selective and untruthful as a family photo album: of vacations at the ocean, parties in New York with old friends, of a marriage that remained a love affair. Her mother obliterated contrary images that were still vivid to Mirie, of her father returning home late at night, and of sullen silences at the breakfast table. Her mother's self-deception took a toll. Old friends drifted away, and her social drinking turned into solitary nightcaps in the living room, the clock quietly ticking.

The psychologist she talked to about her drinking advised her to move and make a new home for herself. She agreed that Manhattan was not what it had been. She said she wanted to move back home to Massachusetts, but she could not afford to give up the apartment. Nor did she want to live far from her daughter.

Her mother had made all the usual stops in her ramble of woes when Mirie finally broke in.

"Jonathan is having an affair." Her mother sat in her Windsor chair impassively sipping instant coffee from the Meissen cup. "It's someone I met," said Mirie, "a girl who works for a movie producer who Jonathan is trying to sell on a movie idea."

Her mother set down her coffee cup. "Are you certain?"

Mirie nodded. She wasn't going to go into detail.

Her mother was pale. She had not been getting out much. There had been some cutbacks at the office, and she was working only part-time. "If you look for trouble, Mirie, you'll often find it."

"It's his deceit. I can't live with that." Was it the first time, the tenth, the hundredth? It was a self-inflicted cruelty that Mirie could so easily picture Jonathan and that girl, the pre-Raphaelite tart, swimming in an abandoned stone quarry, and afterward the girl perfuming herself wrapped in his robe.

Her mother folded her hands. "I know why you fell in love with Jonathan—he's charming in his way. He's so much more interesting than Don."

"Don!" Mirie exploded. Her mother had the most absurd sense of time. "That was ages ago. I was just out of college."

"But you two were so happy, going off to Europe together."

"I was happy in Europe. It was traveling I liked, not Don."

"Evidently. You dropped him fast enough when you came home."

"I was bored. That's not a crime," Mirie said sharply. "Do we have to go into ancient history?"

But her mother was not to be diverted. "After Don—what were you doing, Mirie, experimenting with boyfriends? Every few months there would be a new one. I remember you brought over that young man who was a fireman. What ever happened to him?"

"Oh, Mom," cried Mirie, dismayed at what she had let herself in for. "You have no idea what it's like out there."

"Really?" said her mother archly. "I'm not so foolish as you think. I'm not going to say anything against Jonathan. What you say may be true . . ." Her mother's voice became soothing, distant, like lapping water. "But it's between the two of you. You've been together, what, four years? I don't understand these wishy-washy relationships . . ." The soft desultory reproach hurt Mirie. "Doesn't either of you have any resolve at all?"

o o

Mirie wished she were like the women in Russian novels who jumped into troikas to follow their lovers across the Siberian steppes or hurled themselves under trains. She longed to make a grand gesture. All she could do was not answer Jonathan's phone calls, an act about as satisfying as eating day-old mashed potatoes.

59

Jonathan finally gave up trying to phone her at her mother's apartment and at the office. When she returned from lunch, she found a single red rose on her light table. The secretary said a messenger had brought it. There was no note. Mirie put the rose in a glass, but she did not reach for the phone. Another rose arrived the next day. And the next. Mirie had a stomachache that wouldn't go away.

Liz said she was foolish to break up with Jonathan. Her friend Annie, who was older than Mirie, a lawyer, divorced and caustic about men, said she was right to "leave the horny little bastard." Mirie stopped consulting friends.

The museum was open late. She opted to work late in the library there, to avoid a long evening of listening to her mother. She stopped in one of the halls to look at a glowing glass case of Indian artifacts. At the sound of hurrying footsteps she turned. It was Jonathan. He must have followed her after she had left the office.

"Please. Can I talk to you?" He touched her arm, then withdrew it when she flinched. He groped for a beginning. "That girl . . ."

"She has a name," said Mirie. "Diana." How clever of Jonathan, she thought bitterly, cornering her in her private haven to make peace.

"She's a high-class groupie, a user, a star-fucker who messed up 'cause I'm not a star. I don't know who I am right now. An asshole of the first rank for starters. But I can't see us throwing away four years because of one dumb move. Christ, M, I love you. I was a fucking bandit before we met. You know I stopped that when we started living together."

"You cheapened us. You made us ordinary."

"What happened has nothing to do with us."

"How can I trust you? How do I know that every time you go away or I do, you aren't . . ."

"Because we look out for each other. There's nobody I want as much as you. These last couple of weeks, I feel like half my face has been missing. I was wrong. I'm sorrier than you know . . . . You don't believe me. You're too extreme, Mirie."

Jonathan coughed nervously. Even as she was seething inside, she had let him move closer to her. She didn't know what she was going to do. She put her hand flat against his chest and pushed him back with all her might. He didn't fall, but his hand flew to his chest as if he had been wounded.

She said with quiet ferocity, "I don't want you to touch any other woman. I don't care if your film students fall in love with you. I don't care about your flirting and looking and being charming. But if you do this again, Jonathan, you'll kill us once and for all. I love you, and you've hurt me, and I can't understand that. It's so unfair. Life is not very fair, but you should be. There has to be one piece of firm ground in my life, in our life. Otherwise, what's the point? Maybe sex means too many other things to me, and to you it's only screwing. But I'm not going to share you. If you touch another woman, Jonathan, I'll leave you. I promise."

Her mother had little to say when Mirie repacked the duffel bag. Mirie felt there was relief on both sides. She couldn't wait to get back to her own apartment, and her mother no longer had to hide the sherry bottle.

Hap Raskin never did come through. But that was a couple of years ago, and Jonathan had had a lot of ideas since then.

11

While Max and Mirie were having breakfast, a slim, graying white man strode briskly into the dining area, greeted members of the African staff, then, rather formally, presented himself at their table.

Tom Goode had scarcely sat down before he launched into an involved description of the week of crises that had delayed their meeting. There was the lion hunt, then pumps had broken down, elephants had destroyed an electrified fence, a vanload of tourists had arrived unexpectedly. Now, however, the brochure would receive his full attention.

He sat ramrod straight. His gray hair was precisely combed. Mirie judged he was in his late fifties. His skin was permanently tanned, except for his nose, distressed from sunburn or alcohol or both. The eyes were gentle, Mirie thought, and a little sad.

Over breakfast Goode engaged Max more than Mirie. He talked about the problem of fires and water shortages because the rains had failed for so long; the ranch's difficulty getting stock to the slaughterhouse fast enough; whether or not culling game made sense in overcrowded parklands; how, given entrenched corruption, hunting could be regulated; and the fickleness of the tour business. At times, Max agreed with Goode, but more often than not, in slow, disputatious fashion, he whittled away at Goode's assertions. Goode appeared to enjoy the sparring.

Several times both Max and Mirie attempted to steer the conversation around to the brochure, but they could not pin down the camp manager until he himself was finally ready to talk business. Mirie told him that although she had taken pictures of the tents and immediate camp area during his week-long absence, she now needed his cooperation—as (she reminded Goode) his boss had promised her—in photographing the more remote parts of the ranch.

Goode could not have been more cordial. He reaffirmed that he would help her not only with the brochure but with her personal project as well. Immensely relieved, Mirie was pleased that her work, which she'd planned so carefully, was now right on track.

"You aim to photograph an elephant birth," said Goode. "It's never been done, you understand. A lot of boffins claim they've seen it, but—"

"Boffins?"

"These scientist chaps we see all the time. The owner lets them come. They arrive here with their backpacks and their beards and their grants. Plentiful as termites." He added, "Scientists, they call themselves. Bloody two-year wonders. If you want to know about Africa, talk to the old African hunters and people like myself, who have lived in the bush all our lives, and seen it change."

Goode outlined the safari plans: They would leave after lunch the following day, trek up Rhino Peak, and camp by the river. After the safari he would fly her around the ranch to locate other elephant groups. He would recommend the best campsites, and supply her with whatever equipment she was lacking.

"There's one slight difficulty," said Goode. "My plane seats only two."

"Don't worry about me," asserted Max. "I'm driving up north. It's been a few years since I've been there."

"I'd think twice about going," said Goode. "There's tribal fighting. The government wouldn't care if they wiped each other out, except that AK-47s are being smuggled in and the government doesn't like guns falling into the wrong hands. There used to be game up there, but with the lawlessness . . . Well, I'd best be going. A pity you can't join us, Max."

Goode left, but not before he had had a few words with the African bartender, who hailed him as an old friend.

ɔ   ɔ

"Why are you leaving?" Mirie asked as she followed Max to his tent. They sat in the shade of the canvas porch.

"You're all set with Goode. I want to see for myself what that area is like. Twelve, fifteen years ago the northern territory was packed with elephants. Drought hit and thousands starved to death. Then the price of ivory soared, and everybody and their brother was poaching. The north became an open-air slaughterhouse. The stink of carcasses hung over the place. One day I spotted a man dead in the crook of a tree. I thought a leopard had got him and dragged him up there. When I pulled him down, I saw he'd been shot. He must have climbed the tree wounded, so animals wouldn't get him, and died there. As I was putting the body in the car, there was gunfire. I got the hell out of there as fast as I could. But I was naive. I brought the body to headquarters. I was barred from the area on the grounds that it was too dangerous."

"That makes sense."

"It was a trumped-up excuse. Ivory was white gold and smuggling was big business. The last thing certain government muck-a-mucks wanted was a photographer around. When I was up there six years ago, it looked deserted. I want to see if there's been any change." Max unzipped the tent flap.

"Goode said it's dangerous."

"Goode said a lot of things."

"Why don't you like him?"

"You like to ask questions, don't you?"

"How else can I learn anything? What am I supposed to do—sit there like a lump while you two men discuss the significant issues of the day?"

"There's your answer. This crap of one old Africa hand sniffing out another. Macho games do not interest me, and

64

three's a crowd. Goode is anxious to show you around, so you might as well take advantage."

"But there are technical questions I had hoped you could—"

"You'll pick it up as you go." Max disappeared into the tent. When he returned, his face was pink from sun and shaving. Mirie asked him, "Will you come to lunch tomorrow?"

"I'll pass, thanks. If they ask, tell them their cat makes me sneeze."

He could not be persuaded. Mirie did not relish visiting Evelyn Goode again. It was the drinking that bothered her most, she admitted to Max. "When my dad died—I was eighteen—my mother had a rough time. She began to drink, and then she got sick. She died last year."

"I'm sorry."

"She was elegant." Mirie paused. "I watched her grow old and small." She squinted up at the dazzling sunlight. No shadow at noon, she thought. But in its place was the memory of her mother, which still came to her in painful waves and which she never talked about, not with Liz, or even with Jonathan. So why was she confiding in Max?

"I . . . . Excuse me. You don't want to hear this," she said. "Look, I know you're helping me as a favor to Frank Evans and you don't like talking about personal things. But we photograph cats together and eat breakfast together and watch the sunset together and all we talk about is work. It would be nice to have a friend here. That's all."

His head was cocked, the same quizzical expression she had noticed when they had first met.

She gave up. Max was an onion, she decided, and try as she might to unpeel the layers, she would only end up with more layers, until there was nothing left.

12

"I was a hunter," said Tom Goode, finishing a slice of pineapple. "I'm still a hunter."

"Oh, dear." Evelyn Goode rang a silver bell for the servant to clear the dishes. "When you say that, you give Mirie the wrong idea."

"It's true," said Goode with conviction heated several degrees by the beers he had drunk. "If I could, I'd go off to Mozambique today for a big tusker, before they're all gone—or I am."

His wife clucked as if he were a naughty child. "What Tom is not telling you is how all his life his heart's desire has been to shoot a bongo—a lovely antelope with corkscrew horns. A few years ago he came upon one. It was as close as you and I. He had a clear shot. Do you know what he did? He deliberately broke a twig to make it run."

"What was the point of killing it?" Goode muttered. "There was no sport in it."

His wife looked conspiratorially at Mirie, as if to say, "We women know better."

Throughout lunch Mirie felt as if she had been dropped into a parlor-room drama in a foreign language. She was anxious to get going. While Tom Goode enjoyed regaling her with stories of past safaris, he seemed in no particular hurry to start the present one.

He had another beer as he directed a man who was loading gear onto the truck. The African was even taller than Max and bone-thin. His perforated ear lobes dangled in long loops. Mirie asked the man if he was coming on safari with them. He looked at her blankly. He didn't speak any English, said Goode. His name was Odwana. He would accompany them to scout game, set up camp and cook. Goode said this as if it were too obvious to need explaining—how else would one go on safari? Servants and laborers cost next to nothing and people needed jobs. Goode respected "the chap"; he knew the meaning of work; and many Africans were "lazy buggers."

Goode and his wife fell to bickering over what provisions to take. Evelyn Goode walked off.

"My wife is a bit under the weather."

She returned, however, more composed and smelling of whiskey. The last skirmish was fought over whether or not to pack bottles of soda.

"I'm not taking her on a bloody picnic," snapped Goode. "I've walked all day across the bush without so much as a sip of water. The body gets used to it." He roughly handed the drinks back to his wife. While he went to get more gear, Mrs. Goode told Odwana to put the drinks on the back of the truck under a tarpaulin.

Mrs. Goode bore a grim smile of triumph. She wandered off to her garden to try to revive a flower bed damaged by the elephants' latest raid.

Mirie climbed into the truck and Goode placed the Winchester on her side. Odwana sat in back on a tire, resting an old Lee Enfield rifle across his knees.

Mrs. Goode, now in a dreamy, abstracted state, approached Mirie's window. "You'll have a lovely time. Tom will show you the true Africa."

Tom Goode drove down the rough curving hill too fast. The Winchester bounced as the car hit a dip in the road.

"Evelyn's a city girl," said Goode as if that explained everything.

ɔ ɔ

The sun bore down, flattening the trees and singeing the scrub. The land was dry, flat and monotonous, and Tom Goode didn't stop talking. Every red termite hill and flat-topped acacia sparked a story, of growing up in Africa, of hunting, of hacking through thick bush, of close calls with animals and with armed poachers.

They were good stories and Mirie tried to listen, but a dense fog sat between her and Tom Goode. Perhaps it was because Goode's stories were time-honed reminiscences of a past that for her was foreign and exclusionary. Or maybe it was because the expanse of scorched wilderness unrelieved by river or mountain or herds of animals reminded Mirie, more powerfully than all the naysayers could, of the near impossibility of her project. So far, her best shots of elephants had been in Evelyn Goode's vegetable garden.

At last, faraway doum palms delineated the one permanent river serpentining across the plain. How fine it would be, she thought, to stretch out on a shady bank and drink one of those tepid sodas Evelyn Goode had stowed on the back of the truck.

But there was no time. Tom Goode was determined to climb Rhino Peak, two hours beyond the river, before nightfall. They followed the track parallel to the river, past the waving doum palms and yellow fever trees, to a flood plain of smooth bare rock. There Tom Goode allowed a stop for a brief look around.

The rock was so hot the soles of Mirie's running shoes became sticky when she stood in one spot too long. She asked Odwana for Coca-Cola, figuring whatever dialect he spoke, that word he'd understand.

Mirie pried off the bottle cap with her Swiss Army knife and offered to do likewise with his bottle. Odwana simply twisted the bottle between his teeth and spat out the cap. He chased the cap clattering over the rock, snatched it up and dropped it in his pocket. Leaning on his rifle butt, he tipped the bottle up toward the sun and downed the soda in two gulps. Mirie drank hers almost as avidly. It was warm and vilely sweet.

When Mirie asked Goode why Odwana kept the cap, he said, "It's for his wife, for jewelry—Africans will cut up old tires and make sandals and door hinges. They don't throw things away the way you Americans do." He went on to deplore the fact that Africans' traditional diet had been corrupted by "paleface luxuries."

Goode refused a bottle. "I prefer water to soda, and whiskey to water." The phrase rolled off his tongue with practiced ease. "Until my twenties I drank nothing but orange squash. I couldn't stand the taste of liquor. As I grew older, I came to appreciate whiskey. It's a man's drink."

Out in the African bush in which he had spent his life, Goode was brittle and boxed-in. He seemed so keen to impress her with the ways of the wild. Mirie drank the Coke and said nothing.

From the rim of the gorge Mirie photographed the river cutting through the plain. Its rise and fall over thousands of rainy seasons had worn the pink-swirled rock into smooth elongated forms that looked more alive than the crocodiles below. Jaws gaping, the crocodiles blended in with the bank so well that she did not see them until they slipped into the water.

Goode said, "Given the chance, they'll tear a man to pieces. A few years ago a tourist fell in the river and we never found a trace of her."

If Goode expected Mirie to gasp and back away from the edge, he was mistaken. She peered into the drop as if contemplating a swan dive. "The river's so shallow and slow. How could anyone disappear?"

Goode was used to more credulity from his guests. "It's sluggish, but the rains change everything. A few years ago, when the river was close to overflowing, we caught poachers here. One of the drivers spotted a *basi* on the bridge. He had guests with him and drove back to camp as fast as he could. We radioed the police, but they had no vehicles and asked if we could pick them up—they're bloody useless. I had to do something. I flew over, and the poachers opened fire. I gave them a present. I got the stick between my knees, pulled a pin on a grenade and threw it out."

"You were carrying grenades?" asked Mirie, shocked.

"It's very hard for outsiders to understand. This is a war. Our chaps showed up in vehicles. There was a shootout. A nasty business—they shot one of our men—but eventually they surrendered. The grenade made rather a mess of one man—he lost both his legs." Goode paused. Mirie couldn't tell if it was for dramatic effect or because some bothersome detail had diverted his thoughts. "The others were persuaded, you might say," he resumed, "to take us to the godown. The tusks were small. They shot calves for toothpicks of ivory." He added with disgust, "They were not men. They were vermin."

Goode repeated the story in Odwana's language. He must have done a good job, judging by the man's rapt expression.

"You see," he continued, "the owner thought that setting aside part of the ranch as a wildlife area would be good conservation and good business. Tourists will pay quite a bit to see a piece of unspoiled Africa. But he's beginning to think it's more trouble than it's worth. We didn't anticipate elephants coming in, at least not in the numbers that have entered over the last few years. They moved onto the ranch because it's relatively safer inside than out. Unfortunately, the fire roads give poachers easy access, and we can't station guards everywhere day and night. I've had to keep tourists close to camp because I'm afraid of someone getting shot. It's a constant battle."

"Do you think it does any good, I mean, in terms of saving elephants?"

"I'm not a preservationist. One elephant more or less makes no difference. It's that standards are eroding. The system is breaking down. I say, not on this ranch, not in this country. This is a war, and I'm bloody well determined to fight it to the best of my ability, to hunt down these poachers if necessary."

She didn't see how Goode fought his crusade against poachers when all his time was taken up with banal details of the tourist business. Goode saw himself as a lonely defender of wild Africa and the poachers as emissaries of evil. That stark picture did not fit with what Mirie knew.

Poachers were poor rural Africans paid what to them was a fabulous sum for a night's work. Though they did the actual killing, they were just highly expendable laborers in a big international business. Greed and venality were disbursed along a chain of middlemen stretching from Africa to businessmen in

Japan, Hong Kong, other Asian countries and Europe. Raw ivory was a commodity like gold or oil, to be bought, sold or stashed as a hedge against inflation. Japanese and Americans were the biggest buyers of finished ivory, most of it obtained illegally. The more elephants killed, the scarcer the commodity, the higher the price. How could Tom Goode believe that by running a tourist camp in a small piece of wilderness preserved for well-to-do foreigners, he could win a battle against the overwhelming economics of the ivory trade?

If Tom Goode was aware of what he was up against, he was not the sort to fret. Part of the basic equipment with which he marched into the wilderness was an unwavering belief in his own ability to alter the world. Mirie could not make fun of his missionary zeal without feeling ludicrous herself. She had, after all, given herself a similarly chimerical task, of photographing an elephant being born in the wild, before the elephants and the wild vanished altogether.

o   o

Tom Goode marched up Rhino Peak, Winchester slung over his shoulder. Hiking in sandals, he stepped noiselessly over rocks and roots. Mirie followed, setting off a small avalanche with every step. Odwana stayed well behind her.

Brambles scratched her bare legs. Stinging nettles with poison bladders scraped the cuts. Halfway up the hill her legs were on fire, and the back of her neck had turned a furious red. She had drunk most of her water already and she was still parched.

She doused her bandanna with water and rubbed her legs. That seemed only to spread the poison.

Goode backtracked to where Mirie was crouched in distress. He soaked the kerchief in whiskey from a flask he had brought. She patted her legs all over. At first the alcohol made it hurt more, but finally the sting ebbed.

"Damned fine stuff," he said. "Cures a multitude of ills."

Goode tucked away the flask and resumed hiking at a fast clip, but stiffly, like a toy soldier.

Mirie trudged behind, watching her feet to avoid nettles and loose soil that made her backslide. Every so often she stopped to take in the view. An augur buzzard hovered in the wind. Spreading out below was land the color of dull gold, relieved by a green fringe of doum palms winding along the river.

Wind gusted at the top. Goode took Mirie's arm.

"I don't want you to blow off."

"I'm fine." She extricated herself. Whether Goode was being courtly or timidly lecherous, he made her skin crawl.

She sat near the edge, Goode beside her. Down below, elephants drank at a watering hole. Worn paths fanned out in spokes. From this perspective the largest mammals on earth looked like ants. She had to go closer.

Tom Goode drew an imaginary line in the air where the ranch lands ended and the wilderness began.

"To me it all looks the same," said Mirie.

"To Africans as well. Boundaries and private land are European ideas we imposed on them, but there's no going back. When I was a boy, all this was thick bush. You couldn't walk without fear of being chased by elephant or rhino."

"It's so bare now."

"The elephants knocked down the trees and opened up the land. If it were left alone, it would go back to bush eventually. But it's too late." Goode pointed to something moving far away. Through binoculars Mirie saw cattle heading toward the water hole. They were coming from what looked like a settlement of huts encircled by thornbush.

"They're squatters—worse than poachers in a way. We run them off, but they come in again. You can't shoot them. We tell them this is private land, but they don't understand. They bring their cows and goats to drink and graze because there's no tsetse here. They're nomads, not farmers, but they have no place to go. Next thing you know, they're building huts and growing millet." He looked careworn. "There's no more room for elephants in Africa. No more room for men either."

When they reached the car, Mirie asked Goode to drive closer to the watering hole so she could take pictures. As soon as they heard the car, the elephants walked off. Goode said they had been shot at too often, and, as everyone knew, elephants had long memories.

13

om Goode was long gone.

Seated on a camp chair on the opposite side of the fire, flask in hand, he was telling her how, as a boy, he had been taught by an African hunter to hunt with a bow and poisoned arrow.

"He showed us how to shave the wood for poison, because if we so much as scratched ourselves with it, we would die. He boiled up the shavings with euphorbia, puff adder guts and a hyrax liver, and at the end he threw in a live squirrel. A terrible deadly mess . . ."

Odwana cooked dinner over a smaller fire, his face an illuminated mask.

Lucky for him, she thought, he didn't have to feign being a good listener. More and more, Mirie felt trapped out in the wilderness with Goode and his stories, which had been told once too often. He reminded her of those politicians she used to photograph, who dispensed the same smiles, handshakes and speeches on every occasion. She wished she could go to sleep so that morning would come more quickly and they could be off again searching for elephants. Bad company could certainly wreck beautiful places. She had learned that when she went to Europe. It was her first big trip.

She had loved Don in college. Otherwise she wouldn't have slept with him. It was true, however, that after not dating very much, she made a pact with herself to lose her virginity before graduation. She complicated the job by wanting love to go along with it. Don was her chemistry lab partner. He forgot the instructor's warnings and dropped sodium into a wet sink. It exploded in white light. Don's befuddlement was endearing. They studied for tests together. One night after smoking dope they made love, and because she was stoned, it felt as if she were swimming in warm water.

In the fall following graduation they went to Europe. Mirie had saved up money from her jobs at the university press and working for Dr. Evans. He loaned her his Canon. Sailing to Europe on a budget "students' cruise" was Mirie's idea. Don was seasick for six days. He arrived in Southampton thin and pale, and did not recover until Paris. He headed for Le Drugstore for a hamburger, while Mirie wandered along the Seine taking pictures. Mirie wanted to stay in pensions. But Don, who had inherited money, had a job waiting for him in his father's firm and had already let Mirie talk him into the abysmal voyage, insisted on an American-style hotel. He didn't mind soaking up local color during the day, but at night he wanted a large room and a firm mattress. They shared a joint at night, which no longer helped the sex very much, and the next day Mirie felt tired and intermittently stoned, so she gave up smoking dope.

After six countries in three weeks they ended up in Switzerland. Don wanted to buy her ski clothes for St. Moritz, but Mirie said that blue jeans would work fine. Somewhere between Southampton and Zurich, she had fallen out of love with Don, and she felt guilty and resentful that he was spending so much money on her.

St. Moritz almost rescued Don from terminal blandness. Framed in Dr. Evans' Canon with the Alps behind him, he was handsome in ski clothes. Another skier took a picture of them, with Don carrying Mirie piggyback, skiing double-deck down the slope until they toppled.

On the next slope, Mirie schussed alone. The crisp air stung her cheeks. She didn't know how to stop, and she plowed into people in line for the chairlift. They fell like bowling pins. Don pulled her out of the snow and apologized to the others in primitive German, saying she was a *"jung Frau"* who had never

74

skied before. Everyone laughed and Don assumed he had smoothed over Mirie's gaffe. Mirie, whose German was slightly more advanced, told him later about his own, but he didn't think it was all that amusing.

In Greece Mirie resorted to an evasive maneuver. She developed a passion for broken columns and temples at dawn that Don did not share. While he slept late, Mirie went off on photographic expeditions. She brought back for Dr. Evans a picture of the ruins at Delphi under a subdued pastel sky that still hung in his office.

○ ○

A broken groan came from the other side of the river.

"Is that a lion?" asked Mirie.

"Baboons," Goode said. "There's nothing to worry about."

Who was worried? thought Mirie. She picked at a block of cornmeal that tasted like Styrofoam, and greens that had died under Spam drippings.

"African food is tasty once you're used to it," said Goode. He washed his down with whiskey.

The flames loomed larger and closer than they actually were. Having removed her eyeglasses for the night, she was not seeing very clearly. But then she didn't need to. Across from her, Goode seemed to waver in the flames. Though her attention was drifting, Mirie's myopic stare passed for rapt concentration.

Embers sprayed as Tom Goode laid another log on the fire. Fires reminded him of other campfires, when he was growing up in the bush and the only tracks were those made by animals and hunters. His voice was an incantation that mingled with the crackling wood and wind in the doum fronds.

A bow and poisoned arrow was an astonishingly efficient way of killing an elephant, continued Goode, unless a man missed and the elephant charged. He had shot his first elephant low in the gut. It bellowed in agony and went off. The old hunter and he tracked it for two days before it finally died. Vultures spattered the body with droppings, waiting for the belly to bloat and split. The hunter cut open the elephant. The spleen had turned black and the liver looked like a crumpled shoe. The tusks pulled out easily. The vultures did not feed on the remains; they sensed the poison.

When Goode was older, he learned to hunt with a gun. Properly done, the white man's way of killing was more civilized because it was quick. But he was grateful to the old hunter for teaching him bushcraft that few Europeans knew. At nineteen he became a commercial hunter, killing elephants and selling the ivory. Weary of the business after several years, he started leading hunting parties. He liked that for a time, in particular the admiration of the women who accompanied their husbands on thousand-dollar-a-day safaris. But hunting changed. It was no longer a sport. Men would shoot from cars, kill ten elephants on a license for one and pay off anybody who asked questions. There was no point in reporting irregularities; African officials, their pockets thickly lined with bribes, were deaf.

He took to leading tourists on photo safaris, but that was no better, trying to tell them how to distinguish Tommy from impala. Most people didn't care, anyway. They wanted to snap a picture and move on. That was the trouble with tourists, they were always one gear too high. He preferred the ranch setup, with the tourist business as a sideline. It attracted a better class of tourist, who showed their appreciation with generous tips.

Still, money was a worry. He didn't have bank accounts abroad. He never believed in that sort of thing. Simahali was home, the country where he had grown up and raised a family. But rumors had everyone on edge. Evelyn chided him for not holding on to tusks from his hunting days. If he had, they would have no money troubles now.

Goode had strayed far from the original story that had intrigued Mirie. "What happened to the old man," she broke in, "the ace you hunted with?"

Goode didn't immediately answer. Finally, he said, "I told you about those chaps we caught trespassing a few years ago. When I interrogated one of the poachers in the hospital, I discovered he was the youngest son of that old man. I told him I knew his father, and I wanted to help. I didn't tell him that I had been in the plane, and that I was the one who threw the grenade that tore off his legs. He told me about other

76

poachers. He begged me to see his family. He had two wives and many *totos*. His father was still alive, he said, but he no longer hunted.

"I told the old man about the accident. That his son had been caught poaching. I told him I was responsible for his son's losing his legs. The old man looked straight ahead as if he hadn't heard me. I left food and paraffin for the family. When I went there again with supplies, he had died. He never saw his son again. The son's a cripple. I help the family as much as I can."

This wasn't one of Goode's pat stories. "It must have been awful for you," said Mirie, "to see the old man after all those years, and to have to tell him that."

Goode capped the flask. "I'm going to have a look down-river," he said with false heartiness. "Care to join me?"

◠ ◠

Goode's flashlight beamed a path through low fronds and thornbush down a steep embankment to the strip of sand. He trained the light on the banks of the river silvered with moonlight, searching for something to amuse his guest. Mirie could see little other than Goode's hazy form. The river seemed larger, its sounds amplified in the dark.

Then she heard a reverberant honk, like a tuba player in an echo chamber. The honking continued ominously. Goode's light darted over the water until it hit protrusions Mirie took for rocks. But the rocks disappeared.

"What was that?" asked Mirie.

"Hippo."

She followed Goode downstream as he tried to search out where the hippo would next come up for air. There was a honking snort and Mirie could just make out the pig eyes and glistening nostrils.

Goode cupped his hands around his mouth and made a terrible heaving sound.

"Are you ill?" she asked.

His laughter was mild, constricted. "That's a lion." He did it again. From downriver the hippo answered back with a baleful honk. Goode was delighted. He roared again and the hippo

77

submerged. Goode took a sip of whiskey and continued to follow the animal with the flashlight. Mirie stayed behind him, wondering what the point of the game was.

The instant the hippo's ears popped up and twitched and its pig eyes appeared, Goode roared and the animal sank down again. Goode roared louder and louder.

Then the water exploded.

"Run! She's coming out!" he screamed as a mountain erupted from the river. Mirie ran for the embankment. Goode was beside her, scrambling up the sandy hill. Mirie was running the way she ran in nightmares, going nowhere as her tennis shoes dug deeper and deeper in the sand. She glanced back, only to see peg-leg teeth protruding from an enormous mouth.

She was in the air, hoisted up the embankment by her arms, and she was running again, through sawtooth fronds that tore her legs and wait-a-bit bush that snagged her clothing. She ran until a gunshot shattered the night. There was a resounding splash.

Everything stopped. She could not run anymore. She was stuck fast in the bushes.

Goode laughed uproariously, uncontrollably. He hugged her, she smelled whiskey and couldn't pull away.

"There, there. I'm not a hippo. You're safe." He unhooked her, barb by barb, from the wait-a-bit thicket. "I thought you were behind me. I turned back to get you. You kept sliding down. Then you practically flew over the sandbank." He laughed until Odwana came running up from the river, beating a path through the bush with his gun. He was breathing hard. Goode straightened up, his manner brittle. He commended Odwana.

"He shot over the hippo's head," Goode told her. "It made her think twice about charging. Damned good man." He laughed lightly. "That was a bit of excitement. Is it the first time you've been charged? If I hadn't picked you up, you would have been a meal for her." He put his arm around her.

"I suppose so." She edged away.

Back at camp Mirie refused when he offered her the flask.

"You must be one of those Daughters of the American

Revolution." He strode around the campfire, laughing to himself.

"You made the hippo do that!" said Mirie.

Goode heard her voice, not her anger. "It's instructive. These boffins waste years taking notes and making charts about the relationship of hippos and lions. In five minutes I've proved that lions piss off hippos." He relished the last few swallows from the flask. "Excellent."

Mirie headed for the tent. "I'm turning in. Good night."

"Sleep in peace," said Goode.

The air was too close inside the tent to get inside her sleeping bag. She lay on top. Every scratch on her body had its own distinct sting. When she shut her eyes, she saw the dungeon mouth of the hippopotamus opening and snapping down on her.

Mirie reached for her glasses. Through the net flap, she saw Goode sitting by the dying fire. A trace of a smile remained on his face. He must have been going over the hippo's assault, adding to his repertory the evening's little joke, which he would embellish for another visitor on another night.

She recalled reading that in a lifetime an elephant had six sets of teeth. When the last pair of molars wore out, the animal could no longer feed, so it died. In that way, she thought, the elephant was luckier than the man. It didn't suffer living long past its time.

14

Mirie blew away dead insects, seared by the kerosene lamp, which had fallen on the aérogramme. She had gone only as far as "Dear Jonathan" when she noticed a woman standing over her dinnertable.

"Can I join you?" The woman smiled broadly. "I'm American, too!" she said, establishing their common ground.

The woman bubbled over with presumption: She had seen Mirie eating alone, wondered where her husband had gone and thought Mirie would like some company. She confided, "I'm alone." First names sufficed; she was called Natalie. "Isn't this a fabulous country? The elephants are adorable. Can you imagine anyone shooting one? Hemingway—what garbage!" She leaned forward confidentially. "He *had* to kill. He was tormented by his anima. Follow me?"

She was in her late forties and expensively dressed in camouflage pants, cashmere cape and an amber necklace. Overdressed and overwrought, thought Mirie.

Since Max had gone, tourists had invited Mirie to join them at their table at mealtimes. It was all right when she was in the mood. When she wasn't, she showed up for dinner when everyone else was nearly finished. Natalie's friendly assault made her think it was time to return to the tent to finish the letter.

"Where's your husband?" asked Natalie.

Mirie laughed. "He's not my husband. We're working. We're photographers."

"Oh, that's it. You both looked so serious. When I didn't see him anymore, I was afraid you two had a fight."

"No. Nothing like that."

"Good. I hate to see couples fighting. There's so much divorce where I come from—Marin, that is."

"It's everywhere," Mirie suggested.

"Not here," said Natalie. "Africans respect the family. What beautiful people they are. Our guide told us he has nine children, and they are all a gift from God. Well, he said the boys are a gift from God, which is radically sexist, but I allow for the fact that men everywhere have primitive states of consciousness." Natalie asked Mirie where she was from. "New York! I would have guessed it. You're so intense. What a fascinating city—I was there three months ago on business."

"What do you do?"

"I create colors. I dream up the colors that people use on their hair. Hair color has its fashions like clothing. I've just completed a line of colors that you'll see next fall. I wish I could put my name on people's hair the way Gloria and Calvin do on blue jeans. People would spot a woman on the street, and they'd say, 'That's a Natalie.' It's a tiny claim to immortality, I admit, but you would be surprised how many high-power people wear my colors." Natalie drummed pale pink nails on the table. "Tell me about your work. It sounds incredibly exciting."

Mirie was ready with her exit line. "Actually, I have to go." She gathered up her gear. "Tonight's the night to shoot the mating dance of the sacred golden hornbill. You know about that, don't you?" Natalie looked blank, though her ignorance was more understandable than she realized. "They only dance one night a month, under the full moon."

"Birds doing the samba," said Natalie, mystified. "It's not on my itinerary. I'll have to catch it in reruns."

꙰ ꙰

Dear Jonathan, [She picked up from where she had left off.]
  By the time you receive this letter I'll be with the elephants somewhere. I've gotten a good look at the ranch. I

can set up camp and stay as long as I need to. The trouble is, the elephants are skittish, and the least disturbance sends them on their way. I don't know if they will ever get used to my hanging around. I'm going to ask Howden's advice when he comes back from safari.

I jerry-rigged the camera to the wing of Goode's Cessna with gaffer's tape and a screw and used a remote cable—the way Donner did it. The camera hasn't fallen off yet. I do like small planes. You can appreciate how much there is out there. The wildlife reserve is a tiny patch of the ranch, and the ranch a postage stamp in the bush, and the bush goes on forever in the scrub desert that is most of Simahali. Goode flies so low over the plain, I can't help tensing up my butt to avoid touching the treetops. It's his version of a game drive. I like it, but you really only see the animals running.

Goode and I came close to a falling out on safari because he made a hippopotamus charge me. The way I see it, I was almost bitten in two. The way he sees it, he saved my life and showed me a "bloody good time." Goode likes to play cowboy. Ever since my initiation, he's held me in high esteem.

Do I sound different, Jonathan? I feel like an outsider. In daytime the work keeps me going. At night I miss home. (There are two beds in this tent, and though I know how you feel about camping, I wish you were in the other one.) It's hard to have so much time on my own, though I had better get used to it.

Love, M

ɔ   ɔ

A red and white windsock blew south under cumulus clouds suspended puffy and white in sky so blue it could have come from a child's tempera paint set. On the grass stubble by the airstrip, children who belonged to the African staff kicked a tattered soccer ball. Zebras dyed orange from rolling in the dirt grazed. Cape buffaloes sniffed the breeze through dusty noses. Two men were filling the Cessna with aviation gas.

The children were difficult to photograph, because every time Mirie aimed her camera, they froze in stick-straight poses or collapsed in laughter. They all begged for copies of the pictures, as well as for her to be their pen pal in America. It became too complicated, so she focused on the animals but did manage a few discreet action shots of the soccer players.

She checked her other camera once again to be certain it was firmly fixed to the wing and the remote cable was working. She was all ready, but Goode was late. She hoped this wasn't another of his emergencies. She was looking forward to the flight.

She pulled the brim of her hat down, to keep the sun off her face. She breathed on her glasses and cleaned the dust off with her bandanna. Her eyes smarted from sun and dust. She glanced in a mirror to dab a particle from her eye. The face surprised her. She wore no makeup, hadn't since she left New York. How tanned and honed her features had become. There was a filigree of lines around her eyes. She had lost the bespectacled-gamine look. The reflection did not displease her; but she somehow had not caught up with the change.

ɔ ɔ

Goode drove up looking freshly laundered. His crisp demeanor was marred only slightly by the blood vessels branching on his nose. As he drained fuel from the plane into an empty Coke bottle, he chatted about how the day before, after he had dropped off Mirie, he had arrived home to discover old friends waiting. Never a dull moment at the Goode household, with people always dropping in. Goode examined the pale blue fluid. She asked what he was doing, for on a previous flight she had been too preoccupied with her camera assembly to notice.

"I check for condensation," he said. "And sabotage. You can never tell with these chaps." He spilled out the fuel. Mirie climbed in. Goode secured her door and climbed in on the pilot's side. The cockpit was cramped and Mirie could not see over the instrument panel.

Goode started the engine and checked the flaps. A dew of perspiration appeared on his forehead, though Mirie herself did not find the plane hot. Reaching to check an instrument, he brushed against her leg. She was not about to make an issue—whether it was accidental or intentional—while he was preparing for takeoff.

Goode taxied to the end of the dirt strip and pivoted the plane. The children playing soccer interrupted their game to watch. So did tourists heading out for a game drive. The zebras kicked up their heels and galloped off. The buffalo hardly budged.

Goode checked his instruments again. He looked straight ahead and shook his head, like a swimmer trying to clear his ears.

The plane picked up speed. A golden banner of dry grass streamed past the window. Mirie was pressed back in her seat. She felt the plane lift.

There was a thud. The grass was spinning, the plane pivoting out of control. The tail beat hard against the ground, round and round in an angry dance as if demanding direction from the pilot who lay slumped over the controls.

"Get up!" Mirie heard herself scream. She tried to pull Goode off the stick, as if by righting him, she could bring him out of his faint. But he was dead weight. People ran toward the whirling plane in the jerky motion of a silent movie, their shouts blanketed by the engine drone.

They surrounded the plane, helpless to stop it. She looked at the limp puppet that was Tom Goode. She didn't know how to shut off the engine. She had a vision of the plane turning turtle and exploding on the airstrip. A thin beam of clarity eluded her panic. She unbuckled the seat belt, wrenched the door open and jumped.

A sharp, sickening pain spread up from her foot. Rooted to the earth with her foot twisted in an impossible position, she was telling herself to run when the plane's tail came around and knocked her out of the way.

The plane stalled and there were people surrounding her, Africans and tourists, all talking at once, and she had no idea what they were saying. She crumpled up, clutching her leg, waiting for the swell of nausea to pass. Natalie was there, ordering her to lie down and everyone else to move back. The stench of plane fuel, perspiration and perfume enveloped Mirie. She was going to be sick.

Mirie propped herself up on her elbows and muttered, "I'm going back to the tent."

"Stay still a moment." It was Max. He was standing over

her, his wild sandy hair right up there with the painted cumulus clouds. He was dusty, and his T-shirt was soaked with sweat.

"You're back. See my camera rig?" Mirie asked, forgetting her foot and the commotion.

Max glanced at the plane. Two Africans had managed to lift Goode out. "Nice job. Does anything hurt beside your foot?"

"I don't think so. Did you see any elephants?"

"It's mechanical difficulty, Mirie," Tom Goode had come to and now broke in in a shaky voice. He had extricated himself from the Africans who were trying to persuade him to get in a car. "It's fortunate I realized what was happening in time to abort takeoff. The plane will need a thorough inspection. This demonstrates what I was saying about sabotage." His face was haggard. "We'll be flying in no time."

"No, we won't," said Mirie. "I'm not flying with you. Your boss will have his brochure. Our business is over."

"I promised to help you," said Goode. "What about the elephants? You can't abandon work because of a minor setback—"

"Oh, cut the crap, Goode," said Max. "You've been boozing. If you want to commit suicide, that's your business. But she's not flying with you." He scooped up Mirie, set her unceremoniously in the back of the Land-Rover, and headed for camp.

The pain in her leg where the tail of the plane hit her had subsided to a dull throb. Her foot, however, had swollen to the size of a small cantaloupe and was hurting more by the minute. She was crying from pain and frustration. "How can I work?"

"Relax, Mirie. We'll figure out something."

15

From the back of the Land-Rover, her injured foot propped on a duffel bag, Mirie watched baboons on posts panhandle food from passing tour buses. The clouds thickened and clotted. What lay ahead was the long hot drive back to Kwendela, a night in a hotel room, and after that she did not know what.

"It looks like rain."

"No. It'll burn off," said Max from up front. "How's your foot?"

"Blue and yellow and ugly."

"It could have been a lot worse."

Mirie mulled over the accident. She had never been hurt before, not even the time in exercise class when a stunt man, who was practicing jumps from a balcony, miscalculated a leap and landed on her like a sack of concrete. She wasn't even bruised, and she took this as a sign not of luck but of coordination, or as her instructor said, "You know how to fall." A camera in hand propped up her illusion of invulnerability. Once she covered a crime in progress—a berserk man was shooting wildly from a coffee shop. She finagled to get across the police barricades, closer to the action. Although a policeman twenty feet in front of her was wounded, it never occurred to Mirie that she herself might get shot. And now a broken foot had bollixed her carefully laid plans and jeopardized the rest of the trip.

"If you were me, Max, would you stay?"

"It depends how badly I was hurt and how badly I wanted to work. I'd probably hang around Kwendela, and as soon as I could navigate, I'd go back to the bush—no point in going home."

"What about your family?"

"No one's waiting for me. My daughter's in college and my wife is remarried and lives in New Delhi."

Mirie paused, questioning her recollection. "I thought you lived in Virginia—"

"I do, now and then. Alone. Things change."

"You've mentioned your wife. I thought—"

"She's the only wife I've ever had, so I call her my wife. That ex-wife business never rang true to me, any more than I could call Kate my ex-daughter."

Mirie digested this new information. Max was outwardly gawky and yet seemingly self-assured. The latter quality she didn't associate with the few fortyish bachelors she knew, none of whom seemed to be on especially good terms with their unmarried state.

"I misunderstood. I assumed you were married, and I couldn't help wondering how you worked things out when you were in Africa most of the time."

"And now I've solved the mystery for you," he said with good humor. "Ah, that's the disease of people who think too much, isn't it?—fretting about relationships instead of having them."

"Not instead of. I think it's part of the basic design."

"You don't have to tell me. I wasn't cut out for a conventional marriage. Neither was Sharon. She was a free spirit, and then Kate came along. It's different when you have a child. It's funny—in my pictures I try to avoid clichés, but once Sharon and I had a baby, I felt I had to be the ultimate provider and she was compelled to act like whatever a perfect wife and mother is supposed to be. In Africa life is a lot more fluid—you make it up as you go along—but we still managed to build ourselves a prison. It didn't look like prison. It looked like a nice cottage in the country, with a gardener and a houseboy—very plain compared with the way Sharon was raised. But we did a great job of slowly suffocating ourselves."

Max took a swig of water. He glanced up at the sky. "The clouds sit there, and they aren't going to do anything. I bet you don't even notice the clouds in New York, but here you plan your life around the rains. I prefer that—life stripped down to essentials and balanced on a natural system, however precariously. If the rains come, the crops grow. If there's too much rain or too little, animals and people suffer. They're stark, basic concerns, and they're a good reminder for people like us who complicate our lives unnecessarily."

"If living simply, being closer to nature, were a cure-all, then Tom and Evelyn Goode would be a lot happier than they are."

Max laughed. "Those poor relics . . . They're caught in the cracks between two cultures and two eras. They don't really belong anywhere. Africans are caught, too. The men drift to the cities and drink. The mamas have ten kids and keep their families together as best they can. The old ways die out, the new ways are foreign imports that seldom work. The expats fly in and out, and the Sahara keeps creeping southward." He laughed softly. "And as long as I can, I'll play Indian."

"You keep coming here," said Mirie, "and yet you're cynical."

"Not at all. Sober, is more like it. Twenty years ago I had a sense of excitement and hope, about Africans leading their own countries—an ancient continent in a new era. I could cross borders and travel pretty freely. The corruption didn't seem so blatant, but maybe I was more innocent. I was a dumb kid in love. It was because of Sharon that I first came to Africa. We were in college. She'd just started. But she'd lived all over the world and she couldn't take all the rules and regulations. She split and went back home to her parents' little mansion in Africa. I quit school to be with her. It wasn't smart since I risked being sent to Vietnam, but in those days my brain was not my favorite organ. I lived in a youth hostel. Sharon's dad was in the diplomatic corps and the family lived in an embassy mansion with all the trimmings. The servants had a plot for growing vegetables. Sharon and I took over a patch to grow the finest marijuana ever seen in Simahali. I saw it as a horticultural experiment—I was a botany major and I had figured out ways to improve the plant. The servants helped themselves to our weed, and Sharon's dad caught them stoned and he fired the whole bunch. Sharon was too scared to admit to her dad it was our stuff. The servants' wives did juju on her. They almost convinced her that if her dad didn't rehire their men, she would turn into a cat."

"Did she?"

"Worse than that. She wanted us to get married. She was only eighteen. I would have done it, but her parents insisted that she finish college. Her dad was clever. He knew how to separate us. I'd been tinkering with photography. He helped me get my first good camera duty-free and encouraged me to bum around Africa and photograph wildlife and primitives. Against all odds, I actually sold some pictures to European magazines. Then I came down with malaria that didn't respond to treatment. I was shipped back home as a medical specimen. I was the first more or less living proof of the existence of a quinine-resistant parasite in this part of Africa. The only thing good about it was it got me classified 4F. I finished college while convalescing in St. Louis. Sharon wrote to me from school and visited me on vacations. As soon as I was well, I grabbed my camera and came back. She couldn't take it that I was in Africa and she was stuck in school. College was too confining for her. My letters didn't help. I was kicking around, and a lot of it was just plain miserable, but I guess I made it sound good in my letters. College and her parents be damned, she got hold of some money, bought a plane ticket and met me in Botswana. We were a great team. She loved the bush . . ."

"And?"

"We got married. She was pregnant, but that isn't why. It was what we wanted to do all along. I couldn't wait to be a father. I realized that with the baby we couldn't travel as much as we had. But I figured, how hard could it be for Sharon and me to make a new life with a baby?

"Very hard," he said and paused. "My wife was good at being a free spirit as long as she could go home and wallow in the diplomatic trough. She was very set in her ways. But we tried. Her parents helped us, so did mine, those first few years. I wasn't making much money selling pictures. Her dad got me a job doing photographs and reports on government aid projects. This was in the late sixties, and I wasn't crazy about working for the U.S. government. But it kept the baby fed."

Max stopped to fill the gas tank from the jerry can. Before setting off again, he took a snapshot out of his wallet. It was of a pretty young woman with curly raven hair and a warm, open face. "The kid, twenty years later. Fortunately, she doesn't take after her dad. After Zambia, I'm going to visit her at school." He started the engine and they were off again.

Every mile closer to the city, the brooding sky seemed a more oppressive weight. Mirie regretted Max's imminent departure, and not simply because of his expertise. He had become a reassuring presence. It was only now, as he was leaving, that he offered to tell her something about himself.

She was seized by the discomfiting thought that in the morning when she awakened she would not know a soul in Simahali. Max would be in Zambia and then the States, and Tom and Evelyn Goode, immersed in their bottled pasts—she wouldn't seek them out again. The idea of boarding the next plane back to New York was too fainthearted to consider. Her anxious ruminating was interrupted as the car rolled to a stop, enveloped in a horrible stench.

"What is that?"

Max yanked up the hand brake. "We're near the slaughter-house."

"Why are you stopping here?"

"The tank is empty. *Kwisha, kabisa.*"

"We passed a bunch of gas stations! Why didn't you stop? Didn't you see the signs, '*Hakuna* petrol'?"

"That means out of gas."

"Oh . . . Now what do we do?"

"*We* don't do anything. I walk. You wait here."

They sensed it at the same time: the implosion of air, the sudden stillness. Lightning cracked the clouds and thunder announced a downpour. Drops splattered the windshield, hit the roof in a pinging staccato.

"What a good sound—my first African rain." Mirie shut her eyes to listen better. The car door opened and slammed shut.

The rain fell harder and harder. She thought Max had already gone, but when she looked out, he was standing there soaked, jerry can in hand, gazing up at the sky.

He abruptly started off down the road. He called back, "Lock the doors and windows."

ɔ   ɔ

Needles of rain pierced the dust and etched branching streams on the windshield.

Mirie did not know where the giraffes came from, but suddenly there were four of them browsing an umbrella acacia nearby. Mirie thought the smell of dead cattle might send them running, but it didn't bother them. In haste to get her camera out, she banged her injured foot and cursed. With the window open the stench filled the car.

The giraffes swung their necks around like building cranes and peered down at her through long black lashes, chewing from side to side. If they distinguished Mirie from the car, they recognized nothing edible or threatening and went back to browsing the treetop. She framed them carefully, necks criss-crossing over the acacia.

A speeding car honked, and the giraffes loped off in a slow rocking gait against the dull copper sky. She got them, her ghost giraffes—the best shots since she had arrived in Africa.

She wiped off the camera and shut the window against the downpour. It was nearly nightfall. Max had been gone a long time. He had a plane to make at midnight, and she had to find a room.

A rap on the window made Mirie jump.

It was not Max. Four rain-soaked African children peered in at her: a thin girl in a drenched blue school dress, two younger girls and a bedraggled little boy. Mirie opened the window.

The two younger girls backed away giggling. The eldest girl, who was entering gangly adolescence, spoke hesitatingly.

"Madame, please. Ride? The city is far and the rain is big."

"We're out of gas," said Mirie. "Petrol is finished, *kwisha.*

91

But come in and get dry." She opened the door and the children tumbled in like wet puppies. "Why are you on the road so late at night?"

The girl responded with mute, wide-eyed confusion. Mirie repeated the question more slowly, then riffled through her phrase book. The girl said something and it was Mirie's turn to be baffled.

She tried another approach. She pointed to herself. "I am Mirie." She wrote her name on a piece of paper in big block letters. The girl did the same: R-U-T-H, and with a little encouragement, identified her sisters and brother.

She asked the girl how old she was. How many years? Ruth either did not understand, or was too embarrassed to speak. Mirie dug into her duffel for a bag of hard candies. They had become sticky in the heat, but the children took them eagerly. The little boy tried to snatch the bag but was stopped by one of the giggling sisters.

"How many years have you been in school?" Mirie asked Ruth.

The girl looked down and fidgeted with her worn school uniform. Mirie's questions only made the girl more ill at ease, so she stopped asking them. Mirie rummaged around for a *National Geographic* that Max had left in the car. Ruth slowly turned the pages.

Mirie took up her camera and pretended to snap the shutter. "I take pictures."

Ruth looked at her impassively, then brought out a sheaf of crayon drawings from a school folder. Mirie looked at them by flashlight. There was a crudely drawn map of Africa, stick goats eating brown grass, a skinny woman in front of a thatch hut, with eight smaller figures, and a bent woman with a bundle of sticks on her back. In each of the pictures the sun was a yellow blob with spokes, the way schoolchildren at home drew it.

Ruth pointed to the skinny woman. "Mama." And the old woman. "Mama of my mama."

"Where is your father?"

"Gone," said the girl, and nothing more.

"Do you have more brothers and sisters?"

She paused. "Four brothers, three sisters," she said. "One comes soon."

The car windows steamed from body heat. The children fell asleep.

Finally, Max emerged from the darkness lugging the jerry can.

"Where did you find gas?" she asked as he filled the tank.

"Soldiers sold it to me for the equivalent of seventy-five bucks. There was a big crowd. Whoever dashed most got the gas first. That wasn't me."

Mirie explained about the children.

He said peevishly, "You picked a great time to start a limo service." He jumped in the car, his clothing soaked. "I'm late as it is, and there's barely enough gas to get us back." The children huddled, afraid of Max.

"I couldn't just let them stand in the rain," said Mirie.

He picked up the sheaf of drawings. "What are these?" Leafing through, he came to Ruth's family portrait.

"I like this," he told the girl. "Can I have it?"

"Yes," Ruth said sheepishly.

"Good. Now, how do we get to your house?"

Rain dribbled down the windshield and mud sucked at the tires as they drove through a squatter settlement, a gray wrinkled sea of tin-roof shacks undulating over the hills.

"Just here," said Ruth.

"Just here" went on for many more kilometers. The air reeked of human waste. Skinny goats hid from the rain under a rusting hulk of truck. Under the tin roof of a store, men huddling around a hurricane lamp looked blankly at the Land-Rover. At the last row of shacks the children got out.

From her school bag Ruth took a wooden bell tied with a rawhide thong and without a word gave it to Mirie. Then she picked up her brother, and she and her sisters splashed through the mud to their mother's shack.

"All those kids live in there?" asked Mirie.

"Plus relatives and renters, most likely."

"Everyone here lives like that?"

"What choice is there?"

Mirie hung the wooden bell on Max's mirror. When he hit a bump, it went *tock, tock, tock.* They left behind the squatter settlement. Back on the flooded roads on the city outskirts, rooster tails of spray shot out from the car wheels.

"What happens to kids like her?" asked Mirie.

"In a couple of years she'll get pregnant. And if she's extremely lucky, she'll marry a man with a little farm."

"But if there are seven kids in that house, and eight in the next and ten in the next, all across the hills and valleys—what becomes of them?"

"Nothing," said Max. "They eke out a living, as shadows in their own land."

Thunder rumbled and the rain came down hard again.

"Do you know a hotel that doesn't cost too much?" asked Mirie.

"You're sure you want to stay?"

"I'll be fine." She sounded more confident than she felt. "It's still early. You won't miss your flight."

"Yes. But I have to see someone first."

16

"W here are we?" asked Mirie as Max maneuvered the car around deep puddles and down a dark nave of eucalyptus.

"My estate," was the deadpan reply.

"Lucky you," mused Mirie, playing along.

A large brindle mongrel bounded into the headlights, barking and wagging its tail furiously enough to shake itself to pieces. The hairs on its back flared with excitement.

"That's Humphrey," said Max. "He's not much of a watchdog, but he looks ferocious." Humphrey's barking provoked other dogs, near and far, to bark and bay. An askari who had been dozing jumped to his feet and hailed them with a flashlight and a short bat.

Max said, "That's a traditional weapon. Everybody's afraid of prowlers." The askari herded the dog aside as Max pulled up to the house, but as soon as he was out of the car, Humphrey made a friendly assault.

Max pried the dog's muddy paws off his T-shirt, "Still remember me, Hump." The dog flopped onto its back, beating the wet ground with its tail as Max scratched its belly.

A light went on, a woman's face appeared in the window, there was a shriek.

"I'll be right back," said Max.

The door opened and she burst into Max's arms. Clasping

each other's waists, they went inside, shutting the door before the dog could get in.

Humphrey galloped back to the car and nosed wet tracks on the window. Mirie slid back the glass, letting the dog slobber her hand.

Now she saw things differently. Max had a house, a dog, a lover, a whole life tucked away in Africa. Mirie had had scarcely a glimpse of his girlfriend before Max enveloped her in a bear hug. What an odd relationship theirs must be, with him disappearing for months, then reappearing shortly before flying off again. She had to be awfully tolerant, or, like himself, a hermit.

Mirie followed the askari's flashlight as he patrolled the grounds. She could make out lights through the trees. Other large houses shared the valley. After driving through the fetid sprawl of the squatter settlement, there was once again the luxury of space. Except for the askari with his tribal bat, there was little that could be detected in the dark that placed the house in Africa. She could as well have been in the English countryside or in a wealthy woodsy suburb outside New York. Mirie inhaled the dense aroma of eucalyptus freed by the rains. Bamboo creaked and whined in the wind.

She wished Max would hurry back. He must be explaining to his girlfriend why Mirie was along, though she herself couldn't understand why he had brought her here instead of dropping her at a hotel, as she had asked. Surely, he wasn't going to leave her out there in the dark while he and his girlfriend were inside making love. Max wouldn't do that.

The idea of Max making love was so improbable anyway. He was manly and yet not sexual, as if those energies were directed elsewhere. On reflection, he wasn't ugly. He was awkward, which wasn't due so much to his height but to an almost physical aversion to ordinary social give and take. On the other hand, there was nothing equivocal about the way he greeted his girlfriend.

Though Max didn't seem like the type for hit-and-run affairs, Mirie couldn't rule out the possibility. Her musings ended as his girlfriend returned. Humphrey chased his tail in a new round of ecstasy.

"I'm Frances," said the woman. Her handshake was firm, almost mannish. "Max told me about the accident. He's packing. Here, give me your arm."

Mirie hopped inside, leaning on Frances, who guided her to a lumpy crewel sofa. Humphrey dropped his heavy muzzle in her lap.

"He can't get enough attention," said Frances. "You can push him away."

"I like dogs."

"Me, too, but I'm glad you're here," said Frances, flopping down on the floor. "Humphrey and I have run out of things to talk about." She had short blond hair and a generous mouth. Her clothing was a haphazard concoction, an oversize sweater that flattered her full breasts, an African kanga tied like a sarong, and red tights. Hitching up the kanga, she crossed her legs in a lotus position.

"I'm petrified here alone," said Frances. "It's good you'll be down the hall. You can help me rehearse my lines! He told you I'm an actress, didn't he? Did you bring any books? All they have at the cultural center are classics. And after OD'ing on Shakespeare—professionally speaking—I need books I can read in one night." Frances noticed Mirie's puzzled expression. "You *are* interested in things other than animals. You must be. Max said you're from New York."

"I don't understand . . . What's down the hall?"

"Max's inner sanctum. It's part of the house, really, but it's off by itself. Didn't he tell you about it? Figures. Well, you should be honored—he hardly ever lets anyone stay there."

"But I'm not—I'm going to a hotel."

"New plan," said Frances. "You're staying here until your foot heals." Frances stretched her legs in a wide V and reached for her toes. "I'm getting so fat."

She was not at all fat. She was a big woman, warmly, radiantly sexual and in the full bloom of her late thirties.

Mirie thought that if she were Frances, the last thing she would want would be an unexpected guest, especially when she and Max had so little time alone. And apart from Max's girlfriend, she was hesitant to stay. Spacious as it was, the house was somehow too close, too crowded for her.

"I feel like I'm barging in."

"No way. Max says you're okay, and that's all I need to know. He said you're a nature photographer, too. Have I got nature!" She motioned to the windows where, drawn by the light, large insects with pearly wings beat against the window panes. "Hideous, aren't they? Give me a New York waterbug any day."

Frances went to get drinks, leaving Mirie alone in a room that looked more like a craft shop after a typhoon than a living room. Striped Kente cloth draped the furniture; Oriental rugs covered the floor. A parchment painting depicted Solomon and Sheba surrounded by almond-eyed Abyssinians. There were casts of Benin bronzes, Indonesian dragons, spears and shields, African masks sprouting aigrettes, zebra tails, cowrie shells and pieces of bone and carved totems of devouring devils. Over the fireplace was a gigantic papier mâché lion's head with a lolling tongue, a statue of many-armed Shiva, tiny bronzes of men and women coupling acrobatically. A seated Buddha perched on top of the television was the only serene image in the place. Desks and tables overflowed with *Variety, Billboard, W, Interview, Vogue* and *Elle.* There were books on African history and politics, paperback mysteries, *Madame Bovary,* an anthology of great American plays. A *Portable Shakespeare* lay open, face down, on an overstuffed chair.

The fireplace was full of logs and papers that, had it been lighted, might have provided a warm center in a room that seemed a temporary receptacle for trinkets from everywhere. Removed from the jumble, each might have interested Mirie as an artifact of another culture, but there were too many of them, randomly placed on walls, mantelpieces, tabletops. All looked as if they could be quickly packed up and moved to another house in another country.

Mirie included herself among the foreign artifacts. Her foot hurt and she felt clumsy. The disorderly collection troubled her. She felt as if she were in a room tumbling through space. At that moment nothing seemed stable. She wondered if the room had ever been tidy.

Frances returned with cold drinks. Mirie said, "Thanks for asking me to stay, Frances, but—"

"It's settled. No arguments."

"But I didn't know where Max was taking me . . ." Mirie stopped, hearing her own bluntness.

Frances surveyed the room, as if seeing it through Mirie's eyes. "Hey, it's a little messy—the houseboy's off today—but it's not the house of Usher."

"But three's a crowd, and Max is leaving any minute—"

"Hey, what is this? . . . If you want to have a private good-bye, I'll help you hop back there."

"No, I don't—" Mirie frowned. "I thought *you* did. You have so little time together."

Frances was stunned. "Whoa! You think *we're* an item . . . Oh, man!" She screamed with laughter. "And I thought you and he had a thing, and Max wasn't talking. No, my guy's a hack. He's in Ouagadougou or Wau or one of those made-up places. He and Max are buddies. I adore Max. We all live here, only we hardly ever see each other."

There was an awkward pause as each readjusted her perspective.

"Whew, I'm glad we got that straight," said Frances. "Now what is this about you jumping out of an airplane?"

"That's not exactly how it was. The plane was on the ground at the time." Mirie told her about the accident.

"What a bummer," said Frances. "Well, tomorrow we'll get your foot X-rayed. And Julius—he's my houseboy—he'll get something from the witch doctor. He's got a direct line to the spirits and you might as well cover your bases. Breaking your arm would have been better. You still could have outrun the panga gangs."

"What are they?"

"Bandits who rob and chop up people."

"Mirie doesn't scare easily," said Max, reappearing. He'd showered and changed, and wore a sweater over a blue shirt. His wet hair sprang back in damp curls, and his bald spot was newly apparent. He was unnaturally pink and burnished for a man Mirie was accustomed to seeing in dusty shorts and a worn cap.

Sidling up to him, Frances vamped, "I envy you, dahling. Take me with you." Resuming her normal voice, she said, "So it's gonna be just us chickens, defending ourselves against the panga gangs."

Max hugged Frances. "As long as you don't listen to Frances, Mirie, you'll do fine. Come on. I'll take you back."

He carried Mirie's gear and she hobbled after him, through a musty passageway, a kind of peninsula extending from the back of the house. When they were out of earshot, she said, "You're full of surprises. I didn't know where you were taking me."

"You still don't." He opened a door and flipped on a light.

Mirie found herself in a cabin, twice as tall as it was wide, with a steeply pitched beamed roof perforated with skylights. Occupying almost the entire room was an ornate canopied bed. The headboard was inlaid with porcelain tiles painted with flowers and hummingbirds. The legs were carved birds with lion's-claw feet and the canopy was embroidered with gold. The mattress was higher than in a regular bed, and though more than wide enough to accommodate two people comfortably, it appeared too short for Max.

Max anticipated her thoughts. "I sleep on the diagonal," he said matter of factly. "There's no other way to do it."

In contrast with the main house, the cabin was austere but for the bed. There was just enough room left for a table and chair, a sink and a mirror. Kente cloth covered a crate that served as bookshelf and night table. A bath was off to one side. On opposite sides of the room, windows were enclosed in traceries of grillwork.

"It was a separate guesthouse. The old Brit who owned the estate used it as his chess room. He and his pals would come here and play for hours. Then, when he got feeble and was in a wheelchair, he had the corridor built connecting it to the main house, so that in the rainy season he could wheel himself to the cabin. He died here, playing chess against himself."

Max fell silent. They listened to the white-winged insects bat at the windows, and the whine of bamboo.

Mirie traced the artfully carved vines of the bedpost winding up to the gilt canopy.

"I found it in a house that was being torn down," said Max. "I had to take it apart to get it back here. That was no small feat. It's more than a hundred years old. Back then, couples didn't know each other before they were married. After the ceremony and prayers the groom ate dinner with his friends. Then he joined his bride in the wedding bedroom. There was incense burning and jasmine strewn on the sheets. After the wedding night they had to hang out the sheets to prove they'd done the deed. They stayed in the wedding room for a week before going home together . . . I'm not big on possessions anymore, but when I leave Africa, I'll take it with me."

"Why would you leave?"

Max shook his head. "I've got a plane to make . . . You'll find out. Everybody thinks about leaving. I have a friend who's had his bags packed for fifteen years." Max shrugged. "Never mind. It's different for you. You're only passing through. For as long as you're here, use this as home base."

"You won't be back soon?"

"No." He raised his hands, palms open and apart, as if to amend his reply to "Well, who knows?"

Raindrops pelted the skylights. Max hesitated, loath to be discouraging. "If these freaky rains last, it doesn't make working any easier."

"I know, but I don't have the money or the time to leave and come back again. I have to sell pictures while I'm here. Besides, this is my work now. There's no job waiting for me back home."

"You're brave."

"You did the same thing yourself twenty years ago."

"Africa was a lot easier then. And you're a lot smarter than I was."

The rains came down harder. Max took a last look around. "It's a good place . . . Well, you must want to shower." He paused at the threshold. "Can you make it on your own? I mean—if you need help, Frances can—"

She shook her head. "Max?" She paused. "Thanks for getting me started. And everything."

"You did it yourself." He considered his words. "I envy you, seeing this all for the first time. You have a fresh view."

"To say the least," Mirie said with a laugh. "For a while we were a good team—my fresh view and your experienced eye."

He smiled. "Don't be in too much of a rush. You're on African time now."

She didn't say anything for a moment. "I'm not very good at good-byes." She caught her reflection in the mirror, dusty, thin, thorn-scratched, and perched on one foot. "I look like a stork that got mugged."

"You look okay, Mirie."

o   o

Showering on one foot wasn't easy, especially when she was swatting at insects. They fluttered in the bathroom window and fell like crumpled sails in the drain water. Standing made her foot ache badly.

She dressed and hopped back to the living room. Humphrey thumped his tail at her while he ripped apart a copy of *Vogue*. There was a note taped to the penis of an African carving. "Mirie, I'm taking Max to the airport. If the panga gangs come, wake up the askari and hit the panic button. It's under the bed. *Lala salama.*"

17

Dear Jonathan,

If you have been trying to reach me at Frances' and cannot, it's because the telephone doesn't work when it rains. It doesn't work very well when it doesn't rain, either. Nothing in Simihali works very well and many things do not work at all.

I can hardly complain, though, for I seem to be living in the last days of the Raj. Julius, the houseboy, cooks, cleans, washes my clothes by hand (except for underwear, which for him is taboo), and waits on me so much he drives me mad. When Julius is not working, he stands at the sink staring out the window like a lost soul.

Julius takes care of the house, and Frances in return helps out his family with extra money for school fees, doctors, jail bond, bride price and funerals.

Julius came with the house, and his former employers were proper Brits. They say Brits and other Europeans treat their servants most fairly, while the cheapest employers are newly rich Africans and Asians. Julius is in his twenties. If he were old, he'd be called *mzee*, a title of respect in Swahili, but in English he'd still be referred to as a houseboy.

Julius' English is pretty basic, though probably not so basic as Frances likes to think when she talks about men while he's polishing the furniture. I get the feeling he disapproves of Frances and me, the way we never have formal sit-down meals and instead eat dinner watching pirated movies on the VCR—the main night-time entertainment among expats. There's a buzzer in the floor, which the former tenants used to call the servants (one of whom was

Julius' father). Frances uses lung power instead. When she calls for Julius, Humphrey barks, and that sets off all the dogs in the valley.

Julius doesn't understand why I wear "men's clothes," shorts and pants, rather than skirts or the African kikois and kangas Frances wraps herself in. She'd prefer to run around naked, but with Julius, the gardener, the watchman and all the other locals hovering about, privacy (other than in my cabin) is scarce. Among illiterate Africans there's a puritanical streak, which, I'm told, came from the first missionaries teaching their ancestors to cover up and come to Christ.

Frances and Gary have lived in Africa for almost ten years, Kwendela for two, during which she has run through all possibilities for self-improvement. She's taken tennis lessons, golf lessons, horseback riding, Nautilus, ballet, piano and voice. She has been hypnotized and chiropracted. She's been massaged, waxed, packed in mud, and a Rolfer has stuck his fingers up her nose. She has bought baskets, carvings, pots, beads, wall hangings, musical instruments, stools, gourds and hideous cow-footed drums. She's joined a Gestalt therapy group, an expat women's group, and Kwendela's very own classical theater group. Last year she was Bottom in *A Midsummer Night's Dream* because of a shortage of male actors. I'm helping her learn her lines for *Romeo and Juliet*. If you met Frances, you'd appreciate the challenge of her playing a love-struck virgin.

Gary, Frances' absentee boyfriend, pays for her diversions to keep her from crawling the walls.

She pores over old *Variety*s and *Billboard*s, reading all the casting calls she has missed. When she gets badly homesick, she drives to the airport to sniff jet fumes; it reminds her of New York air.

I hobble around on a crutch Julius carved for me. To be unable to travel is awful, but it's a little consoling that with all the flooding I couldn't follow elephants even if I had two good feet. The ranch owner cabled me that the pictures for the brochure worked out fine. He wired the money plus a small bonus. Every little bit helps.

The *Beacon* has shown lukewarm interest in a picture story. If only I could whet an editor's appetite with REAL news (for real money), but Frances says nothing ever happens here that the outside world would be interested in.

Kwendela looks like a city, with traffic jams, boulevards lined with red roses (the president's favorite) and purple jacaranda trees, drive-in movies and even a shopping center. But it is a sham, a Western city plopped down in the hinterlands of Africa. I take pictures of mamas selling mangoes, sidewalk barbers and deformed beggars. I spent most of yesterday photographing a chain gang building a road. They wore white smocks and shorts; if you disregarded the African guard with the Uzi, you could have mistaken them for students.

When Frances and I were in town, I asked her to leave me at a bank so I could change money. She had a fit: "A bank? No one goes to a bank!" She made a phone call and had me send a check for four hundred dollars to an address in the Channel Islands. Then she comes home with a paper bag stuffed with local currency worth five hundred dollars. This was my introduction to changing money, African-style. Frances says fiddling is the rule, and the president himself has millions in Swiss bank accounts.

Frances and I visited Ruth, the African girl I met. I wanted to take pictures in the squatter city, but I couldn't just walk in there with a white face and a camera and expect the locals to welcome me for taking happy snaps of poverty.

But Ruth was glad to see us, and her mother warmed up because we brought boxes of food: maize meal, sugar, tea, beans, fruit, candies, even a scrawny chicken a guy was selling by the roadside. The mother hid the boxes. She said there are bad people around who would steal it.

Ruth's mother might be my age, but she looks fifteen years older. I took pictures and used Frances' Polaroid to make a snapshot of the family, which the mother pinned to the mud wall beside a light bulb implanted for decoration. There's no electricity, but Ruth's mother wants her home to look modern. The closest water pump is a half mile away, and sanitation in the squatter city is nonexistent.

Ruth's mother has no land and no husband. She weaves baskets for money. She had a job but the memsahib fired her for stealing sugar. And she's pregnant again. Rain and babies, she believes, come from God.

Neighbors wandered in. We shook hands—all very formal. I guess our visit was a big deal. The mother served us sugary tea. (We discreetly poured it out.) She asked us if we were going to visit again. Frances said no, we were going on a long safari. Later she said to me, "I'm already supporting Julius' family. Gary will kill me if I get suckered into adopting another." I gave the mother money to buy textbooks and a school uniform for Ruth.

I'm restless, Jonathan, but here I remain, my foot itching

like crazy in a cast, watching birds in the backyard. This is Africa? Do you think it's true that sometimes you have to go a long way around to get where you're going?

Love, M

o o

"Another day. Another day," sighed Frances. She flopped into a lawn chair as Mirie sealed the letter. "What time is it?"

Mirie checked the position of the sun, which had peeked out after a mizzling morning. "Two, three, maybe."

Frances raked her fingers through her short blond hair, which stuck out in chicken feathers. Gray half-moons of mascara dripped under her eyes. She wore striped lavender pajamas and argyle socks. It continually amazed Mirie how Frances could change from vamp to frump.

Mirie trained her binoculars on a long-legged stiletto-beaked bird pecking at the damp grass. She checked her field guide. Abdim's stork, wooly-necked stork. Ibis. Sacred. Wattled. Glossy. Hadada? *"HAH-dah-dah. HAH-dah-dah."*

"What?" said Frances.

"That's the bird. Hadada ibis." She offered Frances the field glasses.

"I'll take your word for it."

Julius brought a pot of steaming coffee, a basket of scones hot from the oven, butter, jam and an egg in a cup. He was used to Frances' irregular habits.

"You're going to make me fat, Julius. Gary won't recognize me."

"Yes, memsahib," said Julius somberly and left.

"Cheerful," said Mirie.

"He misses Gary."

"When's he coming back?"

"The question of the decade. Hold on."

Frances went inside and returned with a bulging scrapbook. "This is Gary." But she held the cover closed. "Wait a minute—I want to see Jonathan."

Mirie fetched the framed picture from the duffel. It elicited a smacking sound of approval from Frances. In it, Jonathan was wearing his old leather jacket. His thumbs were hooked on his jeans pockets. His dark, wind-mussed hair was haloed by backlighting. "You two could be brother and sister."

"Everyone says that."

"How old?"

"Thirty-nine next month."

"He looks younger."

"The picture is a few years old. He looks even better now."

"What are you doing here if he's there? I'd be on the next plane . . . Where did you meet?"

"I'd moved back to New York after the newspaper job. I wasn't going out much. I took a film class for fun and to meet men. Jonathan's a terrific teacher. I was intimidated by him. There were always women waiting for him after class. I assumed he was a womanizer, which he was, and he thought I was cold and preoccupied, which I was. He asked students to help him on a project for public TV, and I volunteered. He asked me to a few screenings, and afterward . . ." Mirie laughed.

"Heavenly," said Frances, and she obviously meant it.

"When I showed him my pictures, he told me I was too good a photographer not to be making a living at it. I was afraid he was only saying that to put the make on me."

"What is your problem, girl?" Frances thrust the picture at Mirie. "This man is not Godzilla. This man is adorable."

"That was just it," said Mirie. "I wanted to. And the more I wanted to, the more afraid I was. I couldn't take it when guys slept with you a couple of times and then said they didn't want to get serious, or never called again as if the whole thing never happened."

"I suppose you never changed your mind about a guy you'd slept with," said Frances.

"Well, yes," Mirie conceded, "but I was never that mean."

"Of course you weren't," said Frances with mocking earnestness.

"Anyway," continued Mirie, "I hadn't had a thing for anyone for so long, and I really liked Jonathan. It would have been too awful if he turned out to be like the others. It took a long time before anything happened with us."

"Not me and Gary," Frances said brightly. "I met him at a

party. We went to his place and screwed our brains out for the next three months. It was the best I've ever had it." She said, "If only it had continued. . . . So what's Jonathan doing right now?"

"He's in New York, editing, teaching and trying to make movies."

Frances sat up. "Do you think he could get me a job? Even as an extra?"

"It's not as if producers are knocking down the door to get him to direct. Not yet anyway."

Frances slumped back in her seat. "Always a catch. That's what keeps me in *lala* land."

"That's why Jonathan's in New York. He thinks every other place is second-rate."

"All too true," said Frances.

Mirie leafed through the scrapbook of newspaper clippings. Jakarta, Beirut, Cairo, Rome, Dakar, Lagos, Mogadishu, New Delhi, Kuala Lumpur. There was a black-and-white glossy photograph of a dark, bearded man in a dugout canoe paddled by an African. Bearers waded alongside carrying luggage and a portable typewriter over their heads.

"Gary," said Mirie.

"On assignment," said Frances with a sigh. Humphrey looked up soulfully as Frances slathered jam on a piece of scone and popped it in her mouth. The dog whined. "What do you want?" She tossed him a morsel, which he inhaled. "Well, I know what I want . . . The truth, Mirie . . . don't you miss it? . . . you'll see. It'll get to you, too. The rains keep on like this, and it gets steamy, like you're in a pressure cooker, and the only thing in bed with you are insects as fat as robins, and everything around you is growing and ripe to bursting, and all the mamas have babies on their tits and *totos* everywhere. And you know it'll all turn back into dust and drought. And I think, why am I wasting away like this, when it's all going on around me? And just when I can't take it anymore, it's time for Gary to come home, and I think about wearing nice clothes. But instead I get a telex, and he's cursing having to go off on another story and says how much he misses me. Fat help that is . . . I don't know about you, but if I go too long without it, my hormones back up and make me crazy."

"I think you have a plumbing problem."

Frances shook her head. "Maybe. But at least I know what I'm about."

A feeble ringing sound came from the house. The phone had come back to life. Frances ran to answer it.

A party next week, she announced on her return. "We might as well go." Affecting a debutante slouch in her purple pajamas and argyle socks, she drawled, "I do declare—my dance card isn't full."

o o

Dear Liz,

It's raining. Days are hot and nights cold and damp in Kwendela. I sit in front of the fireplace with the dog beside me, helping Frances memorize her lines for *Romeo and Juliet.* Julius, the houseboy, brings *chai* with milk and honey to take away the chill that makes my foot ache more. I am living the way my mother wanted to live, an indolent, gracious life with no responsibilities other than to tell the servants what to do. If this is the Cinderella life, give me the pumpkin.

Frances' friends come by at night to watch the VCR. Most are wives and girlfriends of the foreign press, hack-pack memsahibs who conduct their relationships by telex. There is much more smoking and drinking here than at home.

Since Frances is obsessed with her body, she does neither. (She gobbles jam and scones instead, then exercises like a dervish.) So far, I'm only on aspirin for my foot, and an occasional brandy. The women come by, but they don't say much before staring at the VCR. I feel like I'm living in a posh old people's home. Frances invites them to sleep over after the movie. They're scared of driving home at night, because robbers lay thornbush across the road and attack motorists, stealing cars, money, even their clothes. All of Frances' friends live in houses equipped with watchdogs, night watchmen, locks, chains, fences, grates and alarm systems with panic buttons used to call vans of security guards armed with wooden bats. The security business seems to be Simahali's only growth industry.

The women complain about their servants and swap rumors of slashings by panga gangs, political hanky-panky and what's new on the black market. During the day some of them sit around the swimming pool at the country club, while the *ayahs*—African nannies—keep their *totos,* the kiddies, from drowning.

A woman I like, a Brit in her late forties who grew up in West Africa, says that juju has kept the gangs away from her house, which is even more secluded than Frances'. She's put fetish objects, bones and feathers and stuff, all over the garden and nailed to her door a monkey skeleton rigged with glass eyeballs and a fright wig. She's been in Africa longer than any of us, and works on family planning in rural villages. She has no patience with pessimists. She split from her husband ages ago and intends to stay in Africa.

Frances' boyfriend Gary is a British journalist. He's rarely at home. I don't think fidelity is their strong suit. If I were Frances, I'd be terrified I'd get AIDS. The bars where men pick up hookers aren't packed like they used to be. The African doctor who fixed my foot told me he's visited villages that are dying out from AIDS and other diseases. Officially, the government says it's only a little problem.

The person Frances is most dependent on is Julius. Julius is the one constant human presence in her house. He's a link to its past, when it was a real home, and a connection to life outside the enclaves where all the white expats, Asians and rich Africans live. Mostly, I think Julius stands between Frances and loneliness.

It's raining again. My foot hurts. Somewhere in the bush an elephant is calving and I'm not there to photograph it.

Love, Mirie

18

A Rolling Stones record blasted from the landscaped compound. The odor of roasting meat wafted over tall hedges behind which was a wall embedded with bottle shards and strung with concertina wire. Frances and Mirie drove in past an askari in a torn raincoat, who carried a spear, and a uniformed security guard holding a bat.

The party was already well underway. Frances smiled at the faces she recognized. Men paused in mid-sentence. She bloomed out of a blue strapless gown made of sari silk, artfully wrapped and pinned in place. Draped over the swell of her breasts was a necklace of tiny silver phalluses.

"Oh, oh, prepare yourself," said Frances. "The hostess."

Madeleine Chu, squat and determined, forged past guests to greet them. "Frances, you look magnificent." She examined the necklace. "Conquests?"

Frances smiled like the Cheshire cat and introduced Mirie. The expected question about the cast was asked, to which Mirie replied that she had hurt her foot getting out of a plane.

The hostess showed neither amusement nor sympathy. She was interested in Mirie's injury only insofar as it complicated social logistics.

"How can I circulate you?" she clucked. "I'll put you by the bar. That way you're bound to meet everyone." She turned her attention to Frances. "I'm glad you brought Mirie. I'm tired of the same old faces. Too bad I couldn't invite you last week. But it was purely a Francophone evening and without Gary you would have been out of it. Where is that hunk of yours? We haven't seen him since the sauna party."

"Broiling in Khartoum, the last I heard."

"Donald has consulted there." She said to Mirie, "He's a housing expert, but his talent was wasted in that armpit of a place, *absolument*." She examined Mirie's crutch. "You're into native crafts."

"Frances' houseboy made it for me."

"I'm always hunting for export items, but the workmanship is awful unless a European tells them what to do." She looked intently at Mirie; her thin lips moved slightly, forming a frigid smile. "I've never seen such extravagant eyes."

Madeleine Chu led them up a curving stairway overlooking a ground-floor atrium. The atrium had been transformed into a rock garden and pond that was traversed by a wooden bridge. There a couple nuzzled, dangling their feet in the water and tossing flower petals.

"You two, stop that! Bougainvillea clogs the pump!" Madeleine Chu barked from the balustrade. She said to Frances and Mirie, "People have no idea what it takes to maintain a certain standard of living here . . . Come. You must meet Donald."

Hampered by cast and crutch, and put off by the brusque little hostess, Mirie made her way upstairs as slowly as possible in the hope that Madeleine Chu would leave her and Frances to mingle on their own. But Madeleine stuck with them. She explained how she had acquired the house, the furnishings and the guests, mostly European and a smattering of prominent Africans, some of whom Mirie recognized from pictures in the local papers.

A crush of people danced and shouted conversations over the stereo. Servants drifted among the throng with trays of champagne and canapés.

A tall Asian man smiled as they approached. Madeleine Chu introduced her husband Donald.

"What does Mirie stand for?" he asked. "Miranda?"

"No—"

"Mirabella," said Madeleine. "That's infinitely more beguiling! I'll call you Mirabella."

Mirie met Madeleine's unblinking gaze. "Call me Mirie."

"All right . . . Mirie." Madeleine and Donald Chu exchanged glances, as if they were coming to some sort of agreement. Then Madeleine proceeded to give a rundown of the other guests, who was who, and what and whom they were after.

In contrast with his wife's brisk efficiency, Donald Chu had a suave, easy manner. Mirie noticed—indeed, couldn't help but notice, for in the crush she was pushed up against him—designer initials discreetly woven into his shirt, and his tie, flecked with those of a competing designer. He seemed mildly interested, mildly amused by his wife's nonstop monologue, like a ventriloquist listening to his dummy.

Donald Chu hailed a servant circulating champagne.

"A toast to Mirie, our new arrival." He drank to her, then excused himself to greet other guests.

The champagne tasted good, so good that when a servant came around again, Mirie took another glass, her mood improving.

Madeleine Chu, her pinky finger aloft, bit down decisively on a Ritz cracker topped with caviar. "These always make Americans feel more at home."

"Aren't you from the States?" asked Mirie, for Madeleine's accent was solidly American.

"I'm Chinese-American. Donald is Chinese and French-Swiss. We both went to school in Europe. Donald and I share a very European sensibility. Americans are so . . . eager. *C'est trop.*" She flicked an orange crumb from her lips. "I met Donald at a party. I called my mother that night. I told her, 'I've met the man I'm going to marry.' Donald had all the right qualifications. All this garbage about romance is okay for affairs, but you can't base a partnership on it. Don't you think so, Mirie?"

Mirie demurred politely. Frances aimed a playful salvo. "Mirie's got it made. She has a fantastic guy at home waiting for her while she's out romping among the elephants with Max."

Madeleine seized on the innuendo. "Oh, you know Max

Howden . . . I've been trying to get him to one of our parties, but he's never in town. Are you and he . . . ?"

"He helped me get started. I'm a photographer," said Mirie. "This is my first assignment in Africa." Mirie longed to shake off Madeleine Chu. Frances had already managed to extricate herself and was with some people across the room.

"A professional liaison," said Madeleine. "How charming. Well, there are certainly better-looking men around." Her eyes scanned the living room like a searchlight. "Who would be right? You'll have your pick, Mirie." She pronounced her name Me-*rrray*, with a French accent.

"My name is Mirie," she said coolly. "Just plain Mirie. I'm here for a short time. When the rains end—"

"None of us is here for long." Madeleine brushed against Mirie's arm, a gesture vaguely sexual and intrusive. "The minute Donald's contract is up, we're out of here. *Mon Dieu*, Africa is hopeless. We plan to enjoy ourselves while we can." She left Mirie to go pounce on some new arrivals.

o   o

"Another?" The Canadian bureaucrat replaced Mirie's empty champagne glass with a fresh one. He continued, "There's plenty of money. More than the country can possibly absorb. The rascals in government take it. A few million dollars later, there's still no clean water."

The Canadian introduced Mirie to an engineer from Finland. He was in Simahali to donate his invention, a simple machine that compressed soil into building bricks. Through him she met a young German apprenticing as a coffee buyer. Every day he tasted hundreds of cups of coffee, sipping and spitting into a vat.

"Otherwise," he said, "they would have to scrape me from the ceiling, not true?"

Lately, rumors of devaluation had bombarded the coffee auctions, so he had started buying tires. His apartment was stuffed floor to ceiling with tires. He hoped devaluation would take place soon, so he could unload them at a nice profit and have some living space. He was a nervous man. Mirie supposed it was the coffee.

A compatriot of his, a dour veterinarian, told Mirie about the rampages of the tsetse fly. A nurse described her confinement in a luxurious American compound in Riyadh; she was in Simahali for R and R. A Dane bemoaned his long tenure within the tentacular bureaucracy of the U.N. "Ah, without doubt, it has destroyed me."

She noticed a man nestled in a corner next to a speaker. He had pale-oak hair, wire-rim glasses and a patchy beard. He seemed happily oblivious to the people walking around him.

"Don't bother," said Madeleine Chu. She had intercepted Mirie's gaze as she was passing by en route to a cluster of West Africans dressed in long robes. "He's marginal."

Mirie sipped champagne. She wandered about searching for a bathroom and found the kitchen instead. Madeleine Chu reappeared, and assuming Mirie was admiring the kitchen, commenced a tour.

The kitchen was all white. White tiles, white cabinets, white walls, and neat as an operating room. The pantry was loaded with imported foods: Jiffy mix, taco shells, English biscuits, Campbell's pork and beans, chutney, *crème marron,* caviar and stacks of cases of duty-free liquor. The freezer was full of labeled meats: eland, fowl and shark steaks. The refrigerator was stuffed with cheeses and blood sausage. In the corner were sacks of *posho,* corn meal, for the servants.

"We trade with friends who have diplomatic privileges."

"You must like to entertain."

"Entertain? Naturally. But these are provisions. When the coup comes, Donald and I are going to party on the roof with Dom Pérignon. We'll round up the best people. I'll put you on our list."

Madeleine peered out the window, where the cook was basting a goat roasting on a spit. "He slaughtered it in view of the guests. I was just mortified. These people are so backward." She stormed out of the kitchen to go harass the cook.

Silly woman, thought Mirie, with nothing better to do than fiddle and finagle.

She was feeling less and less well. Where was the bathroom in this fortress?

Mirie hobbled upstairs to the top floor, away from the

blaring music and crowds. The Chus' bedroom was painted a dark plum color. In the center was a round bed covered in a black silk duvet. A scroll depicting cranes among reeds floated down from the ceiling. There was a dresser and a vanity and a low black enamel table with an inlaid mirror.

Mirie lay down on the cold tile floor in the bathroom. Her head spun. *Chus' coup, Chus' coup.* The nonsense rhyme would not stop. She wanted to go home, but Frances, she knew, would not want to leave until every man at the party was after her. Free-floating lust in search of an object. It was a game with Frances. She didn't take herself or the men very seriously.

Mirie was roused by sounds outside in the bedroom. She splashed cold water on her face. When she came out, there were the Chus bent over the mirrored table snorting cocaine through straws.

Donald Chu rose debonairly and guided her to the table. "We're having a little break. Come, join us."

"Thanks. No. I'm going to look for Frances."

"She's busy." Madeleine Chu sniffled between words. She hovered around Mirie. "Look at her eyes, Donald. They're mysterious." She said to Mirie, "You really should do more with yourself. Do you always wear eyeglasses?"

"Only to see," said Mirie. She felt less queasy; the Chus had a certain sobering effect.

Madeleine Chu rooted around her dresser drawer and pulled out a handful of ceramic necklaces. "I design these and teach the locals to make them. I have an export deal with Bloomingdale's. Fifty bucks a piece in the States. Ten for you, because you're a friend." She fastened one around Mirie's neck. "Fabulous."

The amoeboid blobs felt like rocks around her slender neck. "I'll pass. Thanks."

Madeleine consulted her husband. Donald Chu undid the clasp and, resting his hand on Mirie's shoulder, remarked to his wife, "Mirie is exceptional without anything."

Madeleine Chu drew Mirie and her husband closer. "I knew you would think so." Her fingertips grazed the back of Mirie's neck. "Stay until everyone else goes, Mirie. It will be more *intime*."

Mirie backed away.

"*Sois tranquille,*" cooed Madeleine.

Donald added soothingly. "My wife has impeccable taste."

"I have to go," blurted Mirie, and she was out the door, as fast as cast and crutch would permit. As she made her way downstairs, she overheard Donald Chu say, "Madeleine, you frightened our little bird."

o   o

The house was bulging with people and there was no sign of Frances. Something held her in place. Mirie looked down. The pale man, ensconced beside the speaker, had taken hold of the base of her crutch. "Hello," he said.

Mirie crouched beside him and cupped her hands. "Have you seen a big blond woman in a blue dress?"

He shrugged. "People coming. Going. Nothing ever happens."

His British accent threw her off, but only for a moment. "*Grand Hotel?*" she guessed.

He put his hand to his heart. "I think I'm in love."

"My boyfriend teaches film."

"Why are there no women in Africa without boyfriends? Which one is he?"

"He's not here. He's in the States."

"An excellent place for him." He held out his hand. "I'm Andrew, but Andy is fine. You're upset. I don't like crowds either. Shall we go outside?"

Andy spoke in disconnected spurts. He was a consultant. He had been in the bush for six months, trying to persuade pastoralists to trade their cows for camels. They refused.

He had lived in a mud-hut village in a prefab house with its own generator, air conditioning and running water until one of the locals speared the pipe. The first day there his car mysteriously developed four punctured tires. Raggedy children followed him around.

"Cattle were dying everywhere. When the rains finally came, the cows couldn't digest the new grass, and they died even faster. But there were big herds of elephants, and the

117

flowers finally bloomed. It was lovely toward the end, if you didn't mind the rotting cows."

Mirie asked him more about the elephants. He told her to do a "recce," go look for herself. There was an old hunting camp where she could stay, and by now—he was quite certain—the rains were finished and the roads would be passable.

Above them the sky was working itself up into a storm. Winds whipped the eucalyptus. The clouds glowed with lightning, and it began raining. Mirie's crutch kept catching in the wet ground. But Andy was hungry to talk, and he was so entertaining that neither noticed that they were getting soggy.

They followed a path to the end of the garden. A spotlight illuminated a tall wooden cistern. Andy gazed on it, awed. "In my village the women had to dig for water in the dry river bed. That much water would have been a miracle."

From inside the cistern came the sound of splashing and laughter, a man's voice, low and seductive, and a woman's raucous laughter. Mirie started to turn back. Just then, two naked people hoisted themselves up on the edge of the vat. One was a man with aquiline features, dark hair and a thin reptilian body. The other was Frances, wearing nothing but the gleaming necklace.

"Hi, Mirie." Frances, friendly and unflappable, did the introductions. "Well, come on in, you two. The water's heated," she insisted.

Mirie used her cast as an excuse to bow out. "I'm going home. Andy will take me."

Frances looked disappointed. Mirie glanced at Andy. The sight of Frances' breasts had apparently robbed him of his power of speech.

Frances put her arms around her companion and sank out of sight.

ɔ　ɔ

When Frances came home the following morning, Mirie told her that she was going on safari. Frances didn't seem to hear. She hiked up her now-rumpled blue dress, flopped down in the grass, and blew on a blade of grass, making a squealing sound.

Her skin was pale and blotchy, and she was obviously in a bad mood. Mirie returned to studying a map of the area that Andy had recommended.

"Have a good time last night?" Frances asked testily.

"Once I escaped the Chus," said Mirie, perusing the map. "Madeleine tried to serve me up to her husband."

"She's a bore . . . Did you say you didn't do threesomes?"

Mirie made a face. "I bolted and came looking for you."

"And caught me in the act," said Frances, petulant, goading.

Mirie looked up. "I didn't say that."

"You don't need to. I can read it in those funny eyes of yours . . . Sex is like food, Mirie. Once in a while you get a great meal, but regardless you got to eat."

"I'm not judging you."

Frances idly played with Mirie's binoculars, looking through them the wrong way. "You don't lie well . . . Let me tell you something. Gary and I don't make a fetish of monogamy, but we abide by house rules. I don't foul the nest, and he doesn't bring home hookers." Frances shouted to Julius, who was in the kitchen, to hurry up with the coffee. Humphrey galloped over and jumped on Frances. He nipped at her necklace. The string snapped and silver phalluses spilled onto the grass.

"My juju!" Frances wailed and pushed the dog away. On hands and knees she combed the grass for the tiny pieces of silver. "So much for the fertility necklace—for all the good it does." She tugged at the top of her dress, to keep it from slipping down.

Mirie handed her the pieces she had found. "You don't want a baby, do you?"

Frances sat up and didn't say anything for a time. A tight smile appeared on her face. "A hooker gave Gary an infection. He gave it to me. It's a souvenir of Africa guaranteed to last a lifetime." She patted her belly and stood up, clutching the broken strand. "It's great when you know you can't tempt fate. You can do it anywhere, anytime. No hostages to fortune from these hips."

Julius came out with Frances' breakfast. He set down the tray of hot coffee, steaming scones, a rose in a vase and a linen napkin, and left without a word. An ibis repeated its unmelodious refrain.

Frances sighed. "Julius is the only good man I know."

Just then a car rolled up the driveway.

Frances wiped her eyes, smoothed her dress and cursed under her breath as the reptilian man strolled across the grass toward them. "I told that son of a bitch not to come here. Now he's ruined everything."

19

"The great thing about this car," said Frances, abandoning the steering wheel to straighten her broad sun hat, "is that it's absolutely indestructible."

"It may be," said Mirie. "But we're not."

A decade in Africa, and Frances drove like the locals. Her car was a poor man's safari Jeep, an eggbeater on wheels that wheezed up hills and took curves tipsily. It rattled and clattered and hurtled over bumps. It rose as the road dipped, then dropped like a rock. Mirie urged Frances to let her do the driving, but her safari companion, infected with a happy fatalism, refused.

"Look around. If your number's up, it's up," said Frances.

They sped past the bloated, smashed bodies of dogs, goats and a zebra, and a gutted truck turned squatters' house. Unlike during her first days in Africa with Max, Mirie did not stop to take pictures. She wanted to reach camp in time to catch the late-day light, and so begin, as quickly as possible, to make up the time she had lost during the rains.

She felt almost painfully alert, a sensation she associated with being on deadline during her first years at the *Beacon,* when every assignment, however soft or trivial, had challenged her. There was, too, a strong, visceral recollection of driving in the bush with Max, and of something like intoxication with the smells and colors and the sheer extravagance of land and sky. It was as if her private vision of Africa had sprung full-blown from her head and spread out before her—warm, radiant and bedrock real.

"It's crazy," she said. "Now anything's possible." She laughed. "Africa's addicting."

Frances was dubious. "Sex is addicting. But this place? It's all new to you. For me, it's different. Oh, I like it. Clouds and sunset and"—she motioned to the land—"all that. It's great. But it's always here."

"I'm only here for a while."

"Keep telling yourself that."

Mirie knew that Frances had been as eager to go on safari as she herself was, though for different reasons. She had had a fine time with Lizard Man until he broke the rules by coming around for more. Being forced to oust him had left a sour aftertaste to an otherwise delicious night. A change of scenery, "a hit on the wild," as Frances called it, was in order.

A semitruck, avoiding a gaping hole in the road, slid into their lane. Frances braked, the wheels locked, the car spun on tarmac melted in the heat, then stopped, uncannily headed in the right direction. The truck disappeared down the road, not slowing for an instant. Frances, too, drove on as if nothing had happened.

"Let me drive," pleaded Mirie.

Frances blithely reprimanded her. "You're in bongo land. Get into the spirit of the thing. Wait till Gary hears about me going on safari."

"Assuming we live to tell about it. When's the last time you went camping?"

Frances laughed her full-throated laugh. "Gary doesn't like that. He likes the bang-bang, along with first-class hotels, fresh linens, good wine and Africans serving him mangoes and Marmite on toast."

"Brewer's sludge."

"Right. . . . Anyway, you wouldn't catch Gary driving hundreds of miles to sleep on the ground. Now that I think of it, why did I let you talk me into this?"

ɔ ɔ

The hunters' camp was in a sorrier state than Andy had described. The manager, an elderly Briton, remarked that it had been some time since he had had women guests. Mirie doubted that he had been overrun with visitors of any sort, other than mosquitoes, which had bred abundantly in the rains. They first took care of domestic chores. Mirie patched holes in the tent with gaffer's tape while Frances, with much grumbling, darned holes in the mosquito netting.

Then they took a drive, and this time, exchanging duties, Frances navigated and Mirie drove. She discovered more of the car's idiosyncrasies. It bucked and coughed and died between first and second gears, and hiccuped in third and fourth. Though she sped up over washboard road (as she had seen Max do), spine-jolting bumps rattled the car like a box full of keys.

Following a track through acacia and whistling thorn, Mirie spotted elephant spoor. The dung trail became fresher.

"See? We're catching up with them," she said with growing excitement.

"I've heard of people reading tea leaves," mused Frances. "But elephant shit?"

Mirie related that she'd read that elephant manure was central to the bush recycling system. "People think elephants act like demolition crews, that they knock down trees and destroy forests. Actually, they're gardeners. Elephants eat trees. Their digestive juices soften the outer wall of acacia seeds. They dump the seeds out again, but now the seeds can germinate. It's like the tree needs the elephant to eat it."

"Yeah?" said Frances, nonplussed by Mirie's speech on the virtues of dung.

Mirie spotted elephants making their way through the bushes. She at first stayed well behind so as not to frighten them. Then she gradually closed the gap.

Calves suckled while their mothers ate branches and stripped bark from trees. They were soon joined by another group, also females and young. The elephants rumbled, rubbed up against one another in greeting, touched their trunks to one another's mouths, then moved off together.

Mirie followed them to a watering hole. Testing their tolerance, she drove closer to the water. They faced her, trunks raised, and walked off, but not before she had taken several pictures. She parked the car in the bush and waited. They returned after a time. She had a good view of them feeding, drinking and tending the calves.

Frances tried drawing the elephants, but she was soon frustrated. "Damn, they keep moving. I can't keep up with them." Mirie thought Frances' quick sketches were good, and urged her to try more. Frances shrugged off the effort. She put on her headphones, shut her eyes and, while Mirie took pictures, moved to her private music.

A baby elephant charged some blue-speckled guinea fowl. The birds hastily waddled for cover. The baby trumpeted a victory, then playfully tried to mount another calf. The play-mate wobbled and they both sat down hard on their broad baby rear ends.

Adult elephants rolled in the muddy shallows, then stood glistening with mud, fanning their ears and swinging their trunks with all the dignity of elderly matriarchs at a spa. A tiny calf threaded through a forest of elephant feet. He wanted to drink but had not mastered his trunk. He knelt at the water's edge, but his trunk behaved like a necktie falling in soup. He got up awkwardly, managing to step on his trunk, which sent him squealing back to his mother.

From the opposite direction came angry trumpeting. Emerging from the bush, a bull elephant shook its head and shifted back and forth, clearly disturbed to find a car in his path to the water. It would have been simple enough to make a detour, but the elephant did not see it that way. Frances, meanwhile, was deeply, obliviously, immersed in her music. Mirie shut off the Walkman. Then Frances noticed the elephant. It raised its trunk, flared its ears and paced in a minatory display.

"I think we're in trouble," whispered Frances, as if she were trying to keep the news from the elephant. "Mirie?"

But Mirie was following her first impulse, which was to put the camera between herself and the elephant, not only because the pictures were too good to pass up but also as a kind of irrational defense: that by freezing the instant on film, she might actually stop the elephant in its tracks.

Frances shook her. "Move your ass!"

"Got it!" Mirie started the engine, and put the gear in reverse. Or thought she had; the car did not move. She tried again. The gear popped into neutral. The bull trumpeted, set to charge.

Frances wrestled the stick. The elephant tucked in its chin, its ears flared forward. Mirie cursed herself for missing the shot. She did not really believe the elephant would attack until it was running at them full force. Then Mirie threw herself on the carhorn, blasted it over and over. Frances joined in, bellowing with all her lung power, "Buzz off!"

The elephant stopped as if he had been shot, shook his head in fury and trumpeted back at them so loudly Mirie felt the sound waves. To their amazement, he backed off and in blind fury bulldozed a bush, then remembered the real target and went through the angry display again.

Mirie fumbled with the shift stick, and this time it slid into reverse. She floored the accelerator and the car hurtled backward, throwing a curtain of dust before the startled elephant. The car sped out of its path, and the elephant hurried to the watering hole. He rumbled and shook his head nervously and finally settled down to drink. He had the watering hole all to himself; during the commotion the other elephants had left.

Mirie and Frances sat for a time without saying a word.

Finally, Frances said, "How did you know the horn would scare him?"

"It *had* to work. If he trampled us, I never would have known how my pictures came out."

○ ○

Frances sketched, Mirie photographed. Rigging a tarp to the back of the car, they spent the hottest hours of the day under the makeshift sun porch. Mirie invented a pastime, collecting thorns—acacia needles, spikes, wait-a-bit barbs, hooks of ziziphus, an array of plant defenses that pricked, scratched, tore and stung the unwary.

Days revolved around elephants and available light; nights around mosquitoes and unforgiving camp beds. Mirie thrashed in her sleep, toppling herself along with the canvas bed. She righted the frame and remade the bed while Frances slept soundly.

One night clouds stole over the sky and Mirie's mending foot began to ache. It rained until dawn. The camp manager surmised that the rain was the last gasp of the monsoon; it wouldn't last. But it rained the next day and the day after.

Mirie refused to let the rains hamper her work. She and Frances set off every morning. They put the car in four-wheel drive and avoided the gluelike mud.

Frances believed in her car and in her driving. She tore around a curve, panicking impalas crossing the road.

"Slow down!" Mirie clutched the window frame. "I want to photograph the animals, not kill them."

The river was high and fast from the rains, but according to her map, there was a track on the other side. Mirie limped along the bank, using her crutch to test the depth. Though it was shallow in spots, Mirie was doubtful about crossing. Frances said that the car was made for precisely these conditions; it could do everything but the breast stroke.

The tires spewed muddy water as Frances headed into the stream. The wheels strained in the viscous bottom.

"Hold on," said Frances. "I got to go faster or the tires will sink in."

Mirie hugged her camera case. The car bucked forward. Water seeped under the door frame.

Frances scowled. "It's supposed to be watertight. I'm turning back." As she maneuvered the car around, the hood suddenly dipped forty-five degrees, the engine sputtered and died. Frances turned the ignition. There was no sound at all.

"That never happened before," said Frances.

Mirie surveyed the small rapids surging over the submerged front end. "How many times have you dunked the engine in water?" she asked.

"Well, you didn't tell me about the hole."

"I didn't know there was one. My arms don't reach twenty feet out into the river." Mirie pressed the horn and tried the lights, but there was no juice.

Frances said, "You're clever. You know how to fix cars, right?"

"Oh, sure," said Mirie dismally.

"Where's Max when we need him?" moaned Frances. "Oh, well, someone will come by. They'd better come soon. I'm starving."

Mirie and Frances climbed onto the roof of the car. Mirie clutched her camera bag as water gurgled and eddied around the auto. Baboons sat on their haunches eating palm nuts, curiously watching the creatures in the middle of the river.

"It's a pretty spot to be stranded," said Mirie.

"It's okay for you," said Frances. "You're happy as long you're taking pictures. You don't appreciate what the African sun does to us blondes." Frances slathered on the last of her tube of sunblock and checked her face in a hand mirror. "Wrinkles, more wrinkles. When I'm a walnut, no man will love me."

They lay on their backs. Palm fronds waved at the scudding clouds. Mirie told Frances how when she was a child her father used to take her to the playground. She hung by her knees pretending she was right side up and the clouds upside down while her father smoked his sweet-smelling pipe and read the tip sheets. If he was in a good mood, he let her choose a horse, and if it won, he presented her with a crisp five-dollar bill, but each time she had to promise not to tell her mother about the game.

"In a way, it would have been better if he had walked out on us—then it would have all been out in the open, instead of blowing all our savings in secret. Maybe it was good for me in a way. I learned not to rely on anyone but myself. I don't know what I'd do if I didn't work. Who would I be?"

"Don't you know who you are without looking at a résumé?" asked Frances. "God, all this terminal anxiety back in the world. It makes me glad I'm in Africa." She rolled on her side, her head propped on her elbow, a rumpled odalisque. "Gary's right. First-class is the only way to go."

"That doesn't guarantee the car won't break down."

"But, we'd have dozens of locals to dig us out. If only Julius were here. What I'd give for hot scones and jam."

"That's what you wanted to get away from. You were dying of boredom, remember?"

"But now I'm dying of hunger."

"Doesn't it bother you? The servant thing?"

"No—why should it? Julius never says a word unless his family is in trouble. Julius is just . . . there."

Mirie realized that Frances was beginning to get a little tired of roughing it. She was reverting to her role as a pampered memsahib.

"Did I tell you," piped Frances, "about my audition for the road company of *A Chorus Line?*"

"Yes."

Frances scowled. "It's the malaria pills. My memory is disintegrating."

"Frances, if you feel so strongly that you're missing your calling, why not go back?"

"And do what? Wait tables? I'm thirty-nine years old. What will I do till I break into the business?"

"Wouldn't Gary help you?"

Frances considered a moment. "Yes," she said, "he might."

"Then why don't you try it?"

Frances said, "This is between us. You have to promise never to tell Gary—no, for once it's not sex. The last time I was in New York, I came apart. I was crazy, but I pretended I wasn't. I'd been in Africa for three years straight. In New York everything was speeded up, except for me. I would go down supermarket aisles in a trance. I couldn't believe all the food and housewares. I had to have every sieve, spoon, spatula, every gadget in the place. The cart overflowed. Then I realized I didn't know what all this junk was. I put it all back and went home empty-handed." Frances laughed nervously. "The next time I panicked because there were twenty kinds of paper napkins. I couldn't choose. I abandoned the cart and ran out of the store. See what this place has done to me? Don't stay too long, Mirie. You'll never be able to leave."

Mirie sympathized. "Frances, you left Africa where most people have nothing and went back to America where people like us have more than we can ever use. You'd have to be a stone not to feel the difference."

"That's a pretty explanation. I only wish it were true." Frances slapped a fly. "I'm glad Max shanghaied you to the house. I thought I should tell you that in case I get sleeping sickness and die out here."

Mirie watched male baboons grooming one another, combing insects from their fur and eating them. A female baboon sauntered by, displaying her pink, swollen rear end. A small male made a few tentative steps toward her. This enraged the big male. He stared balefully, flattened his ears and bared his fangs. There was a chase and a skirmish. The smaller male had no chance at all, and fled crouched and screeching. The big male mated with the female that had provoked the fight. Then everyone went their separate ways. The top baboon reclined languorously as a small scruffy male, clearly low man in the hierarchy, groomed his fur.

Concentrating on photographing the baboons, Mirie went through several rolls of film before she noticed that Frances was gone. Her clothes were on the hood, and she was down below, doing an energetic breast stroke around the car.

"Come out of there," shouted Mirie. "There may be crocodiles."

"Yum, yum. Thunder thighs for dinner," said Frances. She stood up naked, waist-deep in turbid water. "If you want to hang out here and wait for the baboons to evolve, that's fine. Throw me my clothes. I'm splitting."

"Where?"

"Back to camp."

"How?"

"On foot. How else?"

"What about the animals?"

"There *are* no animals here, Mirie. They're all at the tourist lodges for the dinner show. Didn't anybody tell you?"

The baboons screamed and clambered up the trees. Bushes rustled though there was no wind. Mirie grabbed her camera and searched for Frances. But she was underwater, letting the current pull her downstream.

Finally, Frances surfaced, in the wrong place. She rubbed the water out of her eyes. A lion watched from the bank.

"Don't move," said Mirie. She wondered privately (while she shot a few frames) if she had said this for the sake of safety or of photography.

Frances stood petrified. The lion blinked, bent his scraggly maned head and lapped water daintily.

Frances whimpered, "Do something."

"Go down slowly and swim back here."

Frances swam underwater, back to the car in one breath. She and Mirie scrambled back inside.

The lion took a last drink, walked back from the bank, stretched out his tail and sprayed the bushes. It scraped the ground with its back feet, lay down and began to groom its mane.

"I guess we know whose beach this is," said Mirie, continuing to shoot.

"Lions don't swim, do they?" said Frances, hurriedly throwing on her clothes.

"I'm not too sure. I suppose it depends how hungry they are . . . Still want to walk?"

"Not funny," said Frances, not taking her eyes off the lion.

The lion disappeared into the bushes, but the baboons stayed up in the trees. Waterbuck and impala came, and after them cape buffalo waded around the car. Sunset dyed the sky pink and purple. Elephants came—great, slow, indistinct forms in the darkness.

"No wonder Max likes the nature gig," said Frances. "It's so simple."

"Simple!" Mirie was annoyed at Frances' casual derogation of her work.

"Not the photography—the life. He's always on the move, always seeing something new, no one to complicate his life. He has his books, his elephants, his car and he's happy. When he comes back to the city, he gets weirded out. That's why he doesn't stay at the house anymore, because as much as he likes me and Gary, he can't take the domestic scene."

"Doesn't he ever have girlfriends?"

"I've never seen Max with a woman. Of course, he's so damned private. He could have a harem in his cabin, but I doubt it. He's trained his passion along a very narrow track. You won't see Max in anguish over table napkins. I want everything, and Max wants nothing—only his freedom."

"How smart, to want something he can have."

"You're the same, aren't you? You have the man you want, the life you want. You've got it made."

Mirie didn't say anything. There was something curious and challenging in Frances' gaze, as if she knew better.

o   o

Doum palms stood sentry in eerie symmetry along the river banks. Stars peeked through the waving fronds. Scorpio curled its tail above them. A baboon roared. There was a distant pulse, a heartbeat very faint and far away.

"There must be a village nearby," said Frances. "But those people are smart. They're in their huts." The drums were drowned out by the shearing sound of crickets.

Frances and Mirie sat inside the marooned car wrapped in a tarpaulin. Frances wanted to make a fire on shore on the off chance that someone might see it and rescue them.

Mirie thought it was a poor idea. "What about the lion?"

"Screw the lion. I'm cold, hungry and I want a hot bath . . . If I were a lion, I'd be scared of fire."

"They probably are. But what happens when we run out of wood?"

"We'll find more." But Frances' heart was not in the argument. She didn't want to hunt for wood in the dark any more than Mirie did. "Where's the water?"

Mirie fetched the bottle. "Go easy. That's the last of it."

The little rapids gurgled around the car enticingly.

"Would we get sick if we drank it?" asked Frances.

"I think so." Mirie thought a moment, and came up with what she considered an ingenious solution. "Tomorrow we can sieve it through cloth, build a fire and boil it . . ."

Frances yawned. "That's a lot of work for a cup of water."

Mirie told Frances about how during the drought the African women dug holes in the dry river bed to collect trickles of water.

"Fascinating," said Frances. "But I'm not an African and neither are you."

In the darkness the palm fronds waved; it was a taunting sound, like falling rain.

20

At sunrise baboons with babies clinging to their backs and bellies climbed down from the trees to drink. Mirie was drinking, too. She was crawling around the car, licking condensation off the windshields.

Frances was stiff, groggy and, after two days, in a sour mood. Her face was puffy. "This is the pits. No one is going to find us until our bodies are baked onto this car."

"Let's wait a couple of hours and walk." Mirie peeled off her T-shirt and ripped off the bottom.

"You've sure changed your tune," said Frances. "Now what are you doing?"

Mirie wrapped the cotton swath around the end of her crutch. She had worked out an animalproof escape plan. She announced to Frances, "We're going to walk when it's hottest."

"Brilliant!" said Frances. "With a thimbleful of water between us."

"The lions nap during the hot hours. And just in case . . ." She showed her crutch, now a torch. "We'll dip it in gasoline before we go. I have matches. If animals come around, we can defend ourselves."

o o

Frances rolled in the mud to keep off the sun and the flies. She posed mud-caked in her sun bonnet and sarong for Mirie's camera.

"The photographer at work," said Frances as she in turn snapped a picture of Mirie, torch in hand, camera bag at her hip, bare midriff, torn T-shirt, cutoff running shoe protecting her bandaged foot.

Mirie hobbled along. Her armpit was raw where the crutch rubbed. Her foot, still on the mend, throbbed and swelled. They walked and walked and the landscape never seemed to change, as if she and Frances were trapped on a giant treadmill moving ever more slowly.

Drained by the heat, Mirie no longer feared being charged by animals. She was cloaked in dust. Sweat trails ran down her skin. She was too woozy to talk, or even to swat at flies. A tall secretary bird in black feathered tights crossed the road and sauntered off. Oryx that looked like unicorns grazed far away. With every kilometer her camera bag grew heavier. She could not even muster excitement for the pictures she had taken. She had not eaten in two days but it was water, not food, she craved.

Finally, Mirie and Frances came to a wide dirt road. They perked up, for, as they assured each other, someone, some-time, had to drive by. Frances said her eyes were failing; the road wiggled. Mirie saw it too—heat waves, she reassured Frances. They continued walking until they came to a dip in the road where muddy water had collected in ruts. There was no debate, the wisdom of the idea did not matter. They knelt down and drank the standing water, trying not to stir up the muddy bottom or suck in insects floating on the surface.

"A chocolate milk shake," said Frances, hoarse.

Mirie wiped her mouth, bilious but revived. "Delicious."

There was somebody down the road. They walked faster, as fast as Mirie could go. The figure seemed not to move. As they came closer, they saw an elaborately decked out African youth standing still by the side of the road balanced on one foot. He carried a spear and shield. His ochred hair was twisted in stiff plaits and molded around an arc of bone to form a visor. The plugs in his earlobes were ivory and his neck and arms were adorned with beads, paper clips, pen caps and lion's teeth. Under a loin cloth he wore denim shorts.

"A full-dress warrior," said Frances. "We're saved."

"From the lions?" Mirie asked wanly.

"Better than that," said Frances. "We must be near a hotel. He stands out here waiting for tourists to photograph him. Take his picture, and I'll pay him."

"Why would I want a picture of a tourist attraction?"

Frances, exasperated, said, "Mirie, the primitive is dead. You have to take what you can get. Now, shoot, for heaven's sake. He's not out here to get a suntan."

Mirie reluctantly took the boy's picture. Frances tipped him and launched into negotiations, accomplished with hand motions: she would trade their torch for his warrior's spear. "It will look good above the bed." But the warrior was no more willing to hand over his spear than Mirie was her crutch. Frances gave up. This was one trinket she would have to do without.

Finally, a car came and slowed to a stop, at which point a woman with an instammatic molded to her fleshy face snapped a picture of the warrior. She ignored Mirie and Frances; whatever two women were doing out in the bush alone, oddly dressed and disheveled, she didn't want to know about it. They might as well have been invisible.

She spoke in German to her husband, and he, translating her demands into heavily accented English, ordered the African driver to move on. Mirie poked her head in the window. In English she explained their predicament, that she and Frances had been stranded without food or water and needed help.

The husband responded with a list of his own troubles, how terrible his safari had been, how his wife had a rash, how they had seen only six giraffes. Measured against the thousands of marks they had spent, the trip had so far cost—he took out a calculator—eight hundred U.S. dollars per giraffe.

Mirie commiserated, and again asked for their help. Just as the man appeared to be mellowing, the warrier stuck his hand in the window for payment. The *Frau*'s jowls quivered with rage. She sputtered to her husband.

Mirie translated for Frances. "The *Frau* told her husband that we're dirty hippies trying to freeload off their private safari." Realizing too late that Mirie understood German, the husband made a flustered excuse in English.

Frances climbed on the front hood of the tourists' car, crossed her muddy legs attractively, and in a cool, commanding voice, she said, "Tell the Potato Face to dash the kid. He deserves a little luck today. And while you're at it, tell them that if they don't help us, we're going to die out here, and do they want our vulture-picked bodies on their conscience? Try it, Mirie. See how it plays."

"My German doesn't go that far."

It didn't matter. The unhappy husband, caught in the middle, dropped coins into the boy's hands and offered Mirie the same. She shook her head in disbelief.

"What does he think?" said Frances, descending magisterially from the car hood. "That we're trying to catch a bus?"

Having recorded the pittance in a notebook, the embarrassed husband ordered the driver to get going, and they were gone.

ɔ ɔ

"Charming people," said Frances as the dust settled back on the road. "Our friend should have shishkebabbed them."

The threesome kept walking and were soon overtaken by a dusty Mercedes four-wheel-drive. A short bare-chested Briton wearing a kikoi jumped out. He had a prominent sunburned nose and a helmet of brown curls. He was all muscles and cheerfulness.

"Good afternoon, ladies. Out for a little stoll among the natives?"

His name was Matthew, he said. His eyes moved from Mirie's midriff to Frances' breasts. He offered to help. Frances smiled her warmest smile.

"Get in the car, loveys," said Matthew. There was nothing he wouldn't do for them: water, food, car, anything.

"What about him?" Mirie indicated to the African boy.

"The Kaffir? What about him?" said Matthew as they sped off.

ɔ ɔ

Surrounded by a moat, the hotel was a cross between a gun bunker and a medieval castle. There were four towers, made of

135

concrete poured over sandbags, and connected by bridges. In the moat the permanent residents were crocodiles and hippos. Guests were summoned from their rooms when elephants and other animals arrived. Sunbathers marinating in tanning oil lay around the swimming pool.

Mirie and Frances were too thirsty even to get cleaned up. They sat under a table umbrella downing glass after glass of water and passion fruit juice. Mirie was stunned by the cushy circumstances they'd fallen into; Frances took it all in stride. For his part, Matthew apparently couldn't believe his luck. He was savoring the sight of Frances and Mirie in their torn clothes. He snapped his fingers for the waiter. "More juice? How about a real drink now?"

Drums thumped over loudspeakers, announcing to tour buses on game runs that teatime was near.

"Remember the tribal drums? That was it," Mirie said to Frances.

"Fine with me. This is my kind of safari." Frances and Matthew clicked glasses. She had become happier the instant Matthew came along, and she was happier still at the hotel.

Mirie left them to watch the game down below. Had the light been right, it would have made an interesting angle to shoot from. She decided to rise early the following morning.

Crocodiles basked in the sun, their jaws open wide. Elephants hosed themselves. An elephant, chest-deep in the moat, raised its trunk in an S-curve. Wise, mirthful eyes looked up at her under a fringe of dark lashes.

And then it doused her.

"*Scheisse,*" barked a sunbather who had also been soaked. She grabbed the top of her bikini and ran out of squirting range.

In her mind's eye Mirie made a snapshot of herself, the shocked expression, the cooling water running off her. Her lips tasted of animals, earth and salt. She saw herslf: scratched, sunburned, dirt-streaked. Stepping over sunbathers, Mirie moved like a sleep walker to the edge of the swimming pool. She dove in; her torn T-shirt billowed underwater. She reached out, pulling water past her, her body lengthening and becoming liquid itself.

21

"Did you hear the one about the black man who walks into a bar with a parrot on his shoulder?" asked Matthew, launching into another joke. "The bartender says, 'That's the weirdest looking thing I ever saw. Where'd you get that?'

"'Africa,' squalks the parrot."

Matthew and Frances burst into hysterical laughter. Mirie went back to the hotel room as Matthew began another joke.

"I don't get you," Frances rebuked her later. "He saved our lives. He paid for our room, he's towed out the car and found a *fundi* to fix it. So he tells dumb jokes. So what? I suppose you never laughed at a Polish joke?"

"What do you see in him? All he has is muscles and money."

"And an enormous"—Frances paused for maximum effect—"sense of humor." She slipped into a T-shirt he had bought for her and checked in the mirror the effect of the silkscreened elephant's head emblazoned across her chest. "He's been awfully sweet."

"Sweet, my ass," said Mirie.

"No," said Frances. "Mine."

"That doesn't bother you?"

Frances put her arm around Mirie and gave her a sisterly hug. "Wait till you meet someone who grabs you where you live. You'll change your mind just like you did when you said we should walk, lions or no lions."

"That was a practical decision."

"So is this. I'm reaching my peak. Unlike you," she said loftily, "I'm attuned to my body's needs."

"Well, that's dandy." It was obvious to Mirie they were talking past each other. "I've got other needs."

"If that means Jonathan, he's light-years away."

"Not to me, he isn't," said Mirie.

Frances brushed her blond hair, shook it into wisps and headed for the door. "He'd want you to be happy." Frances checked to see if Mirie was coming, but as the latter showed no signs of moving, she left.

"I'm already happy," Mirie said to herself. "I am."

ɔ ɔ

Mirie was photographing elephants from the bridge when Matthew came up to her. He drummed on the railing with a rolled-up magazine.

Mirie turned to him. "It's hard to concentrate with noise." He smirked. Mirie continued shooting. Matthew continued drumming.

Finally, Mirie put down her camera. "What is it?"

"The car's fixed, better than new."

"That's great," said Mirie in a monotone.

He grinned. "Wild eyes you've got. Underneath the spectacles."

"I'm working," she said. "I'd like to go on working."

Matthew ignored Mirie's blockade. "I'm heading up to the frontier. You should come along. I've seen elephants in the highlands. Lots of 'em—puny tusks but—"

"I'm not interested in tusks."

"Baby pictures, eh? That's what Fran said."

"Yes. That's it."

"I have a little business to conduct up there." He handed her the magazine, a glossy catalogue from:

H. R. GRUBB AND SONS
EXPEDITIONARY OUTFITTERS

138

"I designed it myself," Matthew said proudly. "It's a family enterprise. I'm head of our Africa sales branch."

Mirie flipped through the catalog. It advertised tents, blankets, packs, jungle boots, camping goods of every description, not unlike L. L. Bean, until she came to the Kevlar flak jackets, bulletproof helmets and camouflage uniforms, all modeled by the same grim, pock-faced white man, who brandished lead bats and an array of knives that had lurid names, like the "Widow Maker."

"He's our multipurpose mercenary," said Matthew. "I found him in a pub. He's a poof, but he looks right . . . Big business in Africa."

"Mercenaries?" asked Mirie.

"War. There's plenty of action, all kinds of new markets opening up," chirped Matthew. "We sell only software. My uncle got out of hardware when a twelve-year-old pointed one of his own AK-47 copies at his head and called him a bloody imperialist."

"Who buys this stuff?"

"Anyone. We sell to anyone as long as they come up with the cash, though every so often we do a barter deal. We sell only first-quality material. No *shenzi* merchandise." He caressed her arm.

She pushed away his hand.

"Aw, you're hard on a chappy who hasn't seen a white girl in months. A man gets sick of elephants and nignogs."

"Go back to Frances. She likes you—I don't know why."

"I'll give you a free demonstration."

If her slap had connected, Mirie would have sent Matthew over the railing, but he was too fast. He blocked her hand.

"You're spunky. I like that. You and me could have a good time. Think about it." He walked away, then grinned back at her. "You don't know what you're missing."

ɔ ɔ

She told Frances, but Frances laughed it off. "What do you expect? He's a traveling salesman."

Mirie wasn't about to let it go. "What if he has AIDS?"

Frances blew up. "Always looking on the down side! Not

that it's any of your business, but he wears a raincoat. Satisfied?" Then she sniped, "At least I'm normal. I'm into men, not elephant turds."

"Sorry you're bored," Mirie retorted. "You're the one who said you wanted to get away from it all. But the second that gangster comes along . . ." She didn't finish. The whole situation was dispiriting. Mostly, she was angry at herself, for not going on safari alone as she had intended and letting herself get snarled up in Frances' diversions.

The quarrel dissipated in the face of separation. Frances said, "I'll go back to the city with Matthew—I've always wanted a Mercedes. You keep the car. . . . Never mind what I said, about the elephant shit."

Mirie gave Frances her exposed rolls of film to send to Switzerland for developing, as well as two letters.

The letter to Jonathan was about the trip, about being stuck in the river, and rescued—she didn't go into detail about Matthew—and the elephant pictures she hoped she had gotten.

The second letter, to Liz, was a meandering account, filling in certain areas she had omitted from the letter to Jonathan.

> Dear Liz,
> I was on safari with Frances. We were having a good time by ourselves. The car broke down in the middle of a river, we ran out of water, a lion stalked us, and we were picked up by a British guy with a Mercedes four-wheel-drive and a limitless supply of racist jokes. "When you're drowning, you don't ask who is throwing the life preserver"; that was our situation, or at least mine, because Frances thinks Matthew is adorable, and they have been doing it for two days. While Frances was swimming, the wart tried to attach itself to me.
> Frances changes when she's around men. Suddenly, she becomes entirely bent on seduction, to prove to herself she's desirable, though I don't know how she can doubt it. She works at pleasure the way she works on her tennis game.
> Matthew bragged that in his travels around Africa he goes for fat hookers on the theory that they don't have Slim—AIDS, that is. If I were Frances, I wouldn't go near the guy, but she goes on about sex being the life force, and all that.

I think we all would have been much better off if we had evolved from elephants instead of monkeys. Even though baboons act a lot like we do—they flirt, bully and play tricks on each other—they don't cooperate much. The elephants, however, look out for one another. All the females look out for the young, and they'll even nurse one another's calves. When the older ones get annoyed, they growl and shake their heads, but squabbles are settled peacefully. They touch each other a lot. I suppose this is partly because they have bad eyesight and the trunks are good feelers, but it's also to greet and comfort one another. They use trunks and feet to nudge the calves along, reassure them and discipline them.

I was shooting an elephant in a moat, and without warning it squirted me. You have to admire an animal that has both dignity and a sense of humor. That's not the sort of thing you'll find in zoology textbooks, but it's true all the same.

Love, Mirie

22

The day was too hot and the elephants too far away. Mirie returned to the cabin near dusk, hot and stiff from sitting in the car all day. As she did every day, she set the kettle to boil. Under the relentless eye of the sun, she continually thought about water, how much she had left, how far she had to drive to find more. Although she sipped water all day long, she stayed thirsty.

As the sun's full scrutiny hexed her work, she sought to outwit it; she took pictures in the morning when, veiled in mists, it had barely opened its eye, and toward the end of the day, when weary from its long journey, it was ready to sleep.

She did not waste water, and she kept plastic jugs filled in case the pumps failed. While the kettle heated, she sat on the porch steps, watching weaver birds flit about their hanging nests.

When the kettle shrilled, she dropped in tea leaves. While the brew steeped, she cut a mango. A mango rewarded her for good shooting, or consoled her for a wasted day.

She sliced the ripe fruit on either side of the hard white seed, and scored a grid in the orange pulp. Pushing the flesh side out, she ate it square by square, savoring the sweet-tart taste that made her parched mouth water. She scraped the hard white center against her front teeth. She washed down the sweet fibers with tea so hot and strong it made her skin damp. Then she took up her camera again.

A broad acacia grew on a mound of earth in the middle of

the lake. At dusk black-and-white sacred ibises and snowy white egrets flocked to it. They settled and flared up, circled the island and returned. Again they swirled up, black and white against the melon-colored sky, and resettled themselves on the silhouette of branches. She had photographed the same scene night after night, waiting for the perfect composition of birds in flight. For as long as she stayed at the cottage, she would try for this picture.

She did not know why egrets and ibises flocked to the tree night after night, nor what they fed on. Max would have known, but there was no Max to ask, no Tom Goode full of alcohol and bush lore, no Frances trumpeting her latest escapades, no itinerant ornithologist or field biologist to enlighten her. There was only the African caretaker, and he did not speak a word of English.

She heard him whistling. The light of his hurricane lamp swung like a censer in time to his melody. He was a slim man with a slow giraffelike stride. Every evening he came to the cabin to refill and light the lamps. Taking a blade of dry grass to his own lamp, he lit the lamp in the kitchen hut behind the cabin, then the lamp in the bathroom and finally the one between the two beds. He left whistling the same melody, his lantern swinging to and fro in the enveloping darkness. Though he never said anything, had he failed to come one evening, Mirie would have missed his visit. For though they could not speak to each other, Mirie inferred some fellow feeling, if only because each for a moment lightened the other's solitude.

Mirie made a stew of tomatoes, onions and potatoes for dinner. She was not very hungry, but felt compelled to eat. Her pants were already hanging loosely at the waist.

She had missed a period, but she was certainly not pregnant. Her system had gone on strike, she thought, in reaction to the heat, irregular eating and the physical labor that went with traveling alone. When tires went flat, she had to change them in the blazing sun. Keeping the car running, and herself supplied with food and water, required constant logistical planning. Watching, anticipating and photographing, tending to daily rituals and unexpected hitches, she was fully occupied. Except for those moments in the middle of the night when she woke up hollow-eyed with loneliness, she was as happy as she had ever been.

Mirie had a second helping of stew, threw the remainder in the garbage can and washed the dishes.

Insects drawn by the light batted the porch screens. Hot gusts of wind shivered the thatching and swung the white mosquito netting to and fro.

She stripped off her dusty clothes and examined herself critically before the distorted mirror, lamplight playing across her body. She was very thin, and, she thought, she would have looked better with more flesh on her bones. Her foot was healing well. But for an occasional twinge and a slight lingering swelling, it seldom troubled her now. The crutch remained in the corner.

Her hair had auburn streaks, her nose was red, her arms and legs caramel-colored. The sun had etched lines on her once smooth, impervious forehead. Her mismatched eyes looked pinched from squinting against dust and glare.

When had she last spoken to anyone? Perhaps three weeks ago? Four? Her sense of time was calibrated to the elephants' meanderings. She kept a careful map with dated X-marks showing the group's movements. From across the lake came the sound of elephants rumbling and splashing. Whether or not they were her elephants, she could not know.

Her elephants? Was that how she thought of them? She hoped she was not becoming like those researchers who develop a fierce proprietary feeling toward the animals with which they spend their lives. Not that she imagined she possessed or controlled the wild elephants in any way, nor did she want to; it was their tenuous freedom that drew her to them. If she thought of the group as *her* elephants, it was because she was in an ever-alert, suspenseful state, obsessively devoted to photographing them as best she could.

She pulled out the rubber band and shook her ponytail free. She stepped into the shower, washed her hair, drew the lather over her breasts and down her belly. Lamplight flickered on water falling like tinsel streamers from her spread fingers.

Bending over, she brushed her hair toward the floor. Her scalp tingled as the bristles tugged at the wet spears of hair.

Even after she had patted herself dry, her skin stayed florid and moist.

She unknotted the mosquito netting and arranged the veil around the bed. She shut off the lamp between the beds; glow from the bathroom lamp seeped comfortingly under the door. The springs squeaked as her spine settled into the lumpy mattress. The knotted netting over the empty bed swayed back and forth in the hot breeze. A mosquito barred by the muslin sang in her ear.

Mirie slept until metal clanging jolted her back to nights at home when the empty streets of Greenwich Village belonged to derelicts ransacking garbage cans for food. She sat up in bed, fumbled for her glasses. Her flashlight found disembodied red eyes in the dark. A warthog dangling a potato peel in its mouth scampered off. The overturned can rolled in the wind before coming to a stop against the kitchen hut. She felt pricked by a precise awareness of time, not foolish clock time, but fearsome time made visible in Africa's yawning spaces.

She stayed in bed raging against her loneliness while nature went about its business heedless of her. She could do nothing but observe, carefully and constantly. Hours and hours of waiting for a few moments of shooting. She recalled what Max said about learning patience in Africa, especially when shooting animals. That was difficult enough in itself, but impossible when her confidence ebbed, and she would wonder what in the world she was doing out in the bush alone, searching for a pregnant elephant. She never had any time off from un-certainty, never. She wondered where the elephants were, whether at that moment, somewhere, a baby elephant was being born. She was suspended between boredom and appre-hension, which was like waiting for a hippo to erupt from still water, ivory daggers protruding from gaping jaws.

She longed for sleep. Was she becoming bush-crazed? How could she tell? She had no one to talk to.

Mirie shone the light at the empty bed beside her, where a large black beetle was laboriously making its way up the swaying netting. She shut off the flashlight, removed her eyeglasses and hugged the pillow. Even as sleep came, she hardly loosened her grip.

23

Once a week Mirie made a trip to the nearest village to buy food and gas. It was a long, hot, boring drive on bumpy track. Periodically, she would pick up African women on their way to market. The women would hail her with a slow up-and-down hand motion, nod in greeting, and indicate where they wanted to be left off.

Mirie observed that it was women who went to market, women who sold sacks of charcoal, women who walked miles with heavy water jugs, babies at their breasts, produce on their heads and backs. Women tilled the soil and acted as beasts of burden. Women stayed in the company of other women. They gossiped, prayed, cooked, tended their vegetable plots, watched the children, wove baskets, built houses and came to one another's aid in the slow, incessant business of living.

On market days Mirie took pictures with the idea of making a montage of women at work. The theme was neither commercial nor newsworthy, she realized, but the women's labors had a simple grace that she wanted to capture.

Driving along, she was reminded of an old mama she had photographed the previous week who, surrounded by other women and children, was pumping a pedal-powered sewing machine under a baobab. This image along with her other impressions on film she had to take back to Kwendela to send abroad for processing. She was eager to see how her first pictures had turned out, to see Frances, to receive letters from

Jonathan. She wondered if the birthday present she had sent him from Kwendela had arrived in time.

Mirie was startled out of her reflections when a girl leaped out from the bushes directly in front of the car. Mirie braked and swerved. She screamed at the child, frightened by the close call. How stupid she was to run in front of a car! She had almost gotten them both killed! The girl stood in front of the car, thorn-scratched, breathless and uncomprehending.

Exasperated, Mirie opened the car door and the girl jumped in. Mirie tried a few phrases, but the girl did not speak. She was dressed in a ragged red brown tunic, draped diagonally from the shoulder, revealing a nipple beginning to bud.

Mirie pointed ahead, said the name of the village and resumed driving. As they neared town, Mirie picked up two more passengers. One woman was hauling maize to market. The other, bare-breasted and wearing a long wrap skirt plumped by a kind of bustle, was carrying a jerry can for water. Mirie hoped that one of the women might recognize the child or speak her language. But the other two riders ignored the girl, who sat back mutely, showing no sign of wanting to go anywhere in particular.

The village consisted of tin-roof stalls on either side of a dusty street and an open-air market surrounding a bare baobab that provided minimal shade for the market mamas selling fruits and vegetables. As Mirie did her shopping, the child followed at a distance, from stall to stall, past pyramids of tomatoes, cans full of red, white, brown and speckled beans, bunches of plantains, cabbage, mangoes, onions, bananas, leaves like spinach and collard greens, and pineapples. Gaily printed kangas hanging on low branches flapped in the hot breeze, as mamas beckoned to Mirie. "Special price, madame! Special price!"

The special price was always much higher than what the locals paid. She haggled, for that was expected, and if the mama knocked the price down a few cents, she was content with the transaction. It was too hot to argue over pennies, and, by Western standards, nothing cost very much anyway.

Mirie picked out a dozen green mangoes. As she was about to pay, a squat African woman, her head wrapped in a kerchief, sidled up to her and felt one of the mangoes.

"Very bad, madame. This mama cheats you," said the fat woman in pleasingly syncopated English. "I will help you."

She bade Mirie follow her to another stall, scrutinized the fruit and started a negotiation that sounded like squirrels bickering. Before long the fat woman had deposited two dozen mangoes in Mirie's sisal bag, for half the amount that she ordinarily paid for one dozen.

"I save you so much money," said the fat woman proudly.

"I didn't need so many, but thanks."

Mirie was glad to meet someone who spoke English; the fat woman could perhaps also talk to the girl and find out what she wanted. When she looked around, she discovered that the girl had disappeared.

The fat woman said, "The girl ran when she saw me."

"You know her?"

"Very well. I attended her circumcision."

The fat woman introduced herself as Lesa; she was a nurse-midwife. She had grown up in the region and, with the help of a missionary, was sent to nursing school. She returned to work in a clinic, which much of the time was shut down for lack of supplies. She had trouble visiting distant villages because she had no car. But she made do.

In between haggling over the price of papayas, Lesa told Mirie how female circumcision—cutting of the clitoris—though officially frowned on, still held an important place in tribal culture and that it was one of the "old ways" that would not soon die out. Since it was performed by local practitioners under the most primitive conditions, she tried to be on hand at least to ward off chances of infection.

Mirie shuddered at the thought that girls were mutilated for tradition's sake. Why? she asked. It had always been so, was Lesa's answer. Together they strolled among the market stalls. They moved on to beans, tomatoes and the matter of the runaway girl.

"She is so much trouble to her papa. Always, she is trouble. She must marry, and that is why she runs away. If we bring her back, you can see a wedding. No Mzungu has seen this."

"Can I take pictures?" asked Mirie.

"Many pictures. Special pictures. We will buy food, we will

find the girl, we will go to her wedding. You are the special guest."

Mirie peeled off bills while Lesa filled baskets full of pineapples, tomatoes, onions, coconuts, papayas, coffee, tea, sugar, cocoa and kilos of milled maize meal. Lesa rounded up a retinue of children to carry the bundles to the car, and advised Mirie on the proper tip. There were many children, and even the tiniest *toto,* who carried only a single orange, had to be recompensed.

Mirie was dismayed at all the food. She realized, belatedly, that she had spent about ten times as much as she normally did on her shopping expeditions. "I can't eat all this."

"It is not for you. It is gifts for the people," explained Lesa in a way that forbade argument. Lesa hoisted a scrawny chicken by its feet. The bird squawked and flapped its wings then hung in limp resignation. "Mzungus always bring gifts."

"I thought you said no Mzungus had ever visited," said Mirie, with growing suspicion that she was being had.

"Not for a wedding. That is true. But sometimes, not so often, they come, and when they do, they bring gifts. It has always been so. We will bring this chicken."

"No. No chicken."

"It is a good bird."

"It is not a good bird in my car. No way, mama."

Lesa accepted the minor defeat. Together, she and Mirie managed to stuff all the foods in back.

"Now it looks like a *basi,*" said Mirie, chagrined at the prospect of driving back so heavily loaded she could scarcely see out the back.

Lesa did not argue the point, but that was because she was out of earshot, plowing her way through the market like a small tank. Soon she returned with the runaway girl reluctantly in tow.

She deposited the girl in the front seat and settled herself regally on the spare tire in back, among mangoes, pineapples, maize and bananas. Lesa said something fearsome. The child cowered, her head in her arms, whimpering.

Mirie asked what she had said.

"I tell her she must give thanks that we have brought her from the town, for there she would die with no mama, or papa, or brothers or sisters. The people in town would laugh at her and let her starve, for she is nothing. She would be no better than a dog, to be kicked and starved." Lesa seemed well pleased that she had frightened the girl into submission. The child clearly was not going to give her any more trouble.

They drove along, Lesa bouncing on the tire and talking ever faster.

"Many times this girl has run away," she said. "The man she will marry is a man who paid her papa many cows for a young wife."

"Where I come from, she would be much too young to marry," said Mirie. As she spoke, though, she recognized the irrelevance of the remark.

"She has begun the moon," pronounced Lesa.

Mirie looked around to catch what Lesa said.

"To menstruate."

Mirie turned back—just in time to see the road drop off and the car dip into a crater, sending Lesa caroming off the car roof.

"Stop!" Lesa frowned and rubbed her head as Mirie slowed down. "Car goes like gazelle." She poked the back of the front seat, imitating a gazelle's staccato leaping.

She stuck a pudgy finger into the girl's side and made her exchange places. Lesa deposited her copiously perspiring body in the front seat, and the girl wedged herself in among the produce, jerry cans and camera gear. The child was happy, though. She discovered the rearview mirror. The reflection so astonished her that she seemed to forget her troubles.

Ɔ Ɔ

The whole clan turned out for Mirie's arrival; naked toddlers and children in rags followed by shy women in tunics, beaded collars and bracelets, and crooked old men with walking sticks. The young warriors stood apart, too proud to approach the Mzungu visitor.

Judging by the general curiosity about her, Mirie believed that Lesa had told the truth; the tribe had seen few foreigners. Lesa said that every so often she acted as translator when a missionary or anthropologist or fieldworker in the aid trades came calling, and the elders amused themselves by making up tall tales, which the white people slavishly recorded.

Women touched Mirie's fine straight hair, marveled at the pale skin and examined her eyeglasses and different-colored eyes. The old men gathered around, and the chief, an old man with red-rimmed eyes, made a pronouncement.

Lesa translated: One eye, said the chief, was the color of grass when God in his anger withholds the rains. The other eye was the color of rains when God blesses the people. The chief said he would watch the visitor carefully for signs, for as there had been both drought and rain, he wanted to know what God would do next, a plague of grasshoppers, maybe, as in the old days when his father was chief.

The chief demanded that Lesa clear up a mystery about the guest.

"Are you man or woman?" translated Lesa. "I tell them you are woman, but they do not believe me. I will prove."

Lesa suddenly tugged at the neckline of Mirie's T-shirt, and when she pulled away, Lesa became as stern with her as she had been with the child. "Don't fight! I tell them you are my special friend, but they must see you are a woman, or they will not let you know their secrets."

Mirie swallowed her embarrassment and stood still, as one by one the women peeked in. There was one woman who had a haughty bearing. She was not impressed. She drew away her own tunic to reveal ample bosoms. Then she said something to the men that apparently corroborated Lesa: Mirie was a woman, not as beautiful or bountiful as their women, but most definitely a woman. There was more discussion.

Lesa said, "They ask how many babies you have."

"I have no babies," said Mirie.

Lesa, frowning, relayed the message. The woman with the big bosoms made a remark.

"She says," said Lesa, "she has ten children. Why do you not have children? Where is your man?"

Mirie was flustered. She couldn't think of a simple way to say that, in her world, women were not evaluated strictly by their baby-making ability. But a rational explanation wouldn't work, not with these people. She would have liked to dismiss the probing as the naive questions of a primitive people, but it was upsetting to be surrounded all of a sudden and publicly challenged about so private a matter.

"My man is at home." She hoped that would do.

"He sent you away?" asked Lesa, apparently more for her own edification than for general enlightenment.

"No. He works at home and I work taking pictures on safari. That's how we make money so we can buy food."

Lesa then gave an involved explanation to the tribe that went on for a good half-hour, after which there were no more questions. Mirie asked Lesa what she had told them.

"Nothing," said Lesa.

"What do you mean, nothing? You just told them my whole life story."

"I fixed everything," said Lesa.

"I don't doubt it. But what did you say?"

"I explained how Mzungus divorce."

Mirie was about to protest, but decided that since Lesa's lie had satisfied the group and stopped the interrogation, she should let it go at that.

Meanwhile, all the children were clamoring around the car for a peek in the mirror. They pushed each other aside for a glimpse and tried to touch the reflections. The father of the runaway wrenched his daughter away from her friends and chewed her out in front of everyone. Mirie thought this unnecessarily mean. The girl talked back, and that heartened Mirie.

As Lesa related the argument, the father said, "Girl, if you run off again, hyenas will eat you."

"I don't care," said the girl. "I will not marry that man."

"You must grow up with this man and lie down with this man," said the mother, "cook his food and make him babies."

"If you make me marry him, I will eat the bitter root and die."

"Foolish girl," said the father. "You want to be a child forever. You refuse to work. You refuse to sleep in this man's hut. I will beat you to chase away the bad spirits that make you act against your father."

He began to shake the girl.

Mirie was upset. She had not brought the girl home to be battered.

"Lesa, you tell her father that if he hits her, I'll fix things so it won't rain till every last cow has shriveled into shoe leather."

Lesa didn't seem to think much of Mirie's threat, but she did intercede, bodily, between father and daughter. She rebuked the daughter for disobeying her papa, then scolded Mirie for overstepping her guest privileges. If Mirie wanted to do something useful, she said, she should give gifts and pray for more rain and peace in the family.

While she had no desire to meddle in local customs, Mirie had a plan and needed Lesa's help. Together, they handed out the food and, while everyone else was preoccupied with the bounty, Lesa and Mirie took the girl aside.

Mirie showed the girl her steel camping mirror and said that, if she should decide to marry, this would be her wedding gift. Looking at her reflection, the girl was immediately persuaded. She so much wanted the remarkable object, which no one else in the tribe had—not even the chief—that the prospect of marriage became less onerous.

The sudden change in the girl amazed the parents. She was acquiescent, if not exactly cheerful. They asked Lesa if Mirie had cast a spell on her. Lesa said no; white people had no talent for juju.

o   o

Lesa pulled Mirie along into the smoky darkness and sat her down on a bench covered in cowhide. The hut smelled of goats, sweat and charred wood. Mirie felt a twinge in her abdomen, a dull pain signaling that her period was finally coming. Her eyes, smarting and tearing from the smoke, gradually grew accustomed to the dark. She watched the mother ladle water from a gourd and bathe the girl in preparation for the wedding.

The mother looked very young herself. It was hard to guess anyone's age. Except for the very old women, with sacklike breasts and withered flesh, all the women had smooth skin. And girls in their early teens were nursing babies.

Mirie shot a picture with a flash, but the flash startled the women and left everyone temporarily blinded. There was much discussion and negotiation over this between Lesa and the women. The upshot was that Mirie could stay but the sun box had to go. Though Mirie was disappointed, there was nothing she could do.

The mother rubbed the girl with cow fat and dusted her shaved head with ochre. The girl stood belly-out, mute and impassive, as her mother and relatives adorned her in bracelets, collars and earrings. Mirie had no idea whether she was just going along with all this or was actually enjoying the attention. Maybe she looked wistfully at the other unwed girls her own age, but Mirie didn't trust her intuition about that either.

The girl was led blindfolded to a new mud-and-wattle hut that, as Lesa explained, the women had built for her; this was where she would marry and receive her husband. Only married women were permitted to enter, said Lesa. Being Lesa's friend and a putative divorced woman apparently was her entrance ticket. At least, no one challenged Mirie, and she followed Lesa right in. Lesa sat with her fleshy back blocking the entrance from the eyes of curious children.

The hut was dark and confined. It was hard to breathe. Mirie was crushed up against Lesa, and the twinges had become full-blown cramps.

A wizened crone, taking a stick from the unlit fire, began chanting and gesticulating. Lesa translated:

"A long time ago a girl fled from her husband into the forest. She ran and ran until she could run no more. Then she fell asleep. While she lay sleeping, a cobra came slowly, out of the blue dark." The hag writhed in pantomime. "When the girl awakened, the cobra lifted its head . . ." The old woman raised the stick. "And spit in her eyes." Her hips moved lewdly, the stick no longer a cobra but now a thrusting phallus.

The women laughed heartily, except for the girl, who sat blindfolded and removed from the hilarity.

The blindfold was removed, and the women filed out, leaving the girl kneeling before the unlit fire. Outside, all the men sang and chanted. The fathers of the bride and groom each carried a burning stick brought from their home fires into the hut. They were followed by the groom, a man perhaps in his early thirties. As wisps of smoke escaped, the two fathers came out, leaving the bridal couple alone. The women danced in a circle, bowing and swaying, as one of the men smothered a goat to death.

Mirie was pulled along with the crowd. Her cramps grew worse.

As the sun set, the elders of the tribe, putting down three-legged stools, sat around the fire where the goat was roasting. Women knelt on the ground in back. Scraggly dogs sniffed timidly about, until a hurled stone or a kick drove them away. Over the fire was a pot of evil-smelling brew. Mirie and Lesa sat in the inner circle among the men but on the ground. The stools were for the men. The chief dipped a gourd into the pot and motioned to Mirie. She could not politely refuse. The brew tasted hot and prickly. More, drink more, the chief motioned. The tribe cheered her on. Then the gourd was refilled and passed around.

The chief called for silence and proceeded to make a long speech. He paused to drink when the gourd came round to him, then proceeded, on and on. The other men made an affirmative *"Ay-ee, ay-ee"* to whatever the chief said, but Mirie suspected that after a time they weren't really listening.

At first, Lesa gamely kept up the translation, then she withdrew, resting her elbows on her knees, head in her hands. Mirie didn't mind. She watched the full moon rise. Her cramps subsided; the brew had had a good effect that way.

She was enjoying her place as an invisible guest when Lesa nudged her and said, "Chief wants a story." Mirie was perplexed. "Chief says guests must give stories. People go like dust devils, but stories stay."

"You tell them a story, Lesa. You must know lots of stories."

"Chief wants a Mzungu story."

Mirie looked around the circle. They were all waiting for her. A budding panic brought back the cramps.

She didn't know any stories. She didn't even know any jokes. What had she read lately? No, that wouldn't do at all, but since the elders had begun to grumble and Mirie was growing desperate, she had no choice but to begin.

24

"A long time ago there were two tribes that were bitter enemies. They cursed each other. They took up spears against each other and many people died."

The old men nodded as Lesa translated Mirie's words. They remembered those days.

"There was a great chief, the greatest and wisest of all the land, for he had lived so long he knew all that a man could know. And he brought together the chiefs of the two warring tribes and made them agree to a truce. If warriors passed each other on hunting trails, they were forbidden to speak, raise their arms or do anything that would cause more fighting and bloodshed.

"In the season of the antelopes, when the herds crossed the river, men from both tribes ran swiftly after them with sharpened spears. The hunt went well. It was a time of prayer and rejoicing for all.

"On the night of the full moon, a night like tonight, the warriors of one tribe painted their bodies and wore masks made of ostrich feathers, cowrie shells and lions' manes. Men beat drums and people danced."

Mirie paused for Lesa's translation. The tribe had a long-winded oral tradition, and Lesa provided embellishment of her own, which gave Mirie time to transpose the next part of her tale into terms she hoped the people would understand. Lesa helped her out with recognizable names.

"Now it happened," Mirie went on, "that there was a warrior from the other tribe, who among his own people was the bravest, strongest and handsomest. He was called Kalaba."

"Kalaba," the men muttered, and passed the hooch pot. They liked the familiar name; Kalaba was the name of the man who married the runaway.

"When Kalaba overheard the celebrations and saw the fires burning, he longed to join in, and in so doing play a trick on his tribe's old enemy. Kalaba put on a mask of feathers, shells and lion's mane and painted his body. He stole closer to the home of the enemy, who were chanting, dancing and beating the drums. Kalaba joined in as if he were one of their own.

"The young warriors took part in contests to show off their skills in front of the girls who had begun the moon"—Mirie glanced uncertainly at Lesa, and got the go-ahead—"and were ready for marriage.

"Among all the girls, there was one girl who made Kalaba's heart beat fast. Her name was Mwari."

The group shifted about and burped. Mirie took it for a sign of approval; Mwari was the bride's name.

"Mwari wore bracelets of copper, gold and silver that caught the rays of the sun. Her skin was as soft as rain and her eyes were like the full moon. She was so beautiful she made fires burn brighter.

"Now Kalaba saw only Mwari, nothing else, and he had to prove himself worthy of her. The warriors threw spears, and Kalaba threw his spear the farthest. They ran races, and Kalaba ran the fastest. They had jumping contests, and Kalaba jumped the highest. They stood on one foot, and when all the other warriors had moved, Kalaba stood as still as a dead man. Every contest Kalaba won. In this way he also won Mwari's heart."

Lesa nudged Mirie. "What is it, 'to win a heart?'" Mirie put the courtship another way.

"Mwari smiled at Kalaba. She wanted to marry him. Kalaba was in love with Mwari, and Mwari, who was the chief's daughter, was in love with Kalaba, the bravest warrior. They pledged with their eyes never to be apart, and that bond was so strong that the strongest elephant could not have separated them."

The elders groused when Lesa translated this. The hyperbole had missed somehow. But Mirie continued.

"Mwari's tribe chanted in praise of Kalaba, believing he was one of their own. All, that is, except Mwari's brother, who wished ill on the warrior who made his sister's eyes burn brighter. Something was not right, and he vowed to know who this warrior was who had won all the contests.

"As the chief, Mwari's father, was praising the warrior who was the best in all things, Mwari's brother snuck up behind Kalaba and tore off his disguise. There, surrounded by his enemies, stood Kalaba unmasked.

"The songs of praise for the victorious warrior stopped. The drums ceased. There were angry shouts. 'Death to the enemy,' the people chanted. The chief demanded silence. No, there would be no more fighting. He ordered Kalaba to go away, and if he valued his life, never again to come near the tribe.

"Kalaba went back to his own people with a heavy heart. He lay down in his hut, but he could not sleep. He gazed at the moon and saw instead Mwari's eyes. Without Mwari he would die, as surely as a man in the desert dies without water.

"So Kalaba, as quiet as a leopard in the grass, crept over to Mwari's house. He put his spear through a tiny opening in the hut. Mwari, who lay awake unable to sleep, came out of her hut without a sound. The two of them stole away and that night Kalaba made her his wife."

The men grumbled. "What! He took a wife from the enemy tribe!" said the chief. "He went against his own people and the laws of his elders. That is very bad."

"Very bad," agreed Mirie, satisfied that she had conveyed how Mwari and Kalaba had broken all the rules for the sake of love.

The chief continued, "The girl! She married against the wishes of her father, of her tribe. It is not done."

"No. But she is in love," said Mirie. "And love has the power to make people do things that by custom are not done."

Lesa harrumphed, which was to say, Mirie had better come up with something better than love.

The men began to talk among themselves. In desperation, Mirie sought to draw them into the pact. "None of you must say a word more!" she demanded of the elders. "Mwari and Kalaba's marriage is a secret!"

That worked pretty well. The men drank, as did the women, while Mirie continued.

"The next day Kalaba and the other men his age were on the hunting trail when they met warriors from the other tribe, led by Mwari's brother, who had unmasked Kalaba at the celebration. Mwari's brother would not let Kalaba pass. When Kalaba refused to fight, Mwari's brother called him a woman. That enraged Kalaba's best friend, and he attacked Mwari's brother. The two warriors fought with wrist knives and spears. Blood ran into the dust, and soon Kalaba's friend lay dead on the hunting trail, killed by Mwari's brother. Kalaba was out of his head with anger and grief. He was so angry that he forgot his vow not to fight. And in revenge he speared Mwari's brother in the heart."

"What!" said an old man, "Both warriors disobeyed their elders not to fight."

"But if Kalaba had not fought," said another, "he would have been a coward."

"Yes," said Mirie, "and the trouble becomes worse . . . It was not long before the greatest chief in the land heard of the killings. He was enraged that once more there was trouble between the two tribes. He blamed Kalaba. He ordered Kalaba to leave his land, to leave the land of his ancestors, to leave his father and mother, brothers and sisters, and go far, far away, where few men had gone and from where none had ever returned."

"Why didn't the great chief kill him?" asked someone in the circle.

"The great chief was a wise man. When he made Kalaba leave the tribe, leave his family and friends, leave the land of his fathers, it was a punishment worse than death."

The chief concurred with Mirie's explanation, and everyone

in turn agreed with the chief. Mirie took a sip of brew, and Lesa translated questions.

"Where are the chief's other sons?"

"There are no other sons," said Mirie.

Another man asked, "What chief has only one son?"

"The chief's wives didn't give him other sons?" asked someone else.

"He should divorce them!" said another.

A wife who could not make sons, Lesa told Mirie, was the same as a barren wife. She raised a hand to end the caviling.

"Back in Mwari's tribe," continued Mirie, "Mwari's father promised her to a young warrior. He did not know that Mwari was already married. She could not tell her father that she was secretly married to the man who had killed his son, her own brother. The wedding was arranged. But Mwari did not want to marry this man."

"What does it matter?" protested the chief. "She is only a woman. The chief must beat her for disobeying."

"No. He did not beat her, but said she must marry the young warrior he had chosen for her. Mwari wept. She already had a husband, to whom she had pledged herself forever. But she did not want to disobey her father the chief. So she went to a healer who had great powers; she told him her secret and begged for his help.

"The healer asked Mwari for one of her gold bracelets. He would send his son into the wilderness to find Kalaba, and by the bracelet the boy carried—a bracelet like no other—Kalaba would know he came in peace with news of Mwari.

"Then the healer made a drink for Mwari. It would not hurt her, he said, but it would make her sleep like death.

"Like our drink!" The other men laughed at the chief's joke as he dipped into the hooch pot, sloshing a good amount on the ground.

"Yes. It might have been the same," said Mirie. She continued: "On her wedding day, Mwari drank the potion, fell to the earth, and everyone thought she was dead. Her father cried, her mother cried, the warrior who was to marry her cried. The whole tribe cried."

"Why?" asked another elder. "A great warrior must have many wives."

"Yes, but Mwari was the most beautiful woman in all the land."

The elders complained. What was all the fuss over one woman? Mirie was distressed; the whole story would unravel if the elders believed that all women were interchangeable. Lesa rattled off something, which mollified the old men.

"What did you tell them?" asked Mirie.

Lesa said, "I said Mwari had hips that could bear many sons, that she had a strong back and could build a house without a man's help, that she had a soft voice and never complained or scolded, that she would never cheat her husband or run away." Lesa rested her chin in her jowls and smiled with an air of authority.

"Somehow, I hadn't thought of Mwari that way," said Mirie under her breath. "Well, whatever." There was no time to argue. Already a few men were dozing.

"The healer sent his son to find Kalaba and tell him that Mwari had escaped marriage by taking a drink to make her sleep. Deep in the bush, the boy was stalked by a lion and torn to pieces. In his wanderings, Kalaba came upon the trail of blood, then the boy's body and beside it Mwari's bracelet. Why would she give up her bracelet? It could be nothing other than a sign from God that Mwari was dead.

"Kalaba's heart broke. He squeezed drops from a poison plant into a palm-nut vial, and retraced his steps from the end of the world to his own land, to the field where Mwari's body had been left for vultures to eat."

"Kalaba wept over Mwari's body, and while he wept, the warrior who was to marry Mwari came to mourn. . . ."

All this crying was unseemly, complained the elders.

"The warrior challenged Kalaba. Kalaba told him to go away. If he did not, he would end up like Mwari's brother, as vulture food; but the warrior refused. He attacked Kalaba. They fought with spears and wrist knives, and Kalaba killed him quickly."

The chief snorted and said something derisive. Lesa said,

"The chief asks, 'What man fights over a dead woman? What good is she? She cannot lie with him. She cannot bear him sons. She cannot plant and harvest and bring water. She cannot ease the burdens of his life.'"

This was really very difficult. To Mirie the tragedy was self-evident, but she was having a very hard time conveying it in a culture that valued cattle over women. Perhaps Mwari should have been a prize cow. But it was too late to change; Mirie went on with the story.

"Kalaba cried out to God that he would rather die and in death join Mwari than live alone on earth without her. Then he swallowed the poison and flung himself across Mwari's body. At that very moment Mwari woke up. She saw that her beloved Kalaba was dead. Her heart broke. She cried out and tore at her flesh and with Kalaba's knife pierced her own heart.

"When the chief and people came to grieve, they found the vultures feasting. Drums told of all the deaths, and now the other chief and all his people came to mourn as well. So much blood and death! Kalaba's friend, Mwari's brother, Kalaba's rival, Kalaba and Mwari. All those young people lay dead. Warriors whom the tribe needed to hunt and defend it and who might one day have been chiefs, and Mwari, who would have borne many fine sons. A terrible waste!

"The old chiefs saw that their fighting had brought evil. It had robbed both tribes of the best of their young and cursed their tomorrows. Though the rains were due, there was not a single cloud in the sky. God was angry. So they swore over a sacred drum and over the bodies of those young people that the two tribes would never fight again but would live together in peace."

Mirie looked around. An ominous silence had fallen on the circle of elders. Those who were still awake looked expectantly at the chief for a pronouncement. To Mirie's astonishment, the chief began to laugh. The other drowsy, drunken elders also laughed and the women joined in.

Finally, the chief said, "You do not understand and I the chief will help you. Kalaba and the other men died because they disobeyed their elders. The chiefs cursed the sons of the tribe by sending them Mwari, who carried in her belly a bad spirit."

Mirie protested, "In this story men care so much for women, love them so much, they will die for them. . . ."

The chief said no, Mirie was in darkness. "If the warriors had obeyed the chiefs' command not to fight, they would be alive and only Mwari would have died, which was a good thing, since she was a witch."

Mirie's defense of the star-crossed lovers evaporated like smoke as Lesa, her translator, fell asleep, jowls sunk deeply into her breast. The hooch pot was empty and the dogs were gnawing goat bones. The chief listed back and forth on his stool. The women lay curled on the ground behind their men. Everyone was now in a deep sleep, oblivious to the cows' loud belching.

Mirie's eyes streamed from brew and smoke embers. It was too bad they didn't like the story, because the more she thought about it, the more she sympathized with Mwari. Poor Mwari, in love with one man, betrothed to another, daring to drink poison and sleep among the dead to be with the man she loved. Quite a pickle; at least that much Mirie had gotten across. She was sweaty and aching. And now, she thought, she herself had begun the moon.

25

Mirie sat on the porch, hunched over sheets of stationery, tea and mango beside her. A breeze fluttered the tissue-thin papers. Insects tapped the kerosene lamp and fell singed and dying on the paper. She brushed them off, pondering what to write.

Yesterday she had taken pictures that could be interpreted in contradictory ways. She could not in good conscience sell them. What if her suspicions had nothing to do with reality and were only the product of too much solitude and an overheated imagination? If only he had been there to interpret what she had seen.

○　○

Dear Max,

I have been in the bush for about five weeks, my days planned out for me by available light and generally unavailable elephants.

Most animals don't seem to notice me as long as I shoot from the car. The other night, while I was driving back to my cottage, I saw three lions lying in the middle of the track. They didn't budge as I came closer. I shut off the motor, but not the headlights. The lions were lying in a circle of light, paying no attention to the car or to me. I have no idea how long they, we, stayed there. I've lost my sense of time. When the lions finally went away, my feelings ran against my shooting instincts. I liked having a front-row seat. I felt like I'd been let in on a secret. And in a way I was glad I wasn't equipped to photograph cats in the dark. Chasing after them and dealing with shooting logistics would have wrecked the mood.

In daylight my practical self takes charge. I have to sell some pictures. I've pretty much run through the money I made on the brochure. Frances loaned me her car, which is great, but the thing gobbles gas, oil and spare parts. My travel budget has dwindled, and if I don't make some money soon, I'll have to use my emergency money. That's not so terrible, but after that the pot is empty.

The elephants have been easily spooked lately. I've been careful not to provoke them, but a couple of times I've had to make quick getaways. They've been moving farther and farther from the lake. Yesterday I drove for quite a while and didn't see any.

Way off, where the terrain becomes hilly, I saw lots of vultures circling in the thermals. When I got there, I couldn't see anything, but there was an awful stink. Shutting the windows only trapped the smell inside. I tied a bandanna over my nose and mouth, but nothing really helped.

When I was right under the birds, I still couldn't see what they were after because of grass and bush. Some of the vultures had settled in the trees like gargoyles. I climbed on top of the car. There were five enormous gray mounds spattered with white droppings. One of the elephants, a calf, was split open at the belly. The vultures were hopping over the carcasses, their wings spread out like capes, skulking and lunging at one another, bickering over who was going to preside at the banquet. A bunch of marabou storks—with their red neck pouches all puffed out—were waiting their turn.

There were three adult female elephants and two calves. They looked like stuffed animals—stiff-legged and glassy-eyed. They were all bloated, except for the calf, which was already open. I saw the bullet holes, so small you wondered how they could bring down such a big animal.

I knew these elephants, Max. They were part of the cow and calf group I had been following for weeks. I recognized a female with only one tusk that I had photographed along with her calf, the one the vultures and storks were working on. The group had been on edge for the last few weeks. Do you think the elephants knew they were being hunted, while I, with all my lenses and binocs, was missing everything?

I was sick and angry. Then I had an idea: to do a story called "The Short, Happy Life of an African Elephant." I was going to focus on the calf playing and nursing and doing what elephants do every day, and then, before the calf has even sprouted tusks, it's killed by poachers, along with the rest of the family group.

I thought it was a good, sellable story. (Not for *Ecoworld;* Sam wouldn't touch a grim story.) No, I was aiming for *National Geographic* or *Stern.* They'd pay well and give the story plenty of exposure. I came to Africa to take pictures of the birth of a baby elephant, but what I saw first was a death. You go with what you got, right?

I took a few pictures, but the best light was still a couple of hours away. I drove upwind of the stink and parked under some trees. Sitting on the roof, I could still see the elephants. I hoped I'd see predators and scavengers.

I heard a car motor. A government truck pulled up and three rangers in khaki uniforms got out. They were armed with semiautomatic guns. I was impressed that these guys were that on top of things, and were going to go after the poachers. All the better for the story. I was about to drive down there, but knowing how the locals freeze up when you try taking pictures, I decided first to get some candid shots with a long lens, then go down for closeups.

The rangers, however, immediately spotted my car tracks and, obviously rattled, ran back to the truck. Then I got scared. I jumped in my car and honked the horn. I wanted them to know, preferably before they started shooting, that I wasn't a poacher hiding in the bushes, but just a Mzungu trying to take some pictures.

I drove out to meet them. They were not at all friendly. I passed out cigarettes. The guy in charge asked me what I was doing there. I was a little frazzled. I told them I'd found the elephants, that I was a wildlife photographer, and if they, the rangers, were going to track down poachers, I wanted to go along. All the while the guy was checking me out, my cameras and the car. He asked where my group was and I repeated that I wasn't a tourist, and I showed him my photo permit with all the right seals, stamps and official approvals. I offered him another cigarette.

He took the pack and told me to go to the tourist area. He said I was in a dangerous place that was off limits to visitors.

I argued, thinking I could flatter him the way I did cops and firemen when I was at the *Beacon.* I told him that now that he and his men were there, I was safe and that I wanted to photograph him and his men tracking down poachers, that pictures showing the rangers doing their job could get them all a raise.

He didn't buy that. He said they were doing a special antipoaching investigation, and no one was allowed to accompany them, or even talk about it, let alone take pictures. He told me to leave. The three guys stood there, smoking my cigarettes, cradling their guns, and I didn't have much choice.

I couldn't let it go at that. I made a wide circle, then backtracked behind a hill. I left the car and, taking my camera bag, climbed to an overlook. I was worried they might spot me—these guys could have spotted a chameleon on a leaf from a mile away.

I managed to crawl in nettles. In no time I was all scratches and rashes. Though I could see, more or less, what they were doing, the perch was lousy for pictures. What I would have given for your 600-mm lens! I was not only too far away, but there was this sharp light that made everything flat and colorless; yellow scrub, bloody elephants and Africans in khaki all blended into one another. But I continued watching through binoculars.

The guy who'd ordered me out smoked while the other two worked on the elephants with pangas and knives, like it was all in a day's work. They tried to yank out the tusks, but the carcasses hadn't rotted enough. They hacked them out. They cut off the elephant's trunk and butchered the face digging out the base of the tusk. When they finally tore out a tusk, a tube of bloody nerve fell out.

Remember what you said? To a poor African, animals are food. It would have been easier for me, watching this mess, if I could have seen the elephants that way, too, as meat, or commodity, or great photo fodder, instead of as the peaceful family who'd been my neighbors.

The rangers left the carcasses, loaded the ivory on the truck and covered it with a tarp. I figured they would stake out a place in the bushes and wait until dark for the poachers to return. Instead, they got in the truck and sped off, and not, as I would have thought, toward park headquarters. They headed east where, my map says, there's nothing between here and the border.

I drove back down to the elephants. From the car I took closeups of the mother and calf, or what was left of them. I suppose I should have stayed away, in case the poachers showed up to take their booty. But by that time I had a feeling that the only poachers around were the rangers who'd come and gone, and were heading for their hideout to stash the ivory.

Early this morning I drove straight to park headquarters. In case you've never been there, it's a barrackslike concrete building with a rusting roof. The place was a car graveyard; there were a half-dozen banged-up vehicles baking in the sun, missing wheels, fenders, windshields and assorted car innards. I suppose the maintenance crew scavenges them for parts.

I told a clerk that I had to see the warden, that I had something important to tell him. He told me the warden was very busy. He asked me to state my business. I said, "Poaching," which I thought would get his attention. The clerk acted like he didn't understand. I said elephant killing. He repeated that the warden was busy. I said I'd wait. He said, "No problem."

I sat on a bench outside the warden's office, hoping the warden would be more on the ball than his staff. The anteroom smelled like cigarette butts. Rangers drifted in and out, like they didn't have anything better to do. I kept asking the clerk when I could see the warden, and he kept saying, "No problem." It was going on two hours when I ran out of patience. I stormed past the clerk into the warden's office. Maybe the warden thought I was nuts. He was talking to a ranger in front of a map with stickpins, like a war chart.

He asked me what I wanted. He had a thick oblong face and a body turning to fat. He wore a big gold ring on one hand and—I swear—a gold watch on the other.

I told him I'd been waiting a long time to see him, that I was a photographer, that I had permission to take pictures of wildlife, and that his men— And then I stopped. I couldn't take my eyes off his watch, and I thought, What is this? Park wardens' salaries don't pay for gold watches. And then I got it: ivory exchanged for gold.

The warden asked me again what I wanted. I made up something. I said I was lost. I asked him how to find the road to the tourist lodge. He pointed it out for me on the map, showed me the door and that was it.

I feel pretty foolish. I can't actually prove that the rangers and the warden are foxes guarding the chickens. My pictures don't show that. For all I know, maybe they were just doing their job, and the watch was just an Asian knockoff or the warden has a rich relative who gave him a watch for his birthday.

Should I care? Compared with the slaughter and ivory smuggling elsewhere in Africa, or to hundreds of thousands of Africans being wiped out by war, disease and drought, what are five elephants?

As I write to you, lions, hyenas, vultures, wild dogs and flies are polishing off the elephants. By morning there will be little left but bones and a bad smell, and then not even that.

My lamp is giving out. I'm sorry for prattling on like this, but I think you, more than anyone, will understand. I hope the writing is legible. By the way, my foot is pretty much okay now. This will sound strange, but in spite of all, I'm very happy here, following elephants. Are you returning to Kwendela anytime soon? It would be good to see you again.

Mirie

o o

Mirie rubbed her fingers, got up and stretched. She was surprised by the length of her letter. She stood re-rereading what she had written, hoping Max would understand that what she cared for, whether elephants or people, ought not to disappear unremarked, unremembered. If, that is, the letter ever reached him, which in her overwrought state caused Mirie even more concern than when she entrusted her rolls of exposed film to the precarious African mails.

She figured out the logistics. In the morning, she would drive to the lodge and give the letter to a tourist who was returning to Kwendela. Mailed from the city, the letter would have a better chance of eventually reaching Max.

26

Mirie was sprawled in the dust awaiting the reappearance of a pair of blue-and-gold agama lizards that had been playing hide-and-seek all morning getting ready to mate. At least she assumed that was what they had in mind. She was hoping to follow the courtship to its finale.

At first, using a telephoto lens, she had kept her distance, concerned that she might come too close and scare the lizards away. But the agamas didn't seem to notice her creeping closer on belly and elbows. So she snapped on her macro lens and focused tightly on the sunlit rocks right by the car. The female, of a slightly duller color than her mate, scampered over the rocks, pursued by the male. Mirie was poised, with motor drive and a new roll of film, waiting for the two to come together.

Just then, a small van barreled up. Tourists with cameras poured out. They were sweaty and disheveled. A man shaped like an avocado peered down at Mirie and tipped his cowboy hat. *"Che bellezza."* His wife gave him a dirty look. He appeased her with an affectionate squeeze.

"Andiamo," said the tour leader, with an uncompromising British accent, as he tried to keep the group together to proceed down to the river.

The Italian in the cowboy hat continued to admire Mirie, who was again at work, camera molded to her face, legs spread for balance. *"Che splendore!"* Mirie heard the compliment, but she was fixed on the agamas.

The Italian spotted the lizards. *"Si amano,"* he chortled to his wife, and called his compatriots to have a look. The vacationers ambled over, casting their gazes on the rock. They were amused. The fat man squatted down to try to tickle a lizard's tail. The pair raced off. Mirie cursed; the man in the cowboy hat grinned sheepishly.

"Andiamo," the guide called again, impatient with the group. He wiped the sweat from his sunglasses. Though probably no older than she, he already seemed world-weary. He acted as if he were bored with tourists, bored with answering the same questions over and over, bored with mouthing the same superficialities about Africa, and exasperated with the lack of discipline prevalent among Italian package tourists; they were almost as bad as Africans.

The Briton set off down the path through the thicket to the river. The Italians traipsed behind him lackadaisically. An African ranger carrying a Lee Enfield rifle brought up the rear.

Good, they were gone at last, thought Mirie. They had wrecked the shot, but she thought the lizards might come back to warm themselves on the rocks. She crawled under the car for a moment's respite from the sun and drank from her water bottle. She checked her second camera body to be certain there was ample film.

Mirie had no longstanding interest in lizards, but the agamas were spectacularly colorful. At the very least, she thought she might be able to sell the pictures to *Ecoworld*. Or maybe Liz could use them for a science textbook. Or a stock agency might be able to sell them; they'd take half the money, and she'd wait forever to be paid, but any pictures published were better than none.

The female agama skittered back onto the rock. The male, iridescent gold and turquoise, came out of hiding. Mirie edged forward. From where she was, halfway under the car, she could get both of them full-frame—but only if they would come together. The male's head jerked in the direction of the female. He dashed. She darted off the rock.

"Cooperate, damn it," whispered Mirie. She worried about the tourists. They wouldn't stay down at the river forever.

The lizards were unaware of Mirie's timetable. The female skittered to another rock, the male chased after her. This time, however, she stayed still on the sunny rock. He was right behind her.

The male crawled closer. There was good light, good contrast. Mirie waited for the picture, finger poised on the shutter button.

Suddenly, a scream ripped through the thicket. A woman burst out, then ricocheted backward as thorns snatched her camera strap. The ranger dove over her, rifle gripped in both hands. The guide flew out, sunglasses askew. Bushes broke as people exploded from the thicket as if they'd been shot from a cannon. Cameras flew, clothes ripped, people stumbled and scattered. The fat man was last, waddling on stubby legs like a hedgehog. Red-faced, apoplectic, eyes bulging, he ran. Behind him, a Cape buffalo charged out of the bushes. Mud flecks flew off its hide. It shook its head in rage and found a target. The fat man wasn't fast enough. The buffalo ran him down. The horns pierced him like fork tines in a slab of meat and pitched him high in the air. The Italian seemed to be propelled higher than the horns, suspended in the air an instant then dropped on his back. The buffalo pivoted in a tight circle, then impaled the man through the stomach.

A shot splintered the air. The buffalo bellowed, wheeled and charged at a woman, who saved herself by diving under Mirie's car. There was another shot. The buffalo screamed, turned, breathing hard, searching for a way out. It galloped, panicky and wounded, away from the people, the cars, the river, the gun, across the road toward the open bush. The ranger fired, reloaded, fired again. The buffalo vanished in a trail of dust and blood.

They all ran to the fallen man, then stopped as if they had hit a wall. His wife knelt over him as he quivered, fists clenched over his belly, trying to hold his life in. "Fredo, Fredo," she wailed, arms outstretched. Blood drooled from his mouth. The cowboy hat, still tied around his neck, flopped macabrely to one side.

He moaned. The wife held his hand, repeating his name as the guide and other men lifted him into the van.

With the fat man stretched out, there was not enough room for everyone. Mirie was aware that the guide was shouting to her, then the van sped off. The remainder of the group stood dazed among the blood and scuffle marks. Mirie dragged herself out from under the car. They looked to her, to the young woman cradling two cameras and a heavy bag.

Her mind raced, but she moved and spoke slowly. "Get in," she said in a hoarse whisper. "I'll take you back."

The tourists squeezed together, sitting on each other's laps, in the little jeep. A woman jabbered, her hands windmilling in the air. A man buried his face in his hands. A woman whimpered. By the time they reached the lodge, all were silent.

27

Mirie arrived at Kwendela Airport at two in the morning, having driven eight hours straight on bad roads. She put the film on the first flight bound for New York.

She reached her photo agent at home in Manhattan, where it was early evening. Over static and a gibberish of crossed lines, she gave him the bare details, the plane's flight number and arrival time, and repeated it all slowly to be sure he had heard.

The agent repeated the information back to her in quick bursts, the staccato rhythms of New York racing ahead of the desultory tempo of Simahali. He shouted over a garble of conversations. "I always thought you should have stuck with news. The U.S. rags don't give a damn about Africa. But if you could get me a good assassination, like that Liberian lineup on the beach—now that was a beaut. You'll never make any money off the animal shtick." His voice was engulfed by static and the connection faded.

She called home and was greeted by a tape-recorded voice from ten thousand miles away. "This is Jonathan Stuart Productions. Leave a message after the signal and we'll get back to you as soon as we can . . ."

He had changed the tape. On the old tape he had said both their names. He'd had to change it, obviously, since she wasn't going to be calling anyone back immediately. But the new message was still a little unsettling, coming from her own home, taking her absence for granted. She left word that she was back in Kwendela.

ɔ ɔ

Humphrey's barking woke the neighbor's Rhodesian ridge-backs and the trio of pit bulls on the next estate, and soon all the watchdogs in the valley serenaded her. The askari blinded her with his flashlight, then waved her on.

She was surprised to find the house lights on, since it was the middle of the night. A man opened the door. Mirie recognized him immediately, from Frances' pictures, except that he was wearing glasses. Gary's deep-set eyes were accentuated by puffy bags underneath. The black beard was touched with gray. His rumpled shirt hung out in back.

"You must be Mirie. Fran's asleep. I have a deadline. Welcome back," was his terse greeting.

Mirie tugged at the gear in the back of the car. Gary looked at her askance. "What are you doing? The askari will get those."

"That's all right. I'll do it." But the gear that had been her constant companion hung like dead weight. She wobbled and felt hot and cold.

"For a woman who takes on elephants," he said, motioning to the askari to take the gear inside, "there isn't a great deal of heft on you."

"I photograph elephants," she said wearily. "I don't wrestle with them."

He peered at her over his glasses. "You're shaking. Do you have malaria?"

"It's cold here," she said, following him inside. "I was in the bush."

Gary inquired no further. "Have a brandy. Light a fire," he said, as he retreated into his study and shut the door.

Mirie did neither. She rummaged around for letters that had come in her absence. Dirty dishes were piled up on the sink. There were glasses and overflowing ashtrays everywhere. The lumpy couch was all mounds and depressions and dog hair.

Magazines and newspapers were strewn around Frances' exercise mat. The state of the living room reminded her it was Sunday, Julius' day off. Mirie could not find any letters.

She was too wound up to sleep. She sank into the sofa. A steady ticking drew her attention to the newest acquisition. Hung on the wall among the African masks was a Regulator clock, like the one she and Jonathan had at home. From the study came the metallic patter of a manual typewriter. It stopped, raced, stopped again, the interim filled by the steady tick of the clock among an audience of masks. In this house of trinkets, Mirie felt out of time and out of place.

She tried several times to reach the international operator to place a call home, but the line was always busy.

Gary emerged, went to the kitchen, returned with a soda, coughed, pitched a cigarette butt into the fireplace, lit another and, without acknowledging Mirie in any way, returned to the study.

Again Mirie tried the call, and again the steady, rasping busy signal. Were all the expatriates in Kwendela trying to call abroad to homes back in the world? She shivered. The house was cold. She checked the *International Herald Tribune:* The week before, it had been ninety-eight degrees in New York, the last gasp of summer before the fall.

She wanted to hear Jonathan's voice, or better yet, to be home, instantly, far from Africa. One night in her own bed, his warmth next to hers, breath to breath in dreamless sleep.

She tried the phone again, and this time reached the international operator. The callback came promptly, and Gary, assuming the ringing phone could only be for him, picked up the extension in the study. There was no answer, or rather only Jonathan's taped voice again on the answering machine. Gary muttered, then put down the phone. He came out of the study, his jaw muscles working. "I'm expecting calls. I would appreciate it if you could wait until morning."

Gary paced about the room. He haphazardly tossed kindling and wadded newspaper into the fireplace and struck a match.

"I'm working on a long think piece on the atmosphere of repression"—the paper flamed up; smoke curled out into the living room—"which I view as more significant than a piss-ass item the desk wants about a silly wanker who played matador with a buffalo."

She started. How could he know? "An Italian?" asked Mirie. Gary stopped grousing and looked at her. "You're talking about an Italian tourist?"

Whatever Gary was going to say was lost in smoke filling up the room. He doubled over in a coughing fit, the deep wracking cough of a heavy smoker, as the fireplace spewed plumes of smoke. He opened the windows, but that only pulled the smoke further into the room. Gary stood over the fireplace, enveloped in smoke, coughing and cursing as if daring it to defy him.

Eyes streaming, Mirie ran to the kitchen for a wet cloth. With her hand wrapped, she groped in the fireplace and yanked open the damper. Gradually, the smoke retreated—while Gary raged at the fireplace, at Frances' lax management of the house, at servants, at buffaloes, at broken telephones, Simahali and the whole bongo continent. Why, why, couldn't he be posted to Bonn?

Mirie interrupted the tirade. "Tell me . . . the man who was attacked by a buffalo . . ."

"A Wop who was skewered." He bent over coughing, cleared his throat, lit a cigarette. "I can't fly out there until dawn and the cretinous twits on the foreign desk want the story two hours ago. It's impossible to get anything this late. The Italian Consulate can't even send anyone to deal with the body until tomorrow."

The body? It was the first time since she had left the tourists at the hotel that she had been forced to consider what had happened to the fat man. Having driven back to Kwendela— thinking only of dispatching the roll of film carefully labeled and nestled in her camera bag—she had not speculated on what had happened later. It was a neat trick: She had the man on film; therefore, he was safely packeted and bound for New York.

She was aware that Gary was still speaking. ". . . The hotel management stuck the corpse with the vehicles. It will be a hundred degrees when the sun comes up." Gary puffed on his cigarette, his eyes half-closed, inhaling the fine aroma of absurdity.

Mirie considered the dismal happenstance: that the jocular little man who had waddled over and ruined her lizard pictures was now dead. One moment he was flirting with her, the next he was rotting in a shed full of rusting cars.

". . . He died instantly," said Gary confidently, and Mirie knew, wrongly. "The buffalo gored him a dozen times before a ranger shot it, which doesn't say much for the chap's marksmanship." He puffed on his cigarette.

Mirie shook off her torpor. "He was bleeding badly, but he was still alive. He moaned a lot. And the buffalo"—Gary seemed to take notice of her for the first time—"was wounded but it got away. The ranger never had a clear shot—people were in the way."

Mirie put another log in the fire, picked up the tongs and rearranged the wood. It was burning well now, she noted. She faced Gary. "I was there. I took pictures."

His impassive expression changed. He laughed. He laughed the way Africans laughed when things went wrong, exulting in absurdity, the one thing that was in abundance in their lives. He was doubled over, wracked by smoker's cough and laughter.

It caught her, a laughter that welled up and came out in sobs. In tears she saw the man and the buffalo again, and she choked on her laughter.

Gary recovered. He poured her a brandy and stood over her by the fireplace. "You were there?"

She nodded. She felt warm now, by the fire, listening to the steady ticktock of the Regulator clock. Night was waning.

Gary said, "You photographed it. You were far away, naturally."

"As close as you and I are now."

"Did you get it?"

Mirie shrugged. "I think so, but who knows until it's developed?"

"The film?"

"It's on its way to New York."

Gary nodded. "Clever. I'm relieved to see that you're a

hack at heart, and not one of those misty-eyed defenders of wildlife. The locals are killed by animals all the time. But this chap was white. That's good for a few lines on a slow news night, wouldn't you say?" He jumped up and returned with pencil and notepad. "It would help if you'd fill me in on the details. It'll help you, too—get rid of it once and for all."

He coaxed her, asking questions, taking notes, murmuring encouragement. She told him how she had spent a morning trying to photograph lizards when the tourists showed up and ruined her chance. She described how the supercilious guide had told them to follow him into the thicket, and they never bothered to clap or make noise, as she had been warned to do. And they couldn't have known there was a buffalo down by the river. Mirie described where everyone was and the sequence of events, as if she were reviewing slides, frame by frame, through a magnifying loupe.

Gary closed his notepad. "Thanks. You should try to sleep."

"What are you going to do?"

"Finish the piece and file. Then we'll see. The desk will probably spike the bloody thing, and that'll be the end of it. Good night."

She climbed into the big bed in Max's cabin. The faint sounds of rapid-fire typing came down the passageway between the house and the cabin. The birds were waking up. The typing stopped. A few minutes later there was the roar of a motor-cycle and the crunching of gravel as Gary sped down the driveway.

28

"The question is," said Frances, aiming for the heart of Mirie's malaise, "do you miss him—or it?"

"The 'it' being sex, right?" asked Mirie. She was peering behind the makeshift bookcase and participating minimally in the discussion. Her attention was fixed on finding letters from home that had arrived, then inexplicably disappeared.

"The whole routine," Frances went on, eager to share her unsolicited wisdom. "Regular sex. Home. The snug harbor of a warm familiar body. Everything that spells death to erotic impulses . . . Did you look under the bed?"

Mirie crawled underneath. The bare wood floor smelled of polish. She noticed for the first time the old string reticule supporting the bulky mattress on which she slept, a deceptively fragile-looking network that had once sustained the turmoil of the wedding night and now bore, infrequently, the solitary burden of Max when he happened to pass through Kwendela.

She continued to search the cabin for overlooked corners and crevices where the letters (which, Frances said, Julius had tied in a packet and left in the cabin for Mirie's return) might have fallen.

"I don't get you," said Frances. "I've had such hopes for you. You're an adventuress."

"What do you care? Why's my sex life—or lack of it—such a big deal?"

" 'Cause you're tricky. You get all hot about elephants and lizards, like they're exotic and excessive. They're not. They're just there, going about their lives like they've been doing since long before you ever came around . . . You're looking for something excessive." She pointed at Mirie. "It's all in your head. But you pretend there's nothing going on. You deny everything."

"Come on, Frances. Get off your soapbox and help me find these things," said Mirie, more amused than annoyed. "I'm not denying anything. But I'm here, Jonathan's there . . ."

"Who said anything about Jonathan? Why not the guys here? Why not Gary—?" Mirie quit searching and looked evenly at Frances. Having gone too far, Frances could only go farther. "Yeah, he's fantastic when he wants to be."

"Let's drop it." Why was Frances always testing her? It somehow bugged Frances that Mirie didn't pine away for Jonathan or, better yet, lust after any of the men Frances had introduced her to since she'd been back.

At that moment Frances' attention was diverted by Julius, who appeared at the threshold of the cabin, very much on edge.

"What is it, Julius?" asked Frances. "Did you find them?"

Julius explained. Mirie caught the word *toto*.

Frances became suddenly subdued. "Yeah. Okay." Julius hurried out. "His wife's in labor. I said I'd take her to the clinic. She lost the last one—a boy. Julius talked to a healer, but just in case, he wants a regular doctor, too." Frances shook her head. "Baby number four coming up, and she's half our age." Frances slipped on her sandals, brushed her hair, tucked her red silk blouse into her kanga skirt. "Do I look all right?"

"Fine," said Mirie, relieved that Frances had something better to do than think up novel sexual permutations.

Frances halted halfway down the corridor. "Skip it."

"What?"

"The thing with Gary."

Mirie shook her head.

Frances looked at Mirie, abashed. "I always shoot off my big mouth, just to stir things up, you know? Look at me— waiting for someone else's baby. How dumb can you get? I wish everything would blow up—we could leave Simahali and move somewhere else. Beirut. Lagos. New York. Anywhere. A place with some snap."

ɔ   ɔ

While Frances awaited the delivery of Julius' baby in a crowded rural clinic, and Gary was stalled at the Saudi embassy waiting for a visa, Mirie hung around the house, continuing the hunt for her lost letters. She placed another call to New York. Some satellite carried her voice from Africa to New York, where it was once more greeted by an answering machine. She gave up and idly read the newspapers, hoping the phone would ring.

In the government-controlled *Simahali Gazette,* she came across the following items of local interest.

> KWENDELA—Honourable MP Joshua Mbaganga, who yesterday narrowly escaped death when he was set upon by a leopard at his house in Omburi Estates, today accused his opponent of employing juju to incite the leopard attack in order to hamper the MP's campaign for re-election.
>
> KIJIJI—Frightened villagers today fled their homes after another attack of falling stones. They were awakened in the middle of the night by stones flying inside their houses.
>
> MJI NA CHUMVI—Mrs. Florence Mviki died in hospital after complications arising from a traditional operation performed after receiving a skull fracture from disciplinary blows by her husband. The problem occurred after a healer cut a hole in her skull to release bad blood. The hole was plugged with fat and herbs. Mrs. Mviki is survived by her husband, eight children and 32 grandchildren.
>
> KWENDELA—Members of parliament today criticized the Honourable Ruth Kirunga, the only female MP, who spoke on behalf of family planning. Speaking for the majority, the Honourable MP Daniel Wahare quoted from The Holy Bible, which com-

mands men to "spread their seed and be fruitful." Mr. Wahare accused Western donor nations that promote family planning of conspiring in a "wicked neocolonial racist plot to keep African nations weak and underpopulated."

KWENDELA—Court convened on the case of a housegirl who cut off her employer's penis. She said her employer raped her many times and she could not quit her job because she was supporting her family. She said she was very upset and when he next approached her, she cut off his member in self-defense.

KWENDELA—"Corruption is a cancer eating the heart of our great nation," said our Illustrious President in a radio address. "We will not rest until we have arrested all members of the treasonous cabal who would steal from the common man."

There was no mention of the Italian tourist who was killed by a buffalo.

○ ○

Gary cursed the embassy bureaucrat who never got around to issuing him a visa, but the hell with it, he and Frances were going off on holiday. He'd resume the vigil afterward. He did, however, receive a telex at the office to the effect that his buffalo story made the front page, and—as he knew already, having received the most recent issue of the *Herald Tribune*—had been sold to newspapers outside the United Kingdom.

He basked in the comfort of the couch and the attention his story had received. Mirie congratulated him. He uttered thanks. "By the way"—he twisted on the couch and dug into his pocket—"this came for you at the office." He flipped an envelope across the room and went back to reading his story in the paper.

As Mirie tore open the envelope, Frances walked in, radiant. "You are looking at the godmother of a fat healthy baby girl," she announced. "She's named after me." Gary grunted, not taking his eyes off the newspaper. Mirie was similarly preoccupied with the cable from the photo agency,

which she reread as perplexed as if she were having to decode it.

"What is this? Zombie headquarters?" asked Frances. She
peered over Mirie's shoulder and read the cable aloud.

> BRAVO. SOLD EXCLUSIVES TO PARIS MATCH,
> STERN, TEMPO, LONDON SUNDAY TIMES MAG,
> MANCHETE, NATIONAL ENQUIRER. TWENTY-
> FIVE REPEAT TWENTY-FIVE K, MINUS COMMIS-
> SION.

"Twenty-five thousand dollars?" Frances screamed, and threw
her arms around Mirie.

Mirie did not react. She studied the cable as if there were a
chance she had misread it.

Gary made the supreme effort of getting up from the couch
to shake her hand. "Well done."

She looked at him uncertainly. The accident had taken on
the aspect of a gruesome nightmare, upsetting but unreal. She
had never seen her pictures, nor until now, even known
whether they had come out. Now, suddenly, for the first time,
the pictures had earned her a reprieve from money worries
and, if not the kind of recognition she would have liked, at least
a temporary notoriety. But she couldn't shake the notion that
she had capitalized on a man's death.

Frances nudged her. "You really did it."

"It was an accident."

"Such humility," said Gary, cheerfully sardonic. "Let's cele-
brate." Intuiting her ambivalence, he added, "Wrestle with
your conscience another time. Tonight we'll take you to
dinner. Or better yet"—he took her arm as well as Frances'—
"since you're the wealthiest member of the household, you'll
take us. And I'll grab the receipt—the paper must pay for
having dragooned me to this sinking paradise. Then we'll visit
the casino—it's quite entertaining. Asian grandmothers in silk
saris relentlessly feeding coins into slot machines . . ." He
glanced at Frances. "Did I write that story?"

"Several times," said Frances.

ɔ o

Mirie examined herself in the mirror. Pulling her hair back accentuated the planes of her face. She stared at the cable pasted on the glass, it read like a caption beneath her reflection.

Twenty-five thousand dollars for a freak accident. Making money off misfortune. She could tell herself it was in the nature of the business, but it was ghoulish all the same. Even more so because she was so anxious to see the pictures, to see what she had captured on film that had excited photo editors who wouldn't have looked at, much less published, quiet wildlife pictures from an unknown photographer. She had not dreamed of this kind of quick commercial success. Jonathan would be astounded. Now she could at last stop fretting about paying her way through the next month.

But why did her two-colored eyes belie her happiness? She just had to talk to him. While Gary and Frances were in their room dressing, she dialed the international operator. She was lucky. The callback came almost immediately, and this time it was Jonathan himself who answered.

ɔ ɔ

"Where have you been?" asked Mirie, nervous and excited to hear his voice at last. "I've been calling for days. Did you hear?"

"What, Mirie?" (Why was he calling her Mirie? Why not the fond and familiar "M"?)

"Didn't the agency call you? About the exclusives. Can you hear me? Exclusives. Twenty-five thousand dollars' worth. After the agency takes its cut, I'll get around half, ten or twelve. Will you handle it for me, and tell them to hurry up and send me two thousand? I'm running very low. And send me the *Enquirer,* too—the agency takes forever." No, this wasn't what she wanted to say. Did he understand? She was happy and not happy. "Jonathan, I photographed a terrible accident. It was a fluke . . . Oh, where have you been? Can you hear me? . . . What's wrong? You're so quiet? Did you get my birthday present? If you hated it, you can tell me . . ."

"I did. I wrote to you."

"Oh, that was it. My mail, all the letters while I was on safari, were lost. We can't find them."

"You haven't received my letters then," he said, his voice eerily flat. "None of them."

"No."

Silence again.

"What's wrong?" Mirie persisted.

"I had stuff to tell you . . . it was all in my letter . . . You've been away a long time."

"Tell me now. Why are you being so mysterious?"

"I can't, Mirie. Not now."

"Tell me. Are you all right?"

"I'm fine. I'll call you later, Mirie. Bye." She was disconnected.

The African operator came back on, and said in her singing cadence, "Are you finished, madame?"

"Yes," said Mirie woodenly. "I guess so."

29

Jonathan missed her, Mirie concluded as she lay on the big comforting canopied bed. He had written to her asking her to come home and for all these weeks had received no reply. He was hurt and furious. He missed her. He had encouraged her to take this trip, but he was unhappy without her. Her long stay had become intolerable. He needed her. That was it. That was all.

She would put the picture money to work immediately: round-trip tickets to Paris for herself and Jonathan. They would meet there, perhaps marry there. Why not? What was the sense of knowing a need if not to act on it, when—she played with words she had helped Frances memorize—he was at once so loving and jealous of her liberty. And then she would return to Africa to work on her elephant pictures until the new rains. She had left Jonathan temporarily for Africa, and for a time she would leave Africa to savor her winnings. For once she could exult in being a gambler's daughter.

"Mirie!" Frances shouted from the garden. She had been exercising all morning, working off the excesses of the previous night's dinner in preparation for her and Gary's holiday. She was determined to lose enough weight to stuff her ripest parts into a very small bikini. "Mirie!"

Mirie found her behind the servants' quarters, along with Humphrey. The dog's tail thumped madly.

"Here's the culprit," said Frances. Humphrey grinned and barked. He was quivering to pounce, but Frances held him firmly by the collar as she handed Mirie a gnawed, dirty bundle. It was a moment before Mirie realized what it was.

"Hump thought it was a bone. He's been snacking on them. They're wet, but I think they're readable." Humphrey whined and struggled. She took a stick and hurled it far. Humphrey shot after it. "You better take your love letters inside. He'll be back to play tug o' war."

Frances gripped the flesh on her thighs. "I better get back to work. Day after tomorrow I got to be thin for the Seychelles. Another boring paradise, coming up."

o   o

Mirie opened the letters in her cabin. She had a pain in her stomach. Why had Jonathan hung up? He should have told her in any case. What if the phone lines went down again—and she'd be left with the sense of bad news hovering over her, made unbearable by the time and distance separating them? Was it a work disaster? Had NYU sacked him? Had she caught him during the worst pangs of a setback? But Jonathan had to bounce back. He always did.

She set aside the letters from Liz, Frank Evans and Sam. There were three letters from Jonathan. She opened the earliest one, posted several weeks prior.

Dear Mirie,
   I can't reach you. Every time I call, some guy speaking mumbo jumbo answers. Once I got your pal Frances. She said you were on safari. She also said, without skipping a beat, that she was an actress. So, what's she doing living in Africa?
   The Happy Birthday mask arrived. It's the best. I've hung it in my office at school. When students are pouring out their souls to me, they can't avoid the funny eyes and puckered mouth. I think it frightens the undergrads and has pruned my fan club to a devout few.
   Speaking of fans, Frank Evans called to wish me happy birthday. He also called to see how you were doing.

Birthday dinner at a Village *frogerie,* stuffed myself on chocolate mousse cake served with five sparklers, unrelated to my age. Five for high five-figure deal simmering.

> More to come.
> Love always,
> Jonathan

The second letter was a handwritten note.

> Dear Mirie,
> Bingo! Buzzy Butler, King of the Laundromats *qua* producer, came through. He wants a full treatment of the bathysphere heist concept. He thinks it could be another *Aliens.* I'll believe it when we meet Friday to put numbers on paper. It may not be my best work (as you were superquick to point out), but as long as Buzzy bites and keeps on biting, a body can live well on renewable options.
>
> > Love,
> > Jonathan

ɔ   ɔ

The third letter, six pages long, was dated two weeks after the previous one.

> Dear Mirie,
> I've started a lot of letters and torn them up. I wouldn't be writing at all, but Frances says you're still out with the elephants. A letter is a stinking way to tell you this; it's a one-way street, which our relationship has never been. I have met a woman I love. I was not looking for this to happen. But it has, and the experience has changed me.

An affair, no, not even. He had had a quick lay to pass the time, but why did he tell her? Vengeance in the guise of honesty, because she had gone away on a long project, for the first time, leaving him at home. Why? Even Frances didn't advertise her escapades in front of Gary.

> If you haven't already torn up this letter, I want to tell you about her. I don't care what anybody thinks about me, but you, M, you have to understand.

She was trying to. She thought of Frances and Gary, still together after he had made her sterile. They both continued fooling around, cavalierly ignoring the threat of AIDS. Nevertheless, they were going off to the Seychelles to play romantic duo on holiday. If they could survive infidelity, absences and disease, she and Jonathan could get through what she would charitably consider a momentary lapse. They would meet in Paris. They would come through this. Steeling herself, Mirie read on.

Lynn was my student last year. I may even have mentioned her to you. She was in an interdisciplinary liberal-arts masters program, a catchall for unformed minds. She came to my office because she was having trouble with an essay I assigned. She is not like you. She is tentative and fragile . . .

Then what am I, Jonathan? I'm resilient because I had to be, because Dad was a gambler with lousy luck, and Mom dreamed herself to death, and you helped me get free of all that. Why do you reject now what you helped create?

When I first met Lynn, I was fed up with my students dumping their troubles on my desk along with their preliterate term papers. She was different. She never talked about personal things. She was bright enough, but quiet and contained. All she needed, I thought, was a pat on the back to convince her she could get through the course.

She did very okay. She wrote sturdy little pagodas, nothing thrilling, but all the elements were there. I gave her a B+, and wished her a happy life.

That was it, until I ran into her in front of 1 Fifth Avenue. She was with her dad, a rich, silver-haired, pencil-up-the-ass if there ever was one. He was talking to her, and she was crying. There was a chauffeured limo waiting. I was going to cross the street to avoid them, but she saw me. I said hello and pretended I hadn't seen a thing. Lynn introduced me to her dad, stammering and looking as if she was going to shatter right there on the sidewalk. I thought, What's the big deal? Then I thought of the incestuous Mulwrays in *Chinatown*, which led me straight back to the office, to dim sum takeout and a notion about an updated *Oedipus*, down and dirty, set in the Deep South. I forgot about Lynn and her dad.

You don't even know when you lie. Jonathan Stuart, refinancing his future at thirty-nine, with a new woman who has a rich father, the answer to everything. Jonathan Stuart, lover, baby-sitter, B-moviemaker extraordinaire, financed by his student's daddy.

I bumped into Lynn again, at the library. She wanted to explain what had happened. Her dad pulled some strings and got her a job in a law office. She refused, there was a big fight. He said, how did she intend to support herself and the apartment at 1 Fifth? She said the fancy digs had never been her idea, that they, her mom and dad, had forced it on her because it was safe and prestigious, which was the only thing that counted with them. Likewise the law job. She told her dad she would move if he didn't want to pay for the apartment anymore. Of course, her dad imagined his Greenwich-born daughter having to turn tricks to pay the rent, and he backed down. But then her mother called and tightened the screws to force her to take the job. I asked Lynn what she wanted to do. She said she wanted to be a speech therapist and work with kids. She needed to go back to school to get another degree. Against my better judgment, I got involved.

You leaped at the chance.

I met with the father; I know he thought I was boning his daughter, but I wasn't. There was nothing between Lynn and me then. I hated to see her parents twisting her in knots. It's perverse, what people do to each other in the name of love.

What's perverse is his confiding this as if I, Mirie, were his room-mate, not his lover.

Unlike you and me and everybody we know in New York, Lynn doesn't want to *be* anything. She doesn't need a career or a movie deal to make her feel good. She needs only to connect with me. She's real giving. It's no sappy thing. I want her to do the speech-therapy thing if that's what she wants. She wants children, too. How could I refuse? She's in her twenties; she wants to be a mother now, while she's young. I want this not only for her but for me, too. There's no point in waiting. I want to be a father now. Lynn and I are getting married, Mirie. I'm clearing my things out of the apartment.

You're the last person I want to hurt, Mirie. But I'm not

asking you to forgive me. There's nothing to forgive. We gave each other a lot and we both changed. We aren't right for each other anymore. We could have married and gone on for years as partners, then woken up too late to do anything about it. You and I have always hated marking time. I hope you will see someday that it's better we stopped now while we're both young enough to have second chances. I want to know how your work is going. I want you to bring home the baby picture. Once you're done despising me, you'll see this as a beginning.

Jonathan

Couldn't he spare her the rancid optimism, the flimsy con job. What did he mean, marry this Lynn? Who was he kidding?

30

"She's hopeless," Frances complained to Gary, miffed that Mirie had shut her out of her confidence. It was their last dinner together before Gary and Frances left on holiday. Frances appealed to Gary to help her break Mirie's silence: "I tell her everything, absolutely everything."

"I'm sure you do," said Gary with detachment.

"We can't leave her like this," Frances continued, as if Mirie were not there.

"Isn't it enough that you've adopted Julius' entire family?" asked Gary. "Do you have to appropriate Mirie's problems as well?" He helped himself to another slice of pot roast. "Eat something, Frances. You'll feel better."

"Can't. I'm still fat." Frances stared at her own empty plate.

"The sensitive photographer is perhaps still bothered by the blood-money nonsense," offered Gary, then asked her directly. "Are you, Mirie? If so, you can give the money to me."

"It's nothing," said Mirie quietly. "Africa blues. It'll pass." She glanced from Gary to Frances and back to her dinner plate, wishing the two of them would leave her alone.

"Not necessarily," said Gary. "Frances has had them for ten years."

"Don't listen to him," Frances flared. "Give Gary a visa and a plane ticket, and he'll be an instant expert wherever he lands.

He's good for coups and wars, but what he knows about the human heart you can stick up a mosquito's ass."

Gary inadvertently had done her the favor of deflecting Frances' attention.

"But, Fran," Gary said coldly, "inner quests are your job. You have loads of time for them, since the only stage on which you will ever be at center is your own."

Mirie said good night and wished the bickering couple a happy vacation—however inauspicious its beginning.

Frances hugged Mirie good-bye, an all-out embrace that took Mirie by surprise.

"Will you be all right without us?" asked Frances.

"Stop mothering her, Fran," said Gary. "She may look like a waif, but Mirie's *kali*."

Mirie did not know the word. When she looked it up later, she found it meant "fierce."

○ ○

Alone in the house (Julius had been given time off), Mirie pondered what to do. She placed calls to New York, but failed to reach Jonathan at home, at his office, or at school. The phone became more undependable. At times there was no tone at all, not even static. There seemed little chance of Jonathan reaching her.

Writing a letter, she decided, was fruitless. She refused to commit feelings to paper that might meet ridicule at the other end, or worse yet, Jonathan's patronizing solicitude. A letter he could hold at a distance and judge as he would his students' essays:

"The paper shows dogged research on the subject, but your thesis—the 'gestating catastrophe'—is really overdoing it. What in the world do African elephants have to do with the subject? Elephants are elephants, nothing more. Also, where do you address other points of view—i.e., your prof's? Good luck next term, Ms. Keane. Nice having you in my class. J.S."

A letter was out of the question, and the phone was broken. Mirie made a pilgrimage to the Kwendelan post office. Unruly queues of people were waiting to place calls, send cables and post letters. Men elbowed one another for first place in line, while callers in the booths bombarded the fragile phone lines in a cacophony of foreign tongues. Caught in the pack of people crowding the clerk's window, Mirie questioned her tactics. Why not fight for Jonathan? Why not go back? She could put the picture money to good purpose. Why was it that she, who had taken on Africa, could not face going home to New York?

The answer came as a picture: the eviscerated apartment, her own dusty camera gear in the closet under the bare coat hangers from which Jonathan's suits once hung; nights alone with the Regulator clock.

Africa provided a certain protective isolation. She could ignore the signs, stand apart from the throng whose languages she did not understand. The mess of Africa, after all, was not her mess: blame it on corrupt politicians driving Mercedeses, on peasants cutting down trees, on tribalism, on parasitic neocolonials, on the lopsided world economy. Blame it on the sun and the capricious rains; blame it on the endless land that was not only the cradle of man but also his tomb.

It came down to a simple fact: If Mirie went home, she would lose her observer status. She couldn't go back, but she had no plan for going forward. When Mirie stepped out of line at the post office—for her doubts had snuffed out the inclination to speak to Jonathan—the crowd swallowed up the space as if she had never been there.

Driving back to the house, she focused on the fine grit of rust-colored dust on the car and the trees. It was relentlessly sunny. Already, water was being rationed in the city in anticipation of the rains being late or failing altogether. By executive decree, the president's red roses on the median strip of the main highway were allotted water. Everything else was brown and withered.

At the house the bougainvillea remained vibrantly orange and crimson, but on closer inspection, the petals were papery. The only thing still growing was Julius' vegetable patch, a swatch of earth where he had planted corn, beans, peas and greens. Mirie weeded and watered, using a rusty jerry can that Julius had punctured with holes.

Somewhere in the eucalyptus trees, a bird made a brittle, high-pitched tinging sound, like a finger rubbed across the rim of a crystal goblet. Mirie felt distanced from everything; she was watching Frances' and Gary's affair, examining from afar her own estrangement, tending the African houseboy's garden, sleeping alone in a wedding bed. In essence, she was a tourist, no less laughable than the ones in funny hats and safari-wear.

She thought of her mother in an alcoholic haze in her cavernous antique-filled apartment, living a widow's life defined by what it was not, a picture in which negative background space overwhelmed the primary subject. She was sixty-five when she died, elderly but not old. Sixty-five was akin to Mirie's thirty-three, a limbo between no longer very young and not yet middle age.

What would her own old age be like? She saw herself in a sparely furnished apartment, amidst cobra baskets filled with discarded slides, a riot of fading images from everywhere. There would be a chest of drawers full of folders containing tear sheets of published pictures. And there would be her best slides, and though she would keep them, neatly protected, she would never look at them, for already she was wary of pictures that could atrophy the play of the mind, that were imagination's Procrustean bed.

Her gear sat in the corner of the cabin like a recrimination. To hell with moping, she thought; she was better off with the elephants.

31

"Hello?" she answered the phone breathlessly, having raced from the cabin to the house. "Hello?" She waited for the static to clear. There was a tightness in her chest, a knot of hope and dread at the prospect of hearing Jonathan's voice.

But the voice on the other end was not Jonathan's. It was an African asking to speak to the photographer, Mirie Keane. When she said that she was Mirie, the voice on the other end identified himself as Inspector Ng'bene, Ministry of Immigration. "There is a matter to discuss."

Mirie had had no dealings with Simahalian officials. As far as the government was concerned, she was one of many anonymous expatriates who came and went. She asked the inspector what it was he wanted to talk about.

Ng'bene said, "A routine detail. It is best that you come just now. Please, bring your passport and your cameras."

"What is this about?"

"It is no problem, madame. When photographers come to our country, they must pay us a visit. You have not yet visited us."

"No one asked me to."

"Ah, I see. Now you are asked. I will expect you."

It didn't surprise her that the inspector would not tell her anything on the phone. Even when the phones were working well enough to carry on a conversation, the custom was to conduct business in person. She imagined the worst. What if they had caught Mr. Singh, the money-changer Frances had taken her to who provided Simahalian currency in paper bags in return for checks in U.S. dollars sent to the Channel Islands? Could that be it? But everyone said that Simahali had the safest black market in Africa—there was little chance of getting caught. No, more likely it was a paperwork problem, for the tangled system Simahali had inherited from the colonials had spawned a bloated bureaucracy of civil service workers who did little all day but stamp forms. Probably, there were new forms to fill out and fees to pay. Mirie took a fistful of colorful bills from the paper bag—Monopoly money, Frances called it—and tucked it in her passport case.

Mirie drove around a roundabout, in the center of which goats grazed, and took the road up the hill toward the immigration office. Ahead of her a truck loaded with logs creeped up the hill, slower and slower until it finally stopped. The logs shifted ominously, the brakes groaned, the truck began to roll back toward her. Mirie blasted her horn, waved at the drivers behind her as she threw the car into reverse. The line of cars slipped down the hill. Drivers jerked their cars out of the truck's path as it slipped backward through the havoc and finally settled into the center circle. Goats trotted delicately out of the way and went back to grazing the brown stubble.

The truck driver, red-eyed and jittery from *mrungi*, climbed down from the cab, while stranded drivers honked and cursed, and vendors hawking the *Gazette,* live chickens and tire-tread sandals wound their way among exhaust fumes and paralyzed cars. On the car radio a cheery African song played on and on.

Alone in the car, surrounded by all the other cars and drivers going nowhere under a sky blue and empty but for the noon sun and one fat cumulus cloud enthroned up there for all time, Mirie began to laugh. She laughed until her eyes were tearing. She removed her glasses, and Africa became a blur. Someone honked. She replaced her glasses and saw a turbaned Sikh in a white Mercedes honking his horn to flirt. She laughed harder; the Sikh honked more. An African in the Subaru on the other side, who had been waiting in stolid, angry silence, noticed the Mzungu laughing. He, too, began to laugh, as if he, too, saw the joke in trucks that ran backward, goats that grazed traffic islands, and an estranged Mzungu stalled in a snarled roundabout. When the mess finally sorted itself out, the traffic resumed its mad rush.

In front of the immigration office Mirie was met by a man wearing a badge on his white shirt and a slack, unfriendly demeanor. She asked if he was Ng'bene. He shook his head. She asked why the inspector wanted to see her. He just looked at her.

Lugging her camera bag and the metal Halliburton containing the rest of her gear, she followed him behind the building, past the storefront full of fake-leather furniture and imitation Oriental rugs, and up a steep, poorly lit staircase. At the top of the steps a uniformed guard took down her name with painful slowness, while she caught her breath. She was taken to a bare waiting room where two Africans sat on a narrow bench staring vacantly at a grimy window.

Even for someone as slim as Mirie, the bench was too narrow to sit on comfortably. A dull headache pressed on her right temple and she was perspiring. She tried to open the window, but it was stuck tight.

The room grew smaller. Dust motes floated by, more volatile as time went by. Finally, the guard returned and led her to a small office. There was a bare desk, two chairs and a file cabinet. She was left alone there, though not for long. A stocky African with a policeman's paunch entered and introduced himself as Inspector Ng'bene. He opened the file cabinet and riffled through folders. He peeked inside a gray dog-eared folder and, satisfied it was the right one, sat down across from Mirie with the closed folder between them.

His full title, which he pronounced with excessive sibilance, was "Special Investigations inspector for Section I, Ministry of Immigration." He was cordial and precise. He asked her how long she had been in Simahali. ("Three months.") What part of the States was she from? ("New York.") How long had she worked as a photographer? ("Many years. Since college.")

"Now . . ." His smile showed white equine teeth. He removed some papers from the folder and, leaning back in his chair, he leafed through them, glancing at Mirie every so often. He asked to see her passport and went through it page by page. There was little to see; it was a new passport, with an unflattering picture.

"How do you like Simahali?" he asked pleasantly.

Mirie said slowly, "I like it very much." She adjusted the tempo of her speech to the prevailing pace. "Can you tell me what this is about, Inspector?" she asked in a low-key manner that betrayed no vexation. Some local officials, she had been warned, delighted in petty power games with foreign women. If she showed irritation, he might only dig in his heels more.

Special Investigations Inspector Ng'bene disregarded Mirie's question. "Why are you in Simahali?"

"I'm taking pictures of animals."

"Do you have a research clearance?"

"I have permission to take photographs, if that's what you mean."

"Who sent you here?"

Mirie did not know how to answer. "No one sent me. I came here to photograph animals. Elephants are my main interest. Why have you asked me here, Inspector?"

"I shall come to this point. You are working here. Who pays you?"

"No one pays me. I work for myself."

"Who permits you to photograph animals?"

Mirie smiled, confident, almost happy she could show off the fruits of her careful preparations. She handed him the letters, one by one, the long tedious correspondence with government bureaucrats, the statements stamped and sealed with wax and, most importantly, the letter from Gikuthe, the minister of conservation.

"I see, I see," Ng'bene repeated as he perused the letters. "Now let us follow a different path."

From the file folder the inspector plucked a sheet of paper, a page torn from a magazine, and placed it on the desk. It was a picture of a man canted back on the horns of a buffalo, open-mouthed, feet flailing, hat in midair, camera flying out from the neck strap. People were scrambling out of the buffalo's path. It was a sharp, dramatic picture, so well composed it looked staged. Safely laid out between columns of type, it was pictorial news that was distant and had nothing to do with her life.

And yet below the picture, in tiniest agate type, which grew and swelled and threatened to engulf the whole room was:

MIRIE KEANE/NEWS PHOTOS INTL.

"This is your photograph," said Ng'bene. "And this is you," he pointed to the credit line.

He placed a two-page color spread from the *National Enquirer* on the desk. The headline read, "Last Waltz of the Toreador." The paper had the same picture and a second one, of the wife, horror etched on her face, sunk in grief over her dying husband, with the other tourists behind her. "And this is yours as well. And this, too." Mirie nodded as he covered the desk with the pictures she had taken.

Now she understood: Ng'bene was investigating the accident. She was an important witness. Immigration was involved because the accident concerned foreigners. All he wanted was her cooperation.

"Our embassies in Europe and the United States sent these," said Ng'bene. "These are terrible pictures."

"Terrible" wasn't the right word; she attributed this to faulty English, but agreed with the inspector wholeheartedly. "A terrible accident, yes."

"Our friends in Europe and the United States see these pictures and they do not want to come to Simahali. One might say"—he knit his fingers together—"these pictures lie." (Mirie flushed at the remark. She felt her insides squeeze tight.) "Simahali is a very excellent country, a fine and peaceful country, and wild animals do not harm visitors." He spoke like a lecturing schoolteacher. Still smiling, he said, "Why do you make false pictures? You have no permission to make pictures that lie, only pictures that show Simahali's special natural resources."

Mirie stared at Ng'bene, his double talk reverberating. Her voice constricted with anger, she heard herself explain with painful precision. "I was in the bush photographing elephants. The warden told me I had to leave the area. He said it was too dangerous. I didn't want to leave, but he made me. I returned to the tourist area as I had been ordered to. I was by a river taking pictures of lizards when a tour bus came by. The tourists walked through the bushes leading down to the river. There was a buffalo drinking. They startled it, and it rushed out. The man was in its way. I did not cause the accident, Inspector. I photographed it."

"Exactly my point, madame. You admit that you made these terrible false pictures."

"They are not false! I do not take false pictures," she snapped. Hold on, she told herself. She began again, slowly. "The minister has given me permission to take pictures of wildlife. I have a legal permit to work here."

Ng'bene again looked at her passport. He said mildly, "I see no evidence that you have paid bond for your cameras."

"What are you talking about?"

"You must pay bond, and then when you leave with your cameras, the money will be returned. It is the law, madame. You do not wish to break the law."

"That's a law you just made up. Gikuthe granted me a permit to work here. You cannot—"

"No, madame, you have no permission. You have a letter from Gikuthe. Gikuthe is the *ex*-director," he hissed through his teeth as he tore the letter in half. "He has been detained. His loyalty to the president is in question. You are working without a permit, taking subversive, unpatriotic pictures that hurt the reputation of our young nation, and you have not paid bond for your equipment. This is not allowed."

"But any tourist—"

"Ah, madame, you are not a tourist. You are a photographer who exploits Simahali's wildlife to make money, and for this privilege you must pay. Moreover, we must have assurance that you are not going to sell your cameras for a great deal of money. Do you have any idea, madame, how much cameras are worth in Simahali? A great deal, as you know already. Mzungus are always skillful at exploiting African economies for their own purposes." Ng'bene called out, and the first man, her escort, entered and began collecting Mirie's gear.

For a moment Mirie couldn't react; that a stranger would touch her equipment was inconceivable, and yet the man had seized her Halliburton and was removing a camera from her bag.

She flew at the impassive inspector, her rage translating into a rasping squeak. "What do you want?" Money—that had to be it. She pulled Simahalian bills from her passport. "Here, we'll settle this now. This is my photography fee. Make him return my cameras!"

Ng'bene glanced contemptuously at the bills. "Sit down, madame," he said, his voice calm and authoritative. "We shall find a solution to your troubles. There is no problem."

Mirie said, "You have no right—"

Ng'bene smiled slightly. "The bond is little for an internationally famous photographer." He pulled a calculator from his shirt pocket and tapped out numbers. "A mere seven thousand five hundred pounds. Seven, five, zero, zero, multiplied by . . ." He showed her the conversion in glowing red digital numbers; $10,433. "When you pay, we will return your cameras. And when you go, we will return the money to you. You see, there is no problem."

"You're stealing my equipment. You're trying to extort from me more than the cameras are worth. I'm going to my embassy."

Ng'bene smirked. "Your embassy cannot help you. They will tell you, no doubt, that while you are a guest in Simahali, you must obey its rules."

"There was no rule about paying bond when I applied for my visa. Gikuthe said nothing about it."

"Gikuthe is gone. The rules have changed. You owe the government of Simahali seven thousand five hundred pounds." Ng'bene rested his chin on his fist. "But perhaps arrangements can be made."

Mirie now understood where the game was leading. She had to do it confidently. She turned away from Ng'bene and his assistant. Reaching under her T-shirt, she ripped the Velcro tab holding the money belt. It slipped from her waist, clammy with perspiration.

She drew out two hundred-dollar bills and laid them on the desk.

"If he puts down my cameras, this is for you, Inspector. It will be a transaction between you and me. I won't go to my embassy."

"Two hundred dollars? Your arithmetic is at fault, madame." Mirie laid two more bills on the desk. "Arrangements of this type are complex and can be slow, madame, *extremely* slow," he hissed. Mirie peeled off more bills; Ng'bene continued to allude to ill-defined "arrangements."

"That's one thousand dollars." She took up the bills and held them like a poker hand. "It's all the money I have." She could not believe Ng'bene would pass up a thousand dollars cash; that had to be more than he made, legally at least, in a year.

Ng'bene resettled himself in his chair. "You wish to pay one thousand dollars to facilitate the process."

"That's it. For my cameras and a photo permit." He waited, as if expecting her to place the money in his open palm. But Mirie held on to the fan of bills. "My cameras, Inspector. I want my cameras."

Ng'bene said something. The man set down the gear and retreated to the door.

"Let us finish our business," Ng'bene said amiably.

She let him take the bills. They made a vile scraping sound as he slipped them, one by one, into the folder. Then he shifted contentedly in his chair, his equine teeth resting on his full lower lip.

It was unbearably hot and hard to breathe. What was he waiting for? For her to cry? She wouldn't. What was the protocol of a bribe? Did one ask for a receipt?

Mirie began to gather up her gear. His voice calm, Ng'bene asked her to be seated again; he was not quite finished. The other man waited at the door.

She sat. Ng'bene made notes. She wondered disconsolately if he had a ledger for all his graft. He wrote an inscrutable code on her passport and pounded it with a rubber stamp. The gray file with Mirie's money was replaced in the file cabinet. The passport was shunted across the desk. Mirie stood up to leave. The other man came forward. As she reached for her equipment, he blocked her, whisking her aside with his arm as if she were a mosquito, and before she could do anything, he was out the door and her equipment was gone.

She screamed at Ng'bene. "You lied. You can't do this!"

Ng'bene sat back unperturbed. "You are brave but not wise, madame. You bring the rest of the money—nine thousand four hundred and thirty-three United States dollars—and we will return your cameras. Then you must speak to the new minister of conservation about permission. Without permission, you are forbidden in our parks. Good day, madame."

32

The dog licked the residue of sweet *chai* from Mirie's fingertips as she watched images dance in the flames of the fire. She saw Ng'bene's interlaced fingers atop the dirty folder as he recited the numbers of the extortionate bond, the fan of hundred-dollar bills she had handed over in desperation, his assistant shoving her aside to steal her cameras, the gnawed bundle of letters, the bulbous man punctured on the buffalo's horns, the glazed eye of a dead elephant, the photo of Jonathan buried in her duffel.

The images in the flames overlapped disturbingly; the loss of Jonathan became confused with the loss of the cameras. Certainly, Ng'bene's file included a record of petty betrayals and self-deceptions that had supported a love habit of six years. What else did Ng'bene have on her? Well, she should be relieved. There was nothing more that either Jonathan or Ng'bene could take from her.

She would finish her tea, pop the weekly malaria pill, put Humphrey out for the night and retire to the antique marriage bed reserved for the single and solitary.

No sooner was she under the covers and drifting off than Humphrey started barking. He roused all the dogs in the valley, and with them Mirie's fears, which slipped outside and took shadowy human forms among the stands of creaking bamboo. Reason argued (as she reached for her eyeglasses) that the dogs roared every night. They barked at cars and at Africans walking down the road. They barked at monkeys taunting them from the trees. They barked to communicate in ways humans didn't understand. But on this night she was sure that they barked because thugs with pangas were combing the valley for a house to ransack.

She heard the dog yelp, accompanied by a strange sound outside, like a man cursing and clearing his throat.

Mirie tore down the dark passageway to the main house, to check the doors and windows. She did not switch on the lights, for that would reveal her, half-clad in T-shirt and panties. They would bend the security grates, break the windows, cut her to pieces. When she heard the kitchen door open and someone snap on the light, she screamed and locked herself in Gary and Frances' bedroom.

What stopped her from pushing the alarm was a familiar voice: "What the hell's going on? Frances?" It was Max's voice. She opened the door and there was Humphrey grinning, his tail beating, as if to say, "Look, look what I've found." Hearing the refrigerator door open, the dog scrambled into a U-turn and galloped back to the kitchen. Mirie wrapped an African cloth around her hips.

"Mirie!" Max called to her as he tossed Humphrey a meat scrap. "I thought you were Frances finally gone around the bend."

Emerging from the kitchen, Max walked slightly bent, the posture of a tall man who is every wary of hitting his head on low doorways. He gave her a quick, vigorous pat on the shoulders, as if uncertain if the gesture was too much or too little under the circumstances.

"I had to make it up to the beggar mutt," said Max. "I stepped on his foot. *Your* foot looks better."

Mirie looked down, self-conscious. She felt thin, undressed. "Yes. It's fine now. I . . . I was asleep. The dogs woke me. I was afraid—"

"Frances has you spooked . . . Where is she?"

"In the Seychelles . . . She and Gary . . . together."

Max smiled at the added clarification. "You're alone then."

"Yes."

"Has the house been robbed?"

"No. But while I was on safari, the house across the valley was hit—" She stopped, aware that she sounded hysterical. "No, it's been quiet here. I was imagining things." She wasn't going to tell him about the demons, which were now scurrying like ferrets around his photography gear, taunting her for losing her cameras and her emergency money.

"I got your letter." His steady gray blue eyes discomfited her. "Thanks."

"Oh, sure," she said equivocally. She remembered how, at the time, it had seemed vital to tell him about her discovery that the rangers and the poachers were apparently one and the same, but now, facing him, she was faintly embarrassed. "I guess I went overboard about the dead elephants. I suppose that in time you get used to it."

"Not really." He sat down on the couch.

It sagged under his weight. His arms spanned across the back. He had the pallor of jet lag. Too many hours spent wedged in airplane seats had caught up with him. He sketched his travels after Zambia: back to the States to see his parents in St. Louis, his daughter, Kate, at Oberlin, and his agent, his publisher and Evans in New York.

Mirie tried to imagine Max in the home of elderly, solidly midwestern parents, or on a green manicured campus, or in a classy publisher's office in New York. It did not work. Max was outlandishly disproportionate for conventional settings.

Humphrey wedged his square muzzle between Max's knees, angling for a scratch behind the ears. "You're between safaris?" said Max.

She murmured. She was afraid of the pressure inside her, that at any moment she would start to cry. "How long are you staying?" she asked, controlling her voice, but it felt as if she were speaking from the bottom of a well. Fortunately, Max didn't appear to notice.

"A couple days here, then I'm going on safari with a friend of mine. And you? Where are you off to?"

"I haven't made up my mind." She was deliberately bland. It was best to be quiet, to concentrate her energies on resisting the pressure inside. She resented Max returning. He had come home to reclaim his bed. She felt hateful and ashamed, incompetent to work in Africa and incapable of going home. She would let him think that after three months in the bush she, like he, had learned to keep her own counsel.

"Hey, what's with you?" said Max. "We had good talks."

"We did?" she said lightly. "I talked. You listened."

"That's how I am. At first. What happened to Mirie's thousand and one questions?"

"A few I answered for myself. The rest I'm still working on."

His face seemed more drawn now. He went to the fireplace and idly kicked at a log, unleashing a shower of embers. He spoke so slowly and softly she was forced to lean forward in order to hear him. "Let's stop this, Mirie. What's happened to you?"

She paused, then said without emotion, "I have to forget about the elephants. I don't think I can work here any longer."

Max didn't say anything. He just looked at her a long time. Then he rummaged through his gear, returning with a photo sandwiched in cardboard. "I was going to have Fran give this to you. I didn't think I'd see you again."

It was a picture of Mirie at work, bent over, head to head with the skull of a Cape buffalo, against a background of cracked scarlet earth. Her face was hidden under a shiny helmet of straight brown hair; the camera appeared to have replaced her head. Mirie admired the geometry of the picture, the curves of the whited buffalo horns, the circles of eye sockets, the angle of her own stance.

The picture recalled the exhilaration of that first safari, when everything she saw seemed vibrant with inner life. Oh, Africa!—dream become nightmare. It was another optical trick, as a slide held up to bright light could shift into its negative, its inseparable opposite. Mirie's gaze softened and the picture blurred. She pretended to adjust her glasses, hoping he wouldn't notice the tears. How was it that Max could argue so eloquently without his ever having said a word?

She tried to veil her emotion in protest. "You sneaked a picture! I never saw you take out your camera."

"You were busy . . . The light was good."

"I thought you didn't like to take pictures of people."

"Once in a while, I see something . . ." He waved off the rest of the sentence, as if unwilling to say a word about his own work for fear of sounding pretentious. Then he asked her, "Do you really want to go back to New York?"

She shook her head, then said softly, "I don't know . . . about anything. I've been living in your cabin, sleeping in your bed. It was all temporary. Now it's my only fixed point, and everything else is whirling around."

"A lot of people prefer floating. They couldn't live any other way. Like Fran with her Broadway career. Her dreams are so distant they can never be ruined. You, however, chose to go for closeups."

"No. I . . . The fact is . . ."

"Yes?"

There was no one fact, only images in the fire. And a feeling that she could entrust anything to him, even her confused ravings. "Sit down, Max. You're jet-lagged, and I'm not very clear on any of this. But sit down, now, and I'll tell you . . ."

○ ○

"It doesn't surprise me they jailed Gikuthe," Max said finally. "He was a rare bird, honest and outspoken, too much so for his own good. I knew he wouldn't last long in this regime." He paused, considering his words carefully. "Do you understand, Mirie, that this Ng'bene is playing with you? If the government really wanted to nail you, they would have had you out on the next plane. A lot of these guys think that all the misfits and malcontents and losers from Europe and the United States who can't make it back home come to Africa. To Ng'bene you're a helpless American with bucks to spare, and he's going to squeeze you till you don't have anything left to bleed. You can pay the bond and get your cameras, but you'll never see that money again."

"I know that . . . I'm thinking of flying to Europe to replace the cameras, and coming right back."

"You said he marked your passport—they won't give you a tourist visa, let alone an extended work visa. Or if they do let you back in, they could confiscate the new cameras as well."

"Then I'll buy new cameras in Europe and work somewhere else in Africa."

"That will take more money, time and planning. You'd have to be totally self-sufficient. That means a car, gas, spare parts, camping equipment, the works. You have to be prepared for logistical nightmares that will make Simahali look like Shangri-la. How much money will you actually see from the buffalo pictures after commission—twelve thousand or so?"

She nodded.

"Kiss it good-bye." Plus"—he paused—"you have to consider the rains, and work around them."

"They were late before. They may not come."

"I wouldn't bet on it."

"I'll worry about the rains when I start to get wet."

He breathed deeply, a sigh of frustration. "What's wrong with going home?"

Mirie's stomach contracted. She shook her head.

"Why not? Go home. Buy new gear. Come back when the rains are finished and Africa is green. You look like you need a break." He shrugged. "It's only a thought. If you'd taken that advice three months ago and gone home while your foot healed, you would have been out twelve grand and a great set of pictures." The clock chimed; it was four in the morning. "Are you staying?"

He wanted to turn in. Mirie said, "I'll move my things out of your cabin."

"I mean in Africa."

"Oh, Africa. Yes."

He nodded. "You sleep in the cabin. I'll bed down here."

"Don't you want to sleep in your own bed?" Once the words were out of her mouth, she realized they sounded like a come-on. "I'll move my things out," she reiterated.

"It's no big deal," Max said with finality. "I'm leaving in a couple days." It was not clear whether he had missed the gaffe or was letting it pass.

33

$\mathbf{M}$ax pushed aside the cumbersome bed and pried up a few floorboards. He aimed a flashlight into the crawlspace and, satisfied that whatever he was looking for was still there, eased himself down. It was some feat for a gawky man well over six feet tall to fold himself up to fit into an oversized gopher hole. But as Mirie had already observed, when it came to anything related to work, Max was agile and decisive. It was under more relaxed circumstances that his brain and his body seemed to live separate lives.

From the darkness his long arms emerged with all sorts of equipment: a canvas tent, a camp bed, a sleeping bag, a clatter of cooking utensils, a battered brown suitcase and assorted safari gear. Then Max climbed out, a dusty Lazarus, and scooped up the equipment in two broad armfuls.

"You forgot the suitcase," said Mirie. "I'll bring it."

"No, that's for you, if you can use it," said Max, making his way, fully loaded, back to the main house.

What did she need a suitcase for? Judging from the weight of it, it wasn't empty—more camp gear, she supposed. She brushed off the dirt and snapped the latches. Inside was a camera body, an old Leica dull from years of use, two lenses—a 50-mm and a 300-mm—and a flash. The camera body was heavier than what she was accustomed to. She attached the long lens. The shutter, cocked and released, had the smooth, solid sound of fine machinery. She guessed the camera to be about fifteen years old; it must have been his first Leica, bought after *Cats at Twilight*.

That was Max's strange, diffident way of giving, to offer and back away. Whether he was uncomfortable being with her in close quarters or he assumed that she was uncomfortable around him, she did not know. Whichever, his kindness touched her. She held the camera up to her eye, trying to accustom herself to its heft.

o   o

On the stove the stew simmered in lazy bubbles. The aroma of beef, wine and vegetables permeated the far corners of the house. Outside, Humphrey barked, signaling that Max was coming down the driveway. Mirie lit the candles and straightened a glass.

He savored the aroma as he came in the kitchen door, and followed fingers of steam to the stewpot. They ate avidly, and finished the meal with a dessert of chocolate sponge cake. Made from dense African flour, it had turned out more like a chocolate brick; she tried leavening it with a slice of mango. Mirie could not remember when she had last eaten so ravenously.

While he washed the dishes, and she dried, it seemed like the right time to thank him. "That's a great camera."

Max scrubbed the stewpot. "I've been meaning to sell it, but I never get around to it. As long as you aren't doing anything tricky, it does the job."

"Thanks for being the way you are." He glanced at her. An eyebrow lifted, as if he was not sure what she meant and didn't care to find out.

But all he said, as he handed her the pot to dry, was "You know I'm leaving tomorrow."

o   o

The book, published in 1902, was written by a white hunter.

> It's an infernal place. In what the natives call 'the belly of the dry season,' the rocks heat up and the

merest touch burns a man's skin as if it were roasting meat. Four months a year, the region is underwater. In the short period between these extremes of hell-fire and flood, big tuskers and antelopes are everywhere. I potted them from my tent, but one grows weary of the sport. There's fly and mosquito and all manner of fierce biting insects that draw blood and drive a man mad before he succumbs to an excruciating death. My donkeys died. Camels fared only somewhat better. On the plateau, beautiful to behold from afar, the natives are constantly at war, spearing and knifing each other. I've lost three bearers this year, two boys to insects, one to warriors who speared him as he was fetching water. If civilization is to come to these savages, I doubt that it will be in my lifetime.

"This is where you're going?" asked Mirie.

The bald patch encircled by squabbling curls nodded. Max pointed out a lopsided quadrant penciled in red on a map spread over the dining table.

His next project was to photograph a chapter of a book on the most extreme habitats in the world. The idea was to show how plants, animals and people adapt, even thrive, under spectacularly inhospitable conditions. He and his friend Chris Dahlgren, who was a doctor, were flying to a remote area that Max wanted to check out as a possible location. Chris had flown medical missions there, and had set up a permanent, if primitive, camp; access was precarious at best. In the monsoon season the land flooded and the elephant grass grew ten feet high. In the dry season it was well over a hundred degrees in the shade. After the rains tribesmen burned the old grass to encourage new shoots, and that in turn drew the game. Without the game the people would starve.

"Outsiders have always avoided it. Slave caravans, explorers, commercial poachers, they all bypassed it. With any luck, it should be like looking through a window to the past."

"How long will you be there?"

"Not long, a week. When Chris was up there last month, there were showers. In a month it'll probably be a swamp, so this is the time to go. And you. What about you?"

"Thanks to you, I have a camera. But I still don't have a permit."

"These government guys aren't competent enough to bird-dog you. Pretend you're a tourist, and if anybody asks you why you aren't with the milk-run safaris and wants to see your permit, dash them."

"Dash them?" Mirie laughed. It was an incongruous idea, given that she had already thrown away a thousand dollars in an incompetent bribe attempt. Moreover, her ready cash had dwindled to half a paper bagful of pink, blue and yellow Simahalian bills. As she couldn't count on Jonathan, she telexed the agent to wire money from the picture sales, but they were agonizingly slow in paying. She telexed again for an advance. The reply was, it was against the agency's policy. She shot off another telex, saying she was in a crunch, and the agent replied tersely that it was too bad, he couldn't speed up the process. Nor could she ask Jonathan for more money, not now. Thinking about the money snafu precipitated a chain reaction that collapsed her mood altogether. She didn't tell Max about her troubles on the home front. She said only, "I'm broke. Temporarily."

"No money from the buffalo pictures?"

"Not yet. Maybe it's just as well. No doubt I'd hand it over to Ng'bene."

"Your cameras and the grand were small change. It could have been a lot worse . . . Listen . . ." He paused, then said so quietly and hurriedly she wasn't sure she had heard him correctly, "You could always come with us."

This offhand invitation perplexed her. "Me? Why?"

As if he had overstepped himself, Max immediately disclaimed the idea. "Well, I don't think there's much in the way of elephants. Chris has never seen any. All it is is a desolate, forgotten piece of Africa." Mirie could not decide whether Max was reiterating the offer or retracting it. "It's a little trip to check things out," he continued. "If the place is what I think it is, I'll go back after the rains and set up camp."

"But you're taking your gear."

"Sure. Always. And you should, too. If you're still worrying about the photo permit, forget it. You're only kicked out of the official reserves. This isn't official anything. This is no-where."

"But it's *your* nowhere." He looked puzzled. "You were adamant about working alone."

"I'm already not alone. There's Chris and the kid who's his translator—and you if you want to come along."

"Why would you let another photographer come? What if we end up taking the same pictures? All the photographers I know snarl over turf. Why do you—?"

Max laughed. "All the questions—that's the Mirie I first met. All right." He shifted, stretched out his legs, crossed his arms over his chest. His manner changed. He was direct, businesslike. "If I were going up there expressly to shoot, I'd go alone. But it's not like that. If I—or you—manage to shoot anything worthwhile, that's great; but don't count on it. This is really just a chance to explore a corner of Africa few people ever see or, for that matter, want to see. Consider it a detour, while you decide where you're going and what you're going to do." He considered her for a moment. "It must be tough. If you're not used to being alone. Is your husband—?"

"He's not my husband," said Mirie quickly. She frowned and her mouth twisted. "And we've separated."

"Oh." His feet shifted. "I'm sorry." Max looked like he wanted to bolt. "Is that what you say?"

"I suppose." They fell silent, both looking anywhere but at each other.

Finally, Mirie said, "It doesn't seem real to me. A month ago I told this old drunken chief a love story, and he laughed at me. He said I didn't understand my own story. He was right. I don't understand anything—that Frances, with her beautiful body, can't have a baby, that she and Gary are still together after all their affairs and flirting with disease, that Jonathan and I are finished. It's unreal to me . . . I thought I knew myself better, knew who and what I need. Maybe I don't. I've been by myself a lot, and it's had a strange effect. I hear a different voice inside myself. Oh, don't think I'm getting mystical, Max. It's nothing like that. It's a quiet voice that somehow sounds true to me, a part of me that's removed from this whole mess."

Max waited a few seconds before speaking, slowly. "Back there, where we come from, you're not supposed to stray too far from facts that can be measured and analyzed. Here facts are in short supply. And what few there are are stretched and turned inside out and upside down . . . Africans know about us carpetbaggers. They know we're not only after material things. We're greedy for what we lost inside ourselves. That's why I play Indian and you chase after elephants . . . When Sharon left me, I blamed myself. I told myself I had ruined the marriage because I had my head stuck in a camera and didn't notice anything else. There's a soda lake that is red from algae, and in the right light it's the color of blood. I went down there. All these kids covered with snot and flies gathered around my car. I stood on the roof, and one by one I hurled my cameras into the lake as far as I could throw them. The children laughed. They thought I was *wasiwasi*. I wasn't nuts. I was making a sacrifice."

"And then you felt better."

"No, I felt like an idiot. I'd just thrown away thousands of dollars' worth of equipment that I'd sweated years to buy. I'd drowned my cameras and it wasn't their fault. The camera's a dumb machine. I should have thrown myself in the lake."

"But you didn't."

"I considered it. I sat on top of the car thinking about Sharon and Kate. The light changed and the wind picked up. It made bright red ripples on the water, and the kids were giggling and pointing to me, and then I started to laugh, too. Maybe it doesn't make sense, not our kind . . ."

"Max? What you asked me, before. I'd like to go."

He nodded. Yes, it was decided.

34

A fly was doing the backstroke in Max's beer. He fished it out, flicked it aside and had another sip. The beer was warm. Mirie waved away the flies buzzing lazily around her head. In a moment they were on her face and neck. They were slow and she could have swatted them. But squashed, they'd stick to her damp skin, and that irritated her more than the incessant buzzing.

Max said, "Your poison's coming."

The waiter shuffled across the terrace. He wore a skullcap and a long loose robe, a djellabah, that once had been white. Eyes half-closed, he arrived with two demitasses of espresso, Mirie's third double round of the morning. The coffee was vile but safe; it had been boiled all morning. She drank off the thin layer of muddy liquid, leaving gritty sweet grounds and a burnt odor, which cut the rankness of rotting mangoes strewn about the terrace. Mirie looked at the mangoes ripening overhead. They were maddeningly out of reach and the hotelkeeper seemed not to understand when she asked for a stick to knock the fruit from the tree.

The only food left at the hotel was eggs, warm beer and espresso. The food shipment was on the steamer that had been due two weeks before. Max, Mirie and three German backpackers, who together comprised the sum total of paying guests, complained. The hotelkeeper shrugged and shuffled away, avoiding the hordes of flies feasting on squashed mangoes. Beyond the terrace a laborer listlessly swept a topiary of buried upturned beer bottles. Goats sniffed the dirt for a blade of grass. Humidity sucked the life out of the day.

The tattered boat schedule thumbtacked to the wall in the lobby was dated 1954. The town, in the full heat of decay, was a waystation where they would fly with Dahlgren to a place unmarked on any map. He should have arrived in town three days before, but he had radioed that he would be delayed; there had been a cholera outbreak in an overpopulated settlement where pumps, installed as part of a now-abandoned aid program, had broken. People were desperate for water. Additional medical relief was stalled in Kwendela, but as soon as the trucks arrived, Dahlgren would fly out and continue his rounds in the bush.

Mirie blew, with a kind of Gallic pout, at the fly that had landed on her lips. "You know what this town needs, Max? A swimming pool."

Max sniffed, head propped on his hand. "Write to the Chamber of Commerce."

The town had died in its sleep, but no one had told the inhabitants. They floated by, swarthy men in white djellabahs and black men in loin cloths smoking pipes made of spent bullet cartridges. Mirie had seen no women other than a burned-out German woman who was also staying at the hotel.

The woman, in her mid-twenties, was traveling with two countrymen. Both were her boyfriends, she had told Mirie; she had no preference. The trio stayed in bed most of the day smoking hash while waiting for the boat that would take them downriver. Every morning when Mirie ran into her, in the filthy common bathroom on their floor or on the terrace, the woman spun out the latest rumors. The boat had broken down, but spare parts were being ferried down river. The boat had caught fire. The boat had been blown up. The rumors became more florid as each day passed under the dripping mangoes, while the young woman grew thinner and sicklier from dysentery.

She offered Mirie some hash in exchange for two flashlight batteries. Mirie swapped instead for a tin of pineapple, and shared the treasure with Max.

Max said, "Do me a favor. Stay clear of the *Fräulein*."

"Why?"

"The local police stopped by last night. All white people tend to look alike if they have a mind to round up the druggies. I don't want to get busted." He offered her the last chunk of pineapple on the end of his pocketknife, then returned to his book.

Mirie could only envy Max's equanimity. He had improvised a burnoose out of a cap and a T-shirt. Oblivious of the heat and stench, he read—alternating between a spy thriller and a biography of Gandhi—tilted back in the chair, nursing a beer, as contented as if he were at a seaside resort. As for the flies, Max had perfected the African trait of ignoring them. Mirie, by contrast, could not sit still. She shook her head and the ponytail swooshed them away, but in an instant they strafed again. She slapped, scratched, stomped and periodically sprayed herself with canned bug repellent, much to Max's amusement.

"The flies love that goop," he said.

"It works."

"You sweat it off in five minutes."

"That's five minutes without torment." Perspiration drooling down her body felt like crawling millipedes. She shivered in the heat.

She dumped espresso grounds on the table. Was she going to tell his fortune? asked Max. She spread the grounds, shaping them into a picture she recalled from a book her father had once given her.

"This is Pangaea, All Earth, when the continents were one body and Africa was at the navel. One hundred eighty million years ago Pangaea began to split apart." She drew an irregular line through the coffee grounds. "This is the belly of southern Gondwanaland, brother and sister continents, where the Americas and Africa separated. Do you see?" She drew the S-curve where the east coast of South America fit into the west coast of Africa. "It's like jigsaw pieces . . . When I was a kid, I asked my dad whether, when I was as old as he was—which to me was an impossibly long time away—by that time, would Pangaea bring together her children? I thought they were wandering on the oceans, and sooner or later they would have a family reunion. It all seemed very reasonable to me."

"It sounds like you were an only child who wanted a brother or a sister."

"Not at all. I didn't think I was missing out. I thought we were the right-size family the way we were."

"What did your father do?"

"He was an actuarial statistician. He handicapped people's lives. That's all I know. He never talked about work. Insurance was just what he did for a living. What he loved was the horses. To him picking horses was an art and a science. But he wasn't very good at it. My mom had no idea how much he was gambling and losing. When he died, we found out. It was awful for my mom. He'd lost all our money. But more than that, he had this underground life she knew nothing about, or if she suspected, she just put it out of her mind."

Mirie shook her head. She no longer wanted to talk about old pictures and stories. She scooped the coffee grounds and dropped them in a saucer.

"You might as well throw them in the garden," said Max. "It's the goats' dinner."

"If he serves goat kebab tonight, remind me not to eat it," said Mirie. "I'm going to lie down for a while. Will you come get me if anything exciting happens? . . . If the police come or a mango drops."

The wheezing room fan stirred up the fetid air, and tap water swirled black in the sink. She stripped the bed and lay the sheets over cushions on the screened porch. It was suffocatingly muggy and the porch stank of stale urine. Somewhere a radio blared a whining melody peppered with static, then clipped sounds of the BBC, more static, a broadcast in Arabic, more whining like cats in heat. And far away she thought she heard the faint drone of an airplane.

ɔ ɔ

The Cessna sat on the runway like a fat splay-legged chicken as Dahlgren and the spindly African boy finished loading it. Dahlgren was a beefy Australian in his early fifties. He was squarely built, his legs slightly bowed so he teetered as he walked.

Beside him, Joseph, the boy, was an ebony stick, small-boned with a well-shaped head and almond eyes. He looked no more than thirteen, but when Mirie asked him, he said, after a long embarrassed pause, that he was sixteen years old. Dahlgren said that Joseph spoke English very well but only when he wanted to. Mirie recalled meeting Ruth the night of the first rains, and the girl's pained attempt at speaking English. She still could not understand the confusion, which bordered on paralysis, that afflicted African children in the presence of a white person.

Dahlgren put Mirie up front while Joseph and Max climbed in back. After takeoff, the plane banked sharply to the left. The thatch and tin roofs of the town shrank into brown dots and blazing sunlit rectangles against a yawn of yellow gray earth. An interminable, featureless desert stretched as far as the eye could see.

Shouting over the engine, Dahlgren pointed out scorched earth from old grass fires and cut lines made by oil surveyors. The guided tour ended with a violent curse. Ahead was a swarming black cloud.

"Locusts?" asked Mirie.

"Birds," said Dahlgren.

The plane dropped as Dahlgren avoided a cloud of birds sweeping past them. Mirie clenched her seat as the plane twisted, ducked, dropped and climbed. The plane pitched like a toy, and Mirie's stomach, seemingly independent of the rest of her, jumped and plummeted. Dahlgren and Max were stone-faced, and Joseph was pressed against the side window, staring into the brown storm. No one else appeared frightened, and therefore, Mirie tried to persuade herself, her terror was unjustified. Dahlgren was an experienced bush pilot, and was used to unpredictable flying conditions.

The storm of birds passed. The landscape had changed drastically. Beyond the left wing, green foothills rose up fast and steep. The plane banked steeply, passing over thousands of antelopes swirling in panic over a plain flushed with new grass from recent rains. The stall warning bleated. Before them a red scar of a landing strip ran perpendicular to the hills.

Mirie tightened her buttocks off the seat, the same involuntary reaction she had had when flying with Tom Goode, as if that would somehow stop her from scraping the earth. The plane touched down, bouncing hard before coming to a stop just before the end of the airstrip and the escarpment rising steeply dead ahead.

Their clothing had wet patches of perspiration. Back on earth, Mirie's legs trembled. For a few moments no one said a word.

"That was bloody awful," conceded Dahlgren. "It's hard enough to navigate without the birds. You hit a vulture in a plane like this, and it will put you down. The only decent map is the one I've drawn for myself. And there are tremendous winds spilling off the plateau that can pull you down on landing and flip you over on takeoff. In the dry season, dust storms wreck the engine and heat plays havoc with the compass. There have been times when it's so thick I couldn't see the wingtips let alone the mountains." He turned to Max. "I'm getting too old for this."

But Max wasn't there. He was striding off, seemingly in a fury.

Mirie called after him.

"He'll be all right," said Dahlgren. Max stopped to examine a bush, and it was a moment before Mirie realized he was retching. "Poor bugger," said the doctor. "Flying has never agreed with him . . . Here comes the diplomatic escort."

A party of locals made their way across the scrub. Leading them was an old man in a white robe carrying a spear decorated with strips of hide and feathers. Behind him were younger men in red running shorts, also carrying spears. Women and children brought up the rear. The women wore beaded hide skirts and were bare-breasted, though there was one woman (Dahlgren called her "the glamour girl") who wore a fifties-style boned bra. Dahlgren and the chief exchanged greetings, while the honor guard of spear bearers stood behind him and the women carried cargo up the steep path to the doctor's camp on the plateau.

Dahlgren told Mirie and Joseph to go ahead. He would see to Max, who was kneeling with his head in his arms, waiting for the sickness to subside.

Dahlgren's camp consisted of three huts in a clearing. The main tin-roof hut was the clinic by day, sleeping quarters by night. The second hut was a garage and storeroom. There was also a kitchen shack. Dahlgren and Max arrived, and Mirie observed the choreography of setting up camp. Little was said. The two men and the boy knew exactly what had to be done, and Mirie felt a little left out of the male ritual. Dahlgren and Max loaded barrels on the truck. They were going to fetch water.

"What can I do?" she asked.

"I told Dahlgren," said Max, "that you made the tactical error of demonstrating what a good cook you are."

"We trade off on the cooking," said Dahlgren. "Mine is—"

"Grim," said Max.

"Yes, well, it's not as bad as he says, but if you want to teach Joseph something in the kitchen, I'd appreciate it."

Mirie organized the kitchen supplies while Joseph did other chores. He dug a latrine, rigged with a wooden seat and a canvas curtain, and lashed a shower bucket to a low branch. He started a fire, and when the men returned with two barrels full of brown water, his task was to boil it, treat it with alum, and filter it into a clay urn for drinking water.

Wielding a panga, Max cleared an area overlooking the plain for the tent. He laid the tent out flat, then crawled inside with the center post and hoisted it to the vertical. As he drove stakes into the ground, he remarked to Mirie, "This sleeps two, and so does the hut. You can sleep wherever you want."

Implicit in the question was a choice of roommates: Max in the tent, Dahlgren or Joseph in the hut. Leaving her to decide the sleeping arrangements, Max left to fetch the gear.

His mind was on camp logistics. For her it was different. Everything she said or did, since the breakup with Jonathan, was put through the prism of being alone. Traveling on her own in Africa was no longer a temporary work trip but now the whole of her life. What an impossible weight for daily life to bear! No wonder that this simple decision of where to throw her sleeping bag—in an old canvas tent or a tin hut, with stranger or new-found friend—seemed portentous. Everything she did or said raised the question of who she might become without Jonathan.

"I prefer the tent," she told Max in a way that was too serious for him not to note. "If that's all right?" she added, unsure who was crowding who in this arrangement.

"Why not?" Max angled out of her way as she tossed the bag inside the tent.

After she had arranged her belongings, she found Max staring out at the plain. He glanced at her, then turned his attention once again to the changing swaths of blue, orange and lavender that followed sunset into cooling night.

She was done fretting over where to lay her head. It didn't seem so important anymore. "It's too much to take in."

"Whoever made this," said Max, "wasn't concerned with the limits of the human imagination."

⊃ ⊃

Eggs again. Those that had broken in flight had to be used. Mirie had Joseph chop tomatoes, peppers and cabbage. The rhythms of cooking took the place of conversation. She showed him how to sauté the vegetables, then poured them into the mixture of beaten eggs and powdered milk. She had not counted on the insects, however. Drawn by the kerosene lamp, they dropped into the sauce pan as the eggs congealed.

Mirie cursed. She tried picking out the bugs, one by one, but for every insect plucked out, another two dropped in. Dahlgren poked his ruddy head into the kitchen shed to see how dinner was coming along.

Joseph, who until the doctor appeared had stared mutely at the mess, said, "We cook the sons of the Devil."

Dahlgren chortled. "You do, indeed." He was more interested in dinner than in Joseph's strange way of speaking. He inspected the eggs.

Mirie said, "They're disgusting. I'll throw them out and make something else."

"Absolutely not!" said Dahlgren, taking the pan to the camp table and serving them up. "We won't see fresh eggs for another week."

"Just great," said Max, eating avidly.

"Super omelet," said Dahlgren, finishing off his portion.

"It's fritatta," said Mirie glumly. She watched Joseph eat his

fly-free *posho;* he had wisely cooked his dinner in the dark, and
he wouldn't even try the eggs. Mirie held a flashlight over her
plate, trying to eat around the insects, but that only drew more
of them.

"You have to think of bugs as fresh ground pepper,"
said Max.

"Pepper doesn't have legs." She divvied up her portion
between the two men and contented herself with bread and
jelly.

Joseph went to fetch the coffeepot. "He's so shy," said Mirie
while the boy was out of earshot.

"He has to know you better," said Dahlgren. "He lost his
parents. A missionary couple who lived out here adopted him.
He was quick picking up English, and he helped them learn his
language. Without him I'd have no way of talking to the locals."

"How well does he know the area?" asked Max.

"He knows where there's water, and where his people hunt.
What else is there to know?" asked Dahlgren. "It's bloody
desolate." The boy returned with the coffee.

"What about far up in the hills?"

Joseph looked up at the two men.

"Why should they climb hills when there's meat on the
plains? . . . What is it, Joseph? Let's have some coffee."
Dahlgren continued: "Why do you ask? You're going up there?
It's a fair trek. I haven't explored there myself. No bloody
time." Joseph seemed on the verge of saying something. "What
is it?"

The attention discomfited the boy. After another moment's
hesitation, he found words for his thoughts. "In the old days my
people hunted elephants, but not now. The elephants live with
the spirits and when they are disturbed, the hill shakes like
leaves in the wind . . . Yes. I do not cheat you." Joseph lowered
his eyes.

"All right, Joseph," said Dahlgren. He sent the boy to clear
away the dishes. "He's a good boy, but he's all mixed up with
spirit stories and Bible stories." Dahlgren drained his coffee cup
and wedged it in the crook of a tree. "Sleep well." He retired to
the hut.

"Tomorrow—" Mirie began.

Max interrupted her. "The hills? No. We only have a few days. I can't spend them searching for elephants behind trees when there are plenty of animals on the plains."

"We could split up," said Mirie. "Then I wouldn't be in your way."

"There's only one car. You planning to walk?"

It was an unrealistic idea, she realized; the remote terrain was unlike anywhere she had ever been. Setting off alone into the foothills would be too chancy.

"If we spent a day exploring—"

"Too little time. Listen, when Chris and I went to fetch water, we saw hunters chasing after antelope. It's a fantastic opportunity. Besides, I may need you to drive while I shoot—if that's okay."

"Yes," she said unhesitatingly. For all his help, she owed Max that and more. But she asked, "Isn't it against your religion to have an assistant?"

"Yes—an extraordinary measure demanded by the situation." He added wryly, "I'm glad you came along."

This direct, unaffected statement warmed her. Several years before, she had sworn to herself, after suffering Neil Donner's bloated ego, never again to assist another photographer. Max's request, however, was more like a friendly vote of confidence.

Max tied back the canvas flaps, leaving the tent open to the night save for panels of mosquito netting. Fires dotting the slopes below mirrored the stars.

Mirie pointed to Scorpio rising and reminded Max of what he had said some time ago: "Its head was too small for unhappiness."

"I said that?" asked Max, with vague recollection. "Oh, yes, the scorpion. You learned what you needed to on your own . . . I take it you like this place."

"It's terrible and magnificent all at the same time." Max smiled. "Are you laughing at me?"

"No, I like listening to you. If you stick it out, Mirie, you'll find your elephant being born, someday."

"Someday? I can't wait for someday."

"You'll have to."

"I'm running out of time."

"As long as there are elephants, there's time. Come back after the rains. Keep coming back until you have your picture. You have to."

She shook her head. "It's not the elephants, or the rains, or losing my cameras . . . When I boarded the plane to come to Africa, I thought, Well, now I'm going to do this—the baby elephant—and afterward maybe Jonathan and I will decide to do that."

"That?"

"A family. We never got very far talking about it. But I had a feeling that it was time for us."

"Did you? Really? I had the impression that you packed your whole life in those bags and made an all-or-nothing bet."

"I always meant to go home. I just wanted him, us, for once to be . . . definite."

"If you put your mind to it, Mirie, you could find somebody who would be definite"—Max retreated into his sleeping bag—"but you won't like him."

Mirie sat up watching Scorpio arch his back into a reverse question mark. The sky was full of them—question marks in the galaxy. What if the "we" was a necessary fiction to loving? What if there was something in her that was irrevocably alone, and it was that part that made her feel strangely at home in the solitary otherness of Africa? It pained her, but she had to give Jonathan credit. He had sensed what she had been holding in reserve all along. Applause, please, for an unknown director! What a directing triumph! He had always known she would go far.

35

Antelopes and zebras moved past the car in shimmering waves, thousands and thousands of animals migrating according to a timetable set by nature eons before. The first rains brought the new grass. Grass brought the grazing herds, pursued by cats, jackals, hyenas and hunters.

Mirie and Max watched the spectacle from the top of Dahlgren's car. "It's like being in a time machine," said Mirie.

Max agreed. "There aren't too many places like this left on earth, places man hasn't fiddled with. It's lasted this long because it's so Godawful inaccessible and there's been little here that anyone wants—so far. But that will change. You saw the cut lines. Once they strike oil, they'll put in roads, and wells, and you'll get people settling in with cattle. The migration will be disrupted and the herds will die off. No one needs these animals, except for a few hundred primitives and a handful of people like us, who have the luxury of coming here for our own cockeyed reasons."

The animals broke into a gallop. Max spotted hunters running through the herds. Mirie slid into the driver's seat and drove after them while Max navigated from above. The sunroof gave him a better vantage point from which to follow and photograph the hunters loping across the plain.

There were six of them, muscular blue-black men with ten-foot spears, who could outrun gazelles. They closed in on a buck. A hunter hurled his spear, and the foot-long blade pierced the antelope's shoulder. It was not a fatal injury but enough to slow the animal's flight. Antelopes and zebras galloped by as the hunters closed in.

Under Max's direction Mirie maneuvered the car to give him the best shot. For a moment the hunters were obscured by a moving curtain of animals. One man, grasping the horns, twisted the buck's head, while another clubbed the antelope's skull with a heavy metal bracelet. The antelope collapsed, its legs twitched, but it was dead. The hunters shouted and waved their spears.

Max went in on foot as the hunters butchered the antelope. Mirie also left the car, to watch, not to photograph. Two of the hunters were naked. The others wore raggedy running shorts. Their faces and chests were cicatrized in a cheese-grater pattern. The hunter who had first speared the buck sliced off its ear and displayed his prize to the others. "That's for his mother-in-law," said Max, "to show he can provide for the family."

Max photographed the hunters leaving, spears in hand, slabs of carcass balanced on their heads, with the herds moving off in the background. On the ground there was nothing but a bloody smear where the antelope had been.

Returning to the car, Max said, "You didn't shoot."

"I'm saving my film for the elephants," she said. "Besides, I don't have four hands. I can't drive and photograph at the same time." But of course she had been dying to shoot. He knew that. He also probably knew that she was loath to do anything that might distract him or intrude.

"Let's find some shade," he said, sliding into the driver's seat. "In another hour the light will improve."

o   o

Max explained the efficiency of the hunt. Several men hunting one antelope had a better chance of making a kill than each man going his separate way. The antelope was shared and nothing was wasted. "The women make biltong out of whatever meat is left, or beat it into powder for broth. They use the hides for skirts, beds and sandals. The hooves are for ornaments and the horns are for trumpets."

Mirie wondered how the hunters' bodies differed from her own; they could run for hours in searing heat without even a sip of water while her own thirst, after several sedentary hours on the scorched plain, seemed unquenchable.

They came finally to a ridge of scraggly acacia overlooking a fetid watering hole where zebras were drinking. It wasn't much to look at, but there was at least a little shade. Then, as Max was positioning the car under the broadest acacia, they heard a scraping sound. The car jolted and abruptly stopped. Max accelerated, but the wheels spun, churning up dirt. He put the car in reverse, but it would not budge.

He slammed the dashboard with his fist. His binoculars flew, and Mirie snatched them out of midair before they fell. He didn't seem to notice her quick save. He was already out the door and scrambling under the car to check the damage. It looked bad. The car was pinned fast on a thick elbow of root hidden by ground cover. There was no chance of moving it; it might as well have been hoisted on a hydraulic lift. Max cursed at having to waste the best light of the day hassling with the car. The flies closed in, and Mirie dug out her aerosol can of bug repellent.

"Do me a favor," said Max. "If you have to spray yourself, do it down by the water. I'd rather have the flies than that stinking spray."

"What? Another one of your allergies?" she said, picking up her camera bag.

"Right," he muttered as he scrounged among the mosquito nets, photographic gear, food box, spare tires and battery for tools to free the car.

As she could not help Max, Mirie thought she might as well take advantage of the late-afternoon sun that was bathing some nearby zebras in a rich light. The mishap, at least, was a chance for her to get a feel for the Leica.

She sprayed on bug spray and drank from her water bottle. Sun beat on her back as she framed a shot of the zebras. Heat and the strong smell of animals radiated up from the earth.

Sunlight glistening off the water changed the still, turbid pool into an oasis. She was tempted to jump in.

"Mirie! Dive!" Max shouted. He had seen her staring wistfully at the water; he was joking, of course.

"Get in!" he screamed, and when she turned to make a wisecrack, he was racing down the ridge, shirt flapping, gesticulating wildly against a swarm at his head.

Mirie plunged in, swimming underwater until she was out of breath. When she came up, something buzzed in her scalp. Again she dove under, and swam straight and strong until her lungs were ready to burst. In two more breaths she reached the other side. Bees darted pell-mell over the water. But most of the hive was swarming around the car.

She looked for Max. How ridiculous, she thought, being routed not by lions or elephants, the proud animals of Africa, but by a bunch of bees—she and Max would laugh about this.

Then she spotted him, lying on his side in the shallows.

He rolled over, seemingly not under his own propulsion, but more like a floating tree trunk. She ran, stumbling as her feet sank in the mud-sucking bottom. He was on his back, chin on chest as if he had fallen asleep and been transformed into a grotesque inflatable giant. His face was bloated with angry welts and his hands warped into paws. He wheezed horribly, a whistling intermingled with rasping breath.

She pulled dead bees from his hair as over and over she said his name.

His swollen eyes barely opened. He raised a hand toward the car, where the bees still swarmed. His words were slurred. She tried to understand. He was talking about his cameras, no, about medicine with his cameras. He opened his mouth wider, trying to take in air.

"I'll get it." She started to get up.

He gripped her hand. "Wait!" he whispered.

"I've been stung before."

". . . Not by African bees. They'll kill you." His hand went limp.

She tugged at him, dragging him an inch at a time toward shore, enough to keep his head out of water if he passed out. Then she raced around the water's edge and found the can of bug spray where she'd dropped it. She sprayed herself all over, and, coughing from the fumes, she charged the car. Bees flew like sparks around the car and inside. She released a cloud of spray and shut the windows. But the sunroof was wide open, and she wasn't strong enough to reattach the metal cover. She gagged on the cloying sweet insecticide and batted the air to protect her face. Then she saw the nets. She flung them on, one on top of the other. The center disks balanced on her head like a double-decker Chinese hat, and layers of muslin protected her while she searched Max's camera bag. She found a small case and unzipped it to be sure. It contained a syringe of adrenaline and antihistamines. Clutching the box, she ran from the car, tripping over her long train of white netting sequined with dead bees.

She snatched up the water bottle, too, and raced back to Max. He didn't move. Was he already dead, his heart stopped by a bee sting? No, he was moving. Or was it the water pushing him? She knelt beside him fumbling for the syringe. The instructions were simple. There was no time to worry about her inexperience—just get the stuff into him. Her hands shook as she injected him. He didn't flinch at the needle. He was warm. It was not the sun's heat but the warmth of his own body.

The effect was instantaneous. His eyelids fluttered. The stertorous breathing eased. He squeezed her hand so hard she yelped, not realizing until that moment that she had been gripping his hand as if a handhold alone could have pulled him away from death.

He said, "You're a funny-looking bride." His voice was weak, but his eyes seemed clear. At first, she thought he was delirious, then it dawned on her he was talking about the white netting. Yes, she agreed, seeing herself as he had, in the two-story Chinese hat and the muddy bridal train. She gave him a Chlo-Amine pill, and chewed one herself. It was only then, when there was no longer any doubt that he was fully conscious, that she became aware of the pain radiating from her own bee stings.

Skittish, curious zebras came back to drink. Max and Mirie lay in the shallows of the watering hole, his head cradled against her. They were woozy from stings and the pills. The soft blur wore off too soon, and a fear, which had been buried, came over Mirie.

"You're wasting water," said Max after a time. He was still muddled, she thought, until he touched her cheek, and it was wet with tears. Mirie held him tight and buried her face in his curls.

ɔ o

A zebra stallion brayed an alarm when Max stood up. The herd wheeled and galloped off under a gold and pewter sky. Max fought against his shakiness. "Lie down," Mirie told him. He refused, but his legs wouldn't obey him, and again he crumpled.

They were cold and wet and night was coming. Lions roared intermittently. If they could get to the car, they would be safe from animals, but as long as the bees were still there, the car was out of the question. Even with the bees gone, they were still stuck. Without a radio, they could not contact Dahlgren. The doctor could not fly in the dark, and even if he found them the following day, it was doubtful he could land. If Max were stung again, he might die, but if they sat out by the watering hole all night without so much as a campfire to frighten off animals, they were virtually a free-food advertisement. Lions and hyenas would be quick to respond.

Mirie said, "I'm going back to the car."

"The hell you are." He gripped her ankle, hobbling her. "Listen. Even if you're not especially sensitive, you get enough toxins in you and you're dead."

"I wasn't badly stung," she lied. "What choice do we have?" Max's grip relaxed, either because he had relented or because he was still too weak to fight her decision. She put on the nets again and sprayed herself with more insect repellent.

She was prepared to flee, but the bees had gone. She gathered brush and built a fire for Max. Then, working by flashlight underneath the car, she set to work chopping and gouging at the root with a dull panga and a pocketknife. The root resisted, and in the awkward position in which she had to work, she could scarcely do more than pick at it. Periodically, she called out to Max, ostensibly to tell him what little progress she was making but really because she needed to hear his voice.

Finally, the root was nearly sawed through, and the two front tires rested on the ground. She started the car, rocking it forward and back, until something shifted in the undercarriage, the root gave way and the car slid down the ridge. Mirie blasted the horn and shone the lights. When she had collected all the equipment, she drove around the watering hole to Max. He was standing, shakily; when she embraced him in celebration, he was still so weak that it felt like she was supporting him.

○ ○

"You bloody drongo! What kind of wanker gets stuck under a bloody beehive!" Dahlgren continued his tirade as he spooned more venison stew onto Max's plate. "You, of all, people! One sting would have been enough to kill you, but that's not good enough for you. *You* had to take on the whole swarm. If Mirie hadn't gone for the adrenaline . . . Of course, she was a bloody fool. If I'd been her, I'd have let you croak after the way you conned her into coming to this bloody hellhole." Mirie and Max exchanged glances as Dahlgren blustered on, venting his worries on Max, who was too dopey from the pills to protest.

The stew was gamy but tasty, and while Dahlgren hectored, Max and Mirie ate hungrily. After dinner the night's entertainment was tick removal. Both Mirie and Max were covered not only with bee stings but tiny ticks that had burrowed into their scalps. Working with tweezers and alcohol, Dahlgren removed them from Max's hair while Joseph tended to Mirie's. Holding a tick up to the kerosene lamp, the doctor mused out loud on the simple elegance of the disaster: Max nearly dying from anaphylactic shock because the adrenaline kit, tucked away with the cameras, was guarded by the bees. That was a good one for the annals of bush medicine.

Dahlgren mixed a concoction into water and told Mirie to shower in it. It was a dilute solution of disinfectant and veterinary powder. "Examine yourself, closely. *Everywhere,*" he said.

Even after she scrubbed herself red, ticks still clung to her legs and belly and had burrowed into her pubic hair. She spent the rest of the evening by herself, tweezing out ticks by flashlight.

Max was already deep in sleep when Mirie came to the tent.

Lying down was painful. The bee stings ached, and everything else itched. Max, however, seemed almost restored. He lay on his stomach, arms outstretched as if he and the earth slept in calm embrace. His breathing was even now, in concert with the night breezes. She pulled her sleeping bag closer to his and quickly fell asleep.

36

$\mathbf{M}$ax's mishap was followed by another, graver one among the locals. While chasing zebras, the chief's son was speared by another hunter. The accident left him critically wounded. He lay in the clinic, while Dahlgren, through Joseph, tried to persuade the old man that his son, the tribe's future chief, would die unless he was flown to the hospital in Kwendela immediately.

The old chief knew nothing of hospitals, or of the world beyond the plains, but as there was in the tribe something of a mystique surrounding the doctor and his airplane, he finally relented.

The wounded man was carried down to the plane, and the whole tribe gathered around—blue-black hunters, elders, women in hide skirts, infants and children. But before the doctor could fly off, the chief insisted on prayers.

Dahlgren refused, not only on account of the patient but also because the winds were picking up, making flying ever more perilous. On this point, however, there was no arguing with the chief, nor with his retinue of hunters rattling spears around the plane. Resigned to the delay, Dahlgren sat perspiring at the controls of the Cessna while the tribe of primitives prayed, chanted, ululated and evoked plaintive sounds on antelope-horn trumpets.

Mirie photographed the scene, then waited by the plane

beside Dahlgren's window. The doctor reached Max on the radio. "You're missing the party. Mirie's making me into a bloody hero! She's taking souvenir snapshots of me saving the life of the heir apparent." Max's chuckle came through the static. "Where are you?" Max described his position. "Well, the reception's not bad at all. I'll talk to you in the morning. Watch out for beehives." He signed off. They had moved the radio from the clinic to the car so that Max could maintain radio contact with Dahlgren in Kwendela from wherever he was shooting, and a regular morning radio call had been arranged.

"Do you think this guy will make it?" Mirie asked the doctor.

"He'd better," said Dahlgren. "The old man's not going to be around much longer, and this chap's the only son left. The rest died one way or another. If he goes, the tribe comes unglued all that much faster." A naked toddler, who had one opaque eye and a bloated belly, poked at the plane with a toy spear, then hastily drew back. "The medicine I practice here I never learned in school. I can stop pain, cure a few people, prolong a few lives. But sooner or later the tribe will die out. For the government the primitives who are left are irrelevant, or at worst a bloody nuisance."

"You aren't discouraged?"

"No time for that." Raising his sunglasses, the doctor wiped the sweat from his eyes.

In the previous few days, while Mirie and Max were pursuing herds and hunters, the doctor had treated eye ailments, septic sores, malaria, and worse diseases. Added to the usual caseload were the hunters who had been kicked, trampled, bruised and bloodied during the hunt. Dahlgren worked from dawn to sundown, giving injections, dispensing pills and performing simple operations under the crudest conditions.

For Max and Mirie the emergency evacuation to Kwendela meant they could stay longer, since the doctor had to return anyway. Max was glad to stay, since the safari had turned out to be unexpectedly good for photos.

"Have you known Max long?" the doctor asked.

"Not very," she said. "We met when I first arrived in

Africa." Mirie knew he assumed she had come on Max's account. "We're friends."

"I have trouble with American . . ." the Australian persisted.

"We're mates," said Mirie, with a definiteness she didn't quite feel. "Like you and he are."

"Is that some funny way of saying you don't fancy him?"

"I think the world of him. But we're not . . . together."

"Ah, yes . . ." Dahlgren thought a moment, as the ululations and trumpeting subsided. "When I first saw you, I thought, Max's found himself a sheila, but why the bloody hell's he bringing a bird here of all places?"

"Didn't think I could take it?"

"I was wrong." With that, Dahlgren said good-bye.

Mirie joined Joseph, the white-robed chief, and the rest of the tribe to watch the Cessna speed toward the mountain, lift off the bumpy airstrip, turn crosswind and head in the direction of Kwendela.

o   o

She gave Joseph her shirts, that is, Jonathan's old shirts. The boy took them away without a word. The lack of ceremony for the old shirts was disappointing. Like the chief's son, she thought, departing love deserved more of a send-off.

Joseph scrubbed the shirts in a tin wash pail, laid them out to dry on thornbushes and pressed them with an iron heated in the campfire. And, having misunderstood Mirie's overture, he replaced the shirts in the tent.

Mirie found the shirts cuff-to-cuff on her sleeping bag, so crisp and fresh they seem to have walked there by themselves.

"No, Joseph," she said, returning them immediately. "These are for you to keep." Maybe he thinks they're women's clothes, she thought, and hastened to explain that they were for a man. Joseph took them away, as if she had given him not a gift but an order.

Though small for his age, Joseph was not at all childlike. If anything, he seemed very old, as if he had inherited from his missionary stepparents a sense of purpose that ruled out playfulness. Perhaps he was dour only with white people. But, Mirie reflected, he was no different with the tribal people, with whom he had grown up. When Joseph returned to help her cook dinner, he was wearing one of the shirts. The shirttails reached his knees. The slightest smile came and went, a meniscus vanishing behind a cloud.

ɔ ɔ

Now that there was more time and Max had shot all he wanted to on the plains, he was more amenable to exploring the mountain. It was his idea to hire a local to lead them, which to Mirie seemed more trouble than it was worth.

As the locals had no use for money, Max offered salt, which could be used to cure meat and as currency at the trading post. Nevertheless, no one volunteered, until Joseph negotiated with one of his relatives, a sinewy older man who was an ace tracker, who agreed to lead them in return for salt for his family. The salt had to be disbursed among several wives, kin and cousins— his family seemed to extend to the entire tribe. And there were arguments over portions. But at last the expedition set off.

Max and the tracker walked ahead; Mirie and Joseph followed in the car. The tracker pointed out animal spoor crisscrossing the slopes, but the only animals Mirie actually saw were small ones. Curious hyraxes popped out from nowhere and skittered off. Colobus monkeys screeched and leaped to lower branches for a closer look.

Every so often, they had to stop while Max and the tracker hacked through the underbrush with pangas to clear a path for the car. While the men bushwhacked, Mirie photographed.

She pursued a scarab beetle that, using its hind legs, was pushing a baseball-size wad of dung. But the ball kept rolling away, and the beetle chased after it. Mirie followed dung ball and beetle around the forest floor. Her knees ached from squatting. Then a shadow blocked the sunlight, arm raised, poised to strike. Joseph brought down a stick full force beside her. Mirie gasped and fell backward as a snake slithered within inches of her. Joseph struck it again. The snake reared up from the blow, writhed and curled back on itself. Again and again, the boy beat it until it lay lifeless in the grass, its head smashed.

"It goes under her," said Joseph, as Max came running. The boy made a waving motion with his hand. "Mirie has courage. She does not move."

"You're right, Joseph, Mirie has lots of courage," said Max, and then, with a pointed sideways glance, asked Mirie, "Didn't see it, did you?"

She shook her head. She ran her fingers along the back of the limp snake, a gold and black mosaic of a thousand minute arrowheads. "Was it poisonous?" she asked, almost as an afterthought.

"No, but it could have been," said Max.

"I was caught up in the picture," said Mirie.

"I know. But you were about to sit on a snake." He said to the boy, "Good job," as he tossed the snake aside. Now Max took over the driving, and with the tracker leading the way on foot, they continued the rough ascent.

The farther they went, the more Mirie appreciated the difficulty of tracking game there, in contrast with tracking on the open plain. It would have been hard to see an elephant twenty feet in front of her on the forested slopes. She reflected, too, on Joseph's allusion to the hills that shook. Did this happen centuries before, or in Joseph's lifetime, or in the confluence of dreams and everyday life that in Joseph's mind ran together like two tributaries of the same stream?

"Why do your people live on the plains, Joseph?"

"It has always been so. It is their way, and they know no other," said Joseph. "It is hot there. It is where the devil said to Jesus, 'Turn these rocks into bread.' But here it is worse. It is where the mountain spirits live. When they are angry, they raise their fists and the mountain shakes. This is what my people believe."

"And what do you believe?"

"I am modern. I know how to read and write. When I grow up, I will teach my people to be modern. She told me I must do this."

"Your stepmother?"

"No. *Her*," he said. "I was in church and we were singing. There was lightning and the candles blinked many times and went out. It was then that I saw her. She was fuzzy at first, like television when the picture is not clear."

Mirie went along with Joseph right up until the point where his visions began to suffer from bad reception.

"I do not cheat you," said Joseph, his feelings ruffled by Mirie's incredulity. "I know. At home I watch 'Kojak.' When she became clear, she held out her arms and sang and we closed our eyes and sang, too. She said my name, Joseph, and told me what to do. When the song ended, she was gone, and the candles came alive again. The people cried they were so happy. She visited many places after that. She visited people at wells, and in the market, and people queued up for paraffin—they saw her, too. She told me I must teach my people to be modern and forget the old ways."

"Not all the old ways, I hope," said Max, who had been listening to Joseph's story. "There it is. It's inevitable," he said to Mirie. "He wants to toss out his whole culture for 'Kojak.' "

As they made their way up, the tracker pointed out the spoor of bushbuck. The African pointed but did not speak. Max identified tracks of a small cat, probably a genet. Six hours from camp, deep in the highland forests, the tracker stopped more frequently, as if the higher he went, the more difficult it became for him to go on. Finally, he planted the butt of his spear in the ground.

Joseph jumped out of the car. Mirie wished she could have understood; the man and the boy were having a heated, florid argument. When they finished debating, the guide retreated down the slope.

"He believes all the old stories. He goes no more," said Joseph, but tried to reassure them: "It is no problem. It is just there." And to show that he himself was immune to superstition, Joseph jumped out of the car and ran ahead.

"What's just there? Another vision?" Mirie remarked to Max.

"Come off it," said Max with sudden irritation. "As if you and I don't have even more ludicrous ones."

"Why are you angry?" asked Mirie.

He gave her a long serious look, then jerked the car in gear and continued up the slope.

Ever since the mishap with the bees, Max had been inexplicably cool. His diffidence made her self-conscious. Her inclination a few nights before had seemed natural enough at the time, but she somehow had overstepped the terms of companionship. It wasn't as if she had thrown herself at him, not even close. His mercurial nature irked her: he opened up, then retreated into aloofness.

The climb was now too much for the car. Max said the choices were either to hike the rest of the way, with the risk of running into animals, or to turn back. Mirie would not hear of turning back. Max honked to signal Joseph, then shut off the engine. As Mirie was about to speak, Max motioned for her to be quiet. Mirie immediately thought he was listening for animals. At first she heard nothing, then she became aware of a barely audible white noise.

Taking as much gear as they could carry, they followed Joseph's footprints over narrow switchbacks. Their tracks mingled with the impressions of elephant feet and sharper cloven hoof prints, squashed elephant dung of half-digested vegetation and strong-smelling buffalo manure. Though narrow, the trail was free of obstructions, elephants having pulled down branches and stripped bark from the trees, leaving only a few tattered streamers. The trail flattened and fanned out, and the white noise became the sound of rushing water. At last, they reached a clearing. Water shooting from sheer cliffs high above tumbled into a pool in the rocky glade. After the hot floodplain, where water holes were distant, and every drop of drinking water had to be hoarded, the sight of clear flowing water seemed too good to be true.

37

The water was beckoning, and
the smooth rocks inviting. What a welcoming place Joseph had
brought them to. But where was he? The boy had seemingly
vanished into the forest. Mirie called out. "He'll be back," Max
said.

Max was cooling his feet in the shallow water and studying
the configurations of the rocks, cliffs and falls. He climbed up
beside Mirie. Then, while he examined his feet for leeches, he
said, "Don't look up, but he's watching us . . . Behind the
rocks." He put on his shoes. "I'm going to have a look around,"
he announced, loudly enough to be heard easily over the falling
water. "I'd sure like to know where Joseph went . . ."

Instead of walking around the periphery, Max cut across
the pond. That is, he jumped from rock to cobble, cobble to
rock, arms straight out for balance. He wobbled, recovered and
jumped to the next cobble, big enough for one foot only. But
this time he had judged wrong. The mossy stone was slippery
as oil. He tipped to one side, grabbed at the air, a foot flailed,
and with a resigned "Oh, no," he hit the water full force.

From the rocks above, Joseph's head popped up from his
hiding place. He giggled, a sound that Mirie could not have
conceived coming from him. When he realized that she saw
him, his laughter stopped momentarily, as if it might not be all
right to laugh. But Mirie, too, was laughing, and they shared

the joke. Sitting drenched in the pond, Max glowered at both of them, but they knew he wasn't at all angry. With a dignified air, the toppled giant rose and waded out, wringing water out of his T-shirt.

Then he stopped, transfixed, beneath a high rocky niche near the waterfall.

Mirie joined him at the water's edge. "What do you see?"

"You're too low. I'll help you," he said, swooping her up in his arms, and then, before she realized what was happening, depositing her in the chilly water. Then it was all-out war. They chased and splashed each other, the water having soothed away the discomfort between them. They were intoxicated by the churning, fast-flowing water, enough water to squander in play. Mirie aimed a fan of water at Joseph. The boy jumped back.

"Come on in, Joseph!" Max stripped off his shirt. "I'll teach you to swim." He proceeded to demonstrate. His broad shoulders tapered into a slim, long torso. Max the gawky one, the indifferent one. How was it that he had changed before her eyes, and that she now felt unbearably clumsy?

Joseph approached the water fearfully, and the swimming lesson did not go well. No amount of assurance from Max would convince the boy that swimming like a frog was a natural thing for a man to do. The boy sputtered and scrambled out, happier to watch the play from shore. Max swam behind the falls and disappeared under a jagged tooth of overhanging rock.

"Mirie, come here!" he shouted over the falls.

"No way," she called back, believing he had another trick in store.

"Get the flashlights," he said, and she realized he was serious.

Joseph ran to her, his demeanor suddenly pained and frightened. "You must not. It is forbidden."

"What's forbidden?"

"It is sacred. It is a house of spirits. They command the animals to come in, to make a sacrifice, but man is forbidden. My people fear the spirits. When the spirits are angry, the mountain roars. My people believe this."

And he did as well. If in his adoptive parents' home

Joseph's faith evoked a television Virgin, on the mountain, in whose flank his people lived, it was the spirits that spoke most forcefully. Having brought Max and Mirie to their enclave, Joseph was now torn with fear of having trespassed.

Max called again. Mirie frowned. "Stay here, Joseph. We'll be right back. We won't do anything to make the spirits angry. I promise." The boy scrambled up on a high rock away from the falls. He held his knees and rocked as if in a trance. She had misgivings about leaving him, but she had to follow Max.

She picked her way carefully around the falls over rocks and broken boulders littered with elephant dung. Making her way around the overhanging sheet of rock, she found herself at the opening of a cave. Skeins of moss festooned the opening. Light danced on the walls, reflected from muddy footprints. Small birds blinked from nests in crevices under petrified, crystallized branches, the remnants of ancient trees. A narrow path of unstable rocks, slippery with mud and dung, led downward into darkness.

In the channel dimly illuminated by light from outside, she caught up with Max.

He shone a flashlight into a crevice at the bottom of which were the bones of a baby elephant and an antelope skull. Mirie moved closer to the cave wall.

"Stay behind me and walk where there's dung," said Max. "If the rocks can support elephants, they'll support us."

The deeper they went, the darker it became. Glancing back, the entrance to the cave appeared as a far brilliance in the blackness, then as the channel curved, the light died completely. They picked their way, using flashlights to search the path for loose boulders and gaping holes that ended in forty-foot drops.

Thirty meters inside, the throat of the cave opened into a gigantic cavern. The sounds of the waterfall were amplified in the boulder-strewn emptiness, punctuated by shrieks and squeaks. Max started in the direction of the noises, then stopped when he realized Mirie was not behind him.

"Bats," he said. "You all right?"

She took a deep breath. She was, but she was trembling. Her clothes were wet and the cave was cold. Their flashlight beams were swallowed up in the blackness. The hall was as big as a baseball field, and there were smaller compartments off to the sides. Following the cries, they shone their lights into one of the side cabins. Thousands of eyes shone back. Bats disturbed by the light flew about and rehooked themselves upside down to the ceiling. Mirie shrank back from the breeze of a flying bat. The creatures milling about the ceiling looked to her like a topsy-turvy convention of windup toys wearing capes.

In the main hall, hourglass columns of rock supported the ceiling. The floor was piled high with boulders where the roof had caved in, and elsewhere was rent by cracks and a wide chasm where Mirie saw two more elephant skeletons. There were cul-de-sacs, some tall enough to walk in, others that could be entered only by crawling. Neither Mirie nor Max were keen to try.

They followed the walls around. Mirie's teeth chattered with cold and tension. She fired off questions to ease her nerves. Why did the cave attract so many animals? Why would they come in here when there was plenty to eat outside? How did they navigate in the dark? Was it possible large mammals had better night vision than anyone suspected?

Max had no answers, or he was not offering any. He drew his flashlight beam across the wall. In the cracked, broken, eroded hall, it was the walls that intrigued them above all else. They were chiseled and gouged in a free-form pattern that stopped a dozen feet up.

"Who do you think did that?" asked Mirie as Max scratched at the wall with his pocketknife. The rock fell away in powdery chunks. "Joseph begged us not to go in here. He said people were forbidden. But somebody's obviously mining this. What is he hiding?"

"I don't think he's hiding anything."

"Then who did that?" she asked. "Do you think there's gold in here? Or precious stones?"

"In a way . . ."

"Then Joseph's people *were* mining here . . ."

"Who said anything about people?" said Max. "There aren't any human tracks."

247

"But at one time they must have. What if the people were killed in a rock slide, and they took it as an omen and stopped coming?"

Max shook his head. He switched off Mirie's flashlight and his own. They sat together, amid the shrieking bats and the dull roar of the falls, unable to see each other in the ravening blackness.

"Are you frightened?" he asked.

"No. It's okay this way."

"First thing we need is a hiding place," said Max, "where they can't see, smell, or hear us."

"Or step on us," added Mirie. It was understood that they had been seized by the same idea, to forgo the space and light of the plains for a cathedral of darkness whose pilgrims were animals.

38

Ivory tusks clunked against rock, a hollow reverberation that mingled with rumbling in the blackness. A storm of shrieking fruit bats swept pell-mell through the cavern bound for the moonlit night beyond the roaring curtain of waterfall. Directly below the boulder where Max and Mirie were stationed came a soft scraping sound, an elephant rubbing against their perch.

The intense beam of Max's penlight traced the haunch of an elephant, then darted to the calf beside her.

We're close enough to jump on her back, thought Mirie, but kept the thought to herself, for the elephants would leave at even the hint of a foreign presence.

The mother pushed against the cave wall with the full force of her three tons, her tusks chiseling out the etched pattern that days before Mirie had been convinced could only have been man-made. As the rock gave way in chunks, the cow scooped them up with tusks and trunk and maneuvered them into her mouth.

Her tuskless calf tried to do the same. It pushed the wall with its head, and when a few loose crumbs sheered off, the calf vainly tried to lasso them with its trunk. When that didn't work, it flopped its trunk on the cave floor, raising more dust than rocks. Shaking its head in frustration, the calf went under its mother's forelegs to get the minerals the easy way. It suckled, while the mother munched rock contentedly.

An overpowering odor of elephants permeated the cave. All over the amphitheater, hidden in the blackness, elephants were parked against the cave walls, gouging rock, dropping boulders and kicking up dust. Max and Mirie were used to the pungent smell of elephants and dung, and as the cave was well ventilated, it was not especially unpleasant. The dust, however, had Max perpetually on the brink of a sneezing fit. But this was the least of their difficulties.

Max could not photograph elephants he could not see, and if he tried to see the elephants, by shining bright lights at them, they retreated from the cave as quickly and silently as they had come.

Max had devised ways around this. The first morning, with daylight seeping into the empty cave, he came up with a plan for shooting in the dark.

They mapped out stations—cul-de-sacs and high smooth boulders—where they could position themselves out of the elephants' way. He attached a flash to his camera and jerry-rigged a second, with electronic slave, to a nearby boulder. Exposures were tricky; the cavern absorbed light like a sponge. He loaded fast film, but not too fast or the pictures might turn out grainy. He abandoned the motor drive; the noise would scare off the elephants. In penumbral darkness the tall eroded rocks seemed to metamorphose into elephants, and these Max used as stand-ins as he paced off distances for focusing.

It was ingenious, said Mirie. Max disagreed. He thought it a crude way of shooting. He didn't have the right equipment, but the test shots would help him refine a technique for the return trip.

Station One was in the most dangerous section of the cave, the passageway to the opening behind the falls. But there, the elephants' route was predictable. Chasms and crevasses forced the animals to keep to a known path, less than two feet wide, which they negotiated blindly. Elephants came to the cave in slow procession behind a matriarch, trunk-to-tail, one foot placed carefully ahead of the other. Cows guided calves with their trunks.

Mirie marveled at how noiselessly they moved, while on the same path her own feet crunched crumbling rocks and sent them sputtering into the chasms. Max shined the flashlight back to be sure she was all right.

"If you fall in," he said, "Joseph will always believe that this place is haunted."

"Isn't it?" asked Mirie, hugging the wall as she made her way around a crevasse.

Despite their coaxing, Joseph refused to come with them into the cave. They told him that only animals visited the cave, not spirits. The boy believed it might be all right for white people to enter, but not for an African. Though he himself was "modern," he believed that, at night on the mountain, elephants and spirits were one and the same, and he was not about to risk angering them.

Max and Mirie became nocturnal for the elephants. They slept during the day, entered the cave in the late afternoon and stayed until morning. From their first vantage point, deep in the passageway, they watched the cave entrance, hoping that the head of an elephant would appear silhouetted in the brilliant light. But the elephants never showed in daylight, though other animals wandered in, enticed by the salty rock: buffaloes and bushbucks, monkeys, hyraxes and genets. At dusk the light at the cave opening dimmed and quickly died. Moving to a safe perch in the amphitheater, Max and Mirie sat huddled in their sleeping bags, straining to distinguish anomalous sounds from the falling water and chittering bats.

Bats were their flying alarm clocks. In the early evening the adults left the roosts in a flapping, screeching phalanx to feed in the forest, leaving behind the young. Once or twice, the bats' departure coincided with the elephants' arrival. More often the elephants came after midnight. Sometimes the elephants did not come until the early hours of morning when the bats flew back from the night's foraging. Or they came and, smelling Max and Mirie, left immediately. Or they never showed up at all, and Mirie and Max quit the long night's vigil stiff, chilled and discouraged.

When the elephants did come into the cave's amphitheater, Mirie feared they would hear her heart pounding. Not a word to Max, not so much as a whisper, all sound, all movement suppressed, or the elephants would be gone. Holding Max's Leica, she waited.

The elephants spread out along the walls, rumbling to communicate in the dark. Mirie felt the sound as much as heard it, the air throbbing with the elephants' basso purrs.

Feet sloshing in mud, a tusk digging into rock, hide brushing against a volcanic boulder, these gave away the animal's position. Max aimed a small, intense penlight beam. The tiny light, they found, most elephants tolerated, at least for a short time. Once Max had a glimpse of the elephant, he aimed his camera into the darkness, and light exploded in the cave.

For an instant Mirie saw a ghostly white image of elephants tusking among boulders and hourglass columns, immediately replaced by an afterimage dancing with amoeboid elephants. As for Max, the shutter mechanics of his camera prevented his seeing the elephant he photographed. With the penlight Max checked to see that the elephant had not silently fled, then touched Mirie's arm, to indicate she should shoot. For a fraction of a second they both saw the giants illuminated, a moment of awareness before they were blinded by the flash.

There was no anticipating how the elephants would react. Some fled immediately. Others were unbothered even when flashed at several times. Using penlight and flash, they discovered that the elephants took time off from their diggings. They photographed a female scooping up dust in her trunk and throwing it over her back. A small bull approached, sniffing her tail end to test if she was in estrus. The male draped his trunk over the female's back while she continued her dust bath. His erection dangling to the cave floor, he tried to mount her. She flapped her ears and edged away, indifferent both to his attentions and the repeated flashes.

The matriarch trumpeted a shrill blast that called the herd together to leave. After the elephants had gone, Mirie and Max climbed down from the rock. They stretched to shake off the cold that had settled into their cramped bodies. They compared what they had seen, to separate an image conjured from the darkness to what their cameras might actually have captured. Had Max seen the small bull attempt to mount another female? Did Mirie catch the calf that wandered within range of its mother's shower of falling rock? Did she see the mother nudge the calf out of the way?

They were lightheaded. They drank the last of a thermos of hot tea, trading the cup back and forth as in a libationary ritual. Then, like the elephants, they carefully made their way out toward the brilliance of the cave mouth that, when their eyes adjusted, was only the pale foreshadowing of dawn.

39

"**W**e have a few more days," Max said over breakfast. He was subdued after the morning radio call to Dahlgren. "Chris is delayed in Kwendela."

"What a break!" said Mirie.

"Yeah." Max stirred his coffee.

"What's wrong?" She was happy where they were, though evidently neither Joseph nor Max shared her enthusiasm.

"He said something about an infectious outbreak."

"Yesterday he said the hunter was doing well. What happened?"

"He gave me a roundabout answer about how the patient had taken a bad turn. Trouble flaring up in the extremities. The body's defense system fighting back. Worried about an attack on the central nervous system. He says it's been coming for five years. He said it could be terminal."

"Five years? What's he talking about?"

Max nodded. "I asked him point blank, 'How's the hunter?' He says, " 'Oh, that bloke. He'll be all right.' "

"I'm lousy at riddles."

"Five years. The president's been in power for five years. He's telling us there's trouble. He can't say it on the radio, not flat out. If you talk about it, and military spooks are listening, it's sedition."

"You don't think this is expat paranoia?"

"From anyone else, yes. Not Chris."

"Where does that leave us?"

Max looked up at the pewter sky heavy with rain clouds. "I told him if he doesn't come back soon, he's going to need water wings to land." He turned to Joseph. "The doctor wants you to tell the chief that his son is going to be well and strong."

"We are leaving the mountain?" asked Joseph, suddenly perked up.

"Yes," said Max, then, when he saw Mirie's chagrin, added, "Stay if you want, Mirie. But if we want to keep eating, I have to pick up supplies." He rested his hand on Joseph's shoulder. "And in return for the good news, maybe you can get us some fresh meat." Max continued, "Now listen, Joseph. Mirie and I have stayed in the cave all night long, and it's a good place. There are no bad spirits. When your people say the mountain roared and the earth shook, it's not the spirits. It's the cave falling down. You know why?" Max showed the boy a rock from the cave, then smashed it against a harder piece of basalt. "See, this is soft. Elephants eat rocks like this."

"You make a joke. Elephants eat trees, not rock."

"No, the elephants eat the rock, because it has salt, and they need the salt. When the mountain roars, it's because big rocks like this are falling down inside. And sometimes, when elephants are in there, they are killed."

Joseph nodded wide-eyed, believing Max's explanation, and believing as well that spirits were behind it. He glanced apprehensively at the waterfall.

"You may be modern," said Max sympathetically, "but you don't like camping on the gods' doorstep, do you?" He handed Joseph a chunk of cave rock. The boy stared at it, then dropped it, as if terrified at his own audacity at handling a plaything of the gods. "All right," said Max. "I'll take you down." Joseph, more animated than he had been in days, hurried off to collect his belongings.

"He brought us to the cave," said Mirie, "but he can't go in."

"To him it's a haunted house."

"And to me it's magical. I wish we could stay here."

"You'll change your mind when the monsoon hits. I take it you don't want to come along for the ride."

"If you don't need me to help . . . Will you be back in time for the night shift?"

"No telling." He gave her arm a friendly squeeze. "Don't harass the elephants while I'm gone."

"I wouldn't think of it," she said, vexed by the brotherly tease.

Having been together constantly, the prospect of sudden separation left her feeling unexpectedly at a loss. It was all the same to Max whether she stayed or came with him, and this disheartened her. Not that she considered changing her mind and going with him. To the contrary, she was more resolved to stay behind, alone, to puzzle out her malaise in private.

o o

Standing under the falls, she scrubbed off as best she could the human smell that would frighten off the elephants more surely than the wave of a penlight or a flash. She was not as eager to sit in the cave without Max. Who wants to be alone in the dark? The elephants probably wouldn't even show up. On the other hand, a light rain was falling, and the cave was better shelter than the tent.

She moved the gear into the cave as she and Max had done. After the fruit bats left, the cave quieted down and there were no other visitors for several hours. The only activity was within Mirie herself as she traced the uneven course of her emotions. She was annoyed with herself and angry at Max's wretched neutrality. His loss, she told herself, but it didn't make her feel any better. She rationalized the painful imbalance. This was the trouble with all sexual transactions, actual or unrealized. No wonder Max liked being alone. Sex messed things up between men and women who could otherwise get along quite well. What good was it? Genetic diversity? All this tragicomic fumbling for the sake of scrambled genes? Only a god with a sense of humor could think of that one.

She thought of the variations of lovemaking—sucking, licking, smelling, burrowing into another's flesh—a kind of reenactment of the way a newborn seizes hold of life. Lovers

256

thrashed about as if—no, because—life depended on it, joined momentarily with each other and a dimly remembered nascent self. It was a good joke, this altogetherness of sex, love, life-beginning, baby-making, shitting and pissing, ecstasy and excrement, all tucked between the legs. Oh, Max, when we are out here like the first man and woman on earth, what is stopping us? You are as wary of me as I am of you. We defend ourselves with a vengeance—you from the most natural desire, and I from your indifference. We can pretend we're brave explorers in the wilderness, but we guard our secret souls.

The elephants showed up. It was a small group. With the penlight she counted six—cows and calves and one young male. They parked themselves on the far side of the amphitheater. She could hear their growls and tusking, but they were out of shooting range. She could do nothing but hope they might wander her way. This was, as Max had said, a crude way of doing things. She wondered whether it was raining harder outside, and whether Max was already back and asleep in the tent.

A breeze tickled her ear as a bat flew by on its way to the roost. She realized she had fallen asleep, and when she aimed her light around, she found that the elephants had gone. Max hadn't missed much.

As first light seeped into the cave opening, Mirie packed up her knapsack and climbed down from the boulders. She picked her way carefully across the amphitheater, past the chiseled columns, staying close to the walls, as far as possible from the places where the floor opened up. She followed the elephants' tracks through the amphitheater to where it divided into cul-de-sacs and the long passageway leading to the opening.

She neared a wide, shallow side cabin. Suddenly, there was a shrill trumpeting. An elephant appeared, trunk raised, sniffing and shaking its head threateningly in her direction. Mirie froze. Her heart beat fast, and the air seemed to vibrate in her ears, as if the elephant were still giving voice subsonically to its anger. She was stunned into clarity. She did not believe the elephant would charge blindly in the dark, not with all the obstructions and chasms. Moreover, she was a step from the safety of the first station, the boulder pile closest to the passageway.

The elephant sniffed the air delicately, ears fanned out. It kicked at the dust several times, shook its massive head, then went back into the side cabin. Mirie waited to hear the clunk of tusk on rock, then climbed as quietly as she could.

But not quietly enough. The sound of her scrambling up the boulders brought the elephant out again, but by that time she was well out of reach. The elephant trumpeted. She expected it would leave the cave, but to her surprise it again returned to the cabin. Why didn't the elephant go? The passageway to the falls was clear, even dimly lit. Why was the elephant staying in the cave? Was its desire for the minerals that much greater than its fear of humans?

Making her way to the very top of the boulders, Mirie edged around to the side facing the cul-de-sac. She might as well shoot pictures, since she could not leave until the elephant was gone.

The penlight revealed, to her surprise, that there was not one elephant but three, two adult females and one nearly full-grown youngster. The smallest elephant chiseled the walls. The two adults were having some sort of agitated communication. One female was particularly restive, swaying back and forth and swinging its trunk in a violent, aimless way. It leaned against the wall, its hind legs bent in a half-sit. The other female hovered close, occasionally touching the other elephant with its trunk as if to comfort it.

The distressed elephant stood up and paced, dribbling urine and feces. The second cow rumbled as the first elephant, the sick one, leaned back and lay down, then kicked backward to get up again.

What did Mirie see in that suffering elephant? She thought she was watching the animal die and hoped it would die soon, to end its agony. She thought of her own father's sudden, quick, fatal heart attack without a chance to say good-bye, and her mother's long drifting into death. But those were her parents. This was an elephant, an anonymous animal. Why was Mirie transfixed, watching it kick and lurch, kneeling on its drooling hindquarters, now pushing the wall with its head, now lying down and awkwardly rising, and all the while the other female touching it with trunk and tusks?

She knew what to do, but doubted it would work. It was a gamble, after all, the whole thing. No certainties anywhere, not in old family photos or her dad's horses or in Jonathan's promise of fidelity. Nor in her decision to throw herself into her photographs, as if focusing on work alone would somehow clarify her life. Pretty funny, wasn't it? But there was no one to respond. It was only she and the elephants now.

Yes. Now.

Quietly, Mirie took Max's camera from the knapsack and clipped the battery pack to her belt, telling herself over and over why it was all wrong, it wasn't going to work, bad shooting angle, no light, no way to set up the second flash. She couldn't move without running the risk of further disturbing the elephants. What if she shot, and an elephant panicked and fell into a hole?

The elephant paced in the chamber, shaking its head and touching itself under its hind legs. Mirie took up the camera, the protective frame distancing her from the elephants' suffering. The female battered the wall with its tusks, then collapsed on its forelegs, pushing at the base of the wall as if it were trying to stand on its head. Mirie snapped the shutter. When the flash spots went away, she saw that the other female had draped her trunk over the back of the kneeling elephant. It lay down, then its back leg flailed to push itself up again, back into the praying position. Liquid dribbled from between its legs. Mirie shot again. She was blinded for a few seconds, then she saw that the kneeling elephant was expelling something like a big shiny garbage bag. Mirie shot again. The bag burst and there was a pool of liquid and a large visceralike lump between the elephants' legs. Mirie shot again as the elephant shuddered violently and the lump was deposited on the cave floor. Mirie shot again. The light of the flash did not disturb the elephant in its death throes.

But she did not die. Instead, the elephant turned around and extended its trunk at the wet mass. Then the other two elephants joined in, prodding the mess gently with tusks and forelegs, as if they were trying to raise it. For a moment, all Mirie could see were feet and tusks and trunks. The smallest elephant stepped away, and shook its head and returned to mining the rock, while the other two sniffed and nudged the mass with her feet.

The mound stirred. Did it? Something moved, only a little and all in shadows, but Mirie knew. Now, at last, she knew for sure. That she had witnessed not a dying but the everyday miracle of a birth. She watched in awe as the two females, using trunks and feet, lifted off the remainder of the fetal sac. For a time they seemed more interested in the sac than the baby, tossing it about with their trunks, and finally the mother ate the sac while the other elephant kicked at the ground where it had been. Then, using their feet, the two tried again to raise the calf. But the floor was wet. The calf wobbled and slipped back into a formless heap. The two adults nudged it to its feet, and again the calf staggered and fell down. Mirie shot another picture, and this time the midwife elephant left the mother and newborn and walked directly in front of Mirie's station. She shook her head and trumpeted. Mirie lay down the camera. It was enough now.

Finally, the calf was able to stand unassisted. Its head was flattened and rubbery compared with the sculpted brows of the adults. The calf staggered under its mother's legs, but it seemed to have no instinct guiding it to the right place. It even sucked its own trunk for a second before falling down. After it had made several staggering attempts to find a teat, the mother used her trunk to nudge the baby under her forelegs for its first drink.

Another hour or two passed, then the procession—the adult female in front, cow and calf in the middle and the small female in the rear—walked toward the light of the cave opening and out into the day.

40

She lay inside the tent, wrestling with a gut panic that she had blown the shots, that the exposure was wrong, that the flash hadn't even reached the elephants, that the shots would be blurs, blanks, that she'd made up the whole birth sequence in a boredom-induced daydream. What if condensation had already spoiled the roll? If only she had had a chance to set up a second flash, or a better shooting angle. She felt like she wouldn't sleep until the roll was developed, until she saw absolute proof of a moment that she couldn't entrust solely to the illuminative powers of memory. If only Max had been there with her.

She checked the camera; the roll was partly exposed. She had shot. There had been elephants. And through the miasma of self-doubt, she remembered her elation when she had seen the expelled heap stir with life.

Raindrops spattered the tent, a dull arhythmic pinging against the steady roar of falling water. She rewound the roll of film, popped it from the camera, wrote "Toto" on orange tape and pasted it on the roll, sealed the film in a plastic canister, swaddled it in a plastic bag along with the other exposed rolls of film, and tucked it deep in her camera bag. Insistent raindrops soothed her fretfulness, and she fell asleep in the downpour.

o o

A noise woke her. Max was clearing his throat outside the tent, as if to announce his return. She stared myopically as he negotiated a path around the piles of clothes and equipment. He sat beside her. His wet clothing stuck to him. The brim of his cap appeared to have melted in the rain.

"Sleeping Beauty," he said. "How did it go last night?"

She sat up in the quilted bag and brushed back her sleep-tousled hair. "I am so glad you're back." She reached for her glasses. "Last night I saw something . . ." She stopped, not wanting to burst out with it. "You're soaked, Max."

"You will be, too. Let's move into the cave now. I don't see the rain ending before nightfall."

She would wait to tell him.

"Well, our rescue is at hand," he said.

"Oh," she said, disappointed, though the news was not unexpected.

Max went to wash under the falls, and when he returned to the tent for dry clothes, he seemed to fill up the entire tent.

"Max . . ." she began.

"I'm sorry to leave, too. But there's no choice."

"Yes," she said. "I need to, and it's not just because of my visa and the cameras."

"You have personal things—"

"No . . . Listen, Max."

"Let's go," he interrupted, taking up the equipment. "It's warmer inside."

They moved into the cave, and set up in one of the smaller cul-de-sacs, where the ground was flat and comfortable. With the sky enshrouded with rain clouds, the cave was almost completely dark. It was only early afternoon, though, and many hours before any elephants were likely to appear.

"I have to tell you about last night, Max . . ." In the dark she could not make out his face. She had to imagine his intent eyes as she told him about how there hadn't been any elephants for the longest time and that the night had seemed endless.

"After a while I fell asleep. I woke up in the early morning. There was a little light from the opening. I waited a bit and then got ready to leave, using the flashlight to be sure I wasn't going to run into any animals. Then I followed the regular path.

When I went by the side cabin, an elephant trumpeted. She came out, sort of looming over me, blocking the path." Mirie leaned forward and clasped Max's forearms, to breach the darkness between them. "The dumb part is, I wasn't terrified. I was pretty excited."

"That you were about to have a head-on collision with an elephant? . . . Yes, that would be exciting."

"No. I knew that everything was going to be all right if I kept calm. I didn't move, and when she backed off, I climbed onto the boulders." The contact between them suddenly distracted her. "Are you listening?"

"Yes."

She told him she had seen a baby elephant born. She told him she hadn't known what she was shooting, that she had shot reflexively, thinking she was watching a sick elephant; then the baby had been born. "I have film. Whether the pictures will come out . . ."

"But you saw it."

"Yes, in a way, in the dark, and without knowing. But if the pictures come out—"

"I've never known anyone who has seen the moment of birth."

She longed to see his face, his expression. "I wished you were here."

"Me, too," he said.

"You don't believe the pictures will come out, do you?"

"It doesn't matter what either of us believes. You won't know till you put them on a light table. Then maybe I'll see your pictures double-truck in *National Geographic*."

She felt stung when he said that. Yes, she was talking about the pictures, and he used that as a way to say good-bye. There was a silence.

"What is it?" he asked.

"You know. We do fine, don't we, as long as we restrict ourselves to talking technical stuff? But it isn't so clear-cut." Her insides churned. "Not for me anyway." She tried to withdraw, but he held her arm. "Oh, don't pretend you don't know," she blurted, furious that he was playing with her. What was the difference? She would have it out, and the worst would be over. Maybe it was easier that she couldn't see him. "I don't know why it happened, but it happened, and that's making me feel ridiculous right now. If you're not attracted to me, it's not the end of the world, is it? Sometimes I think you've given up women, so maybe I shouldn't take it personally."

"Given up women?" He laughed softly. "I've tried and failed many times."

"Not sex, but given up on the possibility of it ever working out. You won't take a chance, will you?" She was immediately sorry she had said that. He let go of her arm.

Her mouth had the dry taste of dread. This damned one-sided wanting; it was like being frozen alive. It was like a nightmare when she would try to run away but get nowhere, would try to scream and no sound would come out. Max didn't say a word. He no doubt was hoping that the whole stupid incident would blow over.

She talked quietly, suppressing an ache in the back of her throat. "I admire you, whether we go on knowing each other or never see each other again. That's all you need know. I'll shut up now. It's no better playing the fool in the dark than it is anywhere else."

Then he said very slowly, as if every word were an effort, "If I've been trying to steer away from you, I haven't done a good job. I asked you to come."

"You think I don't understand about you."

She felt his hands on her face. His fingers traced the vein down the center of her forehead, around her eyes and over her cheeks. "I'm afraid you do." He pulled her toward him, as if he were scooping her up and molding her to him. She was surrounded by him, moving with him as if they had been lovers before.

She felt herself cry out when he went inside, but her voice was lost in his tense breath. All other sound was drowned out. Max, the ground beneath them, the darkness above, were all together in a rough motion. She was shaken by her own pleasure, and it shook him, too, with a hard shudder, and then there was nothing but their breathing together.

41

Between the goats and the soldiers the ride back to Frances' house was taking an awfully long time. The rusted taxi stalled when the driver stopped for the goats, and Max had to help push the car to get it started again. At dragon's-teeth roadblocks every few kilometers, a sullen soldier would peer in and wave them on. The repetitive songs on the radio were interrupted by bulletins, a mixture of news and propagandistic pep talks.

". . . Four university professors have been arrested for taking part in the traitorous plot against the president," said an announcer in a dead monotone. "The president declared political assembly by groups of four persons or more against the law." There was the sound of pages riffling, then the announcer continued drearily, "The president welcomed foreign visitors to the International Horticultural Symposium. Wearing a red rose in his lapel, he spoke of the roses planted along Freedom Road and throughout the city in honor of the symposium . . . Kwendela has never looked more colorful . . ."

"Yeah, that's a good idea," said Max. They passed a sprawl of squatters' shacks in a sea of red brown mud. "When they run out of maize, let them eat roses."

o o

Mirie had not wanted to leave, but once they were flying, she felt light and unencumbered. She'd look at Max, and it was as if her whole being lifted on a swell of memory.

For Max the trip back to Kwendela had been rather different. The flight was worse than before; this time the motion got to him immediately. He clutched a paper bag, his face gray with airsickness. Shouting over the engine roar, Dahlgren told Max what he had only been able to hint at during the radio calls: shortly after he, Dahlgren, had returned to the city, a junior army officer had shot at the president. He missed. He and other supposed conspirators were captured and executed. An all-out housecleaning and roundup of the president's enemies followed. A minister who had been the president's chief critic was arrested on vague charges. During class an outspoken professor was kidnapped by soldiers, and when students tried to stop the arrest, the soldiers opened fire. Dahlgren's medical relief organization petitioned, on humanitarian grounds, that the families of the dead be notified and the injured be treated in hospital instead of left to die in jail. In a gesture of calculated magnanimity, the president's office "forgave" the students, and the wounded were moved to a hospital. At the same time, the president publicly decorated high-level army officers—Dahlgren snorted derisively—" 'for their heroic defense of continuing peace and stability in our fine young nation.' "

Dahlgren made a stop on the way back to Kwendela. He landed the Cessna in the village where Joseph's stepparents lived, and the missionaries met the plane at the airstrip. The boy's stepmother had on a limp dress; Mirie guessed she and the woman were about the same age. Her weatherworn face brightened when she saw Joseph. She spoke to the boy in his own tribal language, then switched to a plain, slow American English. "What a nice new shirt," she told Joseph, and thanked Mirie. Their family didn't fuss over clothing, she said, but she was glad Joseph now had some good shirts for church. Her husband remarked on the oversized shirt, "There's twice as much shirt as there is boy." His wife assured Joseph that "any day you'll be shooting up," but that in the meantime she might "take a tuck here and there." How long had it taken her to learn Joseph's language? asked Mirie. She claimed to be very much a beginner. Taking her hand, her husband insisted that she was a real linguist and that she was putting together a dictionary. They hoped eventually to translate the Bible into the local tongue. Good-byes were said, the plane was refueled, and Dahlgren, Max and Mirie flew off for Kwendela.

Flying over open savannah, they spotted a large herd of elephants, two to three hundred animals. The rainy months, she knew, were the elephants' mating season. Then the females tended to come into estrus and the elephants formed up into large herds. Between the rains the females and males went their separate ways. She was seeing wild elephants for the last time—that is (she reassured herself), the last time this trip.

The night before, no elephants had visited the cave. Mirie tried to convince Max that there was no point in leaving the mountain. Not yet. Dahlgren wouldn't be able to land in the wind and rain, and she and Max could share the elephants' mountain refuge a little longer. Max said no; this time the doctor was coming. As they made their way down to base camp, they heard the plane. By the time they arrived, Dahlgren had delivered the chief's son, bandaged but recuperating, to his father. His mission completed, he was ready to be off again.

o o

The taxi turned onto the fragrant wooded driveway of the house. Only the askari and the dog were there to greet them. Inside the house looked neat but deserted, and the quiet haven of Max's cabin seemed especially welcoming.

Mirie pressed her cheek to Max's chest.

It was possible, Mirie discovered, to make love on the diagonal, half-entangled in the mosquito netting draped from the bed canopy. He whispered as he touched her, and she dissolved. She lay lightly on top, moving against him.

"What are we going to do?" she said softly.

He stroked her hair. "You're going back to New York. You have your film, and business to settle. I leave for Cameroon in a couple of weeks. You can join me there. Or meet me in Virginia, when I go back to the States. Or maybe I'll come see you in New York."

"That sounds indefinite enough."

"As far as I'm concerned, it's very definite."

For some time they didn't speak, and then he said, as if they had been continuing the conversation the whole time, "I'm out of practice for this, you know."

She knew what he meant. "Well, we'll go slow. I'm used to going slow now . . . Look—it's still a whole lot easier than photographing an elephant giving birth."

He smoothed her hair, and studied her blue and brown eyes. "I can't stop everything else . . . I need to go off . . . If you get involved with me, you may come to resent me."

"I understand that you and I don't come with a lifetime guarantee. But what are we supposed to do—lie and pretend this didn't happen?"

"Listen." He touched her face. "I want you, Mirie. Much too much. But don't delude yourself pretending I'm somebody I'm not. I've done all my accommodating. This, I'm afraid, is as far as it goes."

She propped herself up and looked at them both, straddled naked, under the floating tent of netting. She shrugged. "All right. It doesn't seem all that bad to me so far."

"Nuts," said Max, abruptly rolling her off and pulling her close beside him.

ɔ   ɔ

The rains fell harder. The phones in the valley went dead, and the lights periodically failed. To make her plane reservation Max and Mirie had to drive into the city. Street barbers had rigged wobbly umbrellas to their chairs and were giving haircuts. Beggars missing arms and legs were posted on their regular corners. Jobless men huddled under corrugated roof sheds along with the mamas selling fruits and vegetables. Traffic stopped and started and soldiers patrolled the streets. The red roses lining Freedom Road bobbed in the rain, while queues for gas and kerosene grew longer. A snatch boy was beaten to death by a mob for stealing an orange. A cuckolded husband tried to commit suicide by throwing himself in front of a *basi* in which his wife and her boyfriend were riding. The *basi* missed the man, but the driver got out and beat him bloody for stepping in the way. Conventioners and tourists came and went, while the black market rate for dollars rose as more residents—African, Asian and white—tried to get their money out. Sales of household goods and good-bye parties for departing expatriates continued. So did dinner invitations extended to new arrivals, who were happy to be posted to a small country in Africa where the comfort level of expatriate life was high and the danger quotient relatively low. But people were circumspect in public, at least, about speaking of the assassination attempt. An Englishwoman ahead of Mirie at the airlines office remarked: "Our leave is long over due. It really is time for us to go. My husband is beginning to compromise his standards."

"Frightening," said Mirie. The woman did not catch her irony.

When it was her turn, Mirie reluctantly made a reservation.

o o

Bamboo grew luxuriantly in the rain. That lovely creaking sound, thought Mirie, as she threw her leg over Max's. Then came the stabbing awareness that it was the last day.

After breakfast Mirie steeled herself to pack. Max lay on the bed reading. Mirie dumped out the duffel bag on the bed and proceeded to repack. There was very little now, but it took her an inordinately long time. She packed blouses and skirts, and was glad that she had given the old shirts to Joseph, remembering how he had mistakenly returned them to her, laid out like headless torsos on her sleeping bag.

She glanced over. Max was looking at her over the edge of his book. "You're moving on African time this morning."

She made a face and he laughed.

She packed the light tripod, which conjured up her fiasco with Inspector Ng'bene. She packed the wooden bell Ruth had given her the night she and Max returned to Kwendela. Had she not lost her cameras, she would have been off on safari when Max returned, and she and Max might have missed each other altogether and forever.

There was the plastic bag stuffed with rolls of exposed film, labeled and marked; there, too, looking much like all the others, was the roll labeled "Toto." She zipped up her camera bag, which she would carry on the plane with her.

"You forgot this," said Max, handing her a small object that had been lying on the bed. It was the picture of Jonathan.

Her gaze moved from it to him, trying to decode his expression. What are you waiting for? she thought. You haven't discovered any secret. I'm not going to throw the picture against the wall, or set it on fire, or laugh or cry. "Don't do that, Max," she said quietly.

"What?"

"You know what. Shut me out." He didn't blink, didn't move a muscle. "If you want to know if I have any regrets, yes, that I didn't admit that it wasn't going to work, and that I didn't leave first."

"You did leave," he corrected.

"By the back door." She looked at the picture, as if she were addressing it as much as Max. "It does matter. It matters that people don't take each other so much for granted, because then it's not love anymore, but rituals of getting by and everyday lies."

"Okay." He lay down his book. "You're in luck. I'm not interested in just getting by, and lying gives me rashes. Moreover, I am too large to take for granted and you are too insistent. We should do very well."

Max scooped up her equipment and in two minutes the duffel was packed and padlocked. "Come on. We're going on safari."

42

A couple of hours from Kwendela, they were in sunny semidesert. Cumulus clouds floated lazily across the sky. A breeze ruffled the red lake. Max and Mirie walked the circumference, stopping now and then for Max to take pictures of desert flowers that had bloomed in the rains. Max photographed. Mirie did not. He had urged her to bring along his old camera, but she left it behind. She wanted to have their remaining time together without the temptation to work.

"How hot is it?" she asked.

"It'll simmer you nicely. Why? Are you thinking of going swimming?"

"I guess not."

Water lapped the shore, depositing wavy lines of red algae. Why had Max chosen to come here? Had the picture of Jonathan precipitated the unexpected pilgrimage, if that's what it was. "Do you suppose they're still there?" she asked as if her curiosity were purely of a scientific nature.

Max cleared his throat to cover a smile. "You mean the cameras that broke up my marriage?" he asked blandly, imitating her seemingly disinterested questioning. "I have never investigated the long-term effects of concentrations of sodium carbonate on cameras." Mirie laughed, a little abashed. He put his arm around her. "Now let's have a truce."

"Why? We haven't had a fight. Have we?"

"No, but I can't help but notice you sniffing around in the past." He ignored her protests. "The experiment failed," he continued. "The past did not go down with the cameras. It travels with me, whether I like it or not. When it's a silent partner, it helps me see farther and more sharply. But we don't always get along. Then it's like being sat on by an elephant."

"And now?"

He raised his arms, stretching luxuriantly toward the sun. "You just had to see this before you left."

Fat clouds rolled in, while Mirie and Max circled the lake. The water darkened to the color of blood. The sky grew ominous, and the air cooled rapidly. Gnarled branches of baobabs grasped at the sky. The first drops of rain painted the earth a deeper red and the dry grass a lustrous gold.

They ran the rest of the way back to the car. Mirie leaned over to his side, her feet pushing against the door for leverage. They kissed and caressed and the more ardent they became, the more they wedged themselves into the driver's seat. Mirie pried herself away, and, clearing the bags out of the way, they made a space to continue, though none too comfortably, what they had feverishly begun.

Afterward, he looked boyish, lips reddened and cheeks flushed. The lines on his forehead relaxed. Mirie felt the coming storm as acutely as she felt his embrace. She saw her time in Africa refracted through the raindrops. She saw the first rains when she and Max had driven Ruth and her brother and sisters to their house in the squatter city, where there were too many people and there was not enough food or drinking water or hope for the children's futures. She saw breakfasts with Frances, fresh-cut roses and Julius' hot scones. She recalled the luxury and grating ennui, waiting for her injured foot to mend and rains to subside. She saw elephants, moving through grass with a swinging, up-and-down gait. She saw the newborn, less than an hour into the world, guided by its mother out of the cave.

At first, she might have equated that wondrous, unsteady beginning with her own. But having spent so much time with elephants, the birth now seemed less a beginning than a continuation. And in her own life the notion of a Brand-New Beginning seemed flimsily artificial, a blind denial of the big, unwieldy force of life around her. It was there, and she was a part of it, the extreme cycles of nature on which all life in Africa turned. That she had witnessed, however murkily, the birth of an elephant seemed, as with the coming of the rains, a sign of changing seasons.

Max looked at her as if he had been listening in on her thoughts.

She nodded. "Let's go back now. It's time."

o   o

It was a slow drive back. The road was washed out in places, and Max could hardly see through the downpour. "It'll be faster once we're on the main road," he said.

He was wrong. The rain had turned the road into a slippery obstacle course of wrecked cars, dead animals and overturned trucks. Night stole in without their ever having seen the sun set.

As they neared the city, they encountered more barricades. Max questioned a soldier.

"No problem. A fire," the soldier replied.

"In this rain?" Mirie asked, though she wasn't surprised when he said "Pass on," refusing, or unable, to elaborate.

Max snapped on the radio. An African song played blithely, unendingly. Max said they were singing about angels, and she laughed. It was true, he said, and they laughed giddily until the song of angels ceased and a newscast came on.

". . . battling a fire in an aviation-fuel storage tank. The fire is contained and is expected to be out by morning . . . Electric power lines are down in parts of Kwendela. Police and army are rerouting traffic. . . ."

He turned off the radio.

The closer they came to the city, the more frequently they were stopped. Military trucks screamed by, forcing cars off the road. Max gave up on the main road and detoured onto a side road that ran past a muddy soccer field and into the low hills surrounding the city.

To the east, between the city and the airport, a fireball billowed, while Kwendela itself seemed to have been swallowed up in darkness. The only illumination came from military roadblocks and from the shantytowns, where people used kerosene lamps. They meandered down dark streets, past shuttered stores and roundabouts strewn with nuggets from shattered windshields.

"What a mess," whispered Mirie.

"Come to Kwendela," said Max, "where the streets are paved with broken glass."

It was raining so hard that even with the wipers going full speed, they could see only intermittently. Suddenly, from nowhere, figures darted across the car's high beams. Max jammed on the brakes. The headlights caught faces stunned with fear, images distorted by water running down the windshield. African men and women moved past the car in all directions, shielding their eyes from the bright lights and peeling off into the night.

"What is going on?" Mirie asked nervously, snapping on the radio again.

Max puffed out his cheeks and exhaled. "That's the last place you'll find out." He turned the music up high.

They took a secondary road that snaked around the back of the shopping center. There were no more people on the road. As they approached the austere concrete edifice, they saw another roadblock up ahead, lit by the headlights of army trucks.

Max beat his fist on the steering wheel. "The whole town's barricaded!"

Soldiers swarmed the shopping center. Some were dragging sandbags from the rose beds. So much for the president's beautification project, Mirie thought, when she was suddenly blinded by the headlights of a truck barreling toward them. The next thing she knew, the car was surrounded and she and Max were staring down the barrels of automatic weapons. A soldier shouted.

Max said to Mirie, "Get out slowly and say nothing."

She couldn't have said anything. Everything was in slow motion, and her tongue was stuck to the roof of her mouth.

They stood in the rain, while the car radio was blasting the same cheery song about angels.

"Where are you going?" demanded a soldier.

"To the airport," Max said, sounding calm. Soldiers ransacked the car. Mirie watched with mute rage as her belongings were tossed out.

A soldier grabbed the carton of cigarettes Max kept for dash. Another aimed his gun at the lock on Mirie's duffel bag. Mirie heard herself shout, "I'll open it!" The soldiers trained their eyes and weapons on her.

"Don't move," warned Max. He said something to them that seemed to lower the tension level. Then he told her to go ahead and open it.

Her hands shook as she removed the padlock. She stepped back as two soldiers poured out the contents onto the road and started going through them. Her camera bag was sitting in a puddle; Mirie reached for it.

"Stop!" shouted a soldier as Max jerked her back.

"Don't be stupid," said Max under his breath as the soldiers dug through her belongings.

It was as if they were doing it to her. She turned away, trying to block out what was happening. Over by the shopping center, storefront windows had been smashed and the pavement was littered with goods. Soldiers scurried to collect armloads full. They butted out jagged shards of windowpane, stepped inside and grabbed anything that was left. Others, meanwhile, continued dragging sacks from the rose beds over the barbed wire, then piled them onto the trucks.

But they were not sandbags. Mirie flushed and her insides loosened at the realization. They were limp forms with arms and legs. They were bodies of Africans who had been caught looting. Or if they hadn't actually been stealing, they were there, and the army's bullets hadn't made subtle distinctions. Who were these corpses: the market mamas from whom Mirie had bought mangoes; the children who begged for money for school fees; the snatch boys who made off with car mirrors and watches; the men who loitered jobless and drunk on home brew; poor people who had been shot dead for stealing shoes and food and cheap radios?

A soldier swaggered over.

"Where are you going?" he asked, examining Max's camera.

"I'm taking my friend to the airport. It's the end of her holiday."

"You take pictures," he accused.

"No. I've taken no photographs in Kwendela."

The soldier held out the camera. "What is this?" In Swahili Max repeated that he had taken no pictures, and that he had been on his way to the airport when the soldiers stopped him.

"Open it!" ordered the soldier. Max took out the film. The soldier pocketed it and threw Max the camera.

Another soldier, who was picking through Mirie's belongings strewn on the ground, found the binoculars and the bag of film. The bag crinkled as he swung it back and forth in the rain. The soldier in charge took the items.

"More pictures."

"They're elephants," said Mirie, her words slow and choked. "We were on safari. It's elephants. Pictures of elephants—that's all." She reached for the bag. "Please."

The soldier spat an order and began to walk away with her binoculars and film.

"It's only animals!" Mirie pleaded. Max called to him in Swahili.

The soldier paused, turned slightly and, motioning with his rifle, shouted to his men to send the foreigners on their way. Then, stepping indifferently over a corpse, he tossed the bag of film into the rose bushes and walked away. Mirie uttered a cry as the film bounced out, and all the rolls of elephants rained into the rosebushes.

The soldier ordered them to pick up their belongings and leave.

In broken Swahili, Mirie begged them. "They are elephants. Only elephants." The soldier ignored her, again ordering them to drive on. Mirie pleaded with Max. "Ask him, please ask him. My film. Everything I worked for."

Max grasped her arm, so tight it hurt. "*Let . . . It . . . Go!*" His words seared her.

ɔ   ɔ

The radio blared as they headed for the airport. When the song ended, the mournful newscaster came on. The fire in the fuel tanks was under control, he said, as a result of the courageous efforts of the Kwendela Fire Department. The music came on again. Off to the east the fire blazed away.

Max spoke at last, to break the oppressive silence. "Not much of a good-bye party, was it?" When she didn't respond, he said, "We got off easy, Mirie. You saw what they were doing."

"I know."

"You know now. Back there, you forgot."

"It was rape!" The words exploded from her. "It was the worst thing—"

"No, the worst thing would have been getting killed for a roll of film. We came *that* close—"

"Oh, Max, the pictures of the birth. I saw it. I had it."

"You don't know that. Because the film is gone, you've made up your mind that you got it."

"You don't believe me!"

Max pulled the car over to the side of the road and shut off the radio. He turned to her. "Yes, I do." He spoke very quietly, and Mirie felt a sickening tension in her gut, worse than when the soldiers had pointed their guns at her. "I also believe that if you had had the finest equipment for shooting in the dark, what moved you, and moved me when you told me, would never have come out in that picture." Mirie tried to stifle her tears. "What are you crying about, Mirie? The film? The money you might have made?"

She shook her head, staring out at the fire. "Next time."

"Next time," he reiterated. "It's over. We made it out of there. That beats having our photos published posthumously."

"Oh, Max, what if it's not over? It's coming apart here . . . Leave with me."

"No. Not now. Not yet."

o o

Traffic crawled between roadblocks, as the military stepped up car searches. People on the edge of hysteria, afraid to miss their planes, bribed the guards to be allowed past the dragons' teeth. For the army, it was turning into an extremely profitable night.

Max said they would never reach the airport if they waited in line. He pulled the car off to the side of the road, gathered up the bags and they walked the rest of the way in the rain. Mirie's feet sunk into the muddy roadside. There were sirens in the distance and the roar of planes taking off.

"Come with me," she pleaded again.

"No. It'll be all right, Mirie. The surface is cracking. But it's not time to take apart my bed." Pushing the wet hair back from her face, he kissed her hard. Maybe it was to make her be quiet. He would not hear any more about leaving.

There were crowds outside the airport, people trying to make planes, buy tickets—at any price—find out what was going on. They surged at the check-in counter, where besieged clerks tried to fend off the avalanche of passports and tickets shoved in their faces.

Finally, with Max standing behind her, protecting her from being mashed, Mirie reached the ticket counter. She was ready for the clerk to say the seat was gone. She wanted to be refused. She needed more time—to go back there after the soldiers had gone, to rummage through the rosebushes to find her film. If only . . .

"Go on," said Max, resting his hands on her shoulders.

The seat was still reserved. The ticket was stamped, the duffel moved over to Customs and Immigration. It was too easy, too fast—efficiency, when she least expected or wanted it. Max guided her to the edge of the crowd as a new phalanx pushed forward.

"If the customs guy says anything about your visa . . ." he said.

"I know," said Mirie, dismally. "I'll pay the fine, dash him, whatever he wants." She opened the flap of her now nearly empty camera bag. "There's a certain advantage this way," she said. "It's easier to carry."

Max drew her close.

"Well . . ." she breathed nervously. He kissed her, and they held each other, saying nothing more. She tried to absorb enough of his warmth to last for the time they would be separated.

Mirie resettled her camera bag on her shoulder and joined the crowds jostling their way into the Customs and Immigration area.

ᴐ ᴐ

She handed the customs officer her ticket and passport and glanced at the bored soldiers on either side. The officer leafed perfunctorily through her passport and set it aside. He asked her what was in her duffel.

She answered blandly, "Clothes and camping equipment. Do you want me to open it?" she asked, thinking to herself, Or would your men prefer to shoot off the lock?

The clerk said there was no need to open it. "Your visa expired"—he counted aloud to himself—"sixteen days ago."

"Yes," she said. There was no more anger left in her, just limp resignation to whatever trouble he had in store for her. "I was on safari and the rains made it impossible to fly back in time."

"I see. Yes, it has been raining very much," he said and puzzled over something. "You came here with a permit to work, but that was suspended. What work do you do?"

"I watch elephants. I like watching elephants."

"Ah, yes, many people come to Simahali to see the elephants . . . You have been in the country illegally for over two weeks. I am afraid there is a penalty."

She nodded, giddy by now. She would miss her flight. Fine. While the officer inserted carbon paper between sheets of a printed form, she calculated how long it would take, allowing for roadblocks, rain, fire and chaotic traffic, to make it back to the house.

The officer painstakingly copied information from Mirie's passport, asked her to sign, stamped each of the five sheets and demanded a nominal fee. He gave her a carbon copy and put the other papers in a cardboard box. Her passport was returned and her duffel thrown onto a cart.

"Good night," he said pleasantly enough, seemingly satisfied with the task accomplished. "You are welcome."

That was the end of it. Mirie numbly followed the other passengers toward the 747 glistening on the rain-soaked tarmac. It was huge and otherworldly, sleek and impervious to the muddle at the airport, accepting of the harried travelers boarding it.

A heavy-set African woman was ahead of Mirie. She was swathed in batik, her head crowned in matching cloth. The folds of her dress shifted and strained around her hips as she climbed the stairs. She was struggling with a wayward umbrella caught in the wind and two uncooperative children. With her free hand she clutched her little boy's hand, who in turn was holding onto his tiny sister. The children climbed the boarding stairs ever so slowly, gawking at the nimbus of fire in the distance. Neither the downpour nor their mother's scolding could make them hurry. Finally, wedging the umbrella under her fleshy arm, the woman virtually dragged the children into the plane.

Just as Mirie reached the door, the little boy reappeared, shot past Mirie, then stopped on the top stair, transfixed by the fire. The African woman pushed her huge girth past Mirie and snatched the boy back into the first-class compartment.

It was Lesa—and for an instant Mirie was no longer on the plane leaving Africa. She was back in the village market with Lesa and the runaway girl!

But it was not Lesa, and there was no point in Mirie rushing into first class to find her. For Lesa could not leave. Unlike Mirie or the wealthy African woman, or any of the other travelers, Lesa could not leave that pocket of forgotten people in the wilderness she called home. It was for Lesa to be on hand for births, circumcisions, marriages, illness, death. She was not only nurse and midwife, but also go-between for the old tribal ways and the new modern ones, a constant, if ill-equipped, healer during her country's growing pains. Lesa would certainly have scolded her. To Lesa, Mirie's frustration and despair would have seemed a luxury, a childish indulgence. What could Lesa count on, beyond her own patience, tenacity and skills?

The air-conditioned cabin made Mirie feel clammy, and she

realized that she was soaking wet. The other travelers were equally soggy and disheveled. Luggage was stowed. There was little talk, just the closing of overhead luggage compartments, the snap of seat belts, travelers settling in for a long trip west, far away from Africa. Walking down the aisle, Mirie saw mostly white faces, Americans and Europeans, with a smattering of Africans, Asians, and Middle Easterners. Many were peering tensely out the windows at the fiery glow. Mirie took her seat by the window.

The plane rumbled down the runway, gathering speed. As the wheels lifted off the tarmac, passengers spontaneously clapped and cheered. Among all these strangers, there was momentary unanimity. The plane rose higher, then banked, tipping its wings down, as if to afford one last magnificent view of the fire in the fuel tanks. The more garrulous of the white people began to swap rumors with abandon.

A man seated beside Mirie leaned over to see the fire. He was mustachioed and wore glasses.

"It sure is going good." He had a trace of the American South in his voice. "It's sure pretty, the way it lights up the sky." He looked over the seats to see where the liquor cart was. "Every time I leave Africa," he continued. "Every time I leave," he repeated, "when the wheels leave the ground, I get a pure, sweet sexual rush."

Mirie looked at him queerly. Her brown and blue eyes seemed to stare right through to the back of his head, then a nervous giggle escaped.

Thinking he had broken the conversational barrier, the man went on: "Every time, I promise myself I'll never come back to this, this . . ." He paused, disconcerted that she was still laughing. He shifted back in his seat. "Well," he said, "you look like you've been here awhile—you know how it is."

HARRIET HEYMAN was born in Chicago. She has worked as a journalist for the *New York Times* and for *Life* magazine and now lives in San Francisco. *Between Two Rains* is her first novel.